IMMUNITY

IMMUNITY

ERIN BOWMAN

An Imprint of HarperCollinsPublishers

HarperTeen is an imprint of HarperCollins Publishers.

Immunity

Library of Congress Cataloging-in-Publication Data

Names: Bowman, Erin, author.
Title: Immunity / Erin Bowman.
Description: First edition. | New York, NY : HarperTeen, an imprint of
    HarperCollinsPublishers, [2019] | Series: Contagion ; 2 | Summary: Teens
    Thea, Coen, and Nova are rescued from a deadly planet, only to be taken
    prisoner on board a government ship and used as weapons in a sinister
    political plot.
Identifiers: LCCN 2018061524 | ISBN 9780062574176 (hardback)
Subjects: | CYAC: Ability—Fiction. | Prisoners—Fiction. | Science fiction.
Classification: LCC PZ7.B68347 Imm 2019 | DDC [Fic]—dc23 LC record
available at https://lccn.loc.gov/2018061524

Typography by Erin Fitzsimmons
19 20 21 22 23 PC/LSCH 10 9 8 7 6 5 4 3 2 1

First Edition

For Jeffrey—
Shine bright, baby boy

UNITED PLANETARY COALITION
KNOWN ALSO AS THE UPC, OR SIMPLY, THE UNION

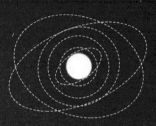

THE CRADLE
(NEW SOL)
MER
PIERRA *
NEW EARTH *#
LARISSA *
DEE
NIMBUS BELT
JUSAURNE

THE TRIOS
(SOL II)
ELPIS
EUTHERIA *#
SOTER *
LETHE BELT

THE FRINGE

FRINGE-1
(F1)
ACHLYS
KERES

FRINGE-2
(F2)
BEV
CASEY *#
SAL

Seven levels underground, in the Paradox Technologies lab that had become her prison, the programmer sat hunched over her keyboard.

It wasn't enough. No matter how many hours she bled into the project, despite bleary eyes and cramped fingers and millions of lines of code, the tech wasn't ready. She could barely think straight anymore, not with the feeds having fallen silent for nearly three months.

Groaning, she turned to the computer beside her, her only window to the outside world. It had been programmed to update with specialized records from the Trios, providing the programmer with a glimpse of her daughter's life via legal documents and report cards, test scores and news reports. Several floors underground and light-years between them, and this *was* what she was supposed to be grateful for?

Finish the tech, and you can go home to her, *Solomon Weet had promised.* Finish the tech, and I'll let you leave.

If the programmer thought she actually had a chance of getting past Paradox's security, she'd have stabbed Sol in the chest thirteen years ago and returned home that instant. But the facilities had proved to be a fortress.

The computer flickered to life for the first time in three months and the programmer jolted. A news anchor appeared on the screen, reporting from Soter's arctic ring. The story was grim, unfathomable.

The programmer frowned, certain she'd heard things wrong. She'd watched travel visas be created just five months ago, read an update when her daughter had landed on Soter in late June. And then silence. Silence for three months that had felt like three years—three sleepless, restless, anxiety-filled years—until this news, today.

She watched the clip again. The anchor recited the chain of events as if it were unremarkable, no different from any other piece of reporting. A Cat-5 blizzard had hit Soter and buried one of Hevetz Industries' research bases. Seven employees died while trying to evacuate. Their identities had finally been confirmed.

The programmer sat rigid as the anchor read off the names:

Dylan Lowe

Dr. Lisbeth Tarlow

Lyndon "Cleaver" Jones

Toby Callahan

Sullivan Hooper

Nova Singh

Althea Sadik

I

THE CAPTIVES

UBS Paramount

Interstellar Airspace

ALTHEA SADIK STOOD IN FRONT of the door to her holding cell. There was no mincing words; that's what it was. Not a room or personal quarters, but a cell. A prison.

She cocked her head, considering the small window in the base of the door. It was meant to serve as a passage for food, so that guards could pass meals to her. At least she assumed there were guards. No matter how hard she stretched the limits of her now-extraordinary hearing, she couldn't make out their heartbeats. There was only Coen Rivli, the boy monster in the cell beside hers. They were monsters together now, forever altered by the contagion they'd encountered on Achlys.

What plan? he whispered in her mind.

She'd told him she had one just moments earlier—her first words spoken to him telepathically. Now she said only, *Follow my lead.*

When she'd first surveyed the room, Thea thought the window in the door was too small to fit her. But Thea was small, too. Little more than a meter and a half tall, roughly forty-seven kilograms in weight, with a figure like an inverted pyramid. The widest part of Thea was her shoulders, not hips, and she'd never been more happy for it. If she angled her body while sliding through the window, her hips would pass easily. But her shoulders . . .

Thea reached across her body, grabbing her left wrist with her right hand. Moving deliberately, she tugged. As her shoulder popped from its socket, a small gasp escaped her. The pain was a tiny blip in her consciousness, and then her brain pushed the feeling aside.

Thea? came Coen's voice. *You okay?*

Her pulse had quickened. He must have heard it.

I'm fine.

The glass was double-paned, secured with a latch on the outside. She kicked with her heel, shattering the first panel.

She froze, listening, stretching her hearing.

No one was coming. Motion sensors or cameras must not be watching the cells. Foolish.

She kicked again, breaking the second panel of glass. Thea was still barefoot, wearing only the T-shirt and leggings she'd been in when the crew of the *UBS Paramount* had taken her and Coen by force. She was still trying to process how the crew that she'd thought would be her savior had turned out to be an enemy. The *Paramount* had pulled in her shuttle not because it had been sent to rescue survivors from Achlys but because it was collecting a resource that would serve their agenda. Lieutenant Burke, *Paramount*'s acting captain, had made that much clear when interrogating Thea just earlier. Once he was done studying the *Psychrobacter achli* swimming in her—and Coen's—veins, he would try to replicate it. And control it.

Like all Radicals, Burke wanted the Trios to secede from the United Planetary Coalition. Even when so many citizens believed the systems were strongest united, he was hell-bent on Trios independence. And from what Thea had pieced together in her interrogation, it sounded like Hevetz Industries had allied with Burke as well, that the company's owner was another Radical lurking in plain sight. If Burke got his way, he'd create an army of soldiers—hosts like Thea—to force the Union's hand.

Thea bent, knocking the remaining shards of glass from the edges of the window frame. Then she lowered herself to the ground and poked her head through.

A dark hallway. No guards.

She wiggled forward. A stray piece of glass dug into her bicep, but she pressed on. Her shoulders slipped through the opening. The rest was easy. Just a quick tilt of her body when her hips reached the frame, and then she was in the hall.

She stood and moved to Coen's cell, her feet tracking blood

on the dark tiles. By the time she reached his door, she was no longer bleeding. The wounds had sealed, her body healing at inhuman speed.

A series of sliding metal bolts secured the door. She unlocked the first, second, third. Then tugged the door open.

Coen stood in the frame. Half of his shoulder-length hair was pulled back in a bun, a dark knot atop his head. The rest hung wildly around his face. His chest swelled with each breath, and beneath the collar of his T-shirt, Thea could make out the edges of his tattoo, black ink against his light brown skin.

Thea. His breathing was labored, as though it had been *him* forcing his way through that tiny window. His pulse beat with excitement.

Silently, he moved to her, crossing the threshold, gathering her in his arms.

Thea wasn't prepared for how the contact softened her resolve. His chest beneath her cheek, his arms warm and reassuring on her back. So unlike the hands that had dragged her to this cell while she was only half-conscious. It almost made her want to linger. Almost.

He backed away quickly, as though he'd heard her thoughts. Perhaps he had. Then he took her wrist in his hand and braced his other palm against her dislocated shoulder. *Don't yell*, he warned her.

She breathed out as he thrust her shoulder back in place. It was no worse than an annoying pinch.

Let's go, she said.

There was only one direction to travel—down a dimly lit, windowless corridor lined with doors. Thea led the way past the cells, all empty based on the lack of heartbeats. A part of her had hoped she'd sense Nova Singh here. Their captors had cut the power to the pilot's cryo pod when storming the *Exodus* shuttle—a gamble that could easily kill a person. Nova's absence from this row of cells could mean only one of two things: she was dead and had been disposed of, or she was in a coma and being held elsewhere on the ship.

None of that's good, Coen said.

Thea flinched; she hadn't realized she'd been sharing her thoughts.

Sorry. I wasn't trying to pry.

It's not your fault if I'm projecting it, Thea said, and hurried on.

At the end of the hall was a service ladder. Thea grabbed the rungs and climbed, coming up against a smooth hatch door. The hand wheel to open it was surely on the other side. She put a palm to the cover, using all her strength to try to turn it. *Help me with this.*

Coen scrambled up the ladder. Working together, they pushed until the cover groaned, then creaked, then began to spin.

A moment later, Thea was shoving it up and stepping through the opening. She squinted in the newfound brightness. The room was a white cube, locked off on all ends. She sensed heartbeats, though, and zeroed in on the guards. Dozens of them, on the opposite side of a sealed door. They spotted her and shouted orders. Gas began to fill the chamber.

Quick! She motioned for Coen.

He joined her at the main door, but the ground sparked to life beneath them. Shock rod plates lined the floor. Heat surged through Thea's bare soles, pain laced her limbs. When her legs betrayed her, she fell to her knees, waiting for the shock to subside. It didn't. The sedative continued to pump into the room, and Thea slumped to her side, writhing.

In his mind, Coen Rivli could picture the window in his cell's door, the tiny opening through which Thea had somehow managed to crawl. Without her, he'd still have no idea what waited on the other side—not the hall or the ladder or the dead-end room they'd never be able to breach. He wondered, momentarily, if not knowing would be better. Not knowing meant he could hope. Now he knew escape was impossible.

He forced his eyes open. Blinked rapidly. Everything was bright and shiny.

For a moment, he thought he was still in the room above the hatch, but then he had the vaguest memory of a mask being put over his face. Not one to fend off the gas, but one to administer it, keeping him sedated as he was dragged . . . somewhere.

Coen pushed himself upright, finding a cot beneath him. Not the cot from his cell, though. One of the walls in this room was made of glass. Beyond was a space he recognized. A table he'd been on some hours earlier, nearly unconscious as medics inspected him and retrieved blood samples.

He was no longer in his cell, but an isolation chamber in the ship's medbay, which wasn't much better. Just a different kind of prison.

Coen swung his legs over the cot. There was a faint throb in his side. Probably a guard had struck him with a baton. He rolled his shoulder, stretched the muscles in his abdomen, and the pain faded with the movement.

A languid pulse beat in his ears. Thea's.

He shot to his feet. Standing, he could see over the operating tables and regenerative beds, to the other side of the medbay. Thea sat in a chamber of her own, massaging the back of her neck.

That went well.

Her head jerked up, and her eyes found his. *Didn't it?*

I wasn't joking, Thea.

Neither was I. Her pulse didn't twitch. Even the tone of her thoughts was even, her expression calm. *We're back on a main level of the ship. That's better than being locked below a hatch.*

It's still a ship, Thea. There's nowhere to escape to.

The medbay's main doors slid open and Lieutenant Burke marched in, a group of men on his heels. Two wore standard military uniforms; the third, a medical jacket.

"How'd they even get out of the cells?" Burke was asking.

"The feed door," one of the officers replied. "The girl dislocated her shoulder." He passed a Tab to the lieutenant, who watched the device, brow wrinkled.

I guess there were cameras after all, Thea mused.

Of course there were cameras. Maybe she hadn't fully processed the direness of their situation yet, but Coen had. They were on a Union battleship, a military vessel that hailed from the Trios. It would be equipped with the very best technology and staffed by officers and soldiers, presumably all of whom were Radicals. If even a single person on this boat was loyal to the Union, representatives from Galactic Disease Control would be present. Instead, Burke had Hevetz employees helping him. Coen had seen the Hevetz logo on the jackets of the medics who had inspected him.

Coen watched Lieutenant Burke take in the surveillance footage, the man's pulse blipping up a hair.

I nearly attacked him when he interrogated me after Achlys,

Thea said. *That why he's scared.*

The image made Coen smile, at least until he realized that a successful attack from Thea could have unleashed *Psychrobacter achli* on the *Paramount*. A small injury to her, a bit of that blood passed to Burke, and that was it. Madness, all over again.

Burke strode to Thea's chamber and stared down at her. "There isn't a scratch on her. She's bleeding in this footage."

"Sir, it is my hypothesis that *Psychrobacter achli* gave the hosts not only enhanced physical strength but incredible healing capabilities as well," the man in the medical jacket supplied. "And who knows what else. I'd love to run some tests on them."

"Negative," Burke said. "I'm putting them in cryo until we reach the research facility. We don't have adequate means of restraining them here."

"But sir—"

"This is not open to debate, Farraday. We only get one shot at this, and I'm not blowing it." Burke turned to the officers. "Get a fully suited unit in here, and tell them to bring shock rods and sedation masks for the hosts. We're moving them immediately."

Coen could guess what would happen next. A sedative would fill his chamber. Once he hit the floor, the suited unit would slip a mask over his face to continue administering the drug, and he'd be dragged to a new location, helpless. And once they reached the destination facility Burke had mentioned, Coen imagined security would only be tighter.

Thea seemed to be running through a similar line of logic because she said, *Maybe our best chance is to try again as soon as possible. Run for an escape pod?*

To what—land on Achlys again? Coen shook his head. *It's the only rock for hundreds of thousands of kilometers.*

What about a shuttle, then? she offered. *Maybe we can make it to a shuttle.*

And fly it . . . how?

"Nova," she blurted out. Thea threw a palm against the glass of her chamber and stared down Burke. "Where's Nova? Our pilot!"

The lieutenant folded his arms over the front of his uniform. "As good as dead. Try anything, and I'll see one of you ends up the same. I only need one host to accomplish what I'm after."

Dread rushed through Coen. Without Nova—without a pilot—they were truly stranded.

"Why are you still here?" Burke barked at the two officers beside him. "I said to get me a unit." They muttered apologies, pressed a hand over their hearts in some type of salute, then fled the room. Burke began to follow, but paused in the doorway, looking over his shoulder at the man in the white coat. "And, Farraday? Make sure they don't talk in the meantime."

The doctor—Farraday—looked between Thea's and Coen's chambers. He was middle-aged, with ashen skin and a red beard peppered with gray. His shaved scalp glinted beneath the operating lights. He didn't look like a threat, and yet Coen could sense a coldness to him. His heart rate was calm, almost lazy, and he eyed them with a look of disgust that made Coen's skin crawl.

The man nodded to Burke, then rolled his eyes once he was alone. "Make sure they don't talk," the doctor grumbled. "Not a word spoken in this entire footage, and he thinks they'll start talking now." Farraday glanced at Coen, gray eyes boring in. "But you don't *need* to talk, do you?"

Don't say anything, Thea whispered.

Obviously, Coen shot back. But he wasn't quick enough to keep his gaze from drifting to her.

Farraday caught it, and looked at Thea. "I wonder if . . ." He let the thought die and instead pulled a Tab from the inside of his lab coat and began recording notes. "Don't mind me," he said, taking a seat where he had a good view of both chambers. "I'm just observing."

"Observe all you want," Coen said. "Maybe you'll crack our fancy code of not talking. Figure out if we're blinking our communications. Or maybe we're relying on sign language.

Let's start with this. Do you know what this means?" He made an obscene gesture through the glass.

The doctor's pulse remained steady.

Don't bait him, Coen. It's not worth it.

Coen glanced Thea's way, but she had her back to him, leaning against the glass door of her chamber. The doctor followed Coen's gaze and frowned, making another note in the Tab.

We'll be out of here soon enough, she continued. *You heard Burke. They're moving us to a research facility. That's when we make our break.*

They're putting us in cryo until we get there.

Which means once we're at the new facility, they'll breathe easier, think we're secure. We'll find a way then. I never thought we'd actually escape today. I just wanted to case our options.

Coen sat on the edge of his cot and sighed. *You said you had a plan.*

I do, and it's evolving. This was step one. Now we know step two comes later.

Coen thought maybe Thea should tell him all her envisioned steps, in detail, that perhaps working together might ensure they weren't captured just minutes after breaking free of their cells.

How do you do it? she asked.

Do what?

Control which thoughts you share and which you don't? I can tell you're annoyed with me right now. Your pulse kicked up, and I can practically feel the heat your emotions are giving off. But I didn't hear any of it. You didn't project anything into my mind. How?

Coen considered this a moment, trying to find the right words. *You have to stop thinking about your thoughts as your thoughts. Nothing is yours anymore, at least not between us— between hosts. If you want a thought to be private, you have to keep it hidden. You have to feel it, not think it. Does that make any sense?*

Dr. Farraday was busy tapping notes into his Tab, so Coen risked another glance at Thea. She'd moved to her cot, wiry forearms resting on her knees and fingers laced together. Her too-thick brows were drawn, and her long, dark hair fell over her shoulders like a river.

It was Dr. Tarlow, wasn't it? she said finally. *Who forced you to learn how to control it?*

Tarlow, he said. *Yes.*

The doctor from Thea's crew. The woman who'd been infected as a child during the Witch Hazel op, who'd become something *more* since setting foot on Achlys fifty years earlier and encountering *Psychrobacter achli*. More strength, slower aging, incredible healing. And of course, an ability for telepathic communication with other hosts.

Coen had been in isolation when Tarlow's voice had suddenly plunged into his head. He'd learned quickly that his thoughts weren't *his* anymore. That as long as another person like him was in his presence, his thoughts were universal, communal, floating in a cloud.

He began to mask them, hiding what he could from the doctor.

But he didn't want to hide anything from Thea. Not anymore.

Is that true? she asked.

He smiled, realizing he'd leaked that last thought to her. He was not as practiced as he let on.

Yes, he responded. *I think the only way we'll get out of here is if we share everything.*

I agree.

So we work together. And get out of this. And then you'll find a cure.

Hopefully.

Coen lay back on his cot, staring at the ceiling. He didn't feel sick or broken, nor did he particularly feel like he needed to be cured. And yet he understood the danger *Psychrobacter achli* posed to the rest of the population—the dangers both he and Thea did as hosts. Images from Black Quarry flashed through his mind. Nosebleeds and hemorrhaged eyes. The crew attacking each other. Clawing. Spitting. Becoming rabid animals in the hopes of passing the bacteria on to a compatible host.

Most of Thea's crew had met the same fate when arriving to help Black Quarry. Thea's captain, Dylan Lowe, had been only twenty-three and still proved unable to host the bacteria. The same proved true of Toby, the crew's tech admin who'd been a year out of university. And now all these Radicals on the *Paramount*—the guards and military personnel, the scientists with Hevetz Industries—were susceptible to infection. Even still, Burke would meddle. He had the research Coen and Thea had salvaged from Black Quarry, including infected blood samples. He was playing with fire.

What do you think they're going to do to us? He knew the answer, and yet he longed to hear a different possibility, a reason to hope.

They'll study us like lab rats, Thea said, confirming his fears. *They'll try to replicate us, and then they'll try to control us.*

Do you think they can do it?

His stomach twisted as she repeated something he'd heard her say before, when they'd fled Achlys aboard the *Exodus* shuttle and he'd asked her if she could create a cure: *Every problem can be solved with enough time.*

Nova Singh opened her eyes. Clamped them shut. Opened them again.

She blinked, but the image wasn't changing.

Dylan Lowe floated before her, suspended in zero gravity, her short hair framing her head like a dark halo. The space station's emergency lighting cast her face in a pallid hue.

"Did you hear me, Nova?" the captain said. "You're in a coma."

Nova turned away, pushed off the wall to propel herself down the narrow hallway. A hand braced against her chest, stopping her cold. Dylan. Somehow right in front of her again.

"You're in my head," Nova said. "You're not real."

"Are your thoughts real? Your feelings? 'Cause I'm as real as them, Nova, and I'm the only thing that's gonna keep you alive."

Nova laughed. Dylan was the reason Nova was in this coma to begin with. On Achlys, Dylan had kept info from her crew so she could continue a search for her father. A search that was pointless. Black Quarry was dead, turned wild by the bacteria that had killed most of the *Odyssey* crew as well. The same infection that had killed Dylan in the end.

"No, *you* killed me, Nova," Dylan said. "You ejected me from the shuttle air lock."

"You asked me to!"

"I was only on that shuttle because you didn't have the guts to shoot me on Achlys."

"Get out of my head!"

"I'm *in* your head. Isn't that what you said a second ago?" Dylan smiled—a rare sight—and held up a patch kit. "You're stuck with me, Nova. Now let's secure this place before you end up sucked from an air lock, too."

A low, metallic groan sounded out of sight. The space station was failing, according to Dylan. They'd nearly been sucked through a malfunctioning air lock earlier, and now they had to patch up additional breaches.

It's in my head. It doesn't matter what I do. It doesn't matter.

"It does, Nova." Dylan grabbed her at the shoulders. "You have to stay busy, keep your brain active. You can't slip deeper or you might never come out."

Another groan.

This is a construct of my mind. I can control it. I can make it all disappear.

Nova slammed her eyes shut again, squeezing tight.

"I'm still here, asshole."

Nova opened her eyes to see it was true. Dylan in her leather jacket. The space station with its flickering lights and groaning metal. A warning panel flashing about a breach in engineering. Droplets of their sweat hung in zero gravity, glistening, morphing.

It was all so lifelike. So detailed. How was she supposed to break out of a dream that felt like reality?

"It's impossible," she muttered.

"You once told me that impossible is just an excuse not to try," Dylan said.

Nova put a hand on the wall to stop herself from twisting away from the other woman. Dylan was merely a figment of her own mind, so it was only Nova herself telling her this bit of advice. But she was suddenly small again, her father teaching her the lesson for the first time.

Maybe this wasn't real. Maybe it was. It didn't matter. Nova had no intention of spinning in somersaults for all of eternity—or until the air locks failed and she was siphoned into space.

Fixing the damn station would at least be a distraction.

She reached out and accepted the kit from Dylan. "Where do we start?"

A scuffle outside Intensive Care Two drew Amber Farraday away from her comatose patient. Peering through the door's glass window and into the general medbay beyond, she caught sight of a pair of unconscious teens being dragged toward the hall by a half dozen armed and suited soldiers, her father and Lieutenant Burke overseeing the whole affair.

Her stomach twisted. This wasn't what she'd signed up for.

When her father had proposed an Alternate Enrichment year several months earlier, she'd leapt at the chance.

Shadowing him sounded like a lot more fun than another
year at Polymire High; she had no doubts that junior year
would be just as bland as sophomore year had been. But
rather than get some true medical insights from her father,
who taught premed at one of Soter's best universities, she'd
been whisked aboard the *UBS Paramount* for god knew what
reason. From what she'd pieced together, her father knew the
acting captain, Lieutenant Christoph Burke, who'd called in
a favor. Something about picking up "cargo" in the Fringe.

Amber still didn't see why her father was needed. *Paramount* had plenty of medical experts and scientists aboard.
Employees of Hevetz Industries, she'd found out. Not to
mention all of Burke's soldiers.

When she'd asked questions, her father told her it was
confidential.

When she'd expressed concerns, and even fear, he insisted
she was being irrational.

When she'd pointed out that a two-month boat hop hadn't
been approved as part of her Alternate Enrichment year, he
simply assured her he'd talk to the school board and everything would be fine. Dr. Chesley Farraday was used to the
universe bending in his favor, after all.

She'd given him the benefit of the doubt at first, but this
was becoming too much. The mysterious cargo the *Paramount*'s crew had flown to the Fringe to pick up had turned

out to be *humans*. The first was intercepted early in their transit—a pilot named Powell who was now locked in isolation. Then the second set of cargo just yesterday: the comatose pilot Amber had been charged with supervising, and these two sedated teens being dragged through the medbay.

One was a scrawny girl with pale skin and inky hair that fell to her chest. The other was a boy, also trim, but with limbs roped in muscle, his skin a light bronze even in the blue-white track lighting of the medbay. Sedation masks were secured over both their faces and neither looked much older than Amber herself.

They disappeared from view as the guards dragged them into the hall.

Amber glanced at her patient quickly—the pilot's pulse had spiked just moments earlier, but was now back to normal—before slipping from Intensive Care and darting through the medbay.

"Did they talk?" Lieutenant Burke was asking when she burst into the hall.

"Not that I could tell," her father responded.

"Excuse me—why are those patients sedated?" Amber called out, running after them.

"Is there a reason you left Intensive Care?" Dr. Farraday said, freezing in his tracks. Burke stopped with him, but the train of officers dragging the unconscious teens continued down the hall.

"I heard a struggle in the medbay and . . ." Amber glanced after the teens, then back to her father.

His eyes narrowed, his upper lip twitching as though he'd just tasted something foul. This was her father's usual expression for disappointment. Amber had witnessed it most recently when she'd questioned what business her father had with Lieutenant Burke. Actually, ever since stepping on *Paramount*, it seemed to be the only expression he shot at her.

No longer able to hold his gaze, Amber looked down the hall. It was quiet now save for a lone officer jogging toward Burke. "Lieutenant?" He pressed the Radical salute—pointer and middle fingers crossed to form an *R* in sign language—over his heart. "That surveillance report you were waiting for just came in from the Inansi Desert."

"Not here." Burke's eyes flashed with warning. "My office. Are you coming, Farraday?"

"Perhaps I should take care of this and find you after?"

"Fine. Let's just make sure these interruptions don't become a reoccurrence."

"Absolutely, sir." Her father crossed his pointer and middle fingers and quickly tapped them to his heart. Burke trudged off, the officer on his heels. As soon as the men were out of sight, Amber's father grabbed her at the bicep, his fingers pinching through the material of her medic-in-training lab coat.

"Where are they taking those kids?" she asked as he steered her back toward the medbay. "And where the heck is the Inansi Desert?"

"On Casey. Clearly the history professors aren't covering the Casey uprising at that school of yours." His lip curled, then morphed into a stern line. "Your focus should be on IC2, Amber. Do you understand me? I don't want to hear from you unless that pilot is alert. There are things more pertinent than what captures your attention in any given moment." He was staring down at her. One day she'd win a staring contest, but today she glanced away.

"I'll focus on the pilot," she said. "Promise. Just tell me who those kids are."

"They're not kids."

"Fine, teens. Whatever. Who are they?"

"They're damaged goods. We planned to keep them quarantined until arriving back in the Trios, but they're giving us problems. They'll be in cryo during transit."

Amber frowned. "If we've begun quarantine procedures, shouldn't Galactic Disease Control be here? And the pilot I'm watching . . ." Her heart stumbled, beating faster. "Wasn't she on the same ship as those teens? That means she should be in quarantine, too!"

"She's fine for now. The medical bed we have her in is completely secure, and we have reason to believe that if she was jeopardized, she'd have already shown signs, even while in a coma. Besides, she isn't Burke's priority."

No wonder I'm the one watching her, Amber thought. *She must be the unimportant half of the cargo.*

"But if she wakes up," her father continued, "if her status changes, you call me immediately, because *yes,* she'll need to be closely monitored." He put a hand on her shoulder, squeezing reassuringly, but all Amber could think about was how those fingers were the same ones to pinch her arm just earlier, steering her like cattle. "You'll be a good doctor someday, Amber. But you need to learn to follow instructions. To listen."

Her father had always said that good doctors follow their intuition, that hunches and gut feelings were just as important as orders and chart data. Sometimes Amber wondered if what her father really meant was that she'd make a good nurse, doing as a doctor requested; if he wasn't quite comfortable with the idea of her earning his title and becoming his equal.

"Where are you going?" she asked as he turned away.

"I need to talk to Burke."

"But Dad . . ."

"Keep an eye on that pilot's vitals, Amber. I'm not going to ask again."

Amber trudged back to the medbay and into a room

labeled *IC2*. The steady, subdued beep of the pilot's vitals greeted her. Where a regenerative bed typically sat was a long, secure compartment. A transparent coffin. There was nothing to regenerate for a comatose patient. Instead, all Amber could do was wait. Monitor vitals. Check IVs and fluids. Empty catheters.

Amber stepped up to the medbed. Beneath the clear lid, the pilot looked as peaceful as ever, mouth relaxed, lips slightly parted.

"Right where I left you."

She bent forward, folding her arms atop the compartment and resting her chin on her forearm as she watched the pilot's chest rise and fall. The patient reminded Amber of Snow White from the Earth Era fables, with dark hair and rosy lips, but bronze skin instead of ivory. Undeniably beautiful, regardless, and she wasn't wearing even an ounce of makeup. Some people had all the luck, genetically speaking.

Amber grabbed the pilot's chart from the foot of the bed, searching the Tab for a name, even when she knew she wouldn't find it. The chart contained only recent medical information, not the patient's name or age or home planet. All things Amber's father probably knew but refused to tell her, even though talking to the pilot—calling her by name—might help bring her back.

It dawned on Amber that her father might not want the

pilot to wake up. That awake, she just might be another nuisance, like the two unconscious teens being transported to cryo.

Amber touched the lid of the medbed. "What happened to you in the Fringe?" she asked. "Was it bad?"

No change in the vitals, no twitch of the pilot's face.

"Of course it was bad. You're in a coma."

No response.

"If you can hear me," Amber went on, "I think things are only going to get worse. I think your friends might be in danger."

The vitals beeped on, unaltered.

Coen could feel the pressure of the officer's grasp beneath his underarms, the knock of his calves against stairs, the bump of his heels passing over thresholds. Clearer than any of these sensations was the subtle pressure of the mask around his nose and mouth. The elastic that held it in place squeezed gently along his temples.

And even while he could feel all this—even while he was being dragged through the ship and to cryo—his limbs were useless. He was limp, leaden.

He couldn't even sense Thea in his drugged state, and that was perhaps the most terrifying of all. He was alone, and it was like being stranded on Achlys all over again, those two months between Black Quarry's demise and the arrival of Thea's crew.

He hated being alone.

Coen's feet bumped over another threshold.

"Put him there. The girl beside him."

"Will it be enough to keep them secure?"

"If the gas is working now, I don't see why not."

Hands moved from beneath Coen's arms to the front of his torso, his shoulders. Another set grabbed his feet. Their pulses were wild now in his ears. They hated being so close to him.

Coen's equilibrium tipped, and then the hands released him.

I'm in the cryo bed, he thought. *I must be.*

The elastic behind his head slipped up, the mask lifted from his face. He heard the door to the chamber slide shut, sensed shadows moving across it. A fan kicked on.

Just as his eyelids began to flutter open, his body returning to itself after the removal of the gas mask, the sedative of the cryo chamber began to weigh on him. He was trading one state of uselessness for another.

"I want a dozen guards stationed here for the next forty-eight hours. Make sure they can't fight this."

Coen's eyelids grew heavy once more. But even as his body became leaden, his mind felt lighter.

During his trip to Achlys, the Black Quarry crew had undergone cryostasis on *Celestial Envoy*. It had been sort of like dreaming, a subconscious state in which he'd had thoughts. His mind had been aware that time was passing even when he'd had no way to count the days.

He felt that way again now, his subconscious surging to life while the rest of his body slept. And in the corners of his subconscious, he was delighted to find that he sensed Thea. Not as crisp as usual. Distant and a bit tinny—like a long tunnel separated them. Muted, too, but there.

Thea, he gasped out, the relief crashing over him.

I didn't think we'd be able to talk in here, she said.

It must be different from the gas sedative.

Cryostasis suspended the body, not the mind, so in a way, it made sense. But the fuzzy, weak quality of their conversations led Coen to believe that if he'd been placed in a pod across the room, rather than directly beside Thea, he wouldn't have been able to hear her at all.

Still, this fuzzy, weak connection was enough. More than enough. If the muscles in his face were capable of smiling, he would have. He could sense Thea's excitement, too. A buzzy, electrified hum.

It's about two months back to the Trios, he said. *Should we discuss escape plans?*

What for? We don't know what we'll be escaping. Not until we get there and see what we're up against.

Coen could see the logic there, but he hated how helpless it made him feel. At least when stranded on Achlys, there'd been plenty of tasks to keep him busy. Inventorying supplies. Gathering water. Charging battery cells. Cleaning the rover. Planning what he'd say to his sister if he ever made it back to her.

But to be stuck in this cryostasis pod, useless, waiting. Doing nothing while the *Paramount* brought him closer to what would essentially be another prison . . .

Thea, I don't want to die like this: on their terms, under their knives, surrounded by strangers.

We're not going to die. And I'm not a stranger.

I barely know you.

Well, we've got two months to fix that. Here, I'll start: I'm an orphan. I've been in child services since I was four. I never knew my dad, and my mom's presumed dead, but I think she's still out there somewhere. I'm going to find her one day, or at least find out what happened to her. After I get out of this mess and attend Linneaus Institute and am making a boatload of unnes a year, I'm going to hire a private investigator to track her down . . .

Coen listened to her talk, and he took it into himself, the fear slowly drowned out by cautious optimism. Thea talked about an after with such certainty he began to picture one for himself. And when it was his turn to talk, he shared the future he longed for.

His sister, Gina, and the tumor along her spine receding. Her regaining strength, leaving the hospital bed. His family, no longer bankrupt from the cost of the care. He'd go back to school, get his GenEd degree, think about attending a trade school for mechanics or robotics.

Maybe, if the stars aligned, Coen just might be able to amount to something more than a scavenger.

Nova lifted the welding mask, sparks from her soldering gun fading.

"Think that will hold?" she asked.

Dylan squinted at the work. "For now."

The breach in engineering had been minor, but this one, in Air Lock 3—a narrow slash in the interior no wider than a hairline, but nearly three meters tall—had proved a nightmare. That Nova had enough scrap to patch it was a miracle, not to mention that she completed the work without an EVA suit. It shouldn't have been possible. In the twenty minutes it took her to seal the breach, the vacuum should have torn the station apart. And she should have run out of air. Or died from the cold.

"It's all in your head, remember?" Dylan chided. "Science doesn't matter here. This is just you making sense of the situation with visuals."

"If science doesn't matter, why can't I just wake up? Something else must be broken." Nova swung the welding mask off her head and dropped it. It spiraled near her hip. Dylan grabbed it and secured it to a holding station on the wall while Nova stowed away the soldering gun. "Let's run diagnostics."

Nova pushed off the air lock door, propelling herself through the station. In command central, static filled the room, garbled and choppy.

If you can hear me . . . things are . . .

Nova pushed off the doorframe, gliding into the room.

Your friends . . . danger.

"Hello?" Nova said into the main comm radio. The static simply continued to crackle, the transmission repeating.

If you can hear me . . . things are . . . your friends . . . danger . . .

"Comms are down." Nova abandoned the radio and turned to the central station, grabbing it at the lip to pull herself in for a better view. "I'm gonna reboot the whole system. Maybe that will get the station rotating again, too; get us out of zero g."

Dylan gave a shrug as if to say, *Whatever you think.*

Nova moved through the interface, which was strikingly similar to the fighters she operated while training at the Academy. It was a relief to be so familiar with the interface, but also unsettling. A space station like this should run on entirely different operations. Then again, it was all in her head.

She found the right command and tapped the button.

"Rebooting." All through the command room, the screens went black. The garbled message repeating from the radio died. For a moment the room was deathly silent.

Then a blinking cursor appeared on the main console.

"Did it work?" Dylan asked.

The screen updated with text.

REBOOTING COMMUNICATIONS . . .

INTERNAL AUDIO AND VIDEO . . . ONLINE.

EXTERNAL NEAR PLANET COMMS . . . ONLINE.

EXTERNAL DEEP SPACE COMMS . . . ONLINE.

COMMUNICATION SYSTEM REBOOT . . . COMPLETE.

"I think that means yes," Nova said.

Another static crackle from the radio, then an alert on the screen before her. *Transmission received via DSC.*

Deep space comms. Figured. Of course help wasn't nearby.

Nova pushed herself over the console, glided for the radio, and played the message.

What happened to you out there in the Fringe? Was it bad? The voice was soft and reassuring, kind. *Of course it was bad. You're in a coma.*

Nova fumbled for the radio's mouthpiece.

If you can hear me, I think things are only going to get worse. I think your friends might be in danger.

"Who is this?" Nova asked into the radio. "Hello? Can you hear me?"

"It's on old transmission," Dylan said sadly. "It's not live."

Nova sat back in frustration. For a long moment, the room was painfully silent. Then a light blinked on the console, indicating a new incoming message, this on the internal lines. Definitely live. Nova straightened.

I'm just going to keep talking, the voice said. *I'm pretty sure you can't hear me, but I'm going to keep at it anyway. You're stuck with me, I guess.*

"I'm here. This is Nova Singh, temp pilot with Hevetz Industries. Do you read me?"

I wish I knew your name.

"It's Nova, dammit! Hello? Hello, do you copy?"

They took your friends to cryo. I think something bad is going to happen to them. Who are they?

"Thea and Coen. I can explain later. Where are you—did you just dock? I don't understand how you're on the internal lines. There's no one else on this station."

Who are you? the voice continued.

"I'm Nova Singh, dammit!" She threw the radio. It clattered against the unit, then bounced back in her direction, floating on its tether. It was no use. Despite being back online, the comms were clearly malfunctioning.

"Morse code," Dylan supplied.

"What?"

"You could try Morse code."

Nova followed Dylan's gaze to the tap lever in front of the radio. It had appeared out of nowhere, as though her brain had conjured it.

Maybe I'm asking questions that are too complicated, the voice went on. *How about this: if you can hear me, blink.*

"Blink?" Nova glanced at the Morse code transmitter, then to the radio. She reached out and pressed the paddle, producing a single, short tap.

Amber froze, certain she'd imagined it.

The pilot's vitals hadn't changed. Her heart rate beeped on, as steady as ever. Her body was rigid in the medbed, and though her eyes remained closed, Amber was certain they'd just twitched.

"I think . . . Did you just hear me? Blink again for yes?"

The pilot's eyelids tightened briefly, then returned to their relaxed, sleeping state.

"Oh my god."

At that, the pilot's eyelids moved rapidly, clenching for varying intervals of time. Amber staggered away from the medbed. The pilot's body temperature was up a single degree, her heart rate just a touch faster than before. Still nowhere near where they should be, but they'd changed.

"I don't understand. Slow down. Let's do yes/no questions."

The pilot relaxed.

"One blink for yes, two for no. You can hear me?"

A blink.

"Are those teens they brought to cryo your friends?"

Another blink.

"Did something bad happen in the Fringe?"

Yes. No.

"So maybe?" Amber paused, sucking her lip. "How about this: Our crew picked up yours and now we're headed home to the Trios. Are we in danger?"

A pause, as though the pilot was considering the situation carefully.

No.

Amber let out an exhale. "That's one silver lining, I guess. But I still think your friends are in trouble. The soldiers sedated them before moving them to cryo. Why would they do something like that?" Amber's thoughts drifted to her father's comments about quarantine procedures. "I wish I knew your name," she added.

The pilot's eyes twitched again, frantic and sporadic.

"Are you okay?"

Yes. Then more panicked twitching.

"I don't understand."

The blinking continued, long and short, with intermittent pauses. It made no sense, except that . . . Amber froze, watching carefully. The blinks weren't as frantic as she'd first thought. They made up a pattern.

"Hang on!" She raced for the Tab, and swiped to a clean page in the pilot's chart. "Repeat it again, slower." As the pilot clenched and unclenched her eyes, Amber recorded the beats. Dashes for long blinks, dots for short.

— • — — — • • • — • —

She stared at her notes, puzzled. Was it a cypher? Some type of code? She lowered the Tab to her lap, shaking her head. The pilot was still repeating the pattern of blinks, but less enthusiastically. The Tab dimmed, and Amber glanced down to see the device had reverted to sleep mode. The Union's military seal now filled the screen.

The *military* . . . Military communications . . . "Morse code!"

Yes.

Amber brought the Tab out of sleep and pulled her notes into the built-in translation software, selecting Morse code as the language. The screen refreshed with a single word.

"Nova?" she asked, reading from the Tab.

Yes.

"Hi, Nova. My name's Amber Farraday. It's nice to meet you."

The pilot began blinking almost immediately. After a moment, Amber had her question: *Where?*

"Where are you? The *UBS Paramount*, somewhere in the Fringe. We're headed back to the Trios, though."

How?

This one was trickier, as Amber didn't know all the details herself. "Our crew was tasked with picking up cargo in the Fringe," she said, explaining what she'd been told. "You and your friends were part of that cargo. I don't know much else beyond that. I'm only an . . . intern, I guess you could say. A medic in training shadowing my father."

Coma? How?

"I don't know. I wish I did. You've been this way since they wheeled you in. Maybe something was wrong with your shuttle's cryo sequence. You might not have been sedated properly and—"

"Amber!"

She jumped at the sudden appearance of her father, the Tab nearly falling from her lap.

"Burke wants all personnel in cryo."

"What about your research?" All Amber had heard since the cargo was picked up was how important her father's research was to Burke's cause and the Radical agenda. She'd seen enough soldiers and scientists making the Radical salute to each other in the halls to assume the entire crew were Radicals. Some even made the salute to her in passing. Amber always mirrored it, feeling like she was in on a secret without the actual details. Everyone on this ship was working toward the same goal—a goal no one seemed to think she needed to know about—only now the crew would be going under for the two-month flight home instead of using that time to work. It didn't make sense.

"I'll pick up where I left off later," her father explained. "I need more equipment than this ship can offer. Plus, Vasteneur will join us there to oversee things."

Aldric Vasteneur, owner of Hevetz Industries. Amber had heard one of the scientists onboard bragging about how close he was with the owner. Another had countered that Vasteneur clearly had faith in her as well, seeing as they'd both been recommended to Burke for this mission. They were like neglected children, Amber had thought, vying for Daddy's attention.

"What about the pilot? I can't leave her now."

"I'll program a med-droid to watch her vitals, change IVs as needed."

"But she's responsive!"

Amber's father perked up. "What?"

"She can hear me. Nova, can you hear me?" The pilot's eyes clenched and relaxed. "See the blink? One means yes, two means no."

Her father peered at the readings on the pilot's monitors and sighed heavily. "Amber, I'm sorry. We don't have time for this. I'll make sure the med-droid pulls me out of cryo if her state changes, but I've got orders from Burke."

Immediately, Nova blinked twice. *No.*

"Dad, I want to stay."

"This isn't negotiable!" He seized her arm and towed her toward the door.

Another two blinks. *No.* Then another, over and over. It was all Amber could see as her father forced her into the hall.

Eventually, their conversations faded, and Thea and Coen sat in eerie silence. Minutes, hours, days passed. Occasionally Thea would reach out to him, confirming she wasn't alone. *I'm still here*, he'd say, the response always calm and warm.

It was like any experience in cryo, in that she knew time was passing, but it was that much more unsettling because conversation was possible. Thea felt like she was stuck in limbo, half awake but still trapped in a sleeping body, unable to move.

She thought of many things as the ship rattled through space. Where it might be headed, what type of facility she and Coen would be moved to, how they'd ever manage to escape it.

One step at a time, she reminded herself.

Before she could attempt to run again, she'd have to be awake. And she'd need to assess the situation fully. No more smash and grabs like her first attempt. The next time Thea would be careful, patient, precise. Her plan would be perfect and she'd execute it flawlessly. Lieutenant Burke and his Radical crew wouldn't even know she was missing.

This was just like any assignment, she reasoned, and Thea had never met an assignment she couldn't complete.

At noon, when he came to check on her as he always did, she attacked. Fists, palms, nails—anything she could get on him.

"Sumi!" he shouted. "Sumi, stop it."

"It's Naree," the programmer snarled, "and it has been for years." Sumi Demir had been dead since the moment the programmer scrambled her records and created Naree Sadik in her place. She'd been a ghost since her involvement with Sol had sent the Radicals after her family. She faulted him completely.

If he hadn't manipulated her, she wouldn't have accepted his briefcase with version one of the tech before he disappeared from the Trios. And if she'd known what he had planned, she never would have left Thea at the bus stop while she delivered said briefcase to a courier at Sol's request. But she'd stuck to her word, and the next thing she knew, she was waking up on a ship bound for Casey. Sol hadn't just wanted the tech. He'd wanted the programmer behind it, too.

She hadn't seen her daughter since.

"I came as soon as I heard," Sol said, his gaze tracking to the computer. The news report featuring Thea's death continued to loop. "It may not be accurate. Word is Hevetz Industries has fallen into Radical hands. They could be covering something up."

"Stop it! Just stop!" She wheeled on him, tears streaming, her pulse pounding in her ears. "You're just trying to find another way to keep me here. Thea was your bargaining chip, and she's gone. I'm finished. Take me home." She collapsed into her seat and cried freely.

"I can't do that." He knelt at her feet, took her hands in his. "I can't do this without you, Sum—Naree. The recharging cycle is the final snag, and you're the only one who can solve it." His eyes gleamed almost catlike.

She yanked her hands from his. "To what end, Sol? What's in it for me?"

"Were you always this selfish or did I miss it all those years ago?"

"Selfish?" She shot to her feet. "You abducted me. You took me from my daughter and held me hostage here, and now Thea's dead. The one thing I was working to get home to is gone. I couldn't care less about your stupid flux drive and changing the universe."

"I recruited you," he said, picking his words carefully, "because it was the only option. Paradox had to go into hiding. Coming to Casey, leaving the Union behind . . . it was the only way to escape the Radicals. They would use this for all the wrong reasons."

"At this point, I wish it would fall into Radical hands so they can tear the world apart. At least then I wouldn't have to see your face."

He touched his tie, wounded. "It pains me that even now, after all these years, you still feel like a prisoner here. That you see me, and not the Radicals, as the villain." Sol was always doing this, twisting her words, making himself the victim. "Besides, Thea is only presumed dead. Why would you give up on her preemptively?"

"I have never given up on her," the programmer snarled. "I've wanted nothing but to go home to her. That is all I've ever wanted."

"So help me with the drive until you have proof."

She raised her chin to look Sol in the eye. "I will ruin you one day," she said calmly. "It doesn't matter if she's alive or not, if you let me go or keep me here forever. I will ruin you for what you've done."

The corner of his mouth quirked upward, amused. "Very funny, Naree."

When she blinked, he was gone.

II

THE TESTING

Unknown Research Base

Presumably in the Trios

NOVA SINGH HAD REPAIRED THE space station to its fullest functionality. It was rotating around its axis again, supplying artificial gravity to her crew of two. No, her crew of *one*. Because even though it was easy to think of Dylan as another occupant, Nova knew the captain wasn't truly there. She even flickered sometimes—a recent development—like a hologram experiencing interference.

Based on the station's number of rotations a minute, Nova had been able to calculate the approximate rotations per hour, and from there, rotations per day. It gave her a grasp on time. Since the artificial gravity had resumed, fifty-four days had passed—enough time for the *Paramount* to return to the Trios. Maybe when she heard Amber again, Nova would finally be home.

She'd stayed busy by cleaning. She scrubbed and polished and shined, the work giving her purpose. She ran system checks daily, confirmed that things were operating smoothly. Debris from a passing asteroid storm took out a solar panel one afternoon, and Nova had the pleasure of donning an EVA suit and spacewalking out to the solar array wing to make repairs. Dylan whispered in her ear via a helmet comm the whole time.

Be careful. Steady there. Take your time.

Nova had never seen this cautious side of the captain, and it made her smile.

There was nothing to eat on the station, and yet Nova felt fine. If hunger ever twanged her belly or thirst coated her tongue, it faded within the hour. When she felt the need to find a restroom, the sensation always passed. She wondered if this was the work of the med-droid Amber's father had mentioned; if somewhere else, IVs and catheters were being seen to. Imagining the droid completing these tasks helped Nova envision the room she was being cared for in. She found herself wanting to truly see it, not just imagine it. And Amber. Nova replayed their short-lived conversation. The medic's voice had been so reassuring, and it looped in Nova's mind like a distress beacon, providing a type of human interaction even Dylan couldn't supply.

And finally, in the twenty-third hour of that fifty-fourth day, Nova heard Amber's voice again.

Right where I left you. How are you doing? Please tell me you can still hear me.

Nova was in engineering, about as far as she could be from central command, but on a whim, she blinked her eyes.

Thank goodness, came Amber's reply. *I'm sorry about before. They didn't give me an option. Your vitals look good, though. Not much has changed in transit. We're docking now and will be able to move you to a nicer room soon.*

A room Nova couldn't even see.

I'm not sure if I'll still be overseeing you when we leave the Paramount. *I hope so, though. If not, now would be a good time to wake up. You know, so we could say hello and good-bye at the same time.*

Nova wanted to. God, did she want to wake up.

She peered out the nearest window and froze.

Instead of the endless expanse that had surrounded her for the past two months, a blue-green planet the size of her fist sat among the stars.

The station suddenly dimmed and a siren whooped. Nova spun from the window to find Dylan hunched over the emergency self-destruction box. The system was armed and her hand hovered over the final lever.

"What the hell are you doing?"

The captain looked at her sadly. "It's like she said, Nova. It's time to wake up." Dylan threw the lever.

T-minus five minutes to self-destruct, the intercoms announced. *All personnel must evacuate via drop pod immediately.*

"What drop pod?" Nova roared. "I've been on this damn

station for almost two months and I've never seen a drop pod!"

"That's the idea. It didn't appear until it was time to take it. Follow me."

Nova raced after Dylan, following her to a docking port for visiting shuttles where a drop pod waited, door open. "It will only hold one." Dylan's hair had lost some of its shine, and her nose didn't seem quite sharp enough. She flickered.

Nova pulled the captain into a hug. "Thanks for everything, Dyl."

"It was never me, Nova. It was *you*. You were everything you needed to get through this, and you will continue to be everything you need moving forward. You are enough. Don't forget that on the other side."

The woman flickered, and for a heartbeat, Nova could have sworn she was looking in a mirror. It wasn't Dylan standing there, but Nova herself. Then Dylan reappeared, smiling. Even now, after hundreds of smiles on this station, Nova still wasn't used to the expression. The captain didn't look like Dylan unless she was scowling.

Nova wanted to say, "I'll see you on the other side," or "Until next time," or basically anything that meant this wasn't good-bye. But it was. She'd said good-bye to Dylan Lowe weeks ago, in that shuttle air lock just beyond Achlys. Everything on this space station had been stolen time.

"Thanks again for the bracelet." Nova raised her wrist, flashing the silver, thread-thin piece of jewelry that Dylan had gifted her. Then she stepped into the drop pod and sealed the door. When she looked back through the small window, Dylan was gone. The hall was empty. The station had only ever held a crew of one.

Thea felt the officers moving her from cryo and into the new facility. Fighting the fog of sedation, she tried to memorize the route but quickly lost track of the numerous turns. When she finally regained enough of her senses to open her eyes, she found operating lights overhead. She attempted to sit, only to find her ankles and wrists in cuffs.

"I wouldn't struggle," said Dr. Farraday, appearing in her peripherals. He wore a full hazmat suit as he drew blood from her arm. The needle felt like the prick of a pin, nothing more. What bothered her more was his pulse—calm and steady, almost indifferent. He wasn't afraid of her. "They'll give you a good zap if you misbehave."

It was then that she felt the strap beneath her chin and the subtle pressure over her skull.

"It's called a hot cap," he went on. "They sound even less fashionable than they are."

Thea turned her head, searching the room. On the far end was a mirror, where she could make out the gear now fastened to her head. The cap itself was a cobweb of woven metal threads. Several of these threads made contact with her skin at her temples and along her forehead. She guessed the *they* Farraday had mentioned were watching on the other side of the mirror, ready to send a wave of electricity through the hot cap if needed.

Glancing the other direction, Thea found a long, narrow window. Light filtered through, warm and yellow. There was a tree in the distance, the green so vibrant it took her breath away. She hadn't seen anything so green in . . . months. A breeze drifted by, rustling the leaves on the branches. Tall grass, golden like wheat, danced at the base of the trunk.

"Where are we?"

"That's confidential." Dr. Farraday kept his eyes on the syringe.

"We're back in the Trios," Thea said, feeling it in her bones. "And when Coen and I break out of here, you'll never catch us. Do you know how fast we can probably run in an open field? How we'll hear you coming kilometers away?"

The doctor set the syringe aside and followed Thea's gaze. "That's simulated natural light and some pretty visuals," he said lazily. "There's no field outside this facility."

"City, then? Even better. More places to hide."

"The window's not real, Thea, because there's nothing to see outside it. This facility doesn't have real windows."

They were underground, then, deep in some Radical-operated complex. It would be hell to get out, depending on how many floors down they were, but she'd manage.

"Type O negative," Dr. Farraday said, applying labels to the tubes of blood. "A universal donor."

"Do you know how dangerous those samples are?"

Before he could answer, the door whooshed open near Thea's feet. "Burke and the others are ready for her," a suited officer said.

Dr. Farraday waved him in, and two other men entered on his heels. One held a palm-sized device in hand.

"Where's Coen?" Thea said, searching the room. "I want to see Coen."

"We're taking you to him," the man with the device said. "But if you don't behave . . ." He glanced at her hot cap and shook the handheld device in her direction.

The threat was clear. If Thea put one toe out of line, this man could fry her brain.

Coen was collared like a dog.

The metal encircling his neck was cold and thick enough that his head was more or less immobile. Beneath each of his ears, metal rods attached to the collar and allowed the guards to steer him forward like meat headed for slaughter.

"Keep moving," one of the guards said, shoving the lead.

Coen stumbled forward, only to feel the collar pinch from the other side, where the second guard hadn't assisted in the thrust.

There was no use trying to overpower them. When he'd come out of a fog, he'd already been collared, and a strange cap had been strapped over his head. He'd been told it could produce enough electric shock to kill him, and the guard had made the threat confidently. Even now, the pair at Coen's side had steady pulses and relaxed postures.

Coen wasn't about to test them.

The room they led him to was spacious, with a shiny floor and immaculate white walls, one of which housed a long, slender mirror. Part gym, part medical room, Coen wasn't sure what to make of the assortment of gear throughout. There were weights and pull-up bars and a boxing ring. Eye charts and regenerative beds and a low table lined with tools that could be used for torture as much as care. At least there were no operating tables. He'd been poked and prodded enough.

He heard footsteps approaching, followed by a swarm of heartbeats.

"Ah, you're here already. Good." Dr. Farraday strode into the room. "Let's get started."

A pair of medics entered on his heels, and then three additional guards, guiding Thea. Like him, she wore a metal cap, but no collar. Perhaps the guards didn't think she had the strength to overpower anyone. Ironic, really, seeing as she was the only one to have broken free of her cell so far.

You okay? he asked her.

Oh, yeah. I'm great.

He'd never heard Thea crack a joke before, and sarcasm sounded wrong on her.

"Let's start in the gym," Dr. Farraday said, motioning toward the area. "Go ahead and unlock the boy."

The guards twisted the metal leads they were holding, guiding them free of the collar. One of the men edged forward, his pulse picking up slightly, and flicked a switch behind Coen's neck. The collar swung open and clattered to the floor. Coen rolled his head with relief.

"The gym," Dr. Farraday said again.

They just want to know what we're good for, Coen said to Thea, the room suddenly making sense. *How much we can lift. How well we can see.* He glanced at the boxing ring. *How well we fight.*

They already know the answers are good enough to try to replicate us, Thea responded. "I'm not doing anything," she announced, and crossed her arms over her chest.

Dr. Farraday gave one of the guards a nod, and Coen felt a burst of heat at his temples, followed by a surge of pain that brought him writhing to the ground.

"Coen!" Thea wheeled on the doctor. "What the hell did you do to him?"

"What I will continue to do unless you cooperate," Dr. Farraday said. "When one of you fails to follow orders, the other will feel the consequences."

Thea hooked a hand behind Coen's back and helped him sit. His stomach surged, and he feared he might be sick.

"That was simply a warning shock. We can provide worse ones without risking any serious damage."

I'm so sorry, Thea muttered in his mind. *I'm sorry. I didn't know he'd—*

"Let's go," Coen said aloud, pushing to his feet. He glanced at the doctor. "Study away."

Farraday ran them through a series of drills, barking out orders and then recording results in his Tab. How much they could bench press, how fast they could scale a climbing wall, how quickly they could run a kilometer. Thea outran Coen by a solid seven seconds—a surprise that made him smile. On Achlys he'd needed to remind himself to slow down so she could follow his lead, and now she was faster.

They moved on to the eye chart, reading from the display with the lights on, off, and in a state akin to twilight. His vision was better than Thea's in the dark, but then she bested him again on a hearing test, where they were asked to point to the speaker in the room that was producing a beeping tone. He'd been certain the test had ended, and then

Thea had raised an arm, pointing to the speaker that had made a high-pitched whistle just moments earlier.

"Incredible," Dr. Farraday had muttered.

All the while, the guards lingered along the room's perimeter, ready to zap Coen and Thea into submission. Eventually, they were shown to the boxing ring, and after stepping under the ropes, each supplied with a shock rod.

They're dumber than they look, Thea said.

Coen scanned the room. The medics had left, and only a few of the guards remained. Notably missing were the pair that had the ability to shock either Thea or Coen. But then Coen caught Farraday giving a thumbs-up to the wall with the slender mirror.

They're still watching. Coen nodded at the mirror. *They'll drop us before we're even out of the ring.* Still, he turned the shock rod over in his hand, wishing he could use it on their captors.

"Disarm your opponent and deliver a knockout blow. Via fist or shock rod," Dr. Farraday said. "We're mostly interested in your technique here."

Coen glanced at Thea. She was half his weight, easily. "I'm not fighting her," he said.

"Same," she spat out quickly, and he realized he'd nearly subjected her to a shock for his unwillingness to follow orders.

Dr. Farraday put a hand to his ear, listening to something

on a comm. Coen could only make out the first few words before Dr. Farraday moved out of earshot. Thea's brows, however, dipped.

Can you still hear him? Coen asked.

"Fight," Dr. Farraday said, lowering his hand from his ear, "and the winner will be granted contact—"

Thea lurched to action, arm swinging.

"—with a family member back home."

She had most certainly heard the conversation between Farraday and Burke.

Coen's body reacted instinctively, leaping back, but her shock rod skimmed his side. A slice of heat curled through him. He breathed out hard, fighting the pain.

It's not personal, she said, angling toward him. *They'd force us one way or another and I need that call.*

She came at him again, swinging wildly. He sidestepped her easily. She lashed out again. He danced away.

Coen laughed and she glared.

What's funny?

You don't know how to use it, he said.

Use what? Another swipe of her shock rod. This time he used his own to deflect it, like a sword.

Any of it. The weapon. Your body.

He understood suddenly why he'd been so unstoppable on Achlys. It wasn't just that the contagion had turned him into a supercharged version of himself. He'd had the skills to begin with. A variety of martial arts training and self-defense lessons since the age of five, ending just two years ago, when Gina had fallen ill and money had to be spent elsewhere. He could fight with his hands, feet, a bow staff, a blade. When he'd become infected with *Psychrobacter achli*, it had merely enhanced everything—more strength, better instincts, eyesight like no other.

Thea had all these things, too, but she'd never been in a fight. It was obvious in her uneven stance, the way she planted all her weight through one foot, how she didn't keep a hand up to protect her face.

Then how'd I manage to hit you once already? she asked.

Luck. And a head start. You heard the offer before I did.

He struck out with the shock rod. Her eyes went wide, surprised to see him fighting back instead of just deflecting. Her improved instincts allowed her to block his first attack, and his second, but his third caught her in the side.

As she buckled from the pain, he dropped low, swiping out her legs. She fell back, and he caught her, softening the fall and straddling her in the same moment. He batted her shock rod away, threw his away, too.

Thea squirmed beneath him, the strength of her own limbs returning to her now that the electric shock had died out. He wound up. As she flung her hands up in an X to protect her face, he threw a punch into the mat just beside her head.

She froze, slack-jawed and stunned beneath him.

Coen turned toward Dr. Farraday. "That would have knocked her out, but like I said, I don't want to fight her." He looked down at Thea, still panting, her mouth caught in a shape of surprise. *It's nothing personal*, he told her, *but I also want that call.*

After hitting *eject*, Nova watched the space station shrink through the pod's lone window until it was no bigger than a silver grain of rice among the stars. The pod jostled violently as it entered atmo, and she clenched the straps of her harness, head braced against the seat and eyes squeezed shut. She wanted a yoke in her hands. She wanted to fly herself to a landing pad, not fall aimlessly.

Something expelled from the pod's rear. A parachute, perhaps.

The computer announced: *Impact in three, two, one . . .*

Nova lurched against the harness.

Water landing. Moderate damage to hull. Evacuate immediately.

She heard the waves next, and the floatation devices expanding from the side of the pod. Nova released the latches on her harness. Something wet lapped at her feet. Water. The pod was flooding.

Pulling her arms from the straps, Nova scrambled onto the chair's headrest and crouched beneath the curved shape of the pod as she grappled with the overhead hatch. The locks slid free, releasing with a hiss of decompression. She stood, using her back to open the hatch as she straightened her legs.

There was soft air on her cheeks.

Blinding light.

And then the silhouette, bent over the pod, reaching in to grab her.

"She's waking!" Amber yelled for the second time, and just like the first, no one responded.

Nova's heartbeat went wild on the monitor. *No, not wild,* Amber told herself as she scanned the readings. *Sixty-five beats per minute. Totally stable, a wonderful resting heartbeat.* It just seemed frantic compared to the average forty-one beats per minute that Amber had grown accustomed to hearing during the coma.

Her father's comments about quarantine rang in Amber's mind, and she darted for the clean room that separated the room from the hallway. Inside, with both doors sealed, she removed a suit from its hook and pulled it on over her clothes in a hurry. Bulky and cumbersome, it was built for the average-sized male. Amber bunched the sleeves up, stuffed her hands into gloves, and pulled a helmet on before racing back into the room.

The pilot was now fully alert, wide-eyed and pawing at the casing of her bed. Amber grabbed the lip of the lid and lifted.

Nova sat up, pulling at the IV and tearing sensors from her forehead and chest.

"Wait! Stop!" Amber lurched forward, grabbing the pilot's arms. Her limbs had been roped with muscle when *Paramount*'s crew first wheeled her into IC2. Now, two months later, they lacked any definition. Amber overpowered her easily.

Nova panted, staring like a child. It was the first time Amber had seen the pilot's eyes open. They were a rich warm brown, like fresh earth.

"Do you know your name?" Amber asked.

"Nova Singh." The pilot's voice cracked on the words, and though everything about her expression was meek in the moment, her answer was confident. That was good.

"Why are you in a suit?" Nova added, her eyes working over Amber. "Where's Dylan?"

Amber could only guess that Dylan was someone important to Nova back home or a deceased member of her crew, left behind in the Fringe. She decided to tackle only the first question.

"The suit's a precaution. There's a slight chance you may be infected or . . . compromised somehow. I've been told to interact with you only while wearing—"

"Infected with what?" Nova's eyes went to the sealed door behind Amber. "Where am I? And who the hell are you?"

"You don't know me?"

"Should I?"

Amber frowned. "What *do* you remember?"

"There was a rescue mission to Achlys." Nova bit her bottom lip, concentrating. "I remember the crew and the transit and the landing, which was a bitch. I've never had to set a ship down on such a pock-ridden, crater-filled, angry slab of land. Black Quarry was missing. Their ship was . . . It was awful. Something bad happened. I don't know what. It's all blurry."

None of what Nova was saying made sense, especially a rescue mission to Achlys. There was nothing *on* Achlys. Still, Nova's lack of memories was concerning. It wasn't uncommon for coma patients to suffer brain damage.

Trying to hide this fear, Amber unlatched the hinges on the corners of the medbed's base and folded the sides down so the unit became more bed than coffin. She propped up the pilot's pillow and helped Nova sit.

"I'm wearing a diaper," the pilot said, staring.

"Yes, well, being comatose isn't very glamorous. There was

a catheter before, but during transit to the new facility . . . Well, *Paramount*'s gear had to stay on the ship, so we had to improvise."

Nova seemed to suddenly realize she was naked save for the disposable wrappings and a military sports bra.

"Who undressed me? Who's been . . ." She glanced again at her hips, the question dying. "I'll use the bathroom on my own now. I'll do everything on my own"—she swung her legs over the edge of the bed—"starting with finding Dylan."

"You're not strong enough yet. Nova, wait!"

"I'll decide what I can and can't do!" She slid from the bed and her legs promptly buckled.

Amber caught her beneath the underarms, keeping the pilot from collapsing fully to the floor. Even in her frail state, she seemed to weigh a ton.

"We'll need to run some tests, get a sense of your state—both mental and physical. It's going to be at least a day before we can get you in PT to start rebuilding muscle." Amber tried to help Nova back onto the bed, but the pilot put her arms out, refusing aid. "Fine! Stay on the floor."

This was the girl she'd tried so hard to connect with, had been so concerned about during cryo. Someone who was so desperate to communicate earlier and now wanted nothing to do with her. Nova had been through a trauma, of course.

A trauma she couldn't even remember. But Amber still couldn't help feeling stung.

She watched as Nova attempted to drag herself back onto the bed. It was too high, her arms not yet strong enough to hoist her onto it. She wouldn't quit, though. She struggled until sweat beaded on her forehead. Finally, when Amber started to worry that the exertion might not be good for someone who'd just come out of a coma, she said, "Can I help you yet?"

Nova glared, her eyes edged with fire. "Yes," she snarled. Then she looked down at her feet and grumbled, "Please." Amber returned to the other girl's side and helped her onto the bed. "It's not easy for me to ask for help," the pilot practically whispered.

Amber nodded. "I doubt any of this is easy. You've been through a lot."

"If I have, I don't remember it."

Because her arm was still around Nova's back and she didn't know what else to do with it, Amber squeezed the pilot's shoulder reassuringly. "They might come back—the memories."

Nova glanced up. Her eyes were big again, hurting. "Does that happen often? With coma patients?"

Amber pulled her arm back and nodded. The truth was that so many coma experiences were different, but she said, "Yeah. All the time."

A knuckle rapped on the door. Through the thick panel of glass, Amber could make out Felix, also suited. Felix was responsible for caring for Decklan Powell, the Hevetz pilot who was the very first bit of cargo the *Paramount* crew had picked up before flying into the Fringe for the second package. *Caring for Powell* was possibly an overstatement. Felix basically just watched him and shoved food through a slot in the pilot's door. It was always locked. Amber had looked through the small window once, curious about the man on the other side.

He'd been sitting on the floor, arms resting on his knees. His jaw was square, his gaze stern. A tiny scar in the shape of a teardrop marked his forehead just above a brow.

Amber wondered how long they intended to keep him in isolation, but she never pressed Felix for an answer. Generally speaking, Amber tried to avoid Felix—both in *Paramount*'s sick bay and now in this quarantined section of their new accommodations. He'd developed a crush on her for reasons Amber couldn't fathom, and his flirting was about as impressive as his inability to read social cues. Felix was nice enough, but he was almost ten years older than Amber, and that was enough to creep her out.

"You were calling for help?" he asked via the intercom system that allowed conversation between quarantined rooms and those outside, but then his eyes found Nova. "Oh, she's awake!" Nova continued to stare at the door as though she'd seen a ghost.

"Is she okay?" he asked. "I think she's trying to kill me with her mind."

Amber rolled her eyes. "Can you watch her for a minute?" It wouldn't be hard work, seeing as Nova could barely move on her own and Powell's room was just across the hall, but Amber didn't want to be insensitive and say this aloud in front of the pilot. "I need to let my dad know she's up. He's not answering his comms."

"Sure," Felix said with a wink. "Anything for my favorite colleague."

Amber forced a smile and darted for the exit. She hit the button to open the door with the back of her fist, and Nova let out a small sob.

"Oh my god." The pilot pressed a hand to her mouth, muffling her words. She was still staring at the door, now open and revealing Felix's fully suited body on the other side. "I killed her."

"Killed who?" Amber asked.

"Dylan. She was sick and I purged her from the air lock."

It came back to Nova in fragments.

The knock on the door had started it, triggering an image of Dylan throwing a palm against an air lock's window.

From there, the images continued, speeding by so quickly Nova could barely interpret them.

Dylan's body suctioned into space. Her bloody nose and hemorrhaging eyes. A smile. A broken ankle. An engine room where Nova should have abandoned the other woman.

Toby, coming after them.

The halls, swarming with infected.

Nova had made it to an elevator with Dylan in tow, then boarded a shuttle. There were two other people on it. Thea and Coen. Nova had flown from Achlys with them, Black Quarry's ship detonating in their wake.

The next memory was of a space station, a construct of her mind during the coma. She'd stayed there with Dylan until the escape pod had appeared. Nova had climbed into it and awoken in this suffocating room, in this foreign body. Her legs didn't feel like her own. Her arms were made of jelly. She glanced down at the bracelet on her wrist. Thin and delicate, a string of silver. It was Dylan's. She remembered now.

A wave of emotions crashed down on her: love and loss, but anger, too. Disgust. How could she feel so many things for the same person?

Love is complicated, she remembered someone saying once, but she couldn't recall who.

"I want to talk to whoever's in charge," Nova said, but when she raised her head, only the male medic remained. Behind his suit's visor, she could make out a small ≠ tattoo beneath his ear, a popular symbol of the Radical movement.

"Not sure if that'll be possible till Amber gets back," he said.

"Amber. Was that who was helping me?"

"Yeah. Amber Farraday."

The name rattled around Nova's skull. She'd heard it before and yet she hadn't recognized the girl. Strawberry hair that fell around an oval face. Skin almost pearlescent behind the visor of her hazmat suit. Deep dimples that had appeared when she'd smiled. Nova would have remembered a face that pretty.

"Is the rest of my crew here?" she asked.

"The hosts? Yeah, they're here."

"They're sick?"

"Nah, more like immune. Actually, that's not the right word, either." The medic scratched his chin through his suit. "I don't really know what's going on. They don't let me visit the research level."

Another wave of emotion hit Nova: loyalty and compassion, an urge to help these friends she could barely remember. They were most definitely friends, though. She was certain of it. And *hosts*, according to the medic. Dread coiled in her stomach as she remembered the bloody-eyed hordes from Black Quarry.

Merely sitting had rendered her exhausted, and Nova leaned back, all but falling into the pillow. The ceiling was white with recessed lights spaced out at even intervals. Having the strength to walk again sounded absurd. She'd be staring at this very ceiling for months. Recovery was impossible.

Impossible is just an excuse not to try.

Someone had told her this once, too. The same someone who'd warned her about love.

Nova closed her eyes and tried to remember.

The offer had been a lie.

Hands fisted, Coen stared at the photo of Gina. *Contact with a family member, as promised*, Farraday had said when he slid the photo beneath Coen's door. They must have found it in his backpack from Achlys.

A photo wasn't what Coen had expected based on Farraday's original offer, and he doubted Thea had, either. And yet here he was, staring at the very photo of Gina that he'd packed before sneaking onboard *Celestial Envoy* as part of the Black Quarry crew. The same photo that had kept him sane when he was alone, all the others dead. Gina's face, smiling up at him. He'd talked to her so many times in that abandoned Witch Hazel bunker, telling her that he'd left to help, promising he'd return no matter what, all while staring at her slouched shoulders.

Between them, a tumor was growing along her spine. When he'd left, she was beginning to lose feeling in her arms and legs. It was possible she had no sensation left in them. She'd been in chronic pain for months, and yet she'd managed to smile for this photo.

This photo in which Coen was grimacing.

This photo that was now his only contact with her.

Coen's fist lurched out, striking the wall. Pain exploded over his knuckles and was gone, all too brief. He punched again, his arm a sledgehammer he longed to drive through the wall. But this new cell was impenetrable. He couldn't dent it.

He kept punching anyway, the pain coming in quick bursts. He punched faster, not letting his body recover from the ache. A wetness covered his knuckles. Flecks of it spattered his face.

Coen was suddenly back in the hospital room, hearing Gina's diagnosis for the first time. His parents were stoic beside him. Gina had forced a smile from the bed, as if the state of her condition wasn't dire, as if the treatment the doctor had just described was something his family could afford. He didn't understand how they were all so calm. The unfairness of the situation was so immense it suffocated. He'd gone wild then, too. Not in that moment, but later, once the doctor had left. He'd put a hole in the wall beside Gina's bed.

Coen, she'd said, and he'd kept punching, ashamed that she needed to console him, that *he* wasn't the one doing the comforting. *Coen, stop.*

But he couldn't—not then and not now, as he continued to punch the cell wall, so much less forgiving than the hospital's. Flecks of blood sprayed from his hands, his knuckles aching with pain.

Coen.

Another punch.

Coen, stop!

He had to get it out. The anger and the helplessness and the fear. If he didn't, he'd break right now. He'd collapse and never get up.

Coen, listen to me!

"STOP!"

He froze, glancing over his shoulder. His current cell was the opposite of *Paramount*'s in almost every way. This new facility was almost blindingly white. White floor tiles, gleaming walls, pale cot, and stark bedsheets. One of the walls was a thick panel of glass, allowing him to see into Thea's cell on the other side.

She stood there, the butt of her fist still pressed to the material. Probably she'd been pounding on it as she begged him to stop.

That isn't going to solve anything, she said, looking at his fist.

He saw the blood for the first time. He'd felt it earlier, been glad for it even, but now he saw the mess. The butchered state of his knuckles, the spatters on the floor and smears on the wall.

It won't, he agreed. *But it felt good.*

He wiped his knuckles clean on his T-shirt. It already had a few blood drops on it, and there was no sense ruining the bedsheets. His hand was already healing, the raw state of each knuckle smoothing over with fresh skin.

He hated this thing he'd become. It had cursed him. Burke and Farraday, the entire research crew—they were never going to let him go home.

I'm sorry about Gina, Thea said.

Me, too. Who would you have contacted?

Does it matter? You won the prize. Tension crackled around her. She was still mad about earlier, in the boxing ring.

Oh come on, Thea. You attacked me first! You wanted to win just as badly.

She turned away, moving for her cot on the far wall. She pulled the sheets down and climbed in, putting her back to him.

Why'd you tell me to quit punching the wall, then? If you're so pissed, why not let me beat my fist to a pulp?

Still facing away from him, Thea said, *It was impossible to sleep with you making so much noise.*

Her words were cool, but Coen could sense the falseness to the statement, a wrinkle in his intuition. The truth was she was still angry about earlier, but she didn't like seeing him hurt, either.

He'd make things right in the morning. But tonight— tonight he'd earned the right to sulk.

He scooped up the picture and crawled into bed, talking to Gina just as he had all those nights on Achlys. He told her he'd be home soon. If he didn't say it aloud, he feared he might forget how to believe it.

Come morning, Thea ignored Coen. Not because she was still angry with him, but because she was busy memorizing what was sure to become a routine.

First, the guards gathered in the hall. The doorframe to her cell was a slight seam in an otherwise pale wall—no visible hinges or handles or access pads and certainly no door windows—but Thea could hear their heartbeats on the other side. Shortly after they arrived, the gas started.

Things went foggy for a few minutes and when she came to, Thea was wearing the hot cap and collar again. The guards had entered the room to secure them after she'd passed out.

Thea, I'm sorry, Coen said for the nth time as they were guided through hallways.

She blocked him out, focusing on the route. Their cells were on a windowless hall that led to a central elevator if you knew where to turn (*first right, third left, right, right, straight until elevator*). From there, the guards brought them to the research and testing room two flights up. Levels were labeled by number only, with the cells held at thirty and research at twenty-eight.

Thea's theory was solidifying. They were underground. If she managed to get to the top level, they might have a chance of escape.

How long are we going to willingly go along with all this? Coen asked as they were ushered back into research.

Until we have a chance at escape that might actually pay off.

Oh, you're talking to me again.

I'll stop if you don't watch it.

She wasn't truly angry with him. She understood why he'd fought her yesterday. It was the same reason she'd attacked him first. His speed had terrified her when he'd countered back, the way his eyes had gone elsewhere and his expression had steeled. But he'd cushioned her fall, and she'd known he wouldn't hit her the moment she'd thrown her arms up. Her brain had jumped ahead, analyzing the position of his wrist, the angle of his arm.

But she was still furious with him. And jealous.

Farraday's offer had been a farce, but Coen's photo was

still *something*. It was a connection to his old life, a reminder of home. Thea longed for that contact. A mere picture of a familiar face—even a worker from child services—would have helped anchor her. It would have been a reminder of Eutheria, of all the things she'd left behind. Her education and grades, a future where she might be able to track down her mother, or at the very least, learn what had actually happened to her. People don't just vanish into thin air.

The collar pinched at her neck as the guards yanked her to a halt. She wasn't at the research lab. Instead, they'd stopped earlier in the hall, just outside a set of locker rooms.

"Both facilities have been emptied," one of the guards said. "You'll have five minutes to shower. Remember that you are wearing a cap that can deliver an electric shock at any moment. If we believe you may be trying to escape, we won't hesitate to use it, and consequences may be dire if you're standing in water."

The metal leads clicked, detaching from Thea's collar and then used to prod her in the back. She staggered into the locker room, catching a final glimpse of Coen disappearing into the male facilities in a similar fashion.

She cased the room with excitement that quickly fizzled. It was empty, as the guard had promised, but there were no windows. No rear exits. No way out but the way she'd just entered.

"Your five minutes starts now!" the guard called from the hallway.

Not sure when her next chance would be to bathe, Thea stripped down and darted into the shower. A dispenser on the wall provided unscented soap, and she scrubbed herself clean as fast as possible. The water was divine. Her skin felt new. She didn't bother with her hair—there was a sink in her cell where she could see to it later, and besides, she was wearing the hot cap. Still, she could have stayed in the shower for hours.

"Last minute!" came a warning from the hall.

Thea turned off the shower and scrambled for her clothes. The guards hadn't even provided a towel, so she used her shirt to dry off, then pulled it on and crammed her legs into her leggings. The material clung to her damp skin. Turning to the mirror, she found the surface fogged with condensation, and cleared it with her palm.

A foreign face peered back.

She'd lost weight in the past months. Thea couldn't remember her last proper meal, and it showed in her cheeks. She frowned, and the strange reflection frowned back.

The guard outside began counting down from twenty.

Thea turned away from the mirror and darted for the hall. As soon as she crossed the threshold, a brief shock came through the hot cap, bringing her to her knees. In that moment of disorientation, the guards secured their leads to her collar.

"Can I . . . ?" a soft voice asked.

"Yeah, she's secure," the guard replied.

Thea glanced up to see a young medic, shower caddy in hand and small pack slung over her shoulder. *Amber Farraday*, the badge pinned to her medical jacket read. *Med Intern*. She had strawberry hair and a slender neck, and while her pulse wasn't hot with fear, it beat unevenly. As she edged around the guard and into the locker room, she made eye contact with Thea. Something lurked there. Pity, Thea realized.

The collar lead was shoved, and Thea scramble-crawled forward before finally standing. Coen sent her thoughts about his shower as they were led off, calling it heavenly. She agreed, but she'd already forgotten the kiss of the water. Her thoughts were stuck on Amber. The way the medic had looked at her: like she wasn't a host to be feared, but a person deserving of help.

Maybe pity wasn't the worst thing to have seen in her eyes. Thea could work with pity better than she could with contempt. She tried to glance over her shoulder, hoping for one last glimpse of the medic, but the collar kept her from turning her head.

❋ ❋ ❋

When Nova woke to the sound of Amber entering her room, the fake window beside her bed glowed with dawn's first light. The medic was in a hazmat suit again, and she smiled from behind the visor. From most people it would be a forced smile. An *I'm smiling so you maybe forget how shitty everything is* smile. But on Amber, it looked sincere. It was more of an *I'm happy to see you again and I promise we'll get through this* smile.

"You don't have to wear that thing," Nova said, nodding at the suit. "I would be showing symptoms by now if I was a danger. I remembered that the nosebleed and spasms started within five minutes of infection. The hemorrhaged eyes, soon after."

"My father said almost the exact same thing this morning. I pressed him for more info as soon as you woke up yesterday."

"And he knows about the answers . . . how?"

"He has some salvaged footage from that Black Quarry operation you mentioned."

Nova frowned, skeptical. Dr. Farraday had come to visit her during the night. She'd recognized him as Amber's father—they had the same eyes—but his touch has been cold and impersonal, and he barked out questions about Black Quarry while checking her vitals. *What is Thea capable of now? Have you observed the boy's healing capabilities? How strong are they, truly? What makes them capable hosts when everyone else is driven mad?* The questions hadn't made sense to her, and the doctor had left disgruntled. Nova wondered what he'd seen in the salvaged Black Quarry footage.

"Yesterday, Felix called my friends hosts," she said. "Hosts to what?"

"I don't know."

"Did they have nosebleeds when you saw them being relocated? Blood-filled eyes?"

"No," Amber insisted. "Nothing like that."

Nova exhaled, relieved. The contagion had been left behind on Achlys.

"As for this suit," Amber said, glancing down at her front, "I've been told to use it for another twenty-four hours, just to be safe. Ready to begin physical therapy?" Another smile, this one bright and encouraging. Nova hated how upbeat it was. "We'll start with the regen bed. It's most effective for healing wounds and slowing bleeding, but it can boost the growth of muscle cells, too. Only a small percentage, sadly. From there, you'll have to do the rest."

"And you're my trainer?"

The other girl's brows slid into a V. "You want someone else?"

"No, you're fine."

"So glad I meet your standards."

"That's not what I—I didn't—" Nova sighed. "Sorry. I just didn't realize you doubled as a physical therapist, that's all."

"I don't. Not really. But everyone else is busy, and you and I are at the bottom of the ladder in terms of priorities here. It's me or no one. Now let's get you out of bed."

Amber pulled one of Nova's arms behind her neck and then helped her to her feet. Nova wanted to ask why everyone else was busy, who was in charge, where she was, but as soon as Amber helped her from the bed, her legs burned with exhaustion. It took all her focus to not collapse right there, even with her arm slung behind the medic's neck.

"This sucks," Nova grunted as they entered the hall.

"It will get better."

She didn't even need to look to know Amber was giving her that supportive smile again. Support and pity mixed together. "Yeah, but right now it sucks and I just want to be able to say that without being coddled or encouraged or pitied. It sucks, it sucks, it fucking *sucks*."

"It's a shit situation," Amber agreed. "One hundred percent."

It was said so sincerely that Nova felt a stab of guilt. "It could be worse," she admitted.

"Of course it could. But here I am, already getting you to think positively."

Nova cocked her head toward Amber. "By tricking me."

Smile widening, the medic winked.

Nova felt an old spark of challenge, a reminder of a game she played at Northwood Point with Dylan. Smiling wouldn't be the prize anymore. Amber handed them out too easily. No, this time it would be winks.

One wink, Nova thought, starting the day's tally.

Coen tested the restraints that held him to his chair. They were tight. Not so tight that he couldn't break them, but with the hot cap on his head, he wouldn't push things.

He was back in the research lab, Thea secured to a chair beside him. A regenerative bed and a tray of medical tools sat nearby. Dr. Farraday hadn't explained what was about to happen, but Coen had a good guess. Their healing capabilities were about to be tested.

It wasn't humane. They should be sedated first, at the very least, but what good were superhuman soldiers if they couldn't heal quickly and under duress?

The testing started simply enough. Injuries no bigger than paper cuts, applied to the meaty part of his arm. Then the knives were drawn deeper and farther. The pain began to blossom and spread. Coen briefly saw stars before his body took over, clotting blood, rejoining skin and tissue. Beside him, Thea let out a gasp.

Tell me about your mom, he said, gritting through pain,

desperate for a distraction.

And she did.

Everything she remembered about the woman and their on-the-move life together. The way she'd disappeared one day as Thea waited at the bus stop. How she was the most loving, caring, protective mother until she vanished, and how records of her didn't exist. Which was why Thea thought she was still out there somewhere. Her mother was hiding, or someone was hiding her, and Thea was determined to get answers.

She spoke through the worst of the knives and into a soldering gun, which tested their ability to recover from burns. The mental conversation didn't mask the pain, but it kept Coen from focusing on it. When it was over, he was breathless and sweaty, his body beat. He felt as though he'd run a marathon, but when he dared a glance at his arm, it was unmarred. No scars. No evidence that he'd just been tortured.

"Excellent," a voice said, cutting through the lab's intercoms. *Burke.* Coen glanced at the mirrored wall. The lieutenant must have watched everything from behind the glass. "Now get them back in the ring. I want to see how they fight after that level of injury."

Without so much as a minute to recover or a drink to quench their thirst, Coen and Thea were shoved into the ring and again supplied with shock rods.

I can't, Thea said, clutching her torso. *I'm exhausted.*

Coen had a stitch in his side as well, but was trying to ignore it. Even during the worst of the fighting on Achlys, he'd never felt this drained. Then again, he'd been able to fight back on Achlys and had only taken a few injuries along the way. But being strapped down, being forced to weather wound after trauma after burn—that was different.

Come on. I can teach you, he said, tossing the shock rod aside. *Start with fists only.*

She stared at him, puzzled.

Go on, toss the rod.

She dropped it by her feet.

Get in a ready stance. Always protect your head from your opponent. Keep your weight light and never planted through one foot. See how I've got my left shoulder angled at you and the rest held back?

Cautiously, she mirrored his stance.

Good. Now front hand up. Shield your face. Always protect.

She moved her left hand up a little, letting it hover near her chin.

Perfect. Now if I come in like this— He threw a light punch and she instinctively danced out of reach. *Right. You can back step. Or you can duck or block. Go on, throw one at me.* She gave him a skeptical look. *Go ahead.*

As her fist hurtled toward his face, Coen brought his

forearm up while circling it away from his body, blocking and deflecting the blow. Thea's eyes narrowed, taking it in.

Your turn. Ready?

She nodded. He threw the punch. She blocked.

Good. And if your opponent gets a hold on you . . . He moved in, and she let him put her in a light headlock from behind. *You're small, but you're bony. That's an advantage. Use your elbows, and use them mercilessly. Go ahead.*

She hesitated, so he tightened the hold around her neck. Her elbow jutted out, slamming into his gut. He coughed, staggering away.

Sorry!

No, that was perfect. Don't apologize. Let's go again.

It went on like that, a sparring session that intensified as Thea's confidence grew. They danced around each other, sweat beading on their limbs, the harsh overhead lights blurring out their spectators. Coen forgot about Farraday and Burke and the soldiers the Radicals wanted to create with Thea and him as their models. He saw only the ring, and Thea's fists, and it brought him a sense of ease.

He hadn't felt so relaxed in months. The fighting set him free.

Amber was roughly the same height as Nova, which made helping her to the regenerative bed relatively easy. It was only once Nova was lying in the chamber that Amber realized she should have brought a wheelchair for the other girl. *Next time*, she told herself.

She lowered the lid of the bed and ran a basic diagnostic. The system told her what she'd already concluded based on her initial assessment and her father's notes from his night visit. Despite a large amount of muscle loss, Nova Singh was healthy. Even the brain scan looked good—expected activity and no serious trauma. If any memories were still clouded or lost to Nova, they were bound to return in time.

She ran a program to stimulate regrowth of muscle cells, and a half hour later, helped Nova sit.

"Next time, tell me how long I'm gonna be stuck in that thing?"

Amber nodded, embarrassed she hadn't thought to warn Nova from the beginning. *There is so much more to being a doctor than treating ailments*, her father was always chastising. *Never forget the human element.* Amber hadn't really understood what he meant, but she thought she might now.

"I'll get a wheelchair and we can head to Therapy," Amber said.

"No, I want to walk. I have to build up the muscle somehow."

"Okay." Amber hesitantly moved to Nova's side, again guiding the pilot's arm behind her neck. They left the medbay and moved down the hall at a terribly slow pace, though

Nova didn't seem to lean on Amber quiet as heavily as earlier.

"I actually feel a little stronger," the pilot admitted. "That's wild."

Amber flashed her eyebrows up, as if to say *Technology!*

When they reached Therapy, Amber helped Nova to a set of waist-high bars in the center of the room, which the pilot would be able to use as handles as she attempted to support her own weight. Amber slowly backed away.

Arms locked and feet planted on the floor, Nova held herself upright. Her limbs trembled. Sweat beaded on her brow.

"Can you take a step?" Amber asked.

"Fuck no," Nova gasped out.

Amber rushed behind her and grabbed Nova beneath the shoulders just before her arms gave out. She lowered her onto a stool and brought over resistance bands and showed Nova a variety of movements she could repeat to help rebuild muscle in her quads and hamstrings.

"You really don't remember me?" she asked as Nova extended her right leg in front of her, stretching the band. "We spoke when you were in a coma. I asked you questions and you blinked yes or no. Blinked whole answers in Morse code, even."

The pilot turned toward Amber, her brow wrinkled. "How did I even end up in a coma?"

"I'm not sure. Something must have gone wrong with the sedation process in the shuttle's cryo pod."

"That's . . . uncommon," Nova said.

Amber held her gaze. "I know."

Neither of them said the words, but Amber could tell they both suspected the same thing: something was being kept from them.

"I asked so many questions when I was first tasked with watching you," Amber went on. "Knowing *how* someone slipped into a coma gives you a good idea of their odds of coming out. They told me they found you like that. Your two friends came willingly and you were already unresponsive. But none of that seems right, because I saw your friends, and they were being dragged around by force, half sedated. People who want to willingly participate in something don't need to be drugged."

Nova licked her lips, thinking. Amber watched beads of sweat trickle across the pilot's temple.

"Can I see them—Thea and Coen?"

Amber's stomach twisted. She'd felt bad enough when they were just *the hosts*, but now they had names. They were real people—teens like her—and she couldn't shake the feeling that something bad was going to happen to them.

"I'll ask," she said finally. "But no promises. I can't imagine Burke will be very accommodating."

"Is that who's in charge?"

"Lieutenant Christoph Burke. He's overseeing this mission . . . whatever it is."

"Trios military?" Nova asked.

Amber nodded.

"And you're military?" Nova's eyes skirted Amber's frame, searching for ID tags, but the medical badge Amber wore was hidden from view beneath the haz suit.

"No, I'm just a medic. Burke pulled some Hevetz scientists onboard when we were tasked with picking up your crew. As well as my father. They're old friends, I guess? I just got caught up in things." Amber explained the Alternate Enrichment year quickly and how far off track her education had strayed in the past two months.

"So where are we now? Somewhere in the Trios, I hope?"

"Yeah. A research base. I don't know exact details."

"And you haven't asked?" Nova looked at her incredulously.

"We only arrived yesterday. You woke up just hours after we got situated, and my key card only gets me to certain levels, so it's not like I can waltz off to hunt down answers on my own. I still don't understand why everything is being treated like a top secret operation. Then again, the Radicals have always been dramatic. Maybe I shouldn't be surprised."

"The Radicals?" Nova let her foot fall to the ground and stared at Amber. "What the hell do the Radicals have to do with anything?"

"Burke's entire crew seems to be made of Radicals. As far

as I can tell, if they dissent, he gets them relocated to different units or—if he thinks they're a liability—gets them discharged entirely. I've seen at least half the Hevetz scientists make the Radical salute to each other while passing in the halls. And Vasteneur called for Burke's help with Black Quarry. He's supposed to arrive in another week or so, so it's safe to assume he's a Radical, too."

"And your father?" Nova prodded. "*You?*"

The pilot was glaring at her in a way that set off warnings in the back of Amber's mind. In the past, plenty of people had questioned Amber's inability to pick a side, but she had no problem defending it. She held nothing against pro-unity people and understood their logic, just as she understood why the Radicals wanted independence, which was precisely why the Trios had been in a stalemate for decades.

"Are you pro-independence?" Nova asked, eyes still boring into Amber.

"My father is," she said. "I'm undecided."

"What's to be undecided about? If the Trios is independent, we'll go belly-up. Our access to the best medicine, ships, education? It'll all be cut off, or at least made so expensive we'll never be able to afford it." Amber must have let something slip on her expression because Nova's eyes narrowed as she added, "Oh, I'm sorry, Miss Enrichment Year. Only *some* of us won't be able to afford it. You know, the less fortunate ones."

"You should work on your calves now," Amber said, desperate to change the subject. She repositioned the band so that Nova could work her lower legs.

"What are the Radicals even after?" Nova went on. "Clearly Hevetz pulled Burke in to rescue Black Quarry. He deliberately went to a Radical friend over Galactic Disease Control, which would mean . . ." Her face went blank. "Last night, your father asked about my friends' *abilities*. What abilities?"

"I don't know," Amber said.

"He implied that they could host what everyone else in Black Quarry couldn't, but that doesn't make any sense. You're sure they didn't have nosebleeds when you saw them being relocated? Blood-filled eyes?"

"No," Amber insisted. "Nothing like that." Just that morning, her father had mentioned that Nova's lack of nosebleed was a promising sign. But Thea and Coen didn't have nosebleeds either, and they were being studied while Nova was all but ignored. "What the hell happened on Achlys?"

Nova didn't break eye contact. "Find out what happened to my friends, and I'll tell you."

When they returned to their cells, every millimeter of Thea was sore. She relished the pain and tightness, knowing it would be gone by morning, just another reminder that she was a thing in the eyes of Burke and his crew. A thing they longed to replicate.

"Clean clothes," the guard said, dropping them at her feet. He was wearing a mask, because the gas had begun to fill her cell now. She stared at the lump of white clothing at her feet, her senses slowing. The collar clinked loose. The cap was lifted from her head.

When the gas wore off, she was alone in the room, slumped beside the fresh clothing.

She shook them out—clean leggings and a tank top— wishing she'd been allowed a trip to the locker room again before being locked in for the night. There was a small wash sink and toilet in the corner of her cell, sheltered from view by a smartly angled, shoulder-high wall. But a sink wasn't a shower. And the wall didn't provide much privacy, regard- less. She could wash her hair now, at least, but she knew that Burke and Farraday were probably watching everything, observing her interactions with Coen, listening. She was again struck by how her wants meant nothing here. Her desire for privacy was meaningless compared to Burke's desire for answers.

We can both turn our backs, Coen said, retrieving his own set of fresh clothes from the floor.

Thanks. He'd heard her wish for privacy. She had to get better at protecting her thoughts.

What else would I do, sit here and leer at you the whole time?

I would kick your ass in the ring tomorrow if you did.

You could try, he said with a smile.

Let me rephrase that: I'd elbow you so hard you'd bruise. At least for a minute or two.

Another smile. Then he grabbed his clothes and moved to his wash station. *Let me know when you're done.*

Even knowing they had their backs to each other, Thea felt exposed. She washed her hair first, then stripped down quickly. After splashing fresh water on her face and limbs, she toweled off and yanked the new clothing on.

All set, she told him. *You?*

More or less.

She turned around and froze. If "more or less" meant "I'm half dressed," Coen's response was accurate. He was still standing at the sink, wearing only his pants and using a towel to dry his hair.

She couldn't tear her eyes from his bare torso. His tattoo was nothing like she'd imagined.

Now that it was fully visible, she could see it wasn't a simple organic design like she'd assumed, but an exquisitely detailed and intricate illustration of an octopus. The creature was positioned along Coen's side, with its arms fanning onto his back and chest. Two coiled up and over his shoulder, ending on Coen's collarbone and neck. These two tendrils were all she'd seen on Achlys, a mere fraction of the actual tattoo peeking into view at the shirt collar.

"Sorry," she murmured aloud, so stunned that the word slipped from her mouth. "You said you were more or less done, so I turned around. I didn't realize . . ." She trailed off, watching the octopus writhe and squirm as Coen finished drying his hair.

"You're staring," Coen said. His voice was deeper aloud than it ever seemed in her head. Rougher, too.

She pulled her eyes up to meet his. "I don't mean to. It's just . . ." Thea looked back at the tattoo. "It's really beautiful."

"Gina drew it. She's so damn talented. Wants to study illustration when she gets to uni."

The ink was black, but the creature had been shaded meticulously, giving it shape and life on Coen's tan skin. He pulled his hair back, securing half of it at his crown, and a ripple moved through the octopus as muscles in his torso stretched.

"Did you know the octopus is the most intelligent invertebrate in the ocean? One of the most intelligent animals, period?"

Thea nodded. There'd been a period in middle school where she was obsessed with the sea. She'd watched about a thousand marine vids at the local library with Mel, marveling at the ocean's ecosystem. One documentary focused specifically on octopuses and how they could learn by observation, opening jars and boxes to reach food.

"It can camouflage itself and fit into impossibly tight spaces," Coen continued. "It can even grow back limbs. The octopus is resilient, and that's why Gina wanted it. This tattoo was supposed to be hers, but by the time she was diagnosed, she was too weak to get the art. The doctor said any exposure to a possible infection was an unnecessary risk. One that could prove deadly. After my parents heard that, they forbade a trip to the tattoo shop. So I got it for her."

"Like a proxy," Thea said.

"Yeah, something like that." Coen slipped the clean T-shirt over his head.

Thea stared at the two tendrils on his neck, the only portion of the tattoo still visible. The only portion she'd known until this moment. She was suddenly overwhelmed by the enormity of it all—the secrets a person could hide in full sight. This research facility and how far she was from home. The very real possibility that Coen might never see his family again—that she would likely never find hers.

"Hey," Coen said.

She glanced up, startled to find an expression on his face that she hadn't seen before. Concern, on every inch of his features, but paired with something else she couldn't place. His brow was wrinkled, but his eyes were soft.

"We'll get out of this." He pressed his palm to the glass, spreading out his fingers.

She didn't know if that was true anymore, but she wasn't

brave enough to contradict him.

"Thea?"

She reached out, pressing her hand to his. Though several centimeters of glass divided them, Coen's pulse beat strongly in her ears. She let hers match it, their hearts beating in perfect unison. She imagined, briefly, what his bare hand might feel like against hers. The thought sent a wave of heat through her and she pulled back as her pulse kicked faster, breaking rhythm with his.

Come evening, Nova couldn't sleep. She was on the IV again, a precaution Amber had insisted on to avoid dehydration. There were sensors on Nova's chest, a clip on her finger. Her vitals ticked on a machine.

She rolled onto her side, muscles protesting, but sore was good. It meant progress. It meant healing. Between the physical therapy and a session in the regen bed every morning, Nova could be back on her feet within a week. Still weaker than she was used to, Amber had warned, but capable of supporting her own weight and using the bathroom alone. Capable of independence.

It sounded glorious. And still it did little to lift her mood.

Too much was wrong. The IV and sensors keeping her chained to the bed. The strange research facility run by Radicals in cooperation with Hevetz Industries. How her cryo pod had somehow plunged her into a coma—a malfunction that happened so rarely Nova couldn't place the last time she'd read about it in the news.

Someone had tampered with her pod while in stasis. It was the only explanation. Likely the same someone who now held her friends against their will. *Burke.*

Her thoughts drifted to Toby and his conspiracy theories about the Radicals staging a coup soon, taking over the government and seizing Trios independence by force with the help of Hevetz Industries. And now she was stuck at this facility, manned by Radicals, all the details lining up with Toby's predictions.

Nova closed her eyes only to see Achlys in the darkness. Black Quarry members slithered into view, crawling from crevices and fissures in the ragged land. Snapping and growling, they chased her into *Celestial Envoy*, pushing her deeper into the ship, trapping her. Toby was there, too, eyes dark with blood. She'd hated him, and yet he didn't deserve what he'd become. No one deserved that.

She blinked and found herself strapped to an operating table aboard *Celestial Envoy*. Toby was upon her, clawing at her face and limbs. Tearing flesh. Driving the infected blood beneath his fingernails into her skin. She could feel the bacteria in her veins—hot, ugly.

Nova screamed, thrashing. She shoved at Toby and pawed

at her own limbs, trying to dig the disease out.

"Nova, stop!"

Hands pressed against her shoulder—Toby, shoving her into the bed.

"NOVA!"

She tried to turn away. Toby was stronger.

"Nova, it's me. You're in your room."

She felt a pillow beneath her back. Medbay operating tables didn't have pillows. There was a blanket over her feet. A window that wasn't a window. A digital night sky.

"You're fine. Come back to me. Come back."

Amber's face appeared where Toby's had been. Nova blinked, confused. Stopped struggling. Her sheets were a mess. She'd pulled the IV from her arm, torn the sensors from her chest and finger.

"Nova," Amber said again.

Nova found the medic's eyes. "I was back there," she gasped out. "They were everywhere. They were attacking me." A sob escaped her, and she buried her face in her hands, crying. Once the tears started, she couldn't slow them. The dam was broken. "I don't know what's real anymore."

"This," Amber said, squeezing her hand. "Me. This room. There's no one here but us."

"I can't slow my heart down. I feel like it's going to explode from my chest."

"It could be PTSD. You've been through a lot and— Here. Try to breathe with me."

Nova forced herself to match Amber's inhales and exhales as the medic got her back on the IV and reattached sensors. Nova's heartbeat soon beeped through the room, fast and urgent.

"Do you want to talk about it?"

She shook her head. She could handle this. They were just memories—nightmarish memories—but she'd lived through them. She already needed help walking. She couldn't bear the thought of needing even more support.

"In that case . . ." Amber pulled an animation up on her Tab—a flat line that morphed into a triangle, then a square, a pentagon, all the way up to an octagon. "Imagine this is your lungs filling as you breathe in," she instructed. "Exhale as it collapses." The octagon folded in on itself, collapsing flat before morphing into a triangle again, the animation looping.

Nova breathed with it for several minutes, her pulse steadying. Her vitals stabilized, the monitor's beeping leveling out.

"Good," Amber said, though Nova could detect some uncertainty in her voice. She was just a medical intern. She was winging this. "Keep doing that."

Nova focused on the animation, barely noticing as Amber

smoothed out the blanket and righted the nightstand that Nova had somehow toppled. Finally, Nova felt as though a weight had lifted from her chest, as if the room was bigger. A steady heart rate blipped on the monitor.

The mattress shifted as Amber sat beside Nova. "Better?"

Nova nodded, noticing that Amber wasn't wearing her haz suit anymore, but jeans and a low-cut tee. Her medical jacket hung askew from her shoulders. One sleeve was rolled to the elbow, the other wrinkled but loose. Probably Nova's doing as she'd thrashed.

"Do you want me to stay?" Amber asked.

Without the hazmat suit's visor, Nova could see that the medic's hair fell to her collarbone, a lob reminiscent of someone else Nova had known. She blinked, and Dylan sat in Amber's place. Another blink, and the medic was back.

The pressure closed in on Nova's chest, threatening to overtake her.

"No," she said. "I need you to leave. Right now."

Amber frowned, standing. "All right. Call if you need anything."

Nova heard her leave, and it was only then that she risked a glance toward the door. The medic was gone. Nova was alone. Safe. She could get through this without anyone. She was enough.

She continued the breathing animation, one hand absentmindedly fiddling with the silver bracelet on her other wrist as she inhaled, and exhaled, and inhaled again.

Thea was awoken by the guards the following morning and again brought to the locker rooms. She whispered the route into Coen's mind, reciting turns and noting levels. His pessimistic thoughts riled her.

What good is knowing the way to the elevator if we're always collared and capped? We'll never get anywhere.

That's not helpful, she snapped, and returned to her work. She didn't care if he thought it useless. The information was important. She ran through it mentally while showering. The mirror was again fogged when she was finished.

"One minute!" the guard shouted from the hall.

Thea scanned the locker room again, searching the corners and ceiling. There were no surveillance cameras to be seen—likely in ordinance with a privacy policy. The locker room was off grid.

She brought a finger to the mirror, tracing a message into the fogged surface.

Is Nova alive?

When she left the room, a quick shock bringing her to her knees, Amber Burke was again arriving. Methodical. Right on time.

It was a bold question, what Thea had left on that mirror.

There was no way of knowing if Amber even knew who Nova was. But the girl was a med intern and at the very least, she'd have access to medical records, so Thea made sure to hold her gaze, thinking, *Help me, help me, please.* She didn't care if it was pitiful or desperate or weak. She wanted an ally outside her cell, and something told her Amber might be it.

Amber was waiting for the water to warm when she spotted the message.

She stared at it, additional steam clouding the mirror, erasing the letters. Within a minute, it was as though the message was never there. Part of her wished this was true. It would be easier to not help the host—Thea, Nova had called her—if the girl hadn't made contact.

But now . . .

Amber considered her options while washing. When she was through—dried and dressed—the locker room was still empty. It was early, but Amber had always been a morning person, up before the sun. Not that there was a sun at this level.

She cleared a section of the mirror with her towel. Her reflection stared back.

What would it be like to be held here against her will, unaware of her location, her purpose, if she'd ever be set free? Amber didn't know what business her father or Burke had with Thea and her friend, but it couldn't be good.

There was no harm in answering the question, she decided. She fished around in her bag until she found a small printout showing Nova's vitals. Amber had requested it back on *Paramount* when the on-site network had malfunctioned one day, failing to back up vitals automatically. She'd entered the data by hand a few hours later when things were back online. The opposite side of the printout was blank.

Amber dug her brow pencil from her makeup bag and wrote: *Nova is fine. Out of coma. Weak but healing.*

She crouched down and tucked the note beneath the sink, cramming it between the vanity and the wall. Lingering there, she wondered if she was making a mistake. She couldn't help Thea, not truly, and just speaking to the host could get her in trouble. It was clear the Radicals were on one side of this and Thea and Coen were on the other.

"Hey, Amber," Cyra said, striding into the locker room. The Hevetz geneticist had a bag in hand and a towel slung over her shoulder. "You all right?"

"Yeah. Just dropped my brow pencil." Amber held it up and stood. No time to change her mind now. "I've got a PT session to run. See you later."

Cyra nodded in farewell, and Amber slipped into the hall.

When Coen was shoved into the research facility, Dr. Farraday and the usual medics were waiting. Today, two desks had been set at opposite ends of the wide room, one right before the mirrored wall, the other on the far side, the chairs positioned to face each other.

Coen was forced into the seat by the mirror. Thea, the other.

He rested his hands atop the desk. Across the way, Thea mirrored him, just as she had the previous night with her palm against the glass. She'd removed her hand quickly, though. It was there, then gone too soon. Coen knew it hadn't been true contact, that the glass wall had divided them, and yet it had been the first human touch he'd experienced since . . . He racked his brain. He'd sparred with her yesterday, but that was different. Full of energy and tension. Last night had been calm, quiet. She had stared at their hands, hovering centimeters apart, and he'd stared at her lips, slightly parted, just as they'd been that day he revived her on Achlys.

He found himself staring at them again now.

What? she said from across the room.

Nothing.

You were thinking about something. I didn't hear it, but I could . . . feel it.

He was a mess. He needed to get it together, guard his thoughts.

It was sort of like when a word is on the tip of your tongue, but you can't place it, she continued.

It was nothing, he said again firmly. Coen didn't want to

think about tongues. That was almost worse than lips. He stared at the top of the desk because it seemed the only safe thing in the room.

"Communication test today," Dr. Farraday said, positioning himself between Coen and Thea. "We will give one of you a message, and you'll have to communicate it to the other host without speaking."

"How is that possible?" Coen said carefully.

The doctor's eyes narrowed. "We have reason to believe you may be able to communicate telepathically."

Don't confirm it, Thea shouted in his ear.

Obviously. Coen didn't look at her when he responded, didn't let his gaze so much as flit from Farraday when he said aloud, "I think if we could do something like that, I'd know."

"Perhaps the skill is repressed," the doctor said with a smug smile. "Let's just give it a try." He walked to Coen's desk and set his Tab on the surface. A giant number 4 filled the screen. "Please pass this information to Thea."

Don't, Thea whispered in his ear. *Once they know we can do this, they'll fear every second of silence between us. Even if we're talking about the weather, they'll think we're plotting an escape.*

We are.

They might separate us if they know we can talk like this, Coen. Do you want to be separated? Do you want to be completely alone again? I don't.

"Any day, Mr. Rivli," the doctor prompted.

Coen put his elbow on the desk and folded his thumb into his palm, wiggling the other four fingers in the air.

"Four?" Thea said from across the room.

Dr. Farraday snatched up the Tab. "We'll try again, and this time: follow directions."

"I did. You said not to talk."

"No hand signals or eye blinking or anything of the sort. I want you to use your mind." He set the Tab back on the desk. It now read *14*. "Focus, Coen. You can do this."

Well, I don't have enough fingers for this one, he thought.

What is it? Thea asked. *Tell me, and I'll guess something else.*

It was a good plan. The doctor would have no way to disprove that Coen hadn't cooperated. He squinted his eyes, made a show of really truly focusing as he stared at Thea. He even gripped the edge of the desk as he passed the number to Thea.

Now you're just being creepy, she said, before adding out loud, "Ten?"

"No," Coen said.

"Twelve then, maybe? I don't know." Thea slumped against her chair. "Maybe I'm imagining things."

"See, I told you we couldn't do this. Can we move on to whatever's next?"

The doctor's brow wrinkled as he consulted with the medics. They were watching a recording of the communication test on the Tab. Coen could hear Thea make her first guess and him reject it.

"Strange," Dr. Farraday said, lowering the Tab. "Your caps picked up increased brain activity on both of you just before Thea made her guess. Almost as if you *were* speaking."

Coen's heart plummeted. If the caps were monitoring their brain activity, it would have picked up multiple abnormalities. Like yesterday, when their sparring session had included a private lesson, whispered just between the two of them.

"Maybe because Coen was trying to do something he can't and I was trying to hear something that wasn't there," Thea said.

The doors slid open and Lieutenant Burke slipped through. The air in the room seemed to thin. The medics stood straighter as the lieutenant marched toward them and plucked the Tab from Dr. Farraday. "We'll try one last time," Burke said. He placed the device on Coen's desk. It still read *14*. "Pass this number to Miss Sadik."

"I would if I knew how," Coen said.

"Oh, I *know* you know how." The lieutenant leaned forward, bracing his weight on Coen's desk and blocking Thea from view. His upper lip curled with annoyance, and his pulse was calm and steady. He wasn't afraid of Coen—because of the collar and the cap—but there was something more. A smugness to his confidence. Like he knew he'd already won.

"You said you were more or less done, so I turned around," Burke recited. "Is that not what Thea said to you last night in your cell? After you'd both changed clothes?"

Dread filled Coen's chest.

"It's funny, because when we checked the footage, you never said anything even resembling that line. In fact, Thea's comment was the first thing either of you said aloud since entering your cells. So please. Pass her the number. Now."

They know we can do it, Coen said.

But they can't prove it. There's no way to prove it unless we confirm it.

"Another spike in brain activity for both of them just now," Farraday said, reading from the Tab.

Burke grabbed the lip of Coen's desk and heaved upward. Coen's instincts were a split second ahead, and he was on his feet in a flash, kicking his chair backward and ducking to the ground as the desk flew over him.

"Pass her the number!" Burke roared. When Coen hesitated, the lieutenant unbuttoned his uniform jacket and extracted a folding knife from a pocket within.

"You just confirmed yesterday that I heal faster than a military-grade regenerative bed. That blade doesn't scare me."

Burke walked away from Coen, closing in on Thea. He grabbed her right wrist. She fought briefly, until a shock warning was sent through the cap and she yelped, folding in defeat. Burke slammed her palm against the desk, spread out her fingers.

He pressed the blade against her pinkie.

"Healing is one thing. Do you think she can regrow a limb?"

It's fourteen still, Coen told her immediately. *It's fourteen, just say it.*

She shook her head. *If it grows back, great. If it doesn't, that's fine. But if I let him take it, they'll think we're being honest. They'll believe we can't talk like this.*

Thea, it's not worth it! Just tell him!

"Perhaps I should find out which hospital is holding Gina Rivli," Burke continued, "and have a Radical loyalist pay her a visit. Might be best to just pull the plug on her, yes? Spare her some pain?"

"Thea, give him the damn number!" Coen screamed. If she withheld this—if Gina suffered any more than she already had because of Thea—Coen would never forgive her. Thea would be as good as dead to him. He'd take being alone again, the only of his kind, a perpetual prisoner in this facility, before spending another day with Althea Sadik if she doomed his sister.

Thea's eyes softened across the way. Her lips fell open. She'd heard it all. Every last thought.

He'd been so angry he hadn't bothered to protect them.

"Fourteen," she said softly. "The number is fourteen."

Burke's smile was thin and wicked. He shared a knowing look with Dr. Farraday, then pressed the knife down, severing Thea's pinkie from her hand.

Thea didn't register the pain at first. The knife cut like butter, at least until it hit bone and protested momentarily. Then the blade connected with the desk and she was staring at her finger, no longer attached to her hand. She blinked, certain she'd seen it wrong. But it was still sitting there, severed. Her blood flowed freely.

Coen was shouting obscenities across the way, his anger a wave that swelled and crashed, sending static through the room. He ran at Burke, but was brought to the ground by a shock wave long before he could tackle the lieutenant.

"Now you know how serious I am," Burke snarled. "Do not try to fight me again, or the consequences will be worse."

Thea felt the pain suddenly, a throbbing sensation where her finger used to be.

"Get it on ice so it can be reattached," Dr. Farraday was saying to a medic. But Thea could already see it would be no use. The blood had begun clotting.

114

"There's no point, sir," a medic said. "The wound's already healing. There are no nerves to reattach."

"Your assumption was correct, Lieutenant," Dr. Farraday said. "Incredible healing capabilities, but no regenerative limb growth. I hope you're happy."

The lieutenant dropped the knife into a container with a biohazard label. "Regeneration would have been nice, but we can't get everything we want, can we? A solider like this is still immensely valuable. They can heal minor injuries in seconds and carry on with the fight, all while communicating without tech. It will be like a giant hive mind. Put them in exoskeleton body armor, and even injuries are unlikely." He shot Farraday a pointed look. "Continue this test. See how far their range stretches. Do they need to be within eyesight of each other? In the same room? What happens when there's walls and floors between them? How about a whole kilometer? More? I expect a report on my Tab by this evening."

Burke left, and the testing continued. Thea and Coen complied because there was nothing to hide anymore, and they quickly learned that their capabilities didn't extend beyond a room or two of separation.

Thea had to be able to sense Coen's presence to make a connection. If she could see him, communication was effortless. If she could hear his pulse, it took a bit more effort, but was manageable. And if she only had a hunch that he might be nearby, passing just a single word between them was exhausting.

All the while he kept apologizing to her, asking if she was okay. Eventually her patience snapped.

Of course I'm okay, Coen; it's my finger, not my head. And I never asked to be the object of your obsessive protection. You've got Gina for that.

It was a cruel blow, but it shut him up. And she needed to think, because they'd likely be separated now, moved to a distance at which they couldn't talk or plan or plot. A distance greater than several rooms.

She'd need to act as soon as possible. There was no point hanging her prayers on Amber Burke. It was more likely she ignored Thea's message than responded to it.

Thea repeated the path from her cell to the elevator in her mind, praying her room would be hers for one more evening.

Nova weathered another draining day of physical therapy, and Amber remained distant through it all. When Nova blinked sweat from her eyes and asked about Thea and Coen, Amber merely said, "Sorry. Don't know anything." When Nova reminded the medic that she'd agreed to ask after them, Amber shrugged and said, "It's like I told you; I only have access to a few levels. I haven't seen them since we left the *Paramount*."

Now, as Amber helped her into bed, Nova couldn't stand it any longer. She needed answers. "You know, I thought you'd have more backbone. But this won't be the first time I've been wrong about someone."

"Like always, call if you need anything." Amber folded the blanket over Nova's lap as though she hadn't just been insulted. "Oh, and let me help with that pillow before I leave."

The pillow was fine. Nova nearly said as much, but Amber had already leaned in to fluff it. Head beside Nova's and lips brushing her ear, Amber whispered, "There's a message on the Tab. Keep it angled away from the cameras." The medic straightened, smiling blithely as she asked loudly, "Better?"

Nova nodded, praying she didn't look shocked. The surveillance camera was mounted in the corner of the room. Anyone watching would have a nice view of the bed right now: Nova reclined on the pillow, Amber with her back to the lens. The Tab—currently propped up at the foot of the bed—had its rear to the camera, too.

"The Tab is locked to patient settings, but that breathing app should be accessible if you need it. I'll be back tomorrow for more PT. Maybe we can get you moving on your own a little." Amber winked. Nova didn't know if it was meant to be encouraging or if it was a nod to the words she'd just whispered in Nova's ear. It counted, nonetheless.

One wink.

Same as yesterday. A sad but legitimate record.

Amber left and didn't look back. Nova waited a few minutes. Then she grabbed the Tab, using care to keep it angled only at herself as she brought it to life.

A message filled the screen.

> *There are too many surveillance cameras in the PT room;*
> *had to wait for now to talk.*
>
> *I made contact with your friend Thea. Communications*
> *are slow: once a day, via the locker room. She asked*
> *about you, and I updated her. I'm still waiting on her*
> *next response. It looks like she's being tested—Coen,*
> *too—but I'm not sure for what. The research lab has glass*
> *windows, but they're fogged, so I can't see anything. Will*
> *talk to my dad tonight and try to learn more. I'll update*
> *you when I can.*
>
> *Delete this after reading and do* not *respond. We can't*
> *risk another medic seeing these correspondences.*

Nova read the note several times before scrubbing it from the Tab.

Her heart beat wildly—not from anxiety, but with hope.

118

She'd misjudged the medic. Sometimes, Nova loved being proven wrong.

She set the Tab at the foot of the bed and practiced her breathing for the cameras.

Amber took the central elevator down to the research lab. She'd called for a dinner tray to be sent to Nova's room within the hour. By then, the pilot should have read and deleted the note Amber had left on the Tab. Now it was time for answers.

She found her father holed up in one of the genetics labs, which was only accessible through a clean room that her key card didn't open. She lingered at the door, anxious, waiting for someone to pass by.

Finally, she had an opportunity: Cyra. The woman was strutting up the hall, one hand in the pocket of her lab coat and the other carrying a Tab.

"Cyra?" The woman looked up from the device, and Amber quickly pressed the Radical salute to her chest. Cyra saluted back. "Can you let me in?" Amber motioned to the clean room.

"Not if your card doesn't."

"My father told me to meet him down here."

Cyra looked over her shoulder, then peered through the clean room. Dr. Farraday was barely visible through the hallway's fogged glass windows. "I really shouldn't, but if he said to come see him . . ." Cyra flashed her key card before the sensor. The clean room door clicked.

"Thanks," Amber said, and ducked inside.

Sterile air rushed over her shoulders. She scrubbed at the wash station, then pulled on a spare clean suit. The material puckered and rippled beneath the moving air. Now in the clean room, the windows looking onto the lab were clear, transparent glass. Beyond, in the lab itself, a series of Hevetz scientists were huddled together, chattering as they reviewed data and tapped notes into Tabs. A DNA helix spun on a screen on the far wall. When a light above the door flashed green, signaling it was clear for her to enter the lab, Amber toed the door open and crossed the threshold.

"So you're convinced youth is a factor?" her father was saying. His back was to Amber, and another scientist was showing him something on their tablet.

A bright orange backpack on a counter caught Amber's eye. Beside it, tubes of blood were arranged on racks. The wall screen refreshed, showing a looping animation of brain activity. It seemed inhuman, too much activity at once, as though every last section of the brain was working overtime. In the corner, she could make out the words *Subject: Sadik, Althea* and a time stamp from just earlier in the day.

"We think so," the Hevetz scientist answered. "Successful injections are nonexistent in the mature rats, and newborn rats are unable to host it as well. But there's a window. Here, look at the numbers. In the youthful rats well out of infancy but not yet fully matured . . . These are your compatible hosts. Chances are it has to do with bodily changes, a flexibility of the host that is only accessible during a small window in time. Rats aren't humans, of course, and the best way to test the hypothesis would be on a person."

"Continue with the rats. If this hypothesis continues to prove sound, then move on to the rabbits. From there, we can discuss a human test."

It was then that Amber saw what had captured the rest of the scientists' attention. Set atop the center counters were three different glass containers, each filled with several rats. In the first container, the rodents were healthy, nibbling at food, suckling from a water feeder, milling about. But in the others . . .

One receptacle was filled with dead specimens, their bodies clustered in a corner, fur matted and wet with blood. In the third, several rats twitched and hissed, surrounding a healthy rodent. There was a flash of fur. Squeals and cries. Blood spattered the glass.

Amber staggered backward, knocking into the door to the clean room.

Her father looked up, spotting her at last. The scientist he'd been talking to hugged the Tab to his chest, covering up the Hevetz logo stitched there.

"What the hell is this?" she muttered.

"Amber, you're not supposed to be down here."

"What the hell is going on?!"

Host, youth, successful injection. Amber stared at the incredible brain activity on the vidscreen, an image of Thea and Coen being dragged through *Paramount*'s halls seared into her mind. *Well out of infancy, but not yet fully matured. These are your compatible hosts.*

Tests on rats. Then rabbits. Then humans.

They were studying the hosts, trying to replicate them. And there were only two other young people at this facility: her and Nova Singh.

Amber turned and fled from the lab.

The instant Thea heard the sedative hissing in the filtration vents, she took a final, deep inhale and held her breath.

She'd been returned to her cell, but Coen's was empty. They'd brought him to a different holding area, just as she'd feared. Now that Burke knew they could communicate telepathically, they'd been separated. Which meant she'd have to leave him behind.

Only temporarily, she reminded herself. *Once you've got help, you can return.*

Thea focused on stilling her body. She let everything go

limp, willed her pulse to slow. The more relaxed she was, the longer her held breath would last.

A minute after the sedative had begun, she slumped to the floor, feigning a loss of consciousness.

Three minutes after the gas had begun, the temptation to gasp down air was strong, but she suppressed it. The guards were entering the room.

Even with her eyes closed she could sense their positions. One at the door, two at her sides; all three pulses beating lazily. They were used to this procedure by now and had nothing to fear. The leads from Thea's collar clicked free and the guard set them on the floor while he unlatched the collar itself. Then he moved on to the cap.

Her chest burned now.

She wanted air.

She thrust the thought away, locked it behind a door where it couldn't tempt her. After today, they'd wait ten minutes before entering her cell, and she'd never be able to hold her breath that long. This was her only chance.

The latch beneath her chin loosened. The cap slid free.

As soon as the sensors were no longer in contact with her skin, Thea reacted. Her eyes shot open and she grabbed the cap from the guard. Shocked, he scrambled away, moving like a crab. She threw out a leg, tripping him. Then she was on top of him, slamming the cap onto his head. The guard by the door was already hitting the shock button in a panic, and as soon as the cap made contact with the other man's skin, he writhed in pain beneath Thea, then went limp.

One down, two left.

Static danced in the corner of her eyes. She yanked the mask off the shocked and unconscious man, and pulled it on. Breathing clean air at last, Thea grabbed the collar from where it had fallen on the floor and hurled it at the nearest guard. It clipped him in the head, causing him to buckle. In his panic, she retrieved one of the collar leads and jabbed it into his gut. Then she spun and struck the final guard still standing by the door. Another spin back to the first man. Thea grabbed his mask and yanked it up and off his face. Spinning back to the door, she struck the guard there again and removed his mask as well.

She watched them grab at their throats, sputter and cough.

Her attack had lasted no more than six seconds, executed with such precision the men hadn't even cried out or alerted anyone via comms.

She stepped over the guard at her feet and fished the key card from his pocket. It was attached to an extractible cord pinned to his pants, and she broke the line with a yank, then waved the card before her cell's door.

It slid open.

The hall was empty.

Thea crossed the threshold and began to run.

First right, third left, right, right, straight.

Straight, straight, straight until she was at the end of the hall, the elevator waiting just ahead. She summoned it by slapping the button. Leapt back as the door opened.

In the ready stance Coen had taught her, she waited for a small army to emerge from the lift, but like the hall, it was eerily empty.

They must have seen what had happened in that cell. The guards might not have had a chance to shout for help, but Thea knew there was surveillance. Maybe she'd face obstacles when she reached the lobby.

She darted into the elevator and hit the button for the very first floor.

The doors slid shut. The car ratcheted upward.

When it eased to a halt, she strained her hearing, listening for heartbeats. Nothing. No one. Were they just going to let her waltz out of here? It felt too easy.

The door opened. She stepped out.

The hall was white, lit with track lighting and tubing that ran the length of the corridor. There were no windows. It was all wrong. This was supposed to be the lobby. The level above ground.

A sign opposite the elevator marked the way toward *Docking* (right) and *Central Command* (left).

Her heart plummeted as she ran toward Docking. It couldn't be. She was in the Trios. They were already home, underground at some research base. But then the hall dead-ended in a ring, and as Thea ran through the curving corridor, she got her first glimpse of a window. No, an air lock. A ship was docked there. And not just any ship, but the *UBS Paramount*, its credentials displayed on a screen beside the docking port.

An alarm kicked on, a robotic voice announcing a Level 1 Lockdown. Thea barely registered it. She staggered on, to the next docking port. It held a freighter. The next, a smaller transit ship. The fourth was unoccupied, its edges framing what waited beyond.

Star fields. Stars and nothing else.

This wasn't an underground research facility.

It was a space station, and there was nowhere to run.

The guards approached from behind—an army of heartbeats and clanking boots, too many for her to fight. When the first shock from a ray-rifle struck her back, she was still staring at the stars, transfixed.

He yelled for Amber to wait and caught up with her in the hall, his hand closing over her wrist. She hadn't bothered to shed the suit—just rushed straight through the clean room and into the hall beyond. She'd been running for the elevator as if the research facility were a place she could escape, as though her key card got her to all levels.

"You better explain," she said, wheeling on her father.

"It's not what it looks like."

"I fucking hope not!"

"Language," he warned.

"Dad, it looks like you're doing some sort of genetic testing on rats. Testing that you plan to do on humans, eventually, too. I don't know what the end goal is, but I know what I saw. Increased—almost inhuman—brain activity in a compatible host, and uncontrollable, violent, destructive behavior in the others." She remembered Nova's nightmare the other night. *I was back there. They were everywhere. They were attacking me.* "I didn't sign up for this. This was supposed to be an enrichment year studying alongside you at the university. This is something else. There's no way it's legal."

"We are on the verge of something huge here." His eyes gleamed with excitement. She'd seen this before, when new treatments were developed or a cutting-edge medicine hit the market. He'd get drunk on the wonder of it all.

"Who's on the verge of something—Hevetz? Did Burke partner with them? Is the surveillance he's running on Casey related?"

"No. Burke's just trying to find someone who's caused trouble in the past—a company, I think—and fugitives always head to the Inansi Desert because security is lax. This is about Burke assiting Hevetz."

"Why? Why would Burke—why would *you*—help Hevetz with random research?"

"I think you know the answer to that."

Her thoughts drifted back to her argument with Nova the other day. There was one thing that united everyone on this ship. One goal that every Radical had in common.

"Trios independence," she whispered.

"This contagion . . . ," her father went on. "With the right host, it can create supersoldiers. Exceptional strength, hearing, and eyesight. Even telepathic capabilities. And that's just what we've confirmed in the past few days."

"And in the wrong host?" Amber prompted. "I saw those containers. The rats had ripped each other apart."

"We know who can host it now."

"No, you have a hypothesis. Dad, if this gets out, this entire facility will be in jeopardy. There's no one on the full-time staff who can be considered 'in their youth.'"

"We know what we're doing."

"Seriously?! How can you know what you're doing with a contagion we know nothing about?"

"Everyone here has been working toward independence for decades, Amber. Some longer than you've been alive. You want what's best for the Trios, don't you?"

She thought of her home, her friends, her entire world. The UPC was a bad deal for anyone who didn't call the Cradle home. She'd devoured enough documentaries and articles and think pieces to see all too clearly what could become of the Trios if its citizens continued to let Union laws strip them of their strengths, forcing them to share their energy, their life force, with the Cradle.

But what was happening to Thea and Coen—Trios citizens themselves—wasn't good for the Trios, either. And independence *could* create new problems, as Nova had pointed out.

"Don't you?" her father repeated.

"Of course," she said quietly.

"Then you will stay in your lane and do what you're told, end of story. This could be a turning point for the Trios, the edge we need to break free of the Union. The Cradle has always had an equally matched military, but with these hosts, the Trios will be unstoppa—" He froze, a finger going to his ear. The intercom there flashed green, transmitting. Amber watched a storm spread over her father's face.

"Level one? I'll be right there," he said to the person on the other end. Then to Amber, "I have to go."

"Dad, I'm not comfortable with this. I want out."

"We can discuss this later." He was already backing down the hall.

"At least tell me this facility is secure; that if this gets away from you, it will be contained."

"Oh, I should think so. I thought you were told after cryo. Amber, we're on Kanna7, one of the Trios's research and development stations. We're orbiting our sun from beyond the Lethe Asteroid Belt. There's no one around for over three hundred million kilometers."

A month after word of Thea's death, the programmer entered the lab to find that Sol had left his personal Tab at one of the stations. Unlike the devices she worked on for the drive, the tablet had a live connection to the Interhub.

She pounced on it, and in seconds had opened a ghosted channel and run a basic search on Thea's name. What came back matched everything from Sol's feeds. The report of the girl's death, two follow-up stories on the tragedy, a death certificate filed in Eutheria's Hearth City. Disappointment throbbed in her chest.

It wasn't that Naree wanted Sol to be keeping anything from her, but she'd hoped for more concrete evidence that Thea was alive and well, even if only through murmurs on conspiracy forums. The galaxy, however, was concerned with more pressing matters: increased taxes on basic meds and growing tensions between UPC loyalists and the Radicals. Some conspiracy theorists were crowing about a big shake-up in the coming months. Even mainstream news outlets were predicting the same.

The programmer sighed and cleared out the search, beginning a new one for Dylan Lowe, the forewoman of Thea's internship *program. Nothing recent came back. She moved on to Dr. Lisbeth Tarlow. Plenty of papers written on the late doctor and coverage from her infamous involvement in Achlys's Witch Hazel operation fifty years earlier, but nothing following her death.*

On the programmer went, working her way down the list of deceased Hevetz employees. She'd all but given up hope when she typed in the final name—Nova Singh—and hit return. There were the standard follow-up stories and the expected IDs, school records, and Academy scores. But the most recent item, a military medical record, was dated just days after the initial report of the crew's death.

Average citizens didn't have access to such content, but the programmer had the locked file open in a matter of minutes, only to find it was scrambled, a shell of what had once been recorded. She scrolled through the illegible lines.

At the bottom was one note that made sense: deleted per Trios Military Guideline XVI, Section C (invalid entry by a medical intern); deletion approved by Lieutenant Christoph Burke, UBS Paramount.

The programmer looked up the guideline, frowning. Invalid entries were rare, but could occur during training exercises or in cases where systems went offline and data recorded manually by a medic was stored publicly by accident, instead of on private military servers. But why a Union battleship would have an intern aboard was beyond Naree.

Poking around the military channels, she located the Paramount's current position: a derelict space station on the outskirts of the Trios system. According to internal memos, Burke was there for training sessions with his unit. He'd made several updates to his superior officer, but none mentioned Nova Singh. There was, however, mention of Hevetz scientists assisting in the training.

She killed the connection, sitting back in her chair. This was it, the cover-up she'd been searching for. If Nova Singh was alive and well on Kanna7, it was possible Thea was being held there as well.

The programmer needed eyes on that station—her eyes. She needed a working flux drive.

THE BOND

Kanna7 Station

Orbiting Sol 2 from beyond the Lethe Asteroid
Belt, Trios System

COEN RIVLI HAD BEEN IN a new cell no more than an hour before he was capped, collared, and dragged back out of it. He blinked the harsh light of the research lab from his eyes after being shoved through the doors.

A giant tank of water sat in the center of the room. Beside it, several steps led to a platform at the tank's lip. Thea stood there, stripped down to her underwear and tank top, her collar in place, but no cap on her head. A guard held the metal leads attached to her collar, pushing her toward the tank. Her energy was white hot with terror.

What happened?

Coen? she managed.

That was it. Just his name as a question, her eyes wide. Then she was submerged. A lid slammed down on the tank, locking her in. Her hands came up against the glass, reaching for him, but this wasn't like in their cells. Even if he put his palms to that glass, it would be no comfort to her. Thea's head snapped up, searching. Her fingers flew over glass. There was no way out, and yet she still searched.

"What the hell are you doing?" Coen shouted at Farraday. "She's going to drown."

"She can hold her breath for an impressively long period of time. Who knows how long, really. We intend to find out—first with her, then you."

Inside the glass, Thea's dark hair fanned out around her face, rippling in the water. The harsh lighting of the room gleamed pearlescent on her skin.

I held my breath. The gas. In my cell. Took a guard's mask and ran. They caught me. It's a space station. We're on a space station.

The words hit him like individual blows, each one worse than the previous. They were truly isolated. There was no escape.

For a split second, he was angry—that she'd left him, that she hadn't tried to seek him out before running, that she'd failed yet again. Then came the fear. It was crushing, her panic in the back of his throat. Her pulse, ticking up wildly as she tried to conserve air.

Lieutenant Burke strode in, calm and authoritative. He fell in line beside Farraday, staring at the tank with interest.

Thea was near the top of it now, her mouth and nose angled upward, trying desperately to find air that didn't exist.

I can't—Coen!—help—I can't . . .

She opened her mouth to try to shout something, or perhaps to gasp for air, but there was nothing but water. Coen watched a giant bubble of air billow from her mouth—the one thing she needed, escaping.

"You have to let her out!" he shouted.

"It's barely been four minutes," Burke said coolly. "She held her breath for longer in her cell, and fought off guards in the process."

Thea was pounding on the glass now. But it was useless, her energy spent, the fight leaving her.

Please . . .

Her eyes fluttered.

Coen . . .

Her mouth fell open.

"She's drowning! Fuck! Get her out of there! Get her out now!"

"Four minutes and twenty-three seconds," Farraday said, reading from his Tab.

Thea's body went limp, sinking to the floor of the tank. Her shirt mushroomed, her hair billowed.

"Goddammit, get her out!"

He could feel the connection to Thea slipping. It wasn't like when she stepped out of his reach during the communication tests, moving beyond the range of their abilities. This was different—and terrifying. It was a tether stretched to its greatest limits, ready to snap. It was a cord about to be severed. And once it broke, there would be no fixing it. Her consciousness was completely gone, her pulse barely a whisper and growing weaker with each moment. And the guards were doing nothing. Burke and Farraday were pouting, like she was a malfunctioning piece of tech, not a human life.

"Get her out," Burke said finally.

The guards fished Thea from the water and dragged her down the steps. She was limp, head lolling.

Burke gave an order to revive her, but the men simply set Thea on the ground and looked at each other. They didn't want to touch her, let alone breathe air into her lungs. "CPR!" Burke snapped. "She's too valuable to lose."

The guards were still regarding each other, neither brave enough to make a move, when Thea's pulse went silent.

A fire lit inside Coen, and he surged forward. The movement was so fast, so sudden, that the guards holding the leads to his collar were caught by surprise. Coen burst free, the leads trailing behind him, the collar digging awkwardly into his neck.

"Let him get to her!" he heard Farraday yelling at the guards.

He was on already his knees, pushing on Thea's chest as a guard slipped a hot cap back on her head. He'd saved her like this once before, damning her in the process. He prayed he could save her again.

● ● ●

There was water in her mouth, her nose, her lungs. She drifted in a thick fog.

Something brushed her lips, a force pressed down on her chest, purposeful, precise. It repeated in a steady rhythm. The fog wasn't so white anymore, but a muted fleshy pink. Her eyes felt heavy.

Another soft pressure on her mouth, the more aggressive thrust on her chest.

His thoughts suddenly filled her mind, pummeling her like waves. *Don't leave me. You can't leave me. Please come back, Thea. Please. I can't lose you. Don't you dare die on me. Thea? Goddammit, Thea. Come on.*

Another thrust on her chest and she lurched beneath the force. Water bubbled at her lips, trickling down her chin. A hand snaked behind her back, helping her sit. She coughed again, expelling more water, gasping and grunting.

Oh my god. Thank you thank you thank you. I can't do this alone. I wouldn't make it without y—

The thoughts stopped the moment her eyes fluttered open. He cut them off, tried to hide them. He hadn't been trying to tell her these things, not consciously, at least, but she'd heard everything.

She stared at his slack-jawed face, the relief in his eyes. His chest heaved.

Thea, he said, her name a whisper in her mind.

Then he grabbed her face and crushed his lips to hers.

He pulled away just as quickly, their eyes locked. She was frozen, cemented to that spot, unable to do anything but stare. For a moment that should have been filled with their thoughts, the world was shockingly quiet. Her lips tingled.

The guards edged nearer and Coen shot to his feet, wheeling on the men. There was a sharp undercurrent to his energy—something hot and filled with hate—a detached expression she'd seen on him as he fought infected Black Quarry members on Achlys.

Coen managed to tackle a guard and bring him to the ground before the cap he wore surged with electricity and he rolled onto his back, twitching.

"Get him out of here!" Burke yelled as the guards descended on Coen. "Get him back in his cell, now!"

"No," Farraday said sharply. The guards paused. Thea turned to the doctor, puzzled. He was eying her and Coen with a calculated gaze, the smile on his lips so thin it unsettled her. "Look at this huge spike in brain activity. It's unprecedented. And their readings are nearly in perfect synchronization." Burke's gaze moved to Thea. "Bunk the hosts together tonight, and keep a dozen guards on watch outside the room. I have a hypothesis I want to test."

Nova tossed in the bed, wrestling nightmares.

She was back on Achlys, searching Black Quarry's drill

site, but in her current physical state. She half limped, half crawled down the catwalks, using the guardrail to pull herself along. Her shoulders burned.

The infected had chased her down to the drilling deck. She'd been separated from her crew, but she couldn't remember when.

A drilling platform waited ahead. She summoned her final bit of energy, staggering onto the platform. Toppling forward, she caught the railing, barely avoiding a fall. Her weight sagged into it.

Nova hoisted herself up. A light on her helmet illuminated the narrow ravine below.

Below, she saw her crew—all of them, dead in the ravine, frigid water trickling over their bodies. Dylan, Thea, Coen, Toby, Tarlow, and Sullivan. *Her cousin.* A memory seared behind Nova's eyes. Sullivan asking her to relay a message to his wife and boys, then a wild version of the man, tackling Nova to the ground. She'd fought back, slitting his throat with a knife. It wasn't a nightmare. It was real.

Nova lurched awake, gagging. She'd killed him. She'd murdered her own cousin.

She rolled from the bed, landing on all fours on the floor and barely crawling to the toilet in time to retch up her dinner.

Behind her, she heard someone enter the room. "Here. Let me help." Amber. She shut the door, closing them in together.

"It's just nightmares," Nova said. "I'm fine."

"You're not. And neither am I."

Nova lifted her head from the seat of the toilet, looked over her shoulder. Amber's fair skin was even paler than usual.

"What's wrong?" she asked.

"Your friends are infected."

"What?! They can't be. They weren't showing symptoms. If they're—"

"They're able to host it. It's made them stronger, Nova. Better hearing and sight and strength. The Radicals are trying to replicate it to create a supersoldier."

A dark ravine.

Hemorrhaged eyes.

Nails scratching and clawing.

Nova squeezed her eyes shut, banishing the images.

"Do they realize how dangerous that is? I've seen what an infected person does if they can't host this. It's chaos. Absolute hell."

"I know. I told my father the same thing. Hevetz is testing the contagion on rats now. Rabbits soon. They want to move on to humans eventually."

Nova pressed a hand to her mouth. She was going to be sick again. She inhaled deeply, breathing as the animation had taught her.

"They've figured out who can host it," Amber went on.

"There's a certain window in age, developmentally speaking."

Thea would be in the first quarter of her senior year right now if she wasn't being held by the Radicals, and if Nova had to guess, she wouldn't place Coen much older. "Teens?" she asked.

"Give or take, and we're the only other young people on this entire station. Yes, *station*. Welcome to one of the Trios's most isolated space stations: Kanna7."

"I have to get out of here," Nova said, fighting the urge to be sick. "I need to find Thea and Coen, and we have to leave."

"You can barely stand."

"I need to leave now! If Hevetz was willing to sacrifice all of Black Quarry just so the Radicals could get their hands on this contagion, do you really think they won't try injecting me?"

"I'm not going to let that happen."

"How old are you, Amber?"

"Seventeen."

"That's more solidly teen than me. What if they get to you first?"

Amber's brow wrinkled. If she'd come to this room hoping that Nova would talk her back from a panic, convince her that she was overreacting and they'd both be fine, she was in for a shock. Nova had always been a realist.

"My dad won't . . ."

"Let that happen?" Nova finished. "If it's not you, it's me. It's one of us, regardless. How far do you think I am from walking on my own?"

"With continued PT and a couple more sessions in the regen bed, you should be pretty steady on your feet after a few days."

"And you said they were only on rats now? That they planned to test rabbits before moving to humans?"

Amber nodded. "We have a couple days, at least. Maybe a week."

There was a knock on the door. Without waiting for a response, the person on the other side nudged it open. Felix. He spotted Nova on the floor and the state of the toilet bowl. His lip curled.

"She was sick," Amber explained.

"I can see that. Get her back in the bed where she can be monitored by surveillance so I can go back to my own responsibilities."

"What responsibilities? I thought they decided to keep Powell in stasis."

"I'm watching the whole wing at night. Just get her back in bed, please?"

Amber pulled Nova's arm behind her neck and helped her stand. Whatever their next step was, whatever plan they needed to form, it would have to wait until tomorrow.

It was Thea's cell, the only one she'd known on this strange space station, but it felt foreign now, wrong. Coen was on *her* side of the glass.

Will you quit pacing? she said. *You're making me nervous.*

He lurched to a halt beside the wall that once divided them. *I can't help it. They almost killed you, Thea.*

But they didn't.

He folded his arms across his chest, clearly not comforted by this statement. He was still looking at her strangely. Like the mere sight of her caused something deep within him to ache.

I heard you during the CPR, she said. *I heard everything you were thinking.* She hadn't stopped reliving it since it happened. Each moment spent in the memory made her stomach twist, like a towel being wrung. She couldn't look at him the same way anymore. His hands, especially. She'd watch them fight off hordes of infected on Achlys, wield weapons and throw blows, but now they'd been on her neck, soft and harmless, holding her face. And his lips . . .

They'd been against her mouth before, too. He'd revived her that very first time in the Witch Hazel bunker, but the kiss in the lab, when she'd come to . . . It was barely even a kiss. It had happened so quickly, she could hardly recall what it felt like. On *Celestial Envoy,* they'd had more physical contact. They'd even been crammed in the dumbwaiter, chests pressed together as they ascended to the escape shuttle, and it hadn't felt as significant as when he'd held her face earlier. It had felt like nothing but surviving, doing what was necessary in that moment.

Now the simplest touch felt like more. They were relying on each other, but suddenly survival wasn't the only thing at stake.

Did you mean it—all of those thoughts?

He looked away. Back to her. Away again. Finally, he asked, *Can I sit on the bed?*

She nodded, but once he sat at the foot, barely a meter away, the cot felt criminally small. His fingers fisted the sheets. He looked at his feet. Her eyes worked over his back— expanding with each breath—and up to his neck, where his tattoo was just barely visible beneath his shirt. Thea swore she could feel the heat radiating off him even from where she sat. She looked at the shape of his ribs along his torso, protesting against the T-shirt. She imagined the tattoo beneath the material, pictured her fingers trailing over the ink marking his skin.

Her heart kicked and she banished the thought, but Coen shifted at the foot of the bed. He'd heard the change in her pulse, Thea was sure of it.

I meant it, he said. *Every word. I spent so long alone on Achlys, and it almost broke me. I was at the brink of something—insanity, maybe? But then you showed up and the reasons I'd been fighting came roaring back. I had hope again. And what they just did to you in that tank . . .* His brow wrinkled. *I can't lose you. This connection . . . It's like I don't know how to live without it, not now that I know what it's like to share it with someone. Does that make sense?*

She nodded, understanding all too well.

Coen pivoted toward her and held his hand up, as he had on the glass that once divided their cells. She reached out, meeting him halfway. Their palms brushed, gently at first, then with more sureness, pressing together.

Her heart seemed to explode in her chest. Contact like this—kind and warm and soft—had become a rarity these past months, practically foreign. She wanted to drink it up, never let it end.

Coen's fingers folded down, threading between hers. His eyes lingered on her pinkie, now a nub from Burke's knife, and he scooted closer, his knee knocking hers. With his spare hand, he cradled the nape of her neck, pulled her nearer. Their foreheads met.

Every thought flying through his mind was clear. Loud and buzzing. Half of them made her blush.

His chest heaved. He was looking at her lips.

This is only happening because we have no other options, she told him.

Do you really think that? Is this how no other option feels?

This wouldn't be happening if we couldn't talk like this, if we didn't have this . . . She searched for the right word. *This bond.*

"I like our bond," he said aloud. The words were a whisper. She felt the heat of them on her lips.

His private thoughts grew louder. *Kiss her. No. She's hesitating. You should wait. Kiss her before the moment passes, you idiot. No, wait for her lead. What the hell is wrong with you? KISS HER.* He'd either quit trying to shield the thoughts from Thea or they were too strong to be contained.

Thea's gaze dropped, finding his mouth. It would be so easy to edge her chin forward, to let her lips meet his. Part of her wanted such a distraction, craved it even.

"I don't get close to people," she admitted. "I've only ever been with Mel, and even that didn't happen until we were incredibly close. Best friends close. Had complete trust in each other close."

"You don't trust me?" Coen asked.

"I do. That's the problem."

"Why's that a problem?"

"Because this is only happening because there's no other option," she said again.

But Thea knew, deep down, that a hundred, a thousand, a million options wouldn't matter. Thea had never been attracted to people in that sense. There was a time in middle school when she'd wondered if something was wrong with her, if part of her heart was faulty for not lusting after this person or that, for failing to crush on someone from afar like her peers.

But with Mel . . . it was like her heart had exploded for him years after meeting him. They'd grown close, and only then had things become physical, had she longed for more.

She didn't understand how she could crave the same type of physical contact with Coen when she'd only known him a few weeks—or months maybe. She'd lost track of time since the *Exodus* shuttle. But one thing remained clear: what they'd been through together on Achlys, then *Paramount*, and now this godforsaken space station wasn't normal. None of this was normal. Not the situation, or their ability to communicate telepathically, or the fact that they were the only two humans alive who were capable of hosting an otherwise deadly contagion.

Coen's energy soured. She'd been silent too long, and shame now flickered in his thoughts, embarrassment. His fingers straightened, withdrawing from their threaded grip in hers. She squeezed, keeping them there.

He found her eyes.

Maybe there's no other option because this is supposed *to happen*, she said.

The corner of his mouth quirked up. *I like that theory.*

She laughed lightly. Shook her head.

What?

It's technically a hypothesis, she explained. *A theory is tested, well-substantiated, and already proven. But a hypothesis is a suggested explanation based on limited evidence that requires further investigation.*

Well, I vote we begin our investigation immediately. It would be irresponsible to delay, agreed?

She smiled and leaned nearer.

Coen's heart raced as she closed the final centimeters between them, bringing her mouth to his. Her lips were cold—she still hadn't shaken the chill from the water tank—but her cheeks were flushed. His hand had moved to the side of her face without him consciously deciding to do it, and he felt her warmth beneath his palm.

He pulled her closer still, and as she deepened their kiss, he lost control of his thoughts. Coen wasn't even trying to control them anymore, and he suspected that he couldn't, even if he wanted to.

He was acutely aware of everything he was passing to her.

How she'd sent his heart pounding. How her need to correct his terminology about theories had only turned him on more. How one kiss wasn't enough and how he wanted to pull them down onto the cot, but wouldn't. Because he wanted to savor this and also because that would be too much. She wasn't ready.

He knew these things because just as his thoughts had

flown wild, hers were rattling around uncontrollably as well. He heard them all. She was flustered and breathless, so he slowed the kiss. He kept his hands on her face instead of moving them to her hips, where they itched to be. Thea's hands were threaded in his hair, loosening the topknot he always wore. Her thoughts grew louder. She couldn't believe she was touching him like this. She wanted to touch more of him. She was thinking about pulling his shirt over his head and tracing the shape of his tattoo with her fingers, starting at his neck, working down his torso toward his hips and—

Coen pulled away, sliding to the foot of the bed. With distance finally between them, he sat there panting, trying to control his thoughts. Trying to block out hers about skin and hands and his tattoo. The tattoo he'd gotten for Gina, because of Gina, and how every battle he'd fought so far—how he'd refused to quit on Achlys—had been done for his sister. And now he was sitting here making out with some girl instead of plotting an escape.

Some girl? Thea said, and Coen realized she'd heard everything.

He'd been lazy during the kiss, but not now. Now he was guarded and cautious. He'd folded those last few thoughts away, deliberately tried to keep them from her, and yet Thea had heard them anyway.

And trying to hide it makes it better? She was dripping with annoyance. Her temperament poised to snap.

That's not what I meant. You're . . . Coen grappled for the right word. *I don't know how to do this, Thea. You know what I was thinking during that kiss. I didn't want to stop. But this—us together . . . It doesn't help me get home. It doesn't get me back to my family.*

Her anger mellowed almost immediately.

I know. We'll figure something out. Her expression was pained, as though she hurt as he did. *I promise we'll get back to her.*

You can't promise something like that. Besides, why would you?

Because I want you to reunite with your family. You have to. Just like I need to get back home so I can learn what happened to my mother. There's no other option.

A desperate sensation passed through Coen's chest—longing, want, *need*. For a truth. For answers. He was suddenly four, sitting on a bench, watching buses pass by in the spitting rain. He'd been abandoned—no, it was bigger than that. Something terrible had happened to his mother. She'd disappeared.

Coen shot from the bed.

"The hypothesis . . . ," he uttered.

"Still needs more testing, I guess," Thea finished with a shy smile.

"Not ours. *Farraday's*. He said to bunk us together, that he had a hypothesis."

Thea's brow wrinkled, then her face blew blank as she felt what Coen did. He was overwhelmed with a desire to find her mother, just as she desperately wanted to reunite with Gina.

Farraday had suspected this would happen. He'd seen a spark between them—their unprecedented, nearly synced brain activity—and blown on the flames. He'd wanted them together, wanted Thea to be completely alert for their next interactions, not caught by surprise. And now their connection had deepened. They wanted what the other wanted. Felt what the other felt. There was no hiding thoughts anymore, no private moments between them, not even if they desired it.

Coen and Thea were bonded in the truest sense of the word.

Thea's head throbbed.

She rolled over on the cot, burying her face in the pillow. It was the worst headache of her life, and there was nothing she could do to banish it.

Coen had pulled a blanket to the floor. He wasn't facing her and hadn't said a word in hours, but she'd heard plenty.

He felt regret at kissing her when they should have been plotting an escape.

He wanted to kiss her again.

His brain was simultaneously replaying the moment their lips had met and trying to push the thought away.

There were memories too: the day Gina had been diagnosed; visits to a man named Rin to purchase black market medications for his sister; stepping aboard *Celestial Envoy* with a fake ID, hope pounding in his chest for the first time in months. This was the turning point, the money their family needed.

The memories were mundane after that: stasis and bunks, meals in the mess hall, construction of what would soon become Black Quarry's drilling base. He was reporting to a drilling shift when Pitch Evans grabbed him by the bicep, tugging him into an elevator, muttering that they needed to run. Things went dark, wild, rabid.

Blood and fluids.

Chaos.

A war among the Black Quarry crew.

He was clawed by a friend outside the Witch Hazel bunker. He was hiding in an air vent. He was fast, strong, never hungry, rarely tired. He was standing over Thea near the air lock, wondering if he should revive her.

Thea saw herself as he did. Smooth skin, narrow nose, brows thick and defined. Ebony hair that framed a striking face. Thea had never thought of herself as beautiful—cute, sure; maybe even pretty on a good day—but the girl in Coen's memories could only be described as stunning. He removed her helmet, starting CPR, and suddenly they were back in the space station's research lab, Thea wet from the tank. There was CPR again, which led to a kiss, which led to Coen battling away the memory and returning to Gina.

The loop continued.

The space between Thea's eyes burned. Her temples ached. Her brain felt like it would explode.

"Get out of my head!" she snapped suddenly.

"You think what I'm getting is a treat?" he retorted. "The car you called home? A mother you can't even picture—just a shapeless ghost? This obsession to find her when she's probably been dead for years!"

"There's no proof of that!"

"What about how you didn't trust me on Achlys?" he went on. "Or how you thought about betraying me multiple times? Or when you finally did? You told Burke I was infected seconds after you came aboard *Paramount*!"

"I had to! He didn't know what he was dealing with. They could have unleashed the contagion on the ship and we'd have had Black Quarry all over again."

He glared at her, eyes narrow. "I would never have given you up like that, Thea. *Never*."

"No, you just used me instead. Every moment until now.

You thought of letting me die when I was electrocuted in the Witch Hazel bunker. You only revived me because you thought I'd help you escape. You kept the truth from me constantly."

"And you used me right back. Do you think you'd have escaped Achlys without my abilities as a defense?"

"Those abilities ruined me, Coen! You made me into this *thing*. And now I'm stuck on this fucking space station with you rattling around my head—all of these hopeless looping thoughts that aren't mine. I have enough problems—enough worries and fears and regrets. I don't need yours, too. My head feels like it's going to split open, and it's entirely your fault." *I hate what you did to me!*

The fact that the last part was a thought didn't matter. He heard it. He heard everything now. There was nothing she could hide from him.

"I saved you," Coen said quietly. "Would it have been better if I let you die?"

"Maybe," she said.

"You don't mean that."

She didn't, and of course, he knew.

Thea looked at him there, sitting on the floor. His arms were draped over his knees. There were bags beneath his dark eyes. He'd never looked tired before.

It's because of you, he said silently. *You're exhausting, Thea.*

The thought of losing you kills me. The thought of never having you out of my head is just as depressing. I can't win.

She sighed, rolling away from him and facing the wall. She couldn't look at him anymore, and yet her head felt slightly better when they were talking because their words had purpose. It was one focused conversation instead of a million thoughts and memories battling for attention.

"Do you think the headaches will get better?" he asked.

"I hope so. Maybe it's like syncing two hard drives. So many of the memories we're getting from each other are new, but maybe once the histories download, the noise will fade and we'll just . . ."

"Be," he finished.

She wondered how long it would take to adjust to this new normal, and if it would ever be easy.

"I don't think so," Coen said. "How could sharing everything with someone be easy? My parents have been married for almost twenty years and I know they have their secrets. Everyone does. But there won't be any between us."

Thea hated the idea. She didn't have anything to hide, but that didn't mean she wanted to share everything. Her thoughts drifted to Mel, who used to get a far-off look in his eyes when their conversations stalled. Thea would ask, *What are you thinking?* and he'd always respond, *Nothing*, even when she was certain something lurked there. There'd been times when she wondered if Mel wasn't happy, if he was cheating on her, if their relationship bored him. These fears happened most frequently in the months before their breakup. It was possible Mel had simply been zoning out and his responses were honest. Whatever the answer, Thea would never know his secrets.

But with Coen, for better or worse, she would know everything.

"I'm not Mel," he reminded her.

"I know." A pause. "And I don't want you to be."

His heart rate spiked. He liked the way that sounded. It was quiet for a long moment.

"I'm sorry I snapped earlier," Thea said. "My head's just killing me. I hate what's happened to us, but I don't hate you. And I don't regret things, not really. Not the choices you made, or the things we decided to do together."

"Like that kiss?"

"I was thinking about blowing up *Celestial Envoy*, trying to hide evidence of *Psychrobacter achli*."

"But the kiss?"

"The result wasn't ideal," she admitted, still facing the wall, "but I don't regret it. It was one of the only good things to happen to me in weeks. I just don't know why it triggered the bond."

"We've been relying on each other for weeks now. It's not

that surprising that an intense connection would result in something like this. Not when things like superhuman healing capabilities are considered normal for a host."

But that wasn't what Thea had meant. Not exactly.

"Ah," he said, understanding. "The kiss after CPR." He rubbed his jaw. "That was pretty one-sided. I kind of just threw myself at you. Maybe it had to be mutual, us both wanting it, both of us engaging. A bond wouldn't make much sense if only one person felt strongly about the other."

She nodded, working over the idea. She'd barely been able to process what had happened after he resuscitated her. But just earlier, in their shared cell . . . She'd wanted it. She might have been afraid to give herself to someone like that again, but she was a more than willing participant.

"You said it was one of the only good things to happen to you all week—the kiss," Coen said. "What were the others?"

"Touching your hand through the glass of our rooms. You telling me about your tattoo. You teaching me to spar. They're all about you, Coen. Every good memory I have from the recent past has you in it."

His heart was pounding now, maybe as much as her own. Even facing away from him, Thea sensed how his eyes flicked to the shape of her back. He was considering coming back onto the cot, wondering if it would be okay.

"It would be," she told him. *But it won't help us escape.*

I know. But that's a problem for tomorrow. There was a rustle behind her, and then he was sliding onto the cot. The noise in Thea's head lessened as he pulled the blanket over both of them.

"Do you feel that?" she asked. "How it's quieter when we're close like this?"

Yes.

He lay down beside her, his chest to her back. He put his arm over her middle. She used to sleep this way with Mel, sneaking into his room after lights-out and curling into him. It was innocent enough, though it sometimes led to more.

A flurry of emotions passed through her: Fear of needing Coen. Fear of losing herself. Fear of being tied to someone, relying on them completely, growing too close.

"You want me to leave?" Coen asked, misunderstanding.

"No," she said. "I want you to stay. And that scares me."

Despite the fact that everything had changed, the next morning began as it always did.

The guards came. The collars and caps were secured and both Thea and Coen were led to the locker room.

It wasn't until Thea was standing before the fogged mirror that she remembered the question she'd left for Amber. She scanned the edges of the mirror, searching for a scrap of paper. Tapped the wall, testing for loose tiles. Then she reached beneath the sink, feeling blindly. Her fingers brushed something.

She plucked the note free and unfolded it, hands trembling.

Nova is fine. Out of coma. Weak but healing.

Thea read the note again. A third time. A fourth. Her heart pounded.

You have contact with someone else? Coen asked, and Thea nearly cried out in shock. His thoughts were always with her now, humming, churning in the background, but she hadn't been prepared for a direct question. It was louder than his private thoughts, sharper.

A medic named Amber, she told him. *She's an intern. Looks about our age. She always comes to the showers after we leave.*

Can we trust her?

I can't just ask outright. No one would ever say no to that question.

The guard called from the hall, giving the one-minute warning.

That's good about Nova at least, Coen added. *Does Amber know where we're stationed? Can she help us escape?*

I'll find out.

Thea squared her shoulders and wrote another message in the fogged mirror: *Where are we? Leave paper + pen pls.*

Today, Amber came to the locker room prepared, paper and pen tucked in her bag. But nothing could have prepared her for how it would feel to answer the most recent set of questions.

You're on Kanna7, she wrote, *a space station in orbit just beyond the Lethe Belt, so technically back in the Trios, but still isolated. Security is dense. There's nothing around for three hundred million kilometers. I'm so sorry. Would it help if you could talk to Nova? Maybe I can arrange a visit.*

Amber reread the note, cringing. It was like telling someone they were dying and then offering them a cookie like sweets could make up for the horrible news.

She crossed off the bit about Nova and added, *I've learned some things. It's not safe for any of us here, but I also have no idea how to get out. You?*

She slid the note into the hiding place, leaving another scrap of paper behind, plus the pen. She'd been foolish to not leave both originally. It would be much easier to communicate with Thea if she could write a non-mirror-length message.

Amber slipped from the locker room, dread coiling in her stomach.

She didn't want herself or Nova to become Burke's newest subject any more than she wanted Thea and Coen to continue enduring . . . whatever testing they were enduring. She couldn't imagine it was better than being treated like lab rats, seeing as their living conditions were akin to being jailed criminals.

If there was a way for them to all disappear—her and Nova and Thea and Coen—Amber would take it. But there wasn't. No matter how many angles she looked at it from, she couldn't find a single way out.

Amber prayed Thea would see a variable she hadn't.

The testing continued.

Farraday confirmed that Coen was no better at holding his breath underwater than Thea, and pulled him out as static began to dance in his vision. But their telepathic abilities had amplified.

They could communicate across vast distances now. Opposite ends of a wing, different floors, from one end of the space station to the other. Coen stood near Docking one day, collared and capped, while Thea stood in a cargo hold at the opposite end of the station.

Her voice was still crystal clear in his head. He confirmed it to the guards. There was no hiding it—Farraday could see their brain activity jumping in sync on his Tab—but they used the opportunity to plan.

They made mental notes of each level: how many guards

worked the halls, when rotations occurred, where air vents might be accessible and how they snaked through the station.

Amber had told them security was dense, and their observations confirmed it. While the medic had no idea how to escape, Thea and Coen had the makings of a plan. They'd escape Kanna7 just as they'd escaped from Achlys: using the air vents to reach a ship. The problem was that the guards they'd need to dodge weren't mindless infected, and the only pilot they knew was Nova, who, according to Amber, was only just getting her feet back beneath her. If Nova couldn't get herself to a ship, Coen and Thea reaching one wouldn't matter. Wings were no good without a pilot.

When Coen wasn't plotting an escape with Thea, he was training with her. Burke's obsession with turning a host into the ultimate soldier became more obvious than ever. The drills grew more militant, tactical. Burke was giving them the very skills they'd need to escape: cardio and strength training, obstacle courses, hours logged in a shooting range. Their aim with both long-distance ray-rifles and standard stun guns was so precise, the only reason to practice was to quicken their reloading and aiming.

Sparring had also changed. Coen was still stronger than Thea, still more practiced, and yet she'd grown impossible to beat. She could see every blow he made coming, anticipate his moves. They'd dance around the ring for hours, punching, dodging, kicking. While he couldn't land a blow on her, she couldn't land one on him, either. Their minds battled, chattering.

"You've gotten exceptionally better," Farraday said to Thea one day.

"Thanks." She smiled at the doctor but said to Coen, *He has no idea how unstoppable we'll be when we fight together.*

Sweat dripped from her brow. She wiped it away with her forearm, and Coen couldn't help thinking that she was the most amazing person he'd ever met. That he'd do anything for her. That she was the sole reason he'd be able to get home.

Part of him wondered if these feelings were real or if they were just a product of their bond. He didn't feel shame at these thoughts, because it was a question Thea routinely battled as well. They were both drawn to each other, yet both constantly torn as to whether this reality was, in fact, real. And still they found themselves wrapped together on the narrow cot each evening. It was the only way to quiet their shared thoughts enough to allow for sleeping.

Eight days after they'd bonded, the door to their cell burst open in the middle of the night. The noise was enough to wake Coen, but the sedative had already been pumping into the room and he was too far gone to fight the guards who descended on them. When he came to, the room was empty.

Thea? He sprang from the bed. *Thea!*

There was no answer. The cell was empty.

He ran to the door, searching on the other side. He could hear the pulse of guards, but not the heartbeat he craved. Thea's matched his now, in exact beat. When he was exhausted after a day of training, their hearts heaved together. When they curled up on the cot, they beat in steady, calm unison.

Each pulse on the opposite side of the door was unique. Foreign. They weren't his, and so they weren't hers.

If they put her back in that tank . . . if they drowned her.

His fingers curled into a fist. He paced the cell, calling out to her every few minutes. Maybe she was unconscious still. Maybe there was no reason to get upset. The logic was sound, yet Coen couldn't calm his breathing.

Finally, without warning, she was in his head: *I'm okay.*

He sagged into the bed, nearly crying.

Coen, I said I'm fine.

They took you.

Only to a lab. They just finished drawing blood.

Why?

Not sure. I was unconscious during it and—hold on. I can hear them. They're talking a room over.

Coen held his breath as Thea listened.

They ran out of blood samples from Celestial Envoy, *the ones*

I took from Tarlow's research on Achlys, she explained. *They wanted more infected blood. I'm type O negative, a universal donor.*

There was only one reason Burke would want more blood. He was ready to infect new hosts. *Thea, if it gets out . . . If they lose control of it . . .*

It's just animal testing right now, according to Amber. Rats and rabbits.

That might still be able to pass it. And eventually it will be more than animals.

I know, but . . . Hang on. Maybe this will be easier if . . .

Her voice faded out and was replaced with Farraday and Burke's conversation. It was the strangest sensation Coen had ever experienced, like listening in on a call without having initiated it. Thea wasn't sending him her own thoughts anymore, she was sending him—in real time—what she, herself, was witnessing.

Burke: You said they've bonded; that it is the reason for their increased abilities. Why can't we re-create that?

Farraday: I don't think it can be forced. It has to happen naturally.

Burke: You forced them into the same cell. They grew attached. There are ten rats here, all hosts, who have been paired off in isolation for a week, but we've seen no change. Same with the rabbits.

Farraday: Maybe it's different with our species. Our brains are far more complex.

Burke: I want to try a human subject.

Farraday: It's too risky. The animals can be easily contained, but look at how many times Thea alone has tried to escape. You say you've got Academy volunteers—Radicals. Even if they're young, with only a year of military training, that training will still make them impossibly hard to control.

Burke: So we don't use a solider. We use someone on board.

Farraday: We are not using my daughter.

Burke: You misunderstand me. We use the pilot.

Farraday: She's nineteen. It might not work. We don't know where the cutoff is. This isn't an exact science, Christoph.

Burke: I don't care. Put the pilot in isolation and inject her. If it doesn't take, space her for all I care. I need results before I can move us to the next stage.

Farraday: Sir, I think we should run a few more tests on the hosts we have. Maybe take one of them out on the shuttle like we proposed—fly Coen away from Kanna7, while Thea stays on the station. Monitor their communications when greatly separated. See just how far their telepathic abilities can stretch.

Burke: We'll do that, too. See to it first thing tomorrow so it's out of the way. But regardless of the results, these abilities are useless to our cause if Thea and Coen are two flukes who can host what no one else can. We must confirm that every human within a certain age bracket is viable, and Vasteneur arrives in thirty-six hours. I want results I can share. Now, are you fully committed to the Radicals, Doctor?

Farraday: You know I am.

Burke: Then inject the pilot during the long-distance communication test. If you fail to do it, I will use your daughter in her place.

The conversation faltered, and Coen heard what sounded like footsteps and a door opening.

Thea's thoughts became a whirlwind as Farraday returned with the guards. The men unstrapped Thea from the operating table, escorted her from the room. She relayed their progress to Coen. When each turn brought her closer to the cell, he began to relax. By the time she was stepping from the central elevator and onto their holding floor, an unseen gas was tugging at Coen's senses. He succumbed to it, slumped on his side.

The next time he woke, Thea was beside him, her skin cool and soft. He kissed her shoulder. She stirred, her thoughts reaching him in a wave—fear for Nova, interest in the shuttle test Burke had mentioned, relief to be back together. He shared them all.

But he also had an idea, something that had come to him when Farraday had mentioned the long-distance communication test. Coen would be moved onto a ship—the very thing they needed to steal. It was the opportunity they needed, delivered on a platter.

He was about to share the detailed plan with Thea when she said, *Don't bother. I can see it right now. It's a good one.*

It requires trusting an outsider.

Honestly? She looked up at him with those wide, glassy eyes. *I think we're out of other options.*

The next morning—the day of the communication test—Thea was brought to the showers while Coen was lugged off to Docking. It would take time for the Radicals to transport him into position and for the ship to detach from Kanna7. Her being allowed to shower in the meantime was a blessing; it made their escape possible.

It *was* a good plan. Thea had meant what she said the previous night. Coen would overpower the ship's personnel while Thea made a run to meet him. But the entire plan hinged on one unpredictable outcome: whether Amber Farraday could be trusted. Without Amber's help, it was unlikely Nova would make it to the ship unassisted and they *needed* Nova aboard it. There was no way Thea was trusting a Radical to fly her to safety.

But what if Amber was caught moving Nova to the ship? What if she hesitated and threw the timing off? What if Amber said she wanted to help, but instead went to her father and told him the plan? Everything would crumble.

Thea and Coen had run through these concerns all night, but they kept coming to the same conclusion. Even with the risks, this was the best chance they had. Waiting meant Nova would face injection.

Thea turned on the shower but didn't undress. Instead, she wrote the plan down on the paper Amber had left. Every last detail. If Amber was in agreement, there would be no time for Thea to confirm it. The communication test was already in the works. It was now or never.

A guard yelled the one-minute warning, and Thea slid the note into place.

Then she loosened the buckle beneath her chin and cautiously—silently—lifted the hot cap from her head. A shock would run through it the moment she didn't emerge from the locker room when shower time was up, but it would be resting in the ventilation system by then, harmless and out of reach.

Thea turned to the vent cover beside the fogged mirror and began to unfasten the screws.

Amber woke early, excited for the day ahead. Between the regen bed and daily exercises, Nova's progress had begun to expedite. She could walk the full length of the therapy room on her own. Slowly and shakily, but she could do it.

The pilot's demeanor had changed with the progress. More optimistic. More upbeat. She still woke with nightmares some nights, and her mood could sour without warning, but that wasn't the real Nova. Amber could see how the pilot went elsewhere in those moments, how she was battling a shadow within herself, a sort of demon that might never leave but she might one day learn to live beside.

On her way to the showers, a pair of guards rushed past Amber, hands on their intercoms. "Start the sweep on level . . ." she caught before they were out of earshot. When she entered the locker room and pulled Thea's note from beneath the sink, she understood.

Amber read the note several times. The escape plan was meticulously detailed.

She glanced at the vent beside the mirror, back to the note, to the vent again. The screws were in place, but loose. It didn't matter that Amber could see a dozen ways in which the plan could backfire. It was already in the works. She needed to get to Nova.

Not bothering to shower, Amber burst from the locker and collided with a white lab coat. And not just any white lab coat—her father's.

"Come with me," he ordered.

"I have a PT session with Nova."

"This is more important."

He snapped his fingers and beckoned her like a dog.

Afraid to look suspicious, Amber followed.

They took the elevator to the research labs, where her father swiped them into the clean room she'd entered a week earlier. Several Hevetz geneticists waited inside, along with Burke. "Just find her," the lieutenant was snarling into his comm. "It's not like she can get far."

Amber needed to get out of here. She had to meet Nova. Every moment she wasted was a moment that pushed Thea's plan off course.

The door clicked shut behind her, and Burke regarded Amber's father. "Finally. You're here. Should we continue?" He motioned toward the wall of windows that looked out onto the lab beyond. On the other side of the glass, Nova was strapped to a chair, struggling against the restraints. Her face was red with effort.

The air in the room seemed to thin.

Amber knew what this meant and yet she didn't want to believe it. This couldn't be happening.

"It's safest if you do it, sweetheart," her father said. "If anything goes wrong, you're a good candidate for a host. It won't destroy you the way it could the rest of us."

Nova glanced up. Their eyes locked through the glass.

A hand materialized in front of Amber. Her father held a portable blood transfusion set. The filter was labeled *Sadik, Althea*, and its contents were red.

* * *

Nova quit struggling as the door creaked open and Amber stepped through. The medic had put on a clean suit, her face visible through the visor. A vial flashed in her hand. Nova saw the tubing next, the needle. She thrashed against her restraints.

"Don't do this," she begged.

"I have to. They're all back there, watching me."

The faces leered at Nova through the glass windows, eager, anxious. The same faces that had pulled her from her bed this morning and strapped her to this chair. She'd tried to fight them, but even with her improving strength, she'd been too weak.

Amber was staring at Nova's bare arm. One of the Hevetz scientists had already rolled up her sleeve and cleaned the injection site at the inside of her elbow. She'd tried to fight that also, but once her wrist was tied to the armrest, it was pointless.

"Please don't do this," Nova said again. "There's no guarantee I can host it."

"I know." Amber glanced up, tears in her eyes. "What else am I supposed to do?"

"You should at least knock me out first!" Nova said, shouting to the faces at the window. "I've seen infected victims break free of restraints like this so they can get to another potential host."

"They'll gas the room if they need to," Amber explained, "but they want to see the natural reaction in humans, regardless of the outcome. They need to know the process of transition—every step."

"You think this chair is going to stop me?" Nova kept yelling. "I will tear your fucking limbs off, you bastards! I'll tear you apart regardless of what this does to me!"

"Nova, stop shouting."

"Don't tell me what to—"

"Nova! You're making this worse."

"They're trying to kill me!"

"I don't know what else to do!" Amber gasped out. She was crying now. Nova couldn't stand to look at her.

"How about don't do it?" she snarled.

"It's not that simple."

"Yes, it is, Amber. Don't do it. Crack the vial. Spill the blood."

"They'll just get more."

The medic sobbed behind her visor, eyes puffy. Suddenly, Nova was furious.

"You don't get to cry about this, Amber. I'm the one getting screwed here. *Me*, not you!"

"I'm sorry," Amber said, and began to unroll the IV cord.

Nova nearly screamed. *This* was how she was going to die—at the hands of the people who were supposed to be her saviors, strapped to a chair on a remote space station? She'd escaped Achlys, killed her own cousin, and spaced Dylan Lowe from an air lock for *this*?

Amber's hand trembled as she struggled to straighten the IV cord.

"I know you think there's no way to avoid this," Nova said, forcing her voice to remain even, "but you just haven't discovered the solution yet."

"It's impossible. If I walk out, one of them will come in in my place. If I spill the blood, they'll get more."

"Impossible is just an excuse not to try."

"You've told me that before."

"If I could remember who told it to me to begin with, I'd tell you about them also. They seem smart. Unlike . . ." Nova glared at the men at the window. "Typical Radicals, risking the safety of the entire universe to get the Trios its independence. They won't stop until they get what they want, will they?"

Amber's head jerked up, her eyes finding Nova's. "Say that again."

"They won't stop until they get what they want?"

Amber's brow wrinkled behind the visor, her face taut with concern. A shadow passed over her features. "They won't stop until they get what they want, so you understand why I have no choice, why I have to do this?"

"No," Nova said. "I'll never understand this."

Amber grabbed Nova's wrist, and she flinched. This was really happening. This was how it was going to end.

She struggled as the needle moved closer to her vein. She yanked at the restraints and bucked her seat and threw every last bit of energy she could into fighting the inevitable. And just before the needle touched her skin, the medic fumbled it. Amber stooped to retrieve the syringe and dropped it again. She glanced up at Nova, and winked.

The first wink of the day, and there was no reason for one given their circumstances.

Time seemed to slow.

"Permission to take my gloves off?" Amber asked, turning toward the window. "I'm not used to doing this type of work in a full suit."

Nova watched as Farraday and Burke discussed the risks. Amber would be exposed to the room, but she could probably host it anyway. If this made it easier . . .

Burke's voice finally projected over the intercom. "Go ahead."

Amber unzipped the gloves from her suit and let them fall to the floor. Then she pushed her sleeves back. Once they were bunched up around her biceps, she moved closer, so close the visor of her helmet brushed Nova's forehead. The medic's back was to the window, her body blocking the men's view of Nova. Amber's grip on the needle was now steady and true.

Nova's pulse was a jackhammer in her head. She was sweating. Her limbs were jelly. But that wink . . .

The needle brushed her skin.

And just as Nova was thinking the wink had meant nothing but good-bye, Amber turned the syringe on herself. The needle hovered above the crook of Amber's elbow for a fraction of a second, then she pressed the plunger on the vial. The blood rushed into its new home.

Amber stared at the needle, barely believing she'd gone through with it.

"What the hell are you doing?" her father yelled through the intercom.

Nova was still staring, too. But what other option had Amber had? It was as the pilot had said—*they won't stop until they get what they want*—and Amber refused to potentially damn her own patient. Now her father and Burke had their experiment. And she had the power on her side.

Amber pulled the needle from her arm, let it fall on the floor as she turned to face the window. Her father was still screaming her name, red in the face. Burke looked dumbstruck with glee. The other men yapped madly.

Increased strength, eyesight, hearing.

"I can hear everything you're saying," she announced.

They froze behind the glass.

"You said it took hours to appear in the animals," Burke said, his voice still transmitting to Amber's side of the glass. "And our video records from Achlys show Thea didn't present immediately."

Her father's response was quieter, barely audible: "Maybe it's faster in certain humans."

It wasn't. Amber felt no different. She couldn't hear most of what was being said in the clean room, only what was being projected via the intercoms, but she'd never let them know it.

Amber picked up her gloves and pulled them back on. Lowered her sleeves and zipped them into the gloves so that she'd be protected if they pumped a sedative into the room.

"I'm going to move toward the door now. You will all gather near the far wall. If anyone comes near me, if anyone tries to follow me, I will attack."

"Amber," her father said pleadingly.

She released Nova's ankle and wrist restraints and offered her a hand. The pilot stared like Amber had gone mad. "Nova!" she urged.

A sedative might not work on Amber in her suit, but it would bring Nova to her knees. And Amber didn't have the superpower strength to carry her. Not yet.

"But where . . . ? How?"

Amber glanced at the clock on the wall. There was still time to carry out Thea's plan. It was supposed to be Nova's escape—the pilot and her friends—but they'd have a fourth passenger now. Amber had seen the line she needed to cross to fall in with the Radicals, and she wasn't willing to cross it. She was her father's enemy now. Burke's, too.

"We're going away," she said to Nova, and because she was feeling extra cheeky, she winked.

Amber extended her palm and, when Nova took it, towed her out of the seat. She moved for the exit, the pilot following behind her. Nova would be tired in a matter of minutes, but right now, Amber needed her to look strong.

She shoved the door to the clean room open. The men had shuffled away, gathering at the far end of the room as instructed. Half the scientists refused to look her in the eye.

"Give me your stun gun," she said to her father. He always carried one, hidden behind his lab coat and holstered to his belt. Burke had a more powerful model—a true military weapon that would shoot bullets—but her father was the easier target. "Put it on the floor and slide it over."

He did.

Amber snatched it up, training it on the men. "And your key card," she told her father.

"Don't you dare hand that over," Burke snapped.

"It would take me approximately three and a half seconds to infect you all. Hand it over, *now!*"

Dr. Farraday removed the card from the lanyard at his breast pocket and slid it across the floor. "Where are you going to go, Amber?"

"Anywhere but here."

He looked sad, broken. His mouth was a crooked grimace. "There's nowhere they can't track you."

"I guess we'll see."

Amber snatched up the key card and fired a stun blast at the nearest scientist for good measure. The man jerked wildly, stumbling into his colleagues, and Amber pulled Nova into the hall.

Thea crawled through the vents, blinking sweat from her eyes. *They're starting to vent a sedative through the system*, she told Coen. *Burke's orders. He's trying to push me toward Docking.*

She could feel his smile, even though he was currently off-station, on a SBT-1200 called *Halo*, to be exact. The model was slightly smaller than *Odyssey*, but more powerful.

Good. They'll be waiting to apprehend you on the wrong end of the station. Did you get a mask?

Yup. Swiped it from a storage closet. Next stop is the cargo hold for an EVA suit, then the hangar. Thea squeezed around a corner, moving easily through the gassed vents thanks to the mask. *How are you doing?*

We're still "waiting for the other host to get into position."

The Radicals on *Halo* hadn't told Coen that half the station was on lockdown, then, that Thea was missing and guards were sweeping Kanna7 for her. When they'd drawn up their plans, they'd worried Coen might get interrogated about Thea's location. But the fact that the Radicals were keeping him in the dark, on *Halo*, was ideal. Burke was playing right into their hands.

The vent Thea was crawling through joined another section, this one running vertically. She popped her head in, glanced up and down. Everything was clear.

How many guards are you dealing with again? she asked as she shifted into the vertical vent. With her hands and feet wedged up against the shaft, she began shuffling toward Kanna7's lower levels.

Two guards on me, each holding a collar lead. Then the guard with the hot cap trigger. He's sitting beside the pilot. Four men total. I'll need to eliminate all but the pilot almost immediately. How long till you reach the hold?

Five minutes or so? Maybe more. I'll let you know when to make your move.

Thea?

Yeah?

He remained silent, but she could sense plenty. He was

picturing her wedged into the vent, sweaty hair in her face. Achlys was fresh in his mind, how vulnerable she'd been in *Celestial Envoy*'s vents. Her abilities hadn't fully matured yet. The infected had still sensed an opportunity in her and had tried to attack. The Kanna7 crew would do the same, and he wasn't there to help her.

I've got this, Coen, she insisted. *Quit worrying about me and focus on your situation.*

Just be careful, he said.

This time it was her turn to smile. *You know I always am.*

She reached her exit point and peered through the grate. In Cargo Hold C, a lone worker was unpacking a recent shipment. No longer in the hangar itself, he'd set his helmet aside. Thea sized up the rest of the EVA suit he wore—fitted but not truly skintight. Very much like the suit she wore on Achlys. This man was bigger than her, but she would take what she could get.

She kicked the vent cover in and dropped into the hold.

Startled, the man turned toward the noise. There was a half second of confusion, then recognition dawned in his eyes. He knew she was the cause for the lockdown, the patient Burke was searching for.

He lunged at her, and all the sparring Thea had practiced with Coen kicked in.

She sidestepped the man's attack easily. It was like it was

happening in half time, maybe even slower. Thea could see the strands of his hair moving as he wound up, follow the folds in his skin shifting as he breathed out air. She blocked his next punch with her forearm and threw a punch into his gut. As he staggered, coughing, she used her left fist to drive an uppercut into his chin. His eyes rolled.

He was unconscious before he hit the floor.

It was almost too easy.

"The cargo hold?" Nova gasped as they burst onto level thirty-two. It was about as far away from Docking as they could be, the complete opposite end of the station. There was only one flight below them, a hangar for freighters delivering supplies.

Nova still couldn't believe what Amber had done to herself in the lab. Was she going to have bloody eyes the next time she turned around? Maybe this was just another nightmare. Nova pinched herself hard, trying to wake up.

"Your friends are this way," Amber urged.

Nova followed, hobbling now. She hadn't walked so much or so fast since coming out of the coma. Her legs felt like they might give out beneath her.

They burst into a small room holding food rations and medicine.

Nova noticed several things at once. A large shipping box filled with supplies on the floor. The busted state of the vent cover on the ceiling overhead. A discarded gas mask and an unconscious Kanna7 crew member slumped in the corner. And Althea Sadik. She wore what was presumably the man's uniform—a gray EVA suit with the words *Shipping and Receiving* on the breastplate and a Trios military seal on the bicep—and smiled at them from behind the visor.

"Hey, Nova." Her voice transmitted through the helmet's external mics. "Ready to get off this station?"

Nova managed a nod.

"Your chariot awaits." Thea nodded at the shipping box. "It's airtight, so you'll be fine while we're briefly in the hangar."

As they'd ridden the central elevator down to level thirty-two, Amber had explained how Coen was already on a ship—something to do with a communication test the Radicals had wanted to run on him and Thea—and he would bring the boat to pick up the rest of them. To save time, the hangar doors would remain open after he flew in. There'd be no time for repressurizing the hold. Dressed in her EVA suit, Thea would move the cargo case onto the ship with Nova inside, and the ship would then cruise through the still-open door.

"I'm coming also," Amber announced. "They forced me to give Nova an infusion of your blood this morning. I took it myself instead."

"That was how long ago?" Thea asked.

"Five minutes. Maybe ten?"

"We'll keep an eye on how things progress. If you can host it, you should start feeling the side effects in about twelve hours. But if there's been no nosebleed yet, you're probably one of us." She shot a crooked smile at Nova. "You're one of us, too, Nova. Don't worry. We were never going to leave you behind."

"And here I was thinking you were only saving me because you needed a pilot you trusted."

"That might have something to do with it, too. Now, in the box."

Nova eyed the airtight container. It was the length of a coffin, but perhaps twice as wide. She and Amber would fit easily, and it was already halfway filled with rations. "How are you going to move that thing?" Nova asked.

"Superhuman strength, obviously. Also, this plate?" Thea stomped a boot on the floor. Nova noticed a seam that ran around the entire crate. "This lowers into the hangar. Hydraulic lifts and conveyer belts are big in shipping and receiving. Now get in so I can give Coen the go-ahead."

Nova didn't need to be told twice.

As soon as he received Thea's signal, he reacted.

Coen dropped to the ground hard, knowing he'd be fighting the tug of the collars. He swiped with his leg out, knocking both the guards from their feet and causing their holds on the leads to slip. Just like that, Coen was loose. Without so much as a breath of relief, he was diving at the man in the copilot chair, bracing for the blow of the shock cap.

Nothing could have prepared him for the pain. As he collided with the copilot, it was everywhere, all-encompassing, white hot and brutal. Perhaps the only thing to save him was the fact that he was already mid-dive. Coen's limp body crashed into the copilot, knocking him to the floor. The remote was dropped in the scuffle.

Coen batted it away, managing a tiny grin as it skittered beneath the flight dash and out of reach. He sensed the pilot zeroing in on the commotion now and threw a punch into the man beneath him, then reached for the latch beneath his own chin. As soon as the cap was off, Coen was truly free. The men stood no chance. The two guards and the copilot were unconscious in under five seconds.

Coen turned on the pilot. The man held his arms up in surrender, shaking.

Coen imagined he looked quite terrifying in the moment. He was breathing hard from the brief fight. One of his knuckles had split open. The pain had been fleeting, but he felt the wetness of the blood against his skin.

"Please don't hurt me," the pilot gasped, eyes on Coen's knuckles. "I'll do anything."

Coen felt blindly along his neck, finding the two collar

leads and releasing them from the collar. They clattered to the floor at his feet.

"Please," the pilot said again, and Coen could feel his fear. Smell it, even. The man's pulse jackhammered. "I just want to go home."

Coen felt a moment of kinship. It was all he wanted, too. Through the bridge window behind the pilot, Coen could see Kanna7, spindle-shaped and dark, massive even from the ship's current distance.

Ready and waiting for you, Thea said. Inside the hangar, she'd already guided the shipping container down a series of conveyer belts and started the depressurizing sequence. Opening the air lock would send alerts to Central Command, so she'd wait until *Halo*'s approach was visible through the windows. It was time to put Kanna7 behind them.

"Keep your hands away from the comms and fly us into the hangar," Coen said to the pilot. "If you do everything I say, I might let you live."

Halo was approaching fast. Through the hangar's air lock windows, Thea could see it bearing down on the station, a beacon of hope against the free stars. Now floating in zero g, she toggled the controls. The doors parted and the transit ship coasted inside.

It was a militarized model, small, but armed with artillery

beneath both wings. It spun about so the rear faced the shipping container holding Nova and Amber, and hovered there as the gangplank lowered.

Thea's heart leapt at the sight of Coen at the top of the ramp. Like her, he now wore an EVA suit, his tan skin glowing behind the illuminated visor. She hadn't realized how desperate she was to reunite with him until the moment was upon her.

You can get sentimental when we're free of this damn station, he teased, and pushed off the edge of the ship to float down to join her.

In another situation she might have thrown a sarcastic comment back, but there was no time. The open hangar door was likely blipping on a dash in Kanna7's central command, and it was only a matter of time before guards came rushing to stop them.

Working together, Thea and Coen unbuckled the shipping container from the conveyer belt and moved it toward *Halo.* It was sort of like bringing a treasure chest up from the depths of the ocean, except they couldn't change their direction with a simple kick. Instead, their very first push off the belt had to be precise. It was. They mentally assured it together. And then once in motion, they just held on to the case and coasted into the ship.

Once inside, they floated until bumping into the far wall.

Thea grabbed hold of a service ladder to stop their momentum, pain flaring briefly in her shoulder. Coen scrambled over the container, floating back to *Halo*'s controls. Once the gangplank was raised, the ship sealed off and its hold repressurized, the container thudded to the floor. Thea fell with it, landing gracefully on her feet.

I'll take care of the old crew, Coen said and flew up the steps, disappearing from sight. They'd be stuffed into an escape pod and dropped right into Kanna7's hangar as Nova flew the stolen ship to freedom. That was, after Thea got their pilot onto the bridge.

Grunting, she heaved the lid of the container open. Nova and Amber blinked up at her, disoriented. "Let's go!" Thea said, grabbing Nova's arm. "On my back. We have to be quick." She helped Nova from the container, and said a silent prayer of thanks that Nova wasn't arguing. Thea knew all too well how proud and self-reliant the pilot was. With Nova riding on her back like a piggybacking child, Thea tore for the bridge.

Coen was waiting there when they arrived, towering over the Radical pilot. Thea dropped Nova in the pilot's chair at the same moment Coen heaved the other man out. The ship shuddered slightly in the awkward transition, but then Nova's hands were on the yoke, holding them steady.

"You'll be lucky if you make it a dozen kilometers," the

Radical pilot grunted. "They'll be on you in a heartbeat. They'll—"

Coen threw a fist into the man's side, cutting off his words. "I'll tell Thea when they're all in the escape pod, then we drop them and bolt," Coen said to Nova. "Clear?"

"Crystal," Nova answered.

Coen disappeared from the bridge, and Thea squeezed the back of the pilot's chair, heart pounding. They'd done it. This was it. They were seconds away from leaving Kanna7 behind forever.

That was when the radio crackled.

"*Halo*, we read you're in the hangar. Do not try to move the host. We're sending additional crew to retrieve you. Do you copy?"

Nova flinched in her seat, jerking her head at something beyond the window. "The doors just closed."

Thea looked up, heart plummeting. Burke had probably ordered them sealed as soon as he registered that *Halo* was in the hangar. If he put the station on a full lockdown before Thea got the doors open again, they'd never make it out.

Thea, don't! Coen shouted. He wasn't even on the bridge, but he'd already sensed where her mind was headed. *We'll figure something out!*

But this was the only solution. Coen was still struggling to squeeze the pilot into the escape pod. It had to be Thea.

"If I'm not back in time, don't wait for me," she said to Nova, and tore from the bridge. Down the stairs. Toward a service air lock. She was out it as fast as possible, sealing it behind her, then pushing off *Halo* and shooting toward the hangar door, all while trying to avoid Coen's mental pleading.

His helplessness and dread were cold and heavy, weighing in the pit of her stomach. But she'd made her choice. She'd made it for all of them.

The doors separating the station from the hangar creaked open behind Thea as she reached the air lock's control panel. She grabbed hold of the unit to steady herself. Guards were surely spilling into the hangar now. They'd be slower in zero g, but they'd reach her eventually. Thea fished the key card from the breast pocket of the EVA suit—it had belonged to the man she'd overpowered in Cargo Hold C—and waved it in front of the sensors.

It blinked in confirmation.

The doors opened.

Turning for *Halo*, she had a clear view of the bridge window. Nova sat in the pilot's chair, reluctance held in every muscle of her face. Coen appeared beside her, breathless from his run back to the bridge. He said something to Nova—probaby that the escape pod had been dropped—but his gaze never left Thea. *Get back here. I'll meet you at the service air lock, open the door. There's still time.*

But a flash of electricity had already appeared in the corner of Thea's vision, fired by a Radical. Not just one flash, but many. Dozens.

Go, Thea said to Coen. *Please.*

This decision of hers had to be worth something. They couldn't throw it away.

She never felt his resolve weaken. His thoughts never shifted toward agreement. The stubborn bond between them would have ruined everything if it wasn't for Nova.

Thea watched the pilot's brows dip, her expression steel. Then the ship surged forward and the discarded escape pod was propelled deeper into the hangar.

The ship had barely passed through the doors when the shock blasts hit Thea in rapid succession. She bounced against the control panel limply. When the first wave of blasts ended, a second came. Her head lolled backward.

She watched *Halo* streak across the stars, Coen screaming in her mind until she fell unconscious.

She slaved over the tech. She worked until her eyes burned, until she fell asleep at her keyboard. She skipped meals, grew irritable, began to make mistakes.

Sol criticized her, and though she hated to admit he was right, she could see she was overexerting herself. She was no help to anyone—especially not Thea—when her mind was exhausted.

The programmer took a week off, and when she returned to her work, she saw it with fresh eyes. It wasn't that she was missing the solution, it was that she was physically incapable of reaching it.

Her code was perfect.

The flux drive was operational.

The issue was in the recharging cycle, and it was power holding the tech back, not her programming.

She glanced at the most recent simulation readings. They'd been holding steady since last month. Impressive, but still not enough. But she'd get it there, because she finally knew what she needed. The answer was just a short flight away.

Sol wouldn't like it. It would be expensive and it would make Paradox Technologies reliant on the help of a second party, but he'd come around. She'd see to it. If she had to lie, pretend to feel something for him again, she would do it. Anything to get back to Thea.

The programer left the lab to hunt down Sol. They needed to talk about the tidally locked planet, Bev.

IV

THE GETAWAY

Halo

Interstellar Airspace

NOVA HELD THE YOKE CONFIDENTLY, guiding them hard and true away from Kanna7.

"We have to go back for her!" Coen shouted.

"Nope."

"Nova, she's the only reason we got away."

"And she'd be pissed if we got caught trying to save her! We need to run!"

Nova could understand her words as reasonable. Rational. Smart. And still they seemed to burn her tongue as she spoke them. Thea had been looking right at Nova when she'd made the executive decision to flee. Thea had even said "Don't wait for me." Why then did it feel like another betrayal? Why was Nova always damning people she cared about?

"I'm with Nova on this one," Amber agreed.

"You would be," Coen argued. "You barely even know her. What do you care?" He lowered his face beside Nova, leaning lightly on the dash. "Please, Nova. We have to go back." She made the mistake of looking at him. His eyes were glossy, filled with water. He blinked, and a tear slipped free. "Nova,

I am begging you. I can't even hear her anymore. What if they kill her?"

"They're not going to kill her," Amber said. "They *need* her."

Coen wheeled on the medic. "You were complacent about all this until your own safety was on the line. I don't want to hear a damn thing about what you think!"

"You wouldn't have your pilot if it wasn't for me!" Amber shouted back.

"Seriously, Coen. Cut her some slack. I'd likely have hemorrhaged eyes and a bloody nose right now if it weren't for Amber injecting herself with—" Nova stopped cold as the dash lit up with warnings. A half-dozen objects were now on the radar, speeding away from Kanna7 to chase after *Halo*. "Buckle in," she told the others.

"Are we going back?" Coen asked.

"Just do it!"

Chances were the Radicals wanted to take the ship whole. They were after Coen, their precious host. They'd want Amber now, too. They weren't about to blast *Halo* into stardust, but Nova was going to have to do some incredible maneuvering to ensure their escape lasted longer than thirty seconds.

As she swung the ship around, turning to face her attackers, a lifetime of memories crashed into her. Her lifelong desire to be a pilot. Her disappointment when a degenerative eye condition barred her from the Academy. It was her father's footsteps she'd been following all those years. He'd died fighting for the Union. *He* was the one who had those beautiful sayings about love and impossible odds.

She could see him, briefly, in her mind. The way he'd held her before leaving for active duty that very last time. He was with her again now, shining in every star, filling the vastness of space, standing beside her seat with his hands resting on her shoulders as she fell into her element.

With nothing left to lose and everything to gain, Nova became invincible.

She fought the way she had at the Academy—wild and scrappy and free. She was daring. She was aggressive. She moved the ship as though it were a part of her, and in the heat of the battle, with Radical ships exploding like fireworks beyond her dash, she forgot that her legs were weak and her mind plagued by nightmares and her eyesight slightly beneath Academy standards. She was simply Nova Singh, the Union fighter pilot she'd always dreamed of being, guided by her father.

He stayed with her until she'd shot down four Radical bastards and caused another two ships to collide based on her impeccable maneuvering. Once the threat was gone and *Halo* was barreling hard and fast away from Kanna7, Nova risked a glance over her shoulder.

Amber and Coen had strapped in, but they'd both been sick from the turbulence. The bridge smelled, but Nova smiled.

"They gone?" Coen grunted, wiping his mouth.

"For now."

"That doesn't mean more won't follow," Amber said.

"They don't need to follow." Nova put the ship on auto-pilot and slid from her seat, all but collapsing onto the floor. Her legs were throbbing. She'd never felt so tired. "This is a military transit ship, meaning *Halo* has tracking software. The comms are linked with *Paramount*, Kanna7, and probably other Trios military channels. Burke can just watch us fly and have forces ready to apprehend us wherever we land. I'm kinda surprised that wasn't his plan from the start."

Nova craned her neck, finding the black compact box beneath the flight dash. She flipped the door open. A mess of color-coded wires stared back.

"So how do we land anywhere?" Amber asked.

"We secure the ship. Get ourselves off-grid." Nova picked at the wires, racking her brain for memories from the Academy and lessons about tracking and comms. Everything was foggy. How could she remember how to fly a damn ship, but not the basics that made that ship function? Maybe it was like muscle memory. Sitting in that pilot's seat was second nature. This box and the wires were just stored knowledge, stuff she'd learned but not something she lived and breathed.

Walking should pull from muscle memory, and yet that leaves you exhausted, too.

She pushed the thought aside and said, "I need someone to pull up a manual."

Amber rushed to the dash. "Tell me what to do." Nova walked her through the interface and soon Amber was reading the color codes from the manual. "Tracking is . . . olive green and black."

"As in two separate wires?"

"No. Sorry. Wrapped together. A set of olive green and black wound together."

Nova found the match and yanked one end free. "Comms?" she asked.

"There's a half dozen."

"Read them all."

"Red for local channels. Navy for internal audio and video. External near planet is black wound with purple. External deep space is black wound with teal. And then there's something called the Union Military Network. That's black, white, and red wound together."

"That's the one that basically links this ship to Burke," Nova explained. "But I'm gonna cut everything except the local and internal lines. It's dangerous—we'll have no way to reach anyone unless they're within a few hours' distance— but it's the only way to be sure."

"Only way to be sure about what?" Amber asked.

"That we can't be tracked. Or spied on. All the other comm systems are part of a greater network, relying on relay points set up throughout the galaxy."

"If there's an external relay point, someone could use it to find us," Coen said, understanding.

Nova nodded from beneath the dash. "Here goes nothing." She gathered the appropriate wires and tugged them free. Several alerts beeped, warning about lost comms. She shuffled out from beneath the dash and struggled to stand, legs wobbling beneath her. She'd feel stronger tomorrow, after some rest, but hated feeling weak in the moment.

Nova collapsed into the pilot's seat. "So," she said, spinning to face the others. "Where to?"

"You know where I want to go," Coen gritted out. His head was frighteningly quiet; a gaping, empty stretch. It was possible the distance between Kanna7 and *Halo* was simply beyond his abilities, but he desperately wanted to confirm that Thea was okay. She was supposed to be on this ship *with* him.

"Coen, you know we can't. It's a death wish." Amber

touched his shoulder reassuringly and he shrugged her off, disgusted. This was Farraday's daughter. This girl was related to the person who had tortured and tested him, who was as responsible for Thea's lost finger and near drowning as Burke. And now she was on *Halo*, standing in Thea's spot.

"The only way we can help Thea is by alerting the right authorities," Nova said. "Authorities who aren't Radicals."

This, Coen could agree with. "We go home, then," he said. "To Eutheria."

Nova shook her head.

"The whole point of escaping was to go home."

"And I want that, too," Nova said. "I *still* want it. But we're in a military transit ship, Coen. Every port in the Trios will have this serial number once Burke reports it stolen. They might let us land, but we'll be immediately arrested, and that's assuming they don't surround us and force a surrender as we approach the planet."

"So the Cradle?"

Nova again shook her head. "The Trios's military and the Cradle's military are all supposed to be playing for the same team. Officials don't know Burke's a Radical. I bet he'll report *Halo*'s serial to the Cradle, too. Nowhere in the Union is safe for us."

"So not only did you leave Thea behind, but we've got

nowhere to go?" Coen's heart was pounding in his chest. His blood was boiling.

"She *asked* me to, Coen! She told me not to wait for her if it came down to it."

"Of course she did! She's selfless and practical to a fault. *You* were supposed to realize it wasn't the right choice. If I was in that pilot's seat, I wouldn't have left her."

"If you were in this pilot seat, we'd all be captured," Nova snapped.

"You think I don't know what happened on Achlys, but I know, Nova. This isn't the first time you've left Thea behind. Your crew abandoned her in that storm. That's how she ended up in my bunker. And you abandoned her again after your captain shot Dr. Tarlow. You've always been okay with leaving her behind."

Nova stood—or tried to. Grimacing in pain and exhausted, she remained in her seat, teeth bared like an animal. "Don't forget that she left you once, too. I wasn't driving that rover when we were attacked while trying to repair *Odyssey*. She was. And she drove on after you fell from the back with Cleaver. She. Drove. On. It's called preservation, doing what's best for the bulk of the group. Sacrificing one to save many."

The memories of that day flared to life for Coen—slipping from the rover, colliding with the hard Achlys ground.

He hadn't been mad at Thea, not truly. He had the skills to survive. It was only mindless infected he had to deal with then. The battle was easy, over within minutes. But he hadn't left Thea on Kanna7 with an enemy she could defeat. He'd left her alone, truly, with Radicals who held all the power. He'd doomed her.

He tried to reach her again, straining his mind, reaching into the depths of black quiet that now filled his head. She was gone. Unconscious, maybe dead. And if not that, she was outside his reach. None of the possibilities brought him any relief.

Amber said, "There is *somewhere* we can go. I overheard some things about a company on Casey. They've caused trouble for the Radicals. That sounds like a good ally to me."

"Casey's in Fringe-2." Coen felt himself frowning. "I'm assuming you got this company's name?"

"No, but my dad mentioned that security is lax in the Inansi Desert."

Nova nodded. "Lots of fugitives and people on the run head there."

"And Casey's an independent rock," Amber went on enthusiastically, "outside UPC jurisdiction. They're not loyal to the Union in any way. Burke will expect us to flee straight home, but with this route, we can disappear. If we manage to find the company Burke fears, even better."

"But it's gotta be a two-month flight," Coen said.

"Given our current position"—Nova glanced at the maps on the dash—"I'd say more like six weeks."

"We still don't have the supplies," Coen argued.

"*Halo* has three cryo pods," Amber offered, and Nova flinched. "You won't lose any of the PT progress you've made," Amber assured her. "When stasis works properly, it's almost like hitting a pause button—no negative side effects."

"I know." The pilot bit her bottom lip. "I can plot our course before we go under. We'd be pulled out as we closed in on Casey."

Coen could almost hear the gears working in the girls' minds. Their hearts were beating slightly faster now, but not with fear. This was something gleeful. Something fueled by hope. It was a good idea, a safe option, but all Coen could think of was Thea, left behind on Kanna7, and Gina, stranded in a bed on Eutheria and growing weaker as he ran.

He was failing everyone he loved.

"What about my family? My sister is dying back home. The whole reason I worked the Black Quarry op was to get the money to help her with treatments."

Nova regarded him sadly. "You're a fugitive now, Coen, wanted throughout the entire Union. Any money you earned through Black Quarry has probably been retracted."

"It's not just about money. It's not even about saving her at this point. It's about saying good-bye. I want to be able to say good-bye, and you're keeping me from her."

"I'm not doing this to you," Nova said. "Burke did this. The Radicals did this. But not me."

He hated that she was right, and yet he was still furious. His chest physically hurt, as though it were being tightened in a vise. It was too much to lose at once—Thea, his family, the future he'd imagined. Everything was spiraling out of control.

"When we get to Casey, you can arrange transit home. You'll be arrested before you even set foot on Eutherian soil, let alone in your sister's hospital, but I won't stop you. Just let the rest of us find some semblance of safety first."

Coen stared at Nova, pulse boiling. She stared back.

Amber shifted uncomfortably. "Coen," she said softly, "what do you think Thea would want us to do?"

He knew the answer immediately, and it made shame kick in his gut. Even with Thea wanting everything Coen wanted—like the reunion with Gina—he knew what course of action she'd argue for. If she was on *Halo*, he'd be having this argument with her, not Nova.

"She'd want us to go to Casey," he said finally. "So I guess that's where we'll go."

As Amber helped Nova move about the bridge, readying the ship for FTL, Coen updated them on *Psychrobacter achli*, explaining how it caused disastrous results in the older population but could be hosted by most teens. How he and Thea had figured this out on Achlys and how, after confirming the same themselves, the Radicals planned to exploit the superhuman skills of hosts to strengthen their military and give them an extraordinary edge when they made their move to claim independence for the Trios.

It was a lot to take in. Amber knew she was gaping. "So you and Thea could speak telepathically?" she asked.

"Yes, but it's even more than that now. I experience pretty much everything she experiences. All our thoughts are linked. We can't hide anything from each other. Distance seems to be the only exception. I can't hear her anymore, and I'm choosing to believe it's because of our location, not the fact that she's dead."

"They need her. She's not dead," Nova insisted.

"How is that sort of connection even possible?" Amber asked.

"Your father had a hypothesis that when two hosts created a strong bond, their abilities might deepen. He was right. After Thea and I bonded, he tried to replicate the bond with the animals but never had any success," Coen went on. "Burke was pretty disappointed."

"Because bonded hosts would be the most powerful weapons," Nova mused aloud.

Amber frowned. "If Burke truly wanted to force another

bond in humans, he'd have injected both me *and* Nova."

"Or he had plans to bring additional potential hosts aboard Kanna7," Nova said.

"I definitely wouldn't put it past him," Coen agreed.

Amber rested her hip against the dashboard, sighing heavily. "If this contagion gets out . . . What if I can't host it?"

"We'd have seen obvious symptoms by now if that were the case," Coen said. "You'll be like me soon, minus the bond to Thea. I'd guess within the next ten to twelve hours."

Amber wasn't sure what was more terrifying: that she might now be like Thea and Coen, something superhuman, forever changed, or that her father and Burke might unleash a plague on the galaxy if they weren't careful.

No, she knew what was more terrifying. An outbreak would be deadly, irreversible. It would mean the end of the Union. What was happening to her would only be dangerous if she passed it on to the wrong person.

"We need to figure out how to cure it," Amber said. "Obviously I don't want more kids subjected to studies and testing and military roles they didn't sign up for. And even *we* could cause an outbreak if we're not careful—you and me and Thea."

Coen nodded in agreement. "Thea's old boss seemed to think there was a possibility of a cure. She implied that she was close to finding one before she died."

Nova said, "So we get to Casey and find this company Amber mentioned. They can alert trustworthy authorities. Thea will be freed. Galactic Disease Control will get to work on a vaccine or treatment or whatever. A happy ending for everyone."

It sounded too neat and clean. Something was bound to go wrong, but Amber bit her tongue. They needed optimism now, not doubts.

Nova glanced up from the dash, where a star map showed their current position and destination. "I'm going to switch us to FTL. Let's head to cryo, and pray that Burke doesn't start an epidemic while we're under."

Cryostasis was torture.

It reminded Coen all too thoroughly that he was alone. The quiet in his head had become a throbbing pain, almost worse than the headache he'd been hit with after bonding with Thea. He wished for the bond fiercely now. He'd take the headache, the endless thoughts, the noise that had filled his mind.

He'd give anything to have her back.

As he lay in the stasis pod, the ship carrying him farther and farther from Kanna7, he began to dream about her.

Sometimes the dreams were nightmares: the torture they'd endured on the space station or the darkness they'd fled on Achlys. Other times the dreams were happier memories, good moments stolen during the bad. Their palms separated by a panel of glass. Her eyes tracing the tattoo on his torso. His lips brushing hers. There were even dreams that delved into fantasy, full of all the things he wished he'd said, the things he longed to do to her, with her.

And sometimes, in the cavernous depth of his subconscious sleep, when everything fell aside in favor of black emptiness, he imagined he could hear her again, nudging at his subconscious, whispering softly, *Coen, Coen, are you there? Please say you can hear me.*

She'd been right—Sol hated her plan—but the company on Bev was the answer.

It was run by Sol's corporate buddies, who'd recently found a unique variety of corrarium on the tidally locked rock. AltCor, they were calling it. The stuff had powered a generator for a month with the fuel line barely dropping. She'd overheard Sol discussing it with the company's owner on a vidcall a month earlier. It's almost . . . sentient, the guy had said. Seems to . . . reproduce, for lack of a better word.

Despite Naree's insistence that this fuel was the solution to their problems, Sol was hesitant. Corrarium was powerful enough. Paradox didn't need something even stronger, especially not something untested or unresearched. But if corrarium didn't give the drive the power they needed for a quick recharging cycle, nothing Naree programmed would. She couldn't make energy out of nothing.

"This new fuel source, however . . . ," she said, straightening Sol's tie and brushing a bit of lint from his shoulder. "It's at least worth a test. You do want us to succeed, don't you?"

He glanced down at her. They were standing very close.

"Are we talking about the drive or us?"

The programmer feigned embarrassment. "Maybe both."

History surged between them. She could see the lust in his eyes and she tried to mirror it, praying her disgust and guilt remained hidden. Sol was the biggest mistake of her life. The affair was what had gotten her into this mess, but if tapping into that history helped bend Sol to her will, she wasn't beneath revisiting it.

"I'll pay Dax a visit," he said. "See if we can obtain a small amount for a few test runs."

"I'll come with you."

"I'd like that."

She smiled for all the wrong reasons and let him think otherwise.

V

THE PRISONER

Kanna7 Station

Orbiting Sol 2 from beyond the Lethe Asteroid
Belt, Trios System

SHE WOKE TO BLINDING LIGHT and a silence that echoed in her ears.

"Where are they?" a voice said, murky at first, then clearer when Thea focused her senses.

She blinked, tried to sit. Straps held her in place. She was on a table again, in isolation. Lieutenant Burke stood before her, fully suited as an extra precaution. It was like her first interaction with him all over again, only in a different room.

"Where *are* they?" he repeated.

Terror raced through her when the quiet in her mind persisted. She reached, called out, shouted mentally, and the silence echoed back. Coen was gone. Out of reach. As good as vanished.

It was nearly enough to bring her to tears. Even now, water welled in her eyes. She blinked rapidly, refusing to let them fall. *Don't let them see you hurt. Don't let them know you're scared.*

Burke nodded to a man in the corner of the room, and something jabbed into Thea's side, delivering a blow of electricity. Her EVA suit had been removed to allow for more effective shock strikes, and she gasped. Tears streamed down her face. So much for not crying.

"Where?"

"I don't know."

"Ask him!"

"I can't!"

Another blast of electricity. She writhed.

"I can't—he's gone. It's broken." Speaking the words was torture. She didn't want to accept this truth. He'd be in her mind any moment. If she just tried harder . . .

Thea clenched her eyes together, strained with every fiber of her being, calling out, begging, praying for his voice in her mind—a whisper, even. The silence was deafening.

"I can't reach him," she gasped between tears. "He's dead or they've gone too far."

"He's not dead, he escaped!"

"Then he's too far. I've got nothing. He's gone!" She was blubbering now, choking on snot that had slid down her face and into her mouth. She was a disgrace.

Burke nodded to his man, and Thea's side again flared with pain. In a stronger state, she'd be able to slip from the cuffs, use her abilities to break free. But her wrists were slick with sweat and she was tired and beaten. Where would she run, even if she managed to get free? How could she ever escape again without an ally?

"This will continue until you talk," Burke warned.

"Sir, I don't think she's lying." Dr. Farraday held out a Tab. Thea registered the strap beneath her chin for the first time. She was back in a hot cap, and yet they were using old-fashioned shock rods to strike her. Maybe torture didn't feel like torture to Radicals unless they got their hands dirty.

"See?" Dr. Farraday continued. "There's no spike in brain activity. She's not hiding anything."

Burke turned on Thea, leveling his gaze with hers. "Where will they go?"

"You tell me. Don't your ships all have track—"

Agony roared. Her vision went white. When the pain passed, her head fell onto her chest and she gasped wildly.

"They disabled the tracking system, the comms—anything we could use to find them has been cut."

Thea smiled despite the pain. Nova had made the ship disappear. She hadn't expected anything less.

"Where. Will. They. Go?"

She refused to speak.

"You didn't have a plan besides steal a ship? I doubt that."

Oh, Thea had formed a plan. She just hadn't noticed its weakness until it was already in motion. When she'd stepped aboard *Halo*, it had hit her. They'd never be able to fly home. It would be suicide, a dead end, a prison cell waiting once they landed. Her mind had flown through alternatives, settling on an independent rock where people often fled for freedom and a chance at a new life. In the excitement of the escape, Coen hadn't sensed this change. They'd been too focused on the ship and the air lock, and the thought had been barely a blip in Thea's consciousness. Even when it occurred to her, she'd considered that maybe she was wrong. Once on *Halo*, once traveling away from Kanna7 with the threat behind her, perhaps she'd see another route. Maybe there'd be a way to go home after all.

Now she knew how foolhardy that hope had been. There were only two habitable destinations outside of UPC jurisdiction where the crew of *Halo* could land: Casey or Achlys. And she knew they'd never set foot on Achlys again.

Burke nodded to his man. The pain scorched Thea's body.

"Go easy on her, please," Farraday said. "She's our only host and you've already pushed her beyond what the average human could withstand."

Thea's heart beat savagely. It was going to burst from her chest. She kept waiting for it to simply stop, for the pain to vanish, for everything to just . . . end. Her vision danced, the room showing in doubles, everything blurry.

"Where do you *think* they'll go?" Burke asked.

"Eutheria?" Thea croaked out. "Coen just wanted to go home."

"There. Now, that wasn't so hard. Was it?" Burke smiled

wickedly and flicked a finger at his fellow Radical.

The shock tore through Thea's side and she clamped her teeth together, writhing as she counted in her head to keep from passing out. At twelve, the pain stopped, and her head sagged forward. Thea vomited down her front.

"Take her to her cell. Keep a half dozen guards posted outside around the clock."

Thea felt a mask being slipped over her face. Her eyes fell shut.

Amid the pain and as she fell unconscious, she reached out to her other half, desperate, delirious. *Coen, Coen, are you there? Please say you can hear me.*

No one came for her the next day, and she spent the better half of the morning crying.

She felt weak and pitiful. She was lying in bed, lamenting her fate instead of plotting and planning, but she couldn't muster the resolve to get up. She wanted nothing more than to feel sorry for herself for a change. She'd earned it.

She spilled tears into her pillow until her eyes were swollen. She screamed until her throat was hoarse. She dug her fingers into her hair, squeezing, scratching, wishing her cursed brain would work properly.

She said his name over and over.

Coen.

Coen.

Are you there?

Please say you can hear me.

The silence was too much. It filled the entire room. It weighed on her shoulders. It blotted out hope.

He was gone. Back to Eutheria if the crew was foolish, where they would be caught upon approach or landing; or to Casey, if they'd been smart about things. And with Nova at the yoke, they'd likely been smart.

There would be Radical spies on that independent rock. Thea wasn't so naive as to believe that the Radicals hadn't infiltrated every fold of the universe by now. She prayed Coen's crew would evade them and land safely. Maybe even devise a way to get Thea help. She'd never know if it was coming for her, not without being able to contact Coen. To hope that blindly, to have such unfaltering faith . . . Thea didn't know if she could do it. She believed in facts and science and reason. What she'd had with Coen had seemed impossible, but she'd lived it, breathed it, felt and heard him in her head. And now he was gone, his absence a gaping hole in her mind, an infection that festered with despair.

Finally, she summoned the strength to clean at the room's small wash station. Her shirt still smelled of vomit. She left it hanging over the sink and paced the quarters in her bra.

She caught her reflection in the glass wall that separated

her cell from the empty one that used to be Coen's. Dark moons sagged beneath her eyes. Her hair hung wild and greasy.

Thea put her palm to the glass and closed her eyes, imagining Coen on the other side and how it would feel for his hand to meet hers now.

When she opened her eyes, his cell was still empty.

Her hand was still alone.

And the quiet was endless.

The following morning, she awoke to find a stranger in Coen's room. A middle-aged man, short but wiry, with ghostly pale skin and eyes that glowed like dark embers. He adjusted the cuff of his jacket, observing her with interest. Burke stood behind the stranger, and Farraday lingered by the far wall.

The men whispered, keeping their voices low, but Thea could hear everything.

The stranger was Aldric Vasteneur, owner of Hevetz Industries. He'd come as quickly as he could. He wanted to see her in the flesh—cameras alone wouldn't suffice.

The shipment was arriving next week, whatever that meant. Vasteneur had brought the implants, whatever those were. Production would begin as soon as possible. Thea was to remain out of it. With Coen gone, she had become Patient

Zero in their eyes. They needed her pure, unaltered. Achlys was too far away to be considered their lifeline, and too dangerous given what they'd learned. Thea was their source. Her blood was their future.

Perhaps they didn't think she could hear them, or maybe they figured it didn't matter even if she could. She was trapped. There was nothing she could do with this information.

She remained in the bed like a statue, not wanting to give them a show. It was obvious Burke and his crew were Radicals, but she'd always harbored some hope that Hevetz wasn't also tied up in the mess, that Vasteneur had loaned scientists to Burke with honorable goals. But watching them now, it was obvious that Vasteneur was as deeply involved as Burke. He wasn't trying to cure a disease or save humanity. He was a Radical, anxious to see the Trios gain its independence, and when it hadn't happened naturally or in a lawful manner, he'd sacrificed Black Quarry to get his hands on *Psychrobacter achli*.

Burke and Farraday eventually left, but Vasteneur lingered. He took meals in Coen's room, watching Thea like a hawk. His eyes on her felt like a second skin, a claw dragging down her body.

"You've taken everything," she finally screamed. "What more do you want?"

Sitting on Coen's cot, one leg folded over his other knee and a cup of tea held centimeters from his lips, Aldric Vasteneur paused. He set the drink aside, adjusted the cuffs of his fitted jacket, then pulled a kerchief from his breast pocket and dabbed at his mouth.

"I want what the Radicals want," he said calmly. "For the greatest find of our generation—an unparalleled resource— to set the Trios free. Hevetz will help bring forth this new resource, but unlike corrarium, the Cradle won't crave it. They'll fear it, fear *us*. They'll surrender. Everyone—even the pro-Union rabble—will submit to Radical ideals."

"If you're talking about biological warfare, you don't understand how fast this spreads. It will wipe out billions."

"I thought you were smart, Miss Sadik. It was why we approved your internship." Vasteneur stood and walked toward the glass. Thea was nearly his height and yet he made her feel small. It was his posture, rigid and confident, combined with the glib way his limbs swayed at his sides. "The contagion is not the weapon. *You* are the weapon. *Hosts*. So long as we can control the hosts, we have an autonomous army. We will no longer be pawns moved by the Union's whims."

Thea's thoughts moved to the implants he'd mentioned. Production. He was going to create more hosts and try to control them. There was no twitch to his gaze, no frenzy to his pulse. His heart beat steadily. His voice was sure. He wasn't bluffing.

"People will look for me. For us," she said desperately. "They'll dig, find the truth before you can make your move."

"What is truth, I wonder? Is it an idea? Documented history? Public record?" He smiled crookedly. "The truth is only as good as the information supporting it. Control the information, and you control the truth. You are dead, Miss Sadik, and you have been since that arctic storm hit Northwood Point. No one is coming for you." He leaned in, nose nearly touching the glass. "No one."

The days began to blend together. She kept track of them by counting dinners, the tally growing in her mind.

At the end of the week, she was brought to the locker rooms and allowed to shower. Like before, the place was emptied for her visit and she was threatened with shocks if she tried to run. The mirror fogged, taunting her. The air vent she'd crawled into was now welded shut.

After the shower, she was transported to the labs, secured to a reclined chair, and left with nothing but the operating light overhead. When she was beginning to wonder if they'd forgotten about her, the door slid open and Dr. Farraday strode into view.

"Nothing but blood work today, Thea. No need to fret." He pulled on a set of gloves and positioned a paper mask over his mouth and nose. Lowering himself into a seat beside her, the doctor readied the needle and leaned closer than seemed necessary.

Thea contemplated yanking her limbs free of the restraints and snapping his neck just for the fun of it. It would get her nothing in the end. There were guards stationed outside the room. She could hear their pulses even now. But the fantasy of revenge, of seeing just one of these men suffer, was tempting. She was thinking about how Farraday's slowing pulse would feel beneath her clenched fingers when he whispered, "Is Amber okay?"

The surveillance camera was behind Thea, mounted above the door. She'd seen it when she'd been dragged into the room. Currently, it would capture nothing but her back, and with Dr. Farraday's mask obscuring his mouth, it was unlikely the camera would capture much from him.

"She was fine when I last saw her on *Halo*," Thea said quietly.

Something glinted in the doctor's eyes. "So no damning symptoms? Hemorrhaged eyes or bloody nose?"

"Nope. She's probably just like me now."

The glint disappeared.

"What's that, doctor? You're concerned for her safety, but

only if she's not a host? You're the one who put her in this situation to begin with."

"Watch your tone. It's showing in your shoulders, and they'll see it on the footage." Thea went still, trying to read his expression, but he'd lowered his gaze to her arm and was now focused on inserting the needle into her vein. Blood zipped through the tubing and began filling the bag.

"Do you know where they'll go, truly?" he asked.

"If I did, I wouldn't tell you."

The doctor glanced up, eyes pleading.

"What's the shipment that arrives today?" Thea challenged him. "Or maybe it already arrived a few days ago. I'm getting fuzzy on time."

"I can't tell you that."

"What about the stuff Vasteneur brought? I heard something about implants."

"Thea." It was said with impatience. He could ask questions, but not her.

"The shipment is a bunch of hosts, isn't it? You're going to infect a bunch of kids and try to turn them into an army. The implants must be some means to control them, snuff out their free will."

Dr. Farraday turned away, drumming the blood bag with his index and middle fingers. "Why ask questions if you've already figured out the answers?"

"And my blood? You don't need this much to infect someone."

"Research."

"Are they trying to find a cure?"

"A treatment of some sort. Maybe a vaccine. You've shown resistance to the negative side effects of *Psychrobacter achli*, so it's reasonable to assume that you hold the key to immunization as well."

"Let me help," Thea pleaded.

The doctor shook his head.

"It would be a better use of my time than sitting in that cell. I'm going crazy in there with nothing to do."

Farraday tested the blood bag again. It was nearly full.

"So this is it? I'll shower once a week, give blood once a week, and sit locked in my room otherwise?"

"That seems to be the gist of it." He withdrew the needle from Thea's arm and didn't even bother putting pressure on the injection site. Thea's blood clotted instantly. "You can't talk to Coen, right? I was correct when I told Burke that the other day? I really want to confirm that my daughter is okay."

"Whose side are you on, Doctor?" Thea growled.

A small pause. "Until recently, I thought I knew."

"Well, that's not good enough. You don't get to pick both. You have to choose."

"It's not that easy."

"Actually, it is. The fact that this is hard for you tells me exactly where you stand."

He stood abruptly and rapped on the door, calling, "We're done in here."

The guards entered, hooking their metal leads back into Thea's collar, unlatching her from the chair. Dr. Farraday was putting her blood on ice when she was tugged into the hall.

The pattern repeated. Daily meals and weekly showers followed by blood draw sessions, but no experiments in between. Not on Thea, at least.

The hosts were a different story.

The first time she heard them—their thoughts loud and wild and confused—it brought her to tears. She was in the shower, close to the room where she and Coen had endured so much testing. She wanted it to be his voice in her head, and instead it was a sea of voices, lost and hopeless. She tried to reach out to them, to tell them it would be okay, to hang in there; but they'd already been infected and weren't listening for Thea. They weren't even listening for each other. They were almost feral, their thoughts propelled through the space station, muddling together, creating a wave of noise. She couldn't break through.

She never saw them, and they never saw her.

Three weeks in, Thea almost found herself wishing to be tested again. Not the torturous type, but the tests where her strength had been measured, where she was allowed to spar in the ring. She wanted to meet the other teens, or even just one of them. The desire to speak with someone of her kind was overwhelming. Being alone had become her torture.

She started working out in her room. Push-ups and sit-ups and jumping jacks. The lip above her doorway allowed for fingertip pull-ups. She did knee-highs until sweat ran into her eyes. It was about remaining sane as much as it was about staying strong.

Thea couldn't envision an end to the nightmare, but she took it one day at a time.

Dr. Farraday appeared to be slipping. He wasn't on the fence so much as he was in the process of climbing over it. He loved his daughter more than the Radicals. During each weekly blood session, he told Thea a little more, until the entire plan was laid bare and Thea was gaping in shock—helpless, hopeless, scared.

The Radicals were ready. Their weapon, the plan of attack, all of it, would unfold in time. They were just waiting for the right moment, an opportunity on the horizon.

Thea saw no way of stopping it. Worse, she saw outcomes where things got away from Burke, where he lost control.

The Radicals were children playing with fire. They were a heartbeat from setting the galaxy ablaze.

She continued to listen, folding away every detail Dr. Farraday shared with her.

She continued her workouts, growing stronger by the day.

And in the dead of the night, when the quiet became too much and loneliness clawed at her heart, she continued to reach out to Coen. He was gone, the connection severed. She'd finally accepted it, but she would never stop talking to him.

The programmer immediately hated Bev.

There were parts of the tidally-locked planet that were surely pleasant, but in the terminator, where Sol's corporate buddies had set up their drilling operation, things were depressing. Sol had told her what to expect during the short flight over, but nothing could prepare a person for this type of dankness, the chill you couldn't shake.

At least the underground facilities spared visitors from the worst of the elements. Now inside, she followed a worker through the halls. Sol had stood too near her on the ship, whispered too often in her ear. He was easily slipping into the role he played thirteen years earlier, and she was grateful when he disappeared to pay Dax and left her to pick up the fuel from Dax's brother, Devon.

The worker led her to the infirmary, where Devon was getting a daily dose of meds. Tall and slight, he sat shirtless on an operating table as a medic checked his vitals. Streaks of bright red covered his chest, arms, and neck, mapping his veins with precision. Sol had warned Naree of his blood poisoning, explaining that Devon had suffered a bad fall while harvesting AltCor several weeks earlier and exposure to the cold had done a number on him. Even still, it was hard to not stare.

"You must be Naree," Devon said, smiling when he saw her in the doorway. "I was hoping to meet you in the warehouse, but I'm tethered to this place lately." He raised an arm, showing off the IV. "Your package is there, by the regen bed. Should be enough for a few tests." He nodded to a dolly stacked with three bright yellow carrying cases. Each was plastered in radiation labels. "It'll do the trick, I promise."

Naree met his eyes. "You don't even know what we need it for."

"I know you need power, and this stuff . . . It's alive, I swear. It knows."

"Knows what?"

"When it's being depleted. It senses it. Reproduces somehow."

"So it's limitless?"

"Of course not. But Bev . . ." He paused and didn't continue until the medic was out of earshot. "Bev tells me it will work. That this stuff can do whatever you need it to do."

"Bev is a planet. It can't talk."

"It talks to me."

Maybe it was the gleam in his eyes, or the way his lips quirked into a smile as he said it, or how Devon's blood poisoning appeared to grow darker when she blinked, his veins taking on a tinge of inky black. Naree believed him. Bev had told Devon something.

Hair stood on the back of her neck. She had the distinct urge to leave the package where it sat and return to ship empty-handed. But she gripped the dolly by the handle, nodded her thanks to Devon, and rolled the AltCor to Sol's ship.

VI

THE DETAINMENT

Halo

Interstellar Airspace

/

Inansi Desert

Casey, Fringe-2 System

THE MOMENT AMBER FARRADAY WOKE from stasis, she knew it was in her. She'd come to before Nova and Coen, and she could hear their hearts pumping languidly in their cryo chambers. The units' slowing fans hummed in her ears. Her entire being felt electrified, hyperaware.

She stepped from the pod, the floor cool underfoot. The ship seemed alive, suddenly. She could make out the thrum of the reactors in the engine room, a steady proximity alert beeping from the bridge.

The pulses behind her quickened, and she knew Nova and Coen were waking. Exhales. Heartbeats. The rustle of their clothes.

"Well?" Nova touched Amber's shoulder, and Amber shrugged away. The pilot couldn't touch her. What if she spread it? What if whatever was now coursing through her veins could also be transmitted in the air?

Impossible.

Thea and Coen would have infected all of Burke's crew long before the *Paramount* had even reached Kanna7 if this were the case, and Coen had explained exactly how the bacteria spread, but still Amber couldn't help but worry.

"I'll meet you on the bridge, then," Nova said, and left quickly.

Without even a glance at Coen, Amber hurried after the pilot. Nova's gait was even, her posture sure. Any soreness she'd been dealing with after escaping Kanna7 had faded during cryo, and she now walked as she had during their last PT session: slowly, but with confidence.

"I'm worried about spreading it," Amber admitted.

"That's not how it works," Nova said, not bothering to turn around.

"I know. But it's strange and terrifying and—did you know I can hear the reactor right now? Yeah, I can hear it humming all the way back in engineering. Also, Coen just slammed his cryo pod shut. I can hear that, too."

If Nova was impressed, she didn't show it. The pilot kept walking, no change to her pace.

Everything seemed brighter: *Halo*'s lighting and the decals on doorways and even the dull metal of the halls. When they stepped onto the bridge, Amber's senses were overloaded. First by the lights on the dash and the brilliance of the stars. Then by two different pulses that battled for her attention. Nova's was fast and impatient as she slid into the pilot's chair. The second, behind Amber, was steady. Almost lazy.

She turned to see Coen standing in the entrance of the bridge. His face was pale, his shoulders slouched in defeat. Suddenly she knew why he'd slammed the door to his cryo pod. "Thea?"

He shook his head. "We're fifty-five light-years apart now. I was crazy to think I'd still be able to reach her."

"No. Not crazy at all. Just hopeful."

His forehead wrinkled as he frowned. Without the hot cap, his jaw was stronger than she remembered, and he stood taller without the collar, too. Amber could see the strength in his shoulders, the roped muscles along his arms, and yet she imagined that if she reached out and nudged him with a forefinger, he'd blow over like a dead sapling.

Coen swallowed, throat bobbing, and looked away.

"I'm so sorry, Coen."

He shook his head more adamantly this time.

We'll get her back, Amber thought. Coen's gaze snapped up. She hadn't been trying to test her abilities, nor was she consciously attempting to speak telepathically with him. It was just an honest internal thought.

Can you hear me? she asked, though she wasn't sure why she was asking. It was obvious he'd heard.

Yeah. I can hear you. There was a hint of frustration to his tone. He'd rather be hearing Thea. *Of course I would*, he added.

Amber froze. "Are we bonded? Like you two were?"

"No. I'd know everything you want if that happened. I'd feel it. You'd feel my wants, too. You're just being sloppy. If you want your thoughts to be truly private, you have to guard them."

"How? Can you teach me?"

He threw the answer to her mentally. He'd already done this once, with Thea. It was too painful to do it again with anyone else, especially her. He turned and strode from the bridge without a backward glance.

"Whatever you guys say in the future, say it out loud," Nova grumbled. "I'm not gonna be in the dark all the time."

"What's there to say?" Amber said. "Thea's gone. I'm a host. And Coen's pissed about all of it. Happy?"

She listened to Coen's retreating boots. Nova flipped a switch on the dash with unnecessary force.

Somehow, Amber had managed to say the wrong thing to both of them.

Coen made his way briskly to the engine room, Amber's frenzied thoughts fading before they could bring him to tears. It was like Thea all over again, how her thoughts had been chaotic at first, projected into his mind. Of *course* he couldn't hear her anymore. Of *course* the fifty-five light-years between them were too much. And still he'd hoped.

He'd spent those weeks in cryo imagining that he might wake to hear her voice.

He burst into engineering and sat beside the reactor. His back warmed from the heat of it. The noise reverberated in his ears.

He closed his eyes and reached out—desperate, heartbroken. Thea was there, and yet she wasn't. There was no response, no connection, but he could picture her lying on her cot. It was like watching a dream. He was there, too, in his own cell. He reached out and put a hand to the glass that divided them, but she couldn't see him. There was fog between them, static in their ears, an invisible disruption to the bond.

It's called too much distance, his brain told him.

But he sat there against the reactor and kept trying. He tried and tried, and he'd never felt more alone.

Casey was the second rock from Fringe-2's sun, and as they closed in on it, Nova was overwhelmed by its beauty. It was smaller than the planets that made up the Trios, but from this distance, it was comfortingly familiar. Blue oceans. Green and brown land. White poles.

She gripped the yoke, confirming the coordinates on the dash before aligning for entry. Amber was buckled in behind her. Nova had made an announcement over the intercoms, telling Coen to come strap in for landing, but he'd yet to appear. It was his superhuman body to take risks with, she figured.

Still, Nova's hands trembled slightly during the approach. She'd landed many ships. She didn't know why she was so nervous. Maybe because the last time she landed on a planet she'd never been to before, half her crew had wound up dead. But this was Casey, not Achlys. It was colonized, developed—modern even, in certain cities. Not that they'd be landing in one of those. Due to the sheer size of the barren land, the Inansi Desert was a popular destination for folks without proper IDs, and Casey prided itself on being separate from the UPC. It practically welcomed anyone looking to escape the Union.

Nova stayed focused and soon they were entering Casey's atmosphere, *Halo* vibrating forcefully.

"This is the Global Security Agency repeating your final warning," a voice said over the radio. "You have entered private airspace without proper credentials. Announce your intentions or we will be forced to fire."

"What?!" Amber yelled from her seat. "That's the first warning we've heard."

"'Cause I cut all the other lines," Nova said. "They were probably trying to hail us on the near planet comms. This is coming through on local channels."

"Well, tell them not to shoot!"

"Hello?" Nova transmitted. "This is *Halo*, requesting permission to land in the Inansi Desert."

"*Halo*, we can see your ship's credentials. The Union military has no business on Casey. GSA rejects your landing request."

Of course. If she were flying a private ship, no one would have blinked twice as she approached. But to a planet that wanted nothing to do with the Union—to people who had already fought a war to maintain their independence—a ship associated with the Trios military had set off a million bells. She should have anticipated it.

"We are private citizens and this is a matter of life or death," Nova said back. "Permission to land at Inansi Desert?"

"Permission denied. Exit our airspace immediately."

"What the hell is going on?" Coen called. Nova risked a glance over her shoulder. He'd appeared in the doorway of the bridge, probably drawn to the commotion thanks to his freakishly good hearing.

"Nova?" Amber said. The desperation was thick in her voice.

"Permission to land at Inansi Desert?" Nova tried a final time. "You can board us immediately and confirm we're all private Trios citizens. There are no military personnel on this ship."

Silence.

"Hello?" Nova tried again.

An alert flashed on the dash, beeping loudly. "Shit," said Nova.

"What?" Amber's eyes were wide.

Coen said, "Nova, what the hell is happening?"

She read the alert again, not quite believing it. *Enemy missiles locked on.* Nova checked the navigational charts, their altitude. There'd be no time to get out of range.

"Nova, what the hell is happening?!"

The map updated. Radar had picked up the incoming weapons. They'd be to *Halo* in less than four minutes.

Nova had no delusions about what would happen. She put the ship on autopilot and turned away from the dash. The others were staring at her, brows pinched and eyes wide.

"We have to get to the escape pod," she announced. "The GSA fired and the missiles are locked on. This ship won't survive."

Coen led the way. The ship supported two escape pods, but they'd already released one back on Kanna7 to ditch the station's guards. Its two-seat, two-person capacity hadn't worried him when he'd crammed all four Radicals inside, but now . . .

He pulled up, letting Amber and Nova claim the pod's two

seats. Both faced a small vidscreen and a dash with limited controls.

"You'll be okay standing?" Nova asked.

"Don't have much of an option, do I?" Positioned behind the two seats, Coen stretched his arms out. He could palm each side of the pod—just barely. Hopefully it would be enough to brace himself during the drop.

"Ready?" Amber called.

"All set!"

She hit the *eject* button, and the pod detached with a hiss, then immediately began to rattle. Coen's arms burned as he held himself in place. There was a murderous sound above them—"That's *Halo* taking damage," Nova yelled over the din—and the pod rocked violently.

Coen's arm slipped and he was thrown upward, his back hitting the top of the pod with such force he was propelled back down to the floor. Pain shot through his spine. He threw his hands out, managing to steady himself as the turbulence mellowed.

The computer announced something about speed and altitude. About impact.

"What does that mean?" he asked.

"Parachutes deployed," Amber said, reading from the small vidscreen.

"We evacuated too low," Nova said. "Chutes won't slow

us enough in time for landing." She pointed to two sets of numbers flashing on the screen. One was shrinking faster than the other. Altitude, Coen realized. The reading for their speed seemed dangerously high.

"What does that mean?" Coen said again.

"Brace for impact," the computer announced.

As Coen steadied his grip, the fog in his mind lifted and the connection came roaring back. Thea was suddenly everywhere, surrounding him, her voice echoing in his head. *Coen, Coen, are you there? Please say you can hear me.*

His arms went slack with surprise. The pod hit earth.

Pain exploded through Coen's body as the world went white.

Nova coughed violently, fanning smoke from her eyes. Her forehead hurt. She wondered if she'd struck it against the computer. Everything was slightly off-kilter and the armrest of her seat was digging into her side. They'd landed at a severe angle, she realized, the pod door now almost overhead. When she tried to stand, Nova's boot slipped in something slick. Blood.

Amber's leg was bleeding, or rather, it had been. The metal edging that surrounded the computer had buckled in the crash and sliced into the medic's calf. Besides a tear in Amber's pant leg, there was no sign of an injury, her body having healed quickly.

Amber gave Nova a quick nod, as if to say, "I'm fine," but Nova couldn't stop staring at the blood on the floor. There was so much of it, and chances were Nova had a gash on her own forehead if the pain throbbing above her right brow told her anything. She had flashbacks from Achlys—the surveillance footage that showed Jon Li infecting himself, passing the bacteria to an open wound on his head; Toby's leg injury and the way he'd passed that blood to her cousin Sullivan.

Nova clenched her eyes shut, envisioning the breathing animation Amber had showed her.

"Coen?" Amber called, fanning smoke from her eyes.

Nova turned around in her chair. Something sparked overhead and she swore as heat lanced her shoulders.

"The pod's still closed," Amber said. "He has to be inside, but he's not responding. Not even when I call out mentally."

"Hang on. Let me try to vent some of this smoke."

Nova stood shakily on her chair and threw the door switch. It creaked open. The smoke slowly dissipated. And there he was, on the floor of the pod, one leg jutted out at an angle so awkward it could only be broken. There was a gash on the side of Coen's brow. Blood marked his temple and neck, but there wasn't much behind his head.

Amber squeezed between the two seats and prodded Coen with her boot. "Coen?" He didn't move. "I can hear his pulse," she told Nova. "He probably just got knocked out."

"I thought you guys were supposed to have superhuman strength."

"Sure," Amber agreed, "but he got thrown around like a pinball when we crashed. It's not like he's wearing an exosuit or anything." She crouched beside him and grabbed his leg, realigning it with a quick movement. Nova heard something crack and wondered if his body had already been healing, if Amber had needed to break the bones again just to reset them.

"You stay with him," Nova said. "I'm gonna see if I can figure out where we are." She grabbed the edges of the open doorway and lifted herself up. It wasn't graceful, and it took a fair amount of grunting, kicking, and cursing, but soon she was standing atop the pod, squinting in the brilliant light.

They'd landed on a rocky outcropping that rose several meters out of the desert. The parachute lay tangled on the rocks, billowing like a dying jellyfish as a hot breeze teased at the fabric. The sun was high overhead.

Nova scrambled off the pod and onto the rocks, climbing the stout structure. Turning slowly at the highest point with a hand held to shield her eyes, she searched the horizon. Sand, dunes, and more sand. It had to be at least forty degrees Celsius. A bead of sweat trailed down her back.

The only sign of civilization appeared far in the distance and low in the sky. A giant cloud of smoke and fumes—all that remained of *Halo*.

Every centimeter of his body ached, and when he regained consciousness, Coen's eyes flew open. The first thing he saw was the buckled shape of the pod overhead and then Amber, crouched before him.

"Are you—?" she began, but he held a hand up to cut her off, pain exploding through his muscles. When she tried to help him sit, he pushed her away.

"Fine. I'll meet you outside," she grumbled as she turned away.

He didn't even feel bad about his rudeness. He could explain it later. In that moment, all he could focus on was the sensation in his chest, the connection buzzing in his mind. It was still there. Her existence, her essence, her every thought crashing into him. She was restless. Pacing, if Coen had to guess. She thought she'd sensed him, and then everything had gone silent, but now . . . Thea paused. She could feel him, too.

Coen?

I'm here.

Oh my god. I thought I imagined it all. She was crying. There was a wetness on his own cheeks. Her voice was beautiful.

I heard you just before our escape pod crashed. I got knocked out for a bit.

You, knocked out? Mr. Invincible?

I wasn't buckled in and hit my head pretty hard. I can't believe I can hear you. I'm not hallucinating, am I?

No, she said. *This is real. The connection was gone, though. I've been trying to reach you for weeks. I thought the ship was just out of range, but maybe it was because of the distance and because you were in cryo. Remember how foggy it felt on* Paramount, *in cryo, even when we were right next to each other?*

Yeah, but that doesn't explain why I couldn't hear you when I came out.

I just got back from medical. They were taking more blood. They do it every week, and they knock me out during transit.

He worked the words over in his mind—delirious with glee, barely able to believe they were talking. Then furious that she wasn't with him. Angry that those bastards were still drawing her blood. Racked with guilt that she was still in their hands.

I never should have left you.

It was the only way.

Still . . . He choked on a sob. How could he explain it to her? That he'd never felt more alone or terrified than when their connection had severed. That he'd been a shadow of himself, how he'd felt as though a critical part of him had gone missing. She'd created an abscess in his side, one that throbbed with every beat and never seemed any closer to healing. She both fueled and destroyed him.

I understand, she said, hearing every last thought. He'd forgotten how annoying it was to have nothing be private. How annoying and wondrous. *I cried almost nonstop the first week*, she admitted.

And recently?

I stopped crying, but I never stopped trying to reach you.

The words made his chest ache, but not in the way it had when they'd been separated. Instead, he felt giddy, as though his heart was beating too fast. It was intoxicating. He wanted to replay this moment for hours, to hear her voice forever. He wondered if he loved her, or if this feeling was just a product of their bond. She wondered the same back, and he found himself puzzled at how they could know everything they were each thinking—how they could be bound so deeply—and still not be able to concretely know how they felt about each other.

Coen, a lot has happened since you left, Thea said hurriedly, her tone turning serious. *Aldric Vasteneur is here. He's partnered with the Radicals. A shipment of teens arrived after you guys got away. They've injected them all. A few were too old and were killed once they changed. The others are all hosts now, a dozen or so bonded like you and me according to Dr. Farraday.*

Farraday's giving you information? Coen could barely process this turn of events.

He loves his daughter more than the Radicals. Don't get me wrong, he's not exactly helping me, just passing along info. But the info is valuable, especially seeing that you and I can talk.

Are you hurt? Are they testing you still?

I'm fine. But she wasn't. He could feel it in his bones. She hadn't been tested in the same way as when he'd been with her on Kanna7, but her time there was slowly breaking her. Coen wondered how much more she could withstand.

They've developed a way to control the hosts, she went on. *A cerebral implant that blocks certain impulses, keeps them loyal. It can shock, too, like the hot caps, but now it's literally inside their brains.*

A cold shiver ran down Coen's spine. His ability to think freely had been all that kept him hopeful during his time on Kanna7.

So if a host tries to fight back . . . ?

They can't, according to Farraday. Or at least, none have tried. Regardless, the shocking capability is there as a backup.

Have they given you one?

No. Something about me being their source host now and wanting to keep me unaltered. But the other hosts . . . He's going to use them soon. To force the Union's hand at—

"Coen, you better come see this!" Nova called from outside

the pod. The pilot's pulse was kicking up. Amber's, too.

What's wrong? Thea asked. *I thought you were safe.*

We're in the Inansi Desert, but Casey's security agency didn't want us to land. I'm gonna go join the others, see what's up. He pushed to his feet. Already, the aches were receding, his body healing. His muscles were stiff, but not useless. *Stay with me?* he asked Thea.

We're bonded, she said with a smile. *It's not like I have a choice.*

The convoy drove across the desert, drawing steadily nearer. Amber could make out six white vehicles with raised chassis and solar panels mounted to the roofs. "Should we hide?" she asked.

"Hide where? They've already seen the pod and are heading right for us." Nova squinted at the vehicles. "Think it's the GSA?"

Coen shook his head. "There's a logo on the side doors. Looks like a *P*, but its broken. Like an optical illusion."

Amber strained her eyesight. She could see it now, too. The logo was designed to appear three-dimensional, and the beams and cross-sections connected in a physically impossible manner. "Maybe it's local citizens," she offered.

"Citizens in a convoy that has a matching logo on all the doors?" Coen scoffed. "My money's on a private company."

"That's better than law enforcement," Nova said.

The vehicles hummed nearer, and soon they were sliding to a stop in the sand. A long tread connected front and rear tires. The doors cracked open, and the barrels of several guns appeared—and not stun guns, but models that shot bullets.

"You were saying?" Coen gritted out. He raised his palms, and Amber hurried to do the same.

The faces came into view next, eyes hidden behind sunglasses. From what Amber could see through the windows, the personnel wore gray uniforms, that same impossibly shaped *P* stitched into their breastplates.

"On your knees," someone barked from behind the door. "Put your hands behind your head."

"Can I ask what this is about?" Nova called.

"On your knees *now!*"

A tiny red dot touched Nova's shoulder, then twitched, settling over her heart. A red dot appeared on Coen's next. Amber didn't need to look to know there was one over her own heart as well.

She slumped to her knees. Laced her fingers behind her head. Coen dropped like a weight into the sand, too. It was Nova who remained stoic, chin raised.

"Nova, get down," Amber pleaded. "Do what they say."

"What if they're the company we're looking for?" she

gritted out. The odds of that seemed impossibly slim to Amber, like finding a single needle among the grains of the desert, but Nova called out to the newcomers. "Can you at least tell us who you are?"

"A company that's worked hard to keep their tech out of the hands of Radicals," the apparent leader said. Hope spiked in Amber's chest. Maybe this really was the company Burke feared. It seemed too easy, but the mere fact that this company opposed Radicals was good news.

"You've landed a little too close to our base for comfort," the man went on. "We're bringing you in for questioning. Now, on your knees."

When Nova hesitated, a warning shot was fired into the sky, and any hope Amber had been feeling vanished. "Nova," she snarled. "Just do what they say."

The pilot reluctantly slumped into the sand.

The convoy's leader smiled, then jerked his head, giving his team a silent order. Four personnel peeled off from the vehicles, weapons still trained as they crept forward.

The sun beat down on the back of Amber's neck. Sweat stung as she tried to blink it from her eyes. The nearest man reached Nova, grabbing the pilot's hands and forcing them down behind her back. Cuffs clinked shut. Then the people were bearing down on her and Coen.

Someone stepped to Amber's side, casting a shadow on

261

her. It offered a momentary break from the sun. Coen was weak beside her, still healing from the crash, but maybe they could take these strangers. She knew how fast he was, what he was capable of. There was a good chance she was just as skilled, too.

No way, Coen snapped in her mind.

Amber had been leaking her thoughts again. Sloppy. Unguarded.

But this close we could get the element of surprise.

I said no! Coen repeated firmly.

So we just let them take us? We could beat them, and then the vehicles are ours.

Ours to go where? We have no clue where the nearest city is, or if the people there will be friendly. We have no food or water, and definitely no citizenship IDs. These guys aren't military or GSA. They're the perfect cover. Let them take us to safety before the Casey officials who shot us from the damn sky show up.

And then? Amber asked. The cuffs clicked shut over her wrists. The man hauled her to her feet.

And then we do what I did on Achlys. Manipulate. Lie. Use others as a means to an end. Get what we're after at all costs, but we have to stay alive first. We have to ally ourselves to someone. So right now, we cooperate.

The weapons stayed trained on Coen, even once he was in a vehicle.

At the mental mention of the red laser on his chest, Thea bristled in his mind. She was thinking of Dr. Tarlow—the woman's skin, healed after a gunshot wound to the abdomen, but her eyes lifeless and her pulse gone.

I'm not going to give them a reason to shoot me, Coen assured her.

It didn't matter. Thea was still on edge, practically breathless.

The vehicles glided over the sand. Nova and Amber were together in the rover behind Coen's. He rested his head on the window, relaying everything he saw to Thea. The ride was smooth until the sand gave way to parched mud cracks. Dust blew across the windshield. They were moving south based on a compass on the dash, heading toward low mesas that broke the flat horizon in the distance.

The company personnel talked about security and a drilling operation on Bev and a man named Solomon Weet. When the clock on the dash informed Coen that he'd been in the car roughly twenty minutes, a barricade appeared ahead. *Standard fencing with barbed wire along the top*, he told Thea.

Security checkpoint?

Not sure.

Fear rippled through him, and Thea sensed it. Had he trusted the wrong people? Maybe they weren't a private company but a contractor working *for* the GSA, gathering up Coen and his friends on the agency's behalf. When they reached the checkpoint, the driver flashed an ID at the guard, and the vehicle slipped through the fencing, entering the gaping expanse of desert beyond.

Five minutes later, the convoy came upon a sprawling, single-story compound. Solar arrays lined every inch of the roof. The garage to the side was taller, likely holding ships in addition to ground transportation, and it, too, was covered in dark panels.

Coen scanned every surface for a name, a logo. There was none. It was only once they'd parked in the garage and been dragged from the vehicles that he got his first glimpse of the impossible *P* he'd seen on the uniforms. A giant version of the logo marked the floor they were ushered across. It was plastered again on the door they pushed through to enter the rest of the compound, only this time a name was spelled out beneath it in neat, narrow letters.

Paradox Technologies, he relayed to Thea.

It made sense now, the way the logo was illustrated, how the beams and cross-sections of the *P* appeared logical at first but failed to add up on closer observation. It was a purposeful contradiction. A paradox.

Who are you? Nova had asked near the drop pod.

A company that's worked hard to keep their tech out of the hands of Radicals, the man had replied.

What the hell were they making here?

Nova was beginning to wonder if she wasn't the pilot she'd thought she was.

She'd landed on Achlys only to watch half her crew die.

She'd flown *Exodus* and ended up a hostage of the Radicals.

She'd escaped on *Halo*, only to crash-land on Casey and be taken hostage again—this time by a private company whose end game she couldn't even begin to fathom.

A better pilot might have out-navigated that missile. A smarter pilot would have anticipated pushback from planet security and launched drop pods earlier. At this rate, Nova was beginning to consider that she might be cursed.

"Miss Singh?" the officer in front of her barked. "Are you listening?"

She was sitting in a chair, arms tied behind her back. Her shoulder sockets ached. The edge of the backrest dug into her biceps.

"Not really," she admitted.

The officer slammed a Tab on the table. The legs rattled against the cement floor. Nova had been struck twice already—once in the gut, another blow to the face—and had expected a third just now. Maybe they were starting to buy her story, see that she wasn't lying.

"We've been telling you the truth," Coen snarled beside her. He was also secured to a chair, though Nova knew he could bust the metal cuffs holding his hands together if he wanted. She knew how strong he was. Amber too now, who was secured to her own chair beside Coen, though maybe the medic still doubted her own abilities. Still, the only reason Nova could figure that Coen hadn't acted yet was fear. Not of the Paradox guards, but of what might happen in a scuffle. The handcuffs would certainly injure Coen in the act of breaking them. If the guard was cut trying to restrain Coen, if Coen's blood entered his bloodstream . . .

"We have no reason to lie," Coen went on. "We were being held against our will by Radicals. We're not working with them."

The officer sucked his bottom lip, thinking. He glanced between Nova and Coen and Amber.

It was true that they hadn't lied. They'd withheld details, certainly. For starters, they hadn't mentioned how Coen and Amber hosted *Psychrobacter achli* in their blood. There was no saying how Paradox might react to that knowledge. Chances were Coen and Amber were communicating right now, discussing the odds.

It stung in a way Nova hadn't been prepared for—to know they could talk and she was unable to hear a damn thing. That even if she wanted to join the conversation, she couldn't.

Then again, she could sit here having these thoughts and no one could hear them. To think that Coen and Thea had shared everything, that they had no private moments . . .

Nova had once longed to know what Dylan Lowe thought—about their friendship that never had a chance to become more, about *everything*. Now she wondered if it had been a blessing to not know. A person needed privacy or they'd suffocate.

"Let me get this straight," the officer said. "You were working a Hevetz job on Achlys, and on the way home, a Trios military ship manned completely by Radicals picked you up, brought you to a remote space station, and held you there against your will until you escaped. Everyone but this Althea Sadik you mentioned."

"That about sums it up."

"Do you realize how far-fetched that sounds? Why the hell would the Radicals do that? And why would Hevetz not fight to get their employees back?"

"They're working together," Nova said. "I've explained this already."

"It still doesn't make sense. What could three teens possibly know that would make the Radicals do such a thing? And why would a random medic"—he glanced at Amber—"risk helping you escape? You're not telling me something."

Nova looked to Coen. *Maybe we should just tell him*, Nova thought, praying he registered the idea in her expression, furious she couldn't send the thought to him so simply.

His brows dipped slightly. His eyes narrowed. "Who knows why the Radicals do anything," he said. "Rational goals have never really been their forte."

The officer scowled.

"Why are *you* so scared of them?" Nova asked. "I mean, you *must* be scared if the GSA shot down our shuttle, but you guys rushed to retrieve us. You're breaking laws just to secure this interrogation."

"I'm not the one being interrogated, Miss Singh," the officer snapped. "I'll ask the questions."

Nova slumped into her seat, spent. They'd been at this for nearly an hour. She was tired and grumpy and thirsty. Her throat scratched. She was thinking about how a warm shower would feel, how amazing it would be to kick off her clothes and wash the sand and grit from her body, when the door burst open.

A woman stood in the frame, face flushed as though she'd been running.

Coen shot to his feet.

He stood so quickly that the cuffs snapped. Blood pooled at his wrists. The officer trained the gun on him. A red radar dot appeared on Coen's chest.

But Coen wasn't looking to attack. He hadn't broken loose to make a move. He was standing there, shell-shocked, staring at the woman.

"What is it?" Nova asked.

The officer's gun twitched between them, uncertain where to aim.

Coen's lip quivered. "Oh my god," he muttered, and a single tear slid down his cheek.

Coen blinked several times, certain he was hallucinating. He'd hit his head too hard in the crash. The desert had been boiling and he'd gotten too much sun. Even now his throat ached with thirst. But he continued to blink, and the woman standing in the entrance of the interrogation room remained unchanged.

She was slightly shorter than Thea, with dark, straight hair cut to her chin and bangs that skimmed her lashes. But her eyes were Thea's. Her mouth, too. He'd never met this woman before and yet he didn't need to. He knew who she was.

This was Naree Sadik.

Coen's heart throbbed as though it were his own mother. He opened the moment up to Thea, letting her listen.

"Where's Althea?" the woman said, looking between the three chairs.

Thea recognized the voice immediately. She'd never forgotten it. It was a dormant memory, something she'd buried deep inside her only to be awoken now, as her mother said her name. Coen could feel the tears streaming down Thea's cheeks. It was her happiness, weighted with disbelief and exhaustion and joy, that brought him to tears as well. He couldn't stop crying.

"She's not here," he managed to say. "We didn't get her out."

"But she's alive?"

He nodded.

"I thought she was dead."

"Everyone told her you were dead, too, and sometimes she even wondered if they were right, but she never truly believed it."

Tears pooled in Naree's eyes. "You know me," she said, staring at Coen. "How?"

"Because I know your daughter, and she looks just like you." A pause. "She wants to talk to you."

"I would love that. Soon. When we get her back."

"She says right now."

"What?" Naree's brow wrinkled in confusion. Coen could feel the girls looking at him, too, their faces drawn with interest. There'd been the crash, then the convoy. He hadn't had time to mention that his connection with Thea had returned.

"We're connected, me and Thea," he explained to Naree. "She knows everything I'm thinking. I know everything she wants."

"Fifty-five light-years apart and you're *connected*?"

"Yes."

Naree shouldn't have believed it. There was no scientific explanation for the phenomenon, no logic that could make sense of something so impossible. But Thea's mother simply closed the space between them and cupped Coen's face in her hands. Her skin was warm. She looked Coen in the eye and said, "Tell her I'm right here."

Coen felt Thea crumple onto her cot. She bawled into her hands.

I'm here, too, she sobbed out, and he repeated the words to Naree.

Up close, the woman smelled of fresh-washed linen and dry summer air. Sharing this with Thea made memories resurface for her: images of the car they had called home in Hearth City; hotels she'd never before remembered; falling asleep on her mother's shoulder, barely four years old.

It should have been *her* having this moment. It should have been Thea standing where Coen stood. They were both sick with the unfairness of it, yet overwhelmed with gratitude that the moment existed at all.

"She can really hear me?" Naree asked.

It was a question, but her eyes were hopeful. There was no judgment, no scorn. Coen didn't know how the woman had such faith. Maybe she could see a piece of Thea in him.

Maybe she sensed the nearness of her daughter in a way only a mother could.

"Yes," he said. "She says she loves you and misses you and she wants answers."

"And I owe them," Naree said. "I do." She ushered the interrogator out and closed the door. But it took her a long time to begin speaking.

She could barely believe it. Her daughter was alive.

After returning from Bev, a security detail had been waiting for Sol in the hangar. He spoke of several teens who had mentioned Thea. Sol's men were always bringing in strangers who wandered too close to Paradox's facilities, most of whom turned out to be Radical spies who never set foot outside again. But teens . . . She'd rushed past the convoy of dust-covered rovers and down to interrogation.

Now looking at this golden-skinned, stern-eyed boy who somehow had a connection to her daughter, Naree didn't know if she could bear hurting Thea any further. There was no easy way to tell the tale. It was full of heartbreak. But that was where she ultimately decided to begin, on the night that her life started to unravel: the evening Solomon Weet had shown up at her apartment with version one of the tech in hand.

He'd slid it across her table and begged for her help, even though she'd left Paradox months earlier, committed to ending the affair and reconnecting with her husband.

The Radicals were aware of what Sol was building, he insisted.

They were trashing the office as he spoke, confiscating everything. Sol would have a cross on his back when they realized he slipped away with the drive. He needed to run.

She'd refused to go with him, so he asked her to deliver the briefcase to a drop point Paradox used to obtain not-quite-legal quantities of black market corrarium for their research. It wasn't safe for him to travel with the tech, not with Radicals looking to apprehend him. To this, Naree had agreed, if only to make him go away.

When she arrived at the drop point two days later, the pier was swarming with Radical agents. They kept fingers on their ears, listening to comms. They ignored the whales migrating offshore that drew tourists to the pier and instead searched the boardwalk for the briefcase—for her. She fled home only to find the apartment ransacked and her husband dead in the shower, a bullet in his temple.

She was lucky she got to Thea's daycare before the Radicals.

That evening was spent in a dingy motel, Thea watching cartoons on the vidscreen as Naree deleted all records of the woman known as Sumi Demir. She even altered Thea's last name to Sadik, then changed her birth records so the girl's father read as "unknown" and her mother pointed to Naree, a woman who would exist only in the fake IDs she planned to procure. A ghost.

They moved around after that, calling their car home and living off meager food credits while Naree worked odd jobs and hunted for Sol. He'd disappeared from the Trios, vanishing like smoke. But she found him eventually, hiding in the Fringe. She arranged a transit for the briefcase because as much as she hated the tech and what it had meant for her family, she couldn't bring herself to destroy it. It had been eight years of her life. Eight years of development and labor. She just wanted it gone.

She left Thea at the bus stop and went to meet the courier. It got blurry after that. A cloth rag over her mouth, strange voices. Then she was waking up from cryo, Solomon Weet towering over her as his ship landed in Casey's Inansi Desert.

He told her he needed her.

He claimed only she could finish the tech.

He insisted he thought Thea would have been with her, that he expected the courier to deliver them all. The briefcase, Naree, and Thea. As though this made the abduction somehow kinder.

She spent a solid month fuming in her quarters, cursing him, hating him, wishing him dead. She plotted and executed several failed escape attempts. And then, because she knew her only way back to Thea was through the completion of the tech, she swallowed her anger and willingly joined Solomon Weet in his labs.

VII

THE COMPOUND

Paradox Technologies

Casey, Fringe-2 System

COEN LET THEA HEAR EVERYTHING. Her reactions rattled in his mind, strong and unyielding. Relief that her mother hadn't abandoned her by choice. Anger that the woman's actions had torn their family apart. Disgust. Fury. But a bittersweet understanding, too. Naree had been the lead programmer on the tech. In the end, Sol would have sought her out regardless of whether they'd been romantically involved. The woman regretted many things, but she never chose to leave Thea. Sol took away that choice.

As Naree finished speaking, a well-dressed man entered the interrogation room. He was tall and bronze-skinned, and his suit was freshly pressed, his shoes gleaming. He touched his tie and moved his narrowed eyes to Coen. "You don't expect me to believe the story you told the interrogators, do you?"

"What I expect doesn't matter. It's obvious you've made up your mind."

The man barked out a laugh and moved to the table. Naree slid away from him like a repelled magnet, and Coen knew instantly who he was. Solomon Weet, dripping with confidence, regarding others as though they were things he could control. "I want the truth," the man said. "No detail left out."

Coen saw no point in withholding anymore. He told them everything—Black Quarry, *Psychrobacter achli*, Hevetz's role with the Radicals, and Burke's goals on Kanna7. Even what Thea had explained to him earlier about the cerebral implants for the newest batch of hosts. In the brief lulls of his confession, Coen mentally assured Amber that it was the right thing to do. She was a jumble of apprehension, and a single glance at Nova's scowl told Coen she wasn't too keen on sharing all this information, either. But Naree Sadik was safe to trust. This was Thea's mom, and even if Solomon Weet had incredibly questionable morals, his company was shaping up to be the very company Amber had heard Burke worrying about. An enemy of the Radicals.

"Great," Nova grumbled when he finished. "You just confessed everything to the asshole who abducted Thea's mom. You think he's gonna let us go after learning about the bacteria you guys are hosting?"

Weet didn't so much as flinch at the insult.

"I don't know," Coen said, gaze never leaving the man. "Paradox Technologies clearly has a complicated history with the Radicals. I think maybe we're on the same side."

"Isn't there an ancient saying about that?" Amber asked.

"The enemy of my enemy is my friend," Nova recited. "It dates back to Earth Era and was hammered into us at the Academy during lectures on war strategy."

"So do we?" Coen asked. He was still looking at Weet, and the man had not looked away, either. His eyes were almost feline, cool and cunning. "Have a common enemy, that is?"

"The tech," Naree said, wheeling on Weet before he could answer. "Sol, this is how I get Thea back."

"No. It's out of the question. Besides, you know how I feel about discussing it with strangers."

"We're several levels underground, with guards stationed at every level. There's nowhere they can go without you knowing."

"According to their story, they broke out of Kanna7."

"But not Thea!"

"This is bigger than your daughter, Naree!" the man spat, eyes flashing.

"Oh yes," the programmer said with a sigh. "This is bigger than Thea. It always has been, right? It's bigger than me and what I want, too. It's all about your noble goals, which mean more than anything, and now you're not even going to put the tech to use." Naree shook her head. "You spent years trying to keep this tech out of Radical hands, but now it sounds like they're creating their own edge—something more powerful than what they tried to steal from you thirteen years ago, and more dangerous, too. I wouldn't be surprised if there's a war on the horizon, and we have a chance to make sure it becomes the war that never was. That's what this has always been about, right?"

Coen watched carefully as Sol shifted, adjusted his tie.

"I know our trust in each other has shattered, but we need to trust *them*." Naree nodded toward Coen. "With this new breed of soldier, the Radicals will reshape the universe into one where power is everything, where the small suffer, where loyalty becomes synonymous with servitude. There's a better way, and that's what you told me this tech was all about. That it was about equality, accessibility. It was for *everyone*. That's how you recruited me for Paradox all those years ago. The droning on about a better world, a better universe—it's what made me fall for you. Please don't tell me that was all a lie. That's it really just about money. That you want to sell it to the highest bidder, so long as that bidder isn't a Radical. Because if that's your moral compass, Sol, it's shit."

Sadness touched Naree's eyes, and Coen got the feeling that the woman already expected it was about money. That Sol wasn't apathetic enough to hand his tech to the Radicals, but that he was greedy enough to sell it to basically anyone else once it was complete.

"You want to go down in history as this great creator?" Naree continued. "Someone who changed the world? Then you can't turn away from this. If you do, what is the point of everything you've built?"

Sol let his hand fall from his tie. He observed Naree for a long moment, then cleared his throat. "You always were my only weakness, Naree. Go on, tell them about the tech."

"It's a drive," Naree said plainly. "Capable of transmitting a ship from one location to another instantaneously. We're calling it the flux drive."

Nova gaped. She'd heard of such tech at the Academy, but it was tossed around with the same skepticism or eye rolls that all impossible tech garnered. The Union was no closer to developing instantaneous travel than it was to achieving immortality.

Amber muttered, "How is that even possible?"

"FTL works by warping time in front of and around a ship, right? The flux drive works with that concept on a larger scale. This is bending time and space completely, folding the universe like a piece of paper until the origin and destination points overlap, then punching a hole straight through so the ship can drop out at its destination like *that*." She snapped her fingers. "As long as the destination is known— a mapped point in our universe—you can travel any number of light-years in the blink of an eye."

"The concept has been around for ages," Sol added. "Even

Earth Era physicists and engineers toyed with it. But we had a breakthrough at Paradox about fifteen years ago, and that's when the Union started offering us money, asking us to sign contracts to create the drives specifically for their military. I took money from private donors, but refused to sign contracts because I couldn't vet every military employee and feared Radicals were likely already in their ranks. Unfortunately, the Radicals caught wind of what we were building anyway, and I could never shake them.

"They asked nicely at first, then resorted to threats, tried to break into our offices. I eventually discovered a few Radicals had infiltrated my staff in low-level positions. They didn't have the clearance to access anything of value, but it was only a matter of time before I lost control of the situation. So I took the tech, burned Paradox to the ground, and fled all in one night. Set up shop here on Casey. The Radicals have been chasing my shadow ever since."

"I'm sorry if I'm being dense," Amber said, "but why is that tech so dangerous?"

"Are you kidding me?" Nova breathed out a laugh. "Drives that can support instantaneous travel across the universe? Any military fleet with that tech would be indestructible. They could outrun enemies with the flip of a switch. They could appear out of thin air, surrounding entire fleets, surrounding *planets*. They could overthrow any military and take control of any system. The Radicals would be able to force *any* hand with that tech."

It wasn't all that different from how Burke planned to use *Psychrobacter achli* to his advantage, Nova reasoned. If his ships couldn't outmaneuver his enemies by using the flux drive, he'd find soldiers who could. Soldiers who were nearly impossible to beat. Soldiers who could think and act together, *and* be controlled.

"This drive is how we stop the Radicals," Coen said. "We figure out when Burke intends to make his move—Thea can help with that, even. She's our inside mol—" Coen stopped abruptly, brows drawn. "Never mind. She already knows." For a moment, he was elsewhere, listening to whatever Thea was relaying. "He'll make his move at the annual UPC trade summit. It's being held at Xenia Station this year."

"That's in roughly two weeks," Sol said.

"I don't know how he expects to bring a small army onto Xenia without anyone realizing it," Nova said. "It's the newest station in the Union. Security will be insane."

Just last year, while working a job with Dylan in the tropics of Eutheria, Nova had watched the news as the station was put into orbit. That evening, she'd even spent an hour at her window, hoping to catch a glimpse of the station in the night sky. It had been too cloudy, but she saw it several days later, a spot of light that streaked across the heavens.

A high-tech gift from the Cradle, Xenia Station was donated to the Trios amid trade disputes and growing Radical resentment. It was a way for the Cradle to say, "we value you, we appreciate you, we're not simply using you for your corrarium." The Radicals, however, saw the station as just that: an appeasement. A distraction from the true goal of independence. At Northwood Point, Nova had heard Toby discuss the political power plays enough times to induce a migraine.

"The *Paramount* is a Union battleship," Coen said. "A military ship would have automatic access to a station like Xenia, right?"

"He can just waltz right in." Nova nodded numbly. She should have put it together on her own.

"Waltz in and force the hand of the various Trios counselors. Cancel corrarium trade agreements and withdraw from the Union entirely. His new hosts will infect someone if they fail to cooperate, showing just how dangerous these new soldiers can be. And there will also be a bluff about how additional host soldiers have traveled to each counselor's home. If they fail to cooperate, their families will be infected."

"He's bluffing with biowarfare?" Nova scoffed.

"Who cares about the bluff?" Amber chimed in. "If he's willing to infect someone on Xenia to illustrate how dangerous *Psychrobacter achli* is, there's a good chance it'll get loose on the station."

"Which is why we need to be there," Coen said. "Use these flux drives to surround Burke and force his surrender. Even make sure an outbreak is contained, if it comes to that. And we break out Thea in the process."

"The drive is operational and we have it installed on nearly every ship here, but we're still having a problem with the recharging sequence," Naree said with a frown. "After one jump, it takes months to recharge."

"That wouldn't be a problem," Coen said. "Not if we only have to make one jump."

"But if something were to go wrong, if we needed to reposition or change our plan of attack, we'd be sitting ducks. Also, we can't jump to rescue Thea without the ability to immediately jump back out once we have her."

"But . . . ?" Nova asked, sensing that there was more the woman was withholding.

"But there's a drilling venture taking place on Bev. They've found something over there. Something corrarium-like. They're calling it AltCor, and we've just secured a small amount for testing. It might be the extra kick we need."

"How long would testing take?" Coen asked eagerly.

Naree smiled. "I was planning on starting tomorrow, small-scale. If we're successful, we'd move on to off-planet tests."

"And if *that* works," Sol said, "I guarantee I can secure us enough AltCor to power our entire fleet. We'd have to make some updates to the fuel intakes on all the drives, but we could be finished within two weeks."

They couldn't be serious. "Am I the only one who thinks this sounds ridiculous?" Nova folded her arms across her chest. "You've got some amazing tech, sure. But you can't take on the Radicals. We should alert Trios authorities, tell them what we know. Let them figure out how to deal with Burke."

Weet shook his head. "Radicals have been infiltrating the Trios government for decades. Many hold positions of power. Look at Burke! But if we act with the element of surprise, the Trios will see ships appearing around Xenia. Trios officials loyal to the Union will aid us, and any Radicals refusing to take part in such aid will immediately out themselves."

"It's still a suicide mission. You're a private company who's been in hiding for years, with only a few hundred staff on hand and, if I'm estimating correctly, about thirty ships in that hangar, only a dozen of which have any serious artillery. If the Radicals are prepared for resistance, we won't stand a chance."

"That's not quite true," Sol said.

"I know how war works," Nova continued. "We are *not* equipped to engage in one—with or without flux drives."

"I meant about being private," the man continued. "Do you think I'd have been able to keep this compound—my company—hidden for so long if I didn't have help on the outside? There are Radical spies in every damn corner of this galaxy. There are dozens in Paza alone, the city forty kilometers to the north, where all our shipments come from. But I have my connections, people invested in keeping Paradox safe, people who believe this tech is worth fighting for. Some of them are even at the GSA. How do you think I've maintained a tap on their communications for so long?" Sol glanced at Naree, like he couldn't quite believe what he was admitting to.

"You've already had a war here," Nova said. "One you were lucky to walk away from without terrible losses. I can't imagine you want another."

"Casey didn't win that war by sheer luck. The Union could have forced us to surrender, easily; could have dragged us into the UPC. But there were Radicals in high-ranking positions, Radicals who knew the flux drive was hiding somewhere on this rock and were afraid of destroying it. We survived because of this tech, and we will defeat them with it now." He straightened, throwing his shoulders back. "Naree, you get to work on that test first thing in the morning and keep me posted. If AltCor fixes the kinks with the recharging cycle, I'll make sure we're able to pick up a larger shipment of the fuel. Meanwhile, I'm going to put a call in to some friends at the GSA and Casey's Integrated Forces— see if I can't secure us an off-planet testing window *and* pull together an organized military fleet ready to take on the Radicals by the UPC trade summit."

"And the rest of us?" Amber asked.

"Sit tight." Solomon's eyes flicked between her and Coen. "Maybe in isolation. There'll be no saving the universe if you wipe us out before we can make our move."

After finally being released from interrogation, they were given a tour of the facilities, or at least the areas that Solomon Weet deemed appropriate for their eyes. Key cards were generated. Rules explained. Meals were at seven, noon, and seven again. Communication rooms were strictly off-limits. In addition to their rooms on SubLevel5, they'd have access to the gym and shower facilities, which were open twenty-four hours a day, and the mess hall for meals. Coen would have access to Naree's lab, providing an ability for her to communicate with Thea, but Nova and Amber would have no such special privileges.

As he followed Weet through the compound, listening to the seemingly endless list of rules, Thea lurked quietly in the corners of his mind.

It had been a lot to take in: the fact that her mother was alive, the possibility of a galaxy-changing technology, the potential showdown with Burke, and a rescue mission for her thanks to the flux drive. She'd been buzzing as it was all discussed, her pulse beating as quickly as Coen's. Now they were both trying to digest it.

When the tour was over, Coen found himself standing before the door to his bunk, Naree lingering. "Is she okay?" the woman asked.

"As okay as she can be." He waited for Thea to elaborate, but she remained quiet. There was a sharp edge to her silence, a heat he hadn't sensed before.

"You should come to the lab tomorrow," Naree said. "I could use some help with the small-scale AltCor test. I'd like to get to know you better. Thea, too."

If silence could grow louder, Thea's did in that moment. Coen merely nodded to Naree and slipped into his room.

It was bare-bones, not unlike the quarters he'd called home during Black Quarry. A bed. A small dresser. Dull overhead lighting.

What's the matter? he asked her.

It's just a lot.

Yeah. I get it.

No, you don't, Coen. You don't get this at all. The heat had returned, slicing, precise.

Are you mad at me?

What? No. I just— She sighed. *It was supposed to be me. I was supposed to find her. I was supposed to look her in the eye and say, "Mom, it's me. It's Thea."*

The heat lingered in his mind, but there was something else beneath it, too. A watery, lapping coolness. It was trying to beat back the . . . jealousy. That's what it was.

I'm not . . . But she didn't say the word. Because she was. She knew it, deep down, and he could feel it in his bones. There was nothing she could hide from him.

You'll still be able to tell her all that, he promised. *You'll see her again.*

He sensed her nodding.

It's late. I'm going to lie down, she said after a moment.

I'll lie with you.

It was dinnertime at Paradox, but food was the furthest thing from Coen's mind. He kicked off his boots and crawled into bed. Fifty-five light-years away, Thea did the same. They lay on their sides. He imagined his arm around her, the scent of her hair.

She fell asleep first, and when her pulse fell into a languid rhythm, an ebb and flow as soft as distant waves, Coen, too, closed his eyes.

Amber was feeling useless.

She'd been overlooked by her father and the rest of the staff on Kanna7, but at least watching Nova's vitals and caring for the pilot after she'd woken had kept her busy. It had given Amber purpose. Now at Paradox, she felt lost. She could stay in her room all day, and no one would miss her.

She forced herself to get up, ran her fingers through her hair. As she was making the bed, a knock sounded on the door behind her. She called for the person to enter and didn't turn until she heard it crack open.

"Morning." Nova was leaning a hip into the jamb, arms folded across a bomber jacket with the name *Lawson* stitched on the front. The sleeves were a bit too short, and the elastic hit so high on Nova's waist that the piece almost looked cropped. Somehow, the pilot still made it look good.

"Nice jacket."

Nova glanced down her front, grinning. "Won it during a game of cards last night. All these big, brawny guys and then this petite meter-and-a-half pilot ends up being the real contender. She'd still have this jacket if I hadn't cheated."

"You don't really strike me as the type that cheats." In fact, the mere idea of it infuriated Amber.

"I didn't have an ace up my sleeve or steal credits or anything. I just counted cards and flirted."

"With everyone or just Lawson?"

"Does it matter?"

Amber shrugged and went back to smoothing the bedsheets. The thought of Nova flirting with pilots up in the hangar bothered her even more than the thought of Nova cheating, though she couldn't say why. Nova could do what she wanted. Just because Amber was responsible for her on Kanna7 didn't mean she had any responsibility for her here.

"You're getting around okay, huh?" she asked.

"I'm mobile enough, but I tire pretty quick. That's why I came here, actually—was wondering if you wanted to train with me."

Amber looked over her shoulder. Nova wasn't leaning on the doorjamb anymore, but simply standing in the frame, picking at dirt beneath her nails. She glanced up to meet Amber's gaze, and while everything in her expression was cool and confident, Amber swore she could hear the pilot's pulse tick up.

"Train?"

"In the gym. They have a boxing ring. We can test out those new abilities of yours and get some PT in for me in the process."

"I'm not really the gym-going type."

"And I'm not really the card-cheating type. Yet here we are."

That made Amber smile.

"Coen's helping Naree with something in the labs," Nova went on, "and Sol told us to lie low. It's not like we've got anything better to do."

For a moment, Amber considered it, pretending it was a possibility. She'd taken basic self-defense classes a few years ago, and with her increased capabilities as a host, a match in the ring wouldn't be fair, especially not when Nova was still healing. It would also be dangerous. If Amber got even a scratch and her blood passed back to the pilot . . .

"I don't think it's a good idea," she said.

Hurt glanced over Nova's features, than vanished behind a forced smile. "Right. Of course. You should train with Coen. It's safer that way." She turned and strode briskly down the hall.

Amber watched her go, wondering why she felt disappointment at something she herself had suggested.

Staring through the double-paned glass, Coen took in the testing room. It was completely white and empty, save for two tables that stood at opposite ends of the space. One table held a cube about a half meter tall.

Naree had met him at his bunk earlier in the morning and led the way to the lab level, then through a heavily guarded set of doors that opened to a hallway so long Coen hadn't been able to see the end of it. Lights were spaced meagerly on the walls and flickered sporadically. By the time Coen and Naree reached the end—another set of doors, these unguarded—he guessed the hall had been nearly a half kilometer long.

"We did all our initial testing here," Naree had explained

as they walked into the secure lab. "A massive amount of radiation is discharged when jumping from one space to another, and . . . well, isolation is important."

Now, on Coen's side of the glass, Naree Sadik was fiddling with a computer.

"Does that remotely control the drive?" he asked.

She nodded. "I'm passing it destination coordinates right now." She glanced up. "Ready?"

Coen glanced past his own reflection, through the glass and to the compact box resting on the table. It wasn't possible—moving a physical object like this, having it disappear from one space only to reappear in another.

Just let her show you, Thea urged. *I want to see it, too.*

She couldn't really see it, not truly. She'd only feel whatever Coen felt. Awe, perhaps. Shock.

Sure, but that will still let me know that it worked, she added. *Tell her to do it.*

You being back is a blessing and a curse. You know that?

She chuckled in his mind, and Coen gave Naree a nod. He heard the programmer tap a key and kept his gaze on the box on the other side of the glass. The rooms were soundproofed and there was nothing to hear, but as the box began to vibrate slightly, its edges blurring, Coen imagined a low humming noise. Then, in the blink of an eye, the box vanished from the first table and appeared a few millimeters above the second, dropping to the table and rattling the legs.

"It's almost impossible to place it directly on the surface," Naree explained. "Better to aim above the table and have it fall to a resting position, than to jump it into another mass. Of course, the falling won't be an issue in space."

Coen stared, trying to make sense of what he'd just witnessed. It was impossible. A magic trick. An illusion. But the box had been on one table a moment earlier and had teleported to the second.

Thea's excitement was apparent, rattling through his mind. Questions for him. Questions for her mother. Questions about the tech.

Hang on, he told her. *I'm still trying to process this.*

"Pretty impressive, no?"

"It's incredible," Coen told Naree.

"Halfway incredible, at least. Until recently, if I wanted to jump that box back, I'd have to wait nearly four weeks for the drive to recharge. The radiation dispelled in the jump practically drains the reactor, and while corrarium has been sustainable for the Union's current needs, it hasn't been cut out for this technology."

"But the AltCor?"

Naree's eyes flashed with excitement. "That's what we're here to test. I had a tech switch out the fuel sources this morning. Do you want to do the honors?" She nodded to the keypad before her. "Coordinates are already programmed, all you have to do is hit *return*."

Go on, Thea urged. *What are you waiting for?*

Staring down at the key, he was reminded of a moment back on Achlys, when he and Thea had stared at the lever that would activate *Celestial Envoy*'s self-destruct sequence. It had been their final prayer, a shot in the dark, a way to bury the evidence of *Psychrobacter achli* and escape that dark planet to a better future.

This felt similar. If the AltCor worked, it meant a chance to secure that better future again. It meant the very real possibility of getting Thea off Kanna7 and stopping Burke in the same breath. But if it didn't work, the contagion could get out. Thea might never be free. It was too much for one person to initiate. He didn't want to be the one to bring the bad news.

You're not alone, Thea whispered. *I'm right here. I'll be doing it with you.*

Coen reached out, finger hovering above the key. Thea counted to three in his mind. He pressed the button.

Behind the glass, the box shook. Its edges blurred. Then it was suddenly gone, reappearing above the first table and falling to its surface.

"Ha!" Naree hit the return button again. At first nothing

happened, but after a few seconds, she tapped the key again. This time, the box returned to the second table. Again she waited, then pressed the button. A third jump. Naree squealed. "It works! I can't . . . It's better than I could have . . . Do you know what this means?"

She tackled Coen in a hug before he could form a response, practically crushing the air from his lungs. Thea's elation buzzed in his mind, an undercurrent of jealousy battling her excitement. She was overjoyed, truly. And yet she still resented that she wasn't there with them, that this was another moment she would never have with her mother.

"What now?" Coen asked.

"I'll need to run some more tests, see exactly how long the recharge cycle takes, but it's looking like a matter of seconds. From there, we'd just have to do an off-planet test. The drives are already installed on most of Sol's ships, so after that, it's just swapping out the fuel source."

"And how long until you can do that off-site test?"

Naree's brows dipped. "Depends on how quickly engineering can get the corrarium reactor switched out for an AltCor one, but I'm hoping by the end of the week."

Three days.

Three days until you know if you'll be coming for me, Thea said.

I'm coming for you regardless. This will just make things a heck of a lot easier.

They were fifty-five light-years apart, but he could feel her smile, and when he closed his eyes, it was almost as if she was standing there before him. He wouldn't waste a single moment the next time they were together. He'd kiss her immediately.

"Was there something else?" Naree said, slamming Coen back to reality. He opened his eyes to find the programmer standing before him, gaze pointed.

"Um, no, ma'am," he managed. "Thea's just really impressed by all this. I was explaining everything."

Liar, she teased.

"I'm not surprised she is." Naree smiled, and Coen felt exactly as he did so often with his own mother: as though secrets were impossible, his feelings written on his skin like a tattoo. It was frightening and wonderful to be understood like this. And yet it stung at the same time. He was so far from his own family.

You're almost back to them, Thea said. *You'll see them soon. I'm sure of it.*

And the thing was, Coen was finally, truly, starting to believe it. The end was in sight now. He dared to hope.

After a morning loitering at the infirmary, Amber made her way to the gym, triumphant. She'd convinced the head physician to let her work as a volunteer. He had an annual inventory cleanout to tackle, and Amber would be in charge of sifting through medications and synthetic blood and discarding anything expired. She wasn't sure if the physician had believed her when she said she was excited to start. But she was. Anything to keep her busy. To feel *useful*.

"Whatever," the man had grumbled. "Just be back for second shift. That's in three hours."

Now lunch hour, Amber was surprised at the syncopated *thump-thwack* she heard as she approached the gym, followed by a heartbeat that became audible as she pushed inside. It was steady and calm, barely elevated. Coen was in the far corner of the gym, throwing his fists into a punching bag.

He paused at the sound of the doors clicking shut behind Amber, arms hanging at his sides. He'd ditched his shirt—it lay draped over a nearby bench—and the tattoo of an octopus on his torso glistened as though it were truly submerged in water.

"You want company?" she called. Her voice echoed in the cold space. Interlocking rubber tiles covered what she assumed was a concrete floor, and racks of dumbbells, scuffed-up benches, and weight equipment lined the walls where mirrors reflected the room back to her like an endless kaleidoscope.

Coen shrugged. "An opponent with more brains than a punching bag wouldn't be bad."

Amber jerked her head at the boxing ring and they both ducked beneath the ropes. She got into a ready stance, and lost spectacularly. Even with her enhanced hearing and eyesight, she couldn't manage to block Coen's blows fast enough. He was stronger, faster, more at ease in his host body, and each time she hunched over, gasping for air, he'd fall back, kindly letting her catch her breath.

Again? he'd ask when she straightened.

Again, she'd respond, because for some delirious reason, Amber believed *this* might be the time she'd beat him.

They spoke mentally as they went. He told her about the flux drive and the test jump Naree had let him witness. She told him about her gig at the infirmary, which seemed inconsequential given what he'd just shared. By the end of the sparring session, Amber had broken her nose (Coen helped her reset it) and she was sporting multiple bruises. Within the next few hours, she imagined they'd disappear entirely. She was never going to get used to this advanced healing stuff.

"Well, that was embarrassing," she said, wiping sweat from her eyes with the crook of her elbow.

"You clocked me that one time." Coen touched his jaw gingerly.

"One time. Pretty pathetic."

"No, you did good. Way better than Thea when she started training."

"Can't she hear that?"

"Sure, but she won't argue with me. It's the truth."

"I've got a few years of defense classes in me," Amber admitted. "It's like all those skills got amplified after I was infected."

"Same, so I completely understand." Coen ducked from beneath the ropes and pulled on his shirt. It clung to him like a wet rag.

"Will Thea care that we were training?"

"Why would she care?"

Amber shrugged. "I don't know. You're not exactly horrible to look at, and you just danced around a ring with me for an hour, half naked."

"I'm not interested, Amber. Sorry if that's blunt, but it's the truth."

"I'm not interested in you, either," she said quickly. "Not like that." God, she was blushing. Why was she blushing if she didn't care?

"So why would Thea mind if we sparred?"

"She wouldn't."

"Exactly. And for what it's worth, she's telling me right now she doesn't. She says the only thing we've made her feel envious about is that she doesn't have access to a gym of her own."

Amber forced a smile and followed Coen out of the ring. The gym was crowded now, lunch hour well behind them.

Paradox employees were scattered throughout, running on treadmills or lifting weights. Nova was at a pull-up bar, floating up and down as though there was no gravity working against her.

"Isn't it awful, knowing everything about each other?" Amber asked Coen.

"It isn't easy," he admitted. "But it's not awful. I know when she's upset. I know what she wants. I can feel what she needs before she has to say a single word."

Nova dropped from the pull-up bar, panting. Amber wondered briefly what it would be like to know exactly what the pilot was thinking.

"I could argue that knowing everything Thea wants takes the work out of the relationship," she said to Coen. "Relationship experts say the strongest couples are the people who listen, who support each other, who really work at it every day."

"Oh, it's still work. Having someone in your head constantly doesn't mean you don't argue. If anything, you do it more, because you can't hide anything." Coen's gaze flicked across the gym, finding Nova, who Amber was still watching. He smiled like he'd just read Amber's mind, which he couldn't have. Amber wasn't Thea. "Look, it's a blessing to not know everything. I love what I have with Thea. Truly. But I wonder sometimes what it would have been like to fall in love with her naturally—with all the awkwardness and jitters and second-guessing."

"You're in love with her?"

"Yeah. I guess I am." He smiled crookedly and for a moment he was elsewhere, Thea surely whispering something into his mind. Then his eyes slid back to Amber. "What I'm saying is falling the old-fashioned way is its own kind of special. So if there's something you're after, Amber, you should just be honest."

She tore her sights from the pull-up bar. "Honest?"

"With yourself. With *her*." Coen jerked his head toward Nova.

"I don't know what you're talking about." But Amber did. Her heart was thrumming like a jackhammer between her ribs.

"Right. Sure." Coen laughed loudly. He had a beautiful laugh. Then he punched Amber playfully in the arm and said, "You're going to be late for work, you know."

Amber glanced at the clock. If she wanted a shower, it was going to be the speediest one she'd ever taken. She bolted from the gym.

The days bled into each other.

Nova stayed busy by working out twice a day and following Lawson around the hangar between meals, helping her switch out corrarium reactors for AltCor ones. An off-planet test was scheduled for tomorrow with one of the already updated ships, but Sol and Naree were so confident it would work that they already had Lawson's crew working on the rest of the fleet. This morning, Nova was assisting with the updates.

And Amber . . . Well, Nova couldn't quite say what Amber was up to. She didn't speak to the medic anymore, and the only time Nova saw her was from afar in the gym, sparring with Coen. The two hosts barely spoke a word to each other, she'd realized, and yet she'd catch them smiling, laughing.

Nova recognized the ugly feeling in her stomach as jealousy. She wanted that sort of connection with someone—was tired of being left out, of not being enough.

At the Academy, it was her eyesight.

With this contagion, it was her age.

Crouched inside an AeroCo Python, Nova gripped the metal casing that held the corrarium reactor in place and yanked. She'd loosened the bolts, but the casing refused to lift free.

When she first began helping Lawson, she'd wondered if it was even worth installing the drives on such small fighters. Paradox didn't need all their ships to jump individually. Ideally, they only needed one battleship to make a jump—the same battleship that would carry all the smaller fighters. But Sol had insisted they get the drives installed wherever possible. They'd be testing things before the summit, but not extensively. If anything went wrong—and it certainly could, given the amount of energy needed to jump an entire battleship—Sol wanted every fighter to have flux drive capabilities as a backup.

"Come on, you piece of . . ." Nova tugged at the casing, and the metal finally lurched free, the sharp edge slicing across her bicep. Pain blossomed. "Son of a . . . !" She clapped a hand over her arm and jumped from the Python.

"You all right?" Lawson called.

"Just a cut. Where are the medkits?"

Lawson's face paled. "Someone from the infirmary came to collect them this morning. Something about updating all the contents, making sure nothing's expired."

"Guess I'm headed to the infirmary, then."

"You need a hand? You're not light-headed or anything, are you?"

Nova lifted her palm. Blood pooled up quickly. "Nah, I feel okay, but this definitely needs a Seckin. I'll be back in a bit."

Lawson nodded and Nova ducked beneath the Python's wing, making quickly for the exit. Back inside Paradox, she took the elevator down to SubLevel1, and by the time she reached the infirmary, she *was* feeling a little light-headed.

"Hello?" she said, staggering inside. Medkits were strewn out across the beds, contents emptied out and organized into various piles. She moved to the nearest bed, eyeing the organized contents. There were no Seckin bandages, only standard gauze dressing. That would have to do. Nova grabbed one only to fumble it, dropping it on the floor. She stared at the item now between her feet, fearing that if she bent over to retrieve it, she might actually pass out.

"Can I help you?" Drawn by the commotion, a medic had appeared from a storage closet. And not just any medic. Amber. So this was where she'd been spending her time.

"Hey, Doc. Long time no see." Nova tried to keep her voice light. The last thing she wanted was to seem desperate.

"I see you every day in the gym."

"Yeah, but you never say hi."

"You told me to train with Coen, Nova. You agreed it was safest if I stayed away, so I've been doing that. Besides, saying hi works both ways. You could have said hi to me." The medic gave Nova a once-over, her gaze skimming from boots to brow. "Did you need something?"

Nova pulled her hand away from the wound, showing the ragged cut that ran across her bicep. Without pressure, it started to well with fresh blood. "I was installing new reactors on the Pythons and got cut on some scrap metal. Was told all the medkits are up here for some reason and not all of us can heal in the blink of an eye, unfortunately."

"Sit," Amber said dryly, pointing to the one empty bed.

Nova sat—she felt phenomenally better sitting—and watched the other girl rummage around in the cabinets. When she returned, it was with a Seckin.

As Amber bent to apply it to Nova's arm, her hair slid from behind her ear, falling like a curtain around her face. Her lips pinched into a pout with focus. Nova wondered what it would be like to kiss her. As soon as the thought entered her mind, she couldn't think about anything else. Amber smoothed the bandage in place with the palm of her hand, and Nova's whole body clenched as she blew out a breath.

"That hurt?"

"No. It's fine. I'm fine."

Amber inspected the rest of Nova's arm, looking for any cuts the bandage might not have covered. Even wearing medical gloves, her touch was personal, soft and delicate. When she'd helped Nova around on Kanna7, guiding her from the bed or assisting her in PT, her grip had always been firm, a necessity. This was different. This made Nova consider how Amber had never really touched her before, not truly.

"All set," Amber, stepping back. The personal moment was gone. The air between them formal. "Guess I'll see you across the gym tomorrow and talk to you again next time you're injured." Her fair skin was ashen beneath the infirmary lights, her expression bitter.

"You look like hell, Amber," Nova said. "Maybe you shouldn't train so hard with Coen. He's too rough with you."

"I think it's been going just fine, so your opinion doesn't really matter."

"He's with Thea. You know that, right?"

"Of course I know that. What the hell is your problem? Ever since I said that us sparring might be dangerous, you've been avoiding me, and then when we do talk, you're a jerk. I took that injection for you on Kanna7. I saved your ass and this is how you thank me?"

"You did that because it was the only way out, not because you actually cared about me."

"Of course I cared! I watched over you when you were in that coma, and then after, and . . . I felt personally responsible for you, Nova."

"Yeah, well, I didn't ask for that. I never wanted your pity. I can take care of myself fine."

Nova shouldn't have come here. She should have bandaged her arm with a rag. Anything but appearing weak and needy in front of this girl.

She swung her legs off the bed and stood.

Amber didn't back away. Instead, she looked Nova square in the eye and said, "I *still* care about you. That's why I've been training with Coen; because *you* asked me to. I'm trying to respect that request."

Nova was breathing hard. Centimeters separated her nose from Amber's. The medic's lips were back in that pinched pout. Again, Nova wanted to kiss her.

"Every time I watch you guys, I want it to be me," she said. "Every time he makes you laugh or smile, or pins you to the mat, I wish I were the one doing it."

"Nova," Amber said softly.

"That's all." Nova took a step back. "Now you know."

She left before she could say anything else foolish.

The morning of the off-planet AltCor-powered flux drive test, Coen was restless. He'd slept poorly and woken well before dawn, the digital window on his wall still displaying an indigo sky.

What if it doesn't work?

We can't think like that, Thea said.

We can't be realistic?

He could sense her sighing. She was in her cell—like always—only this was supposed to be one of the few hours she had to herself. Fifty-five light-years between them, and their days and nights still managed to mostly line up. She went to bed before him, giving him a few hours of privacy each night, and she spent her mornings alone. Except for today. Because he was awake early, fretting.

It worked in the small-scale test underground, she said. *It will likely work off-planet, too.*

But if it doesn't—

If it doesn't, you can still jump once, and the element of surprise might be all you need. Surround Xenia. Hold Burke and the Radicals in place until Union backup forces can arrive.

And what about you, Thea? What good is jumping to you if I can't jump back out once I have you again?

It was quiet a moment. Coen pressed a hand on his chest, wishing the pressure on his heart would stop. All the healing abilities in the world and he still couldn't will away his anxieties.

Getting me doesn't matter, Thea said.

What the hell are you talking about? You matter more than anything.

That's just the bond talking. What about your family?

They matter, too, of course. But I meant it the other day—when I was talking to Amber. I meant it when I said I love you. I don't know if it's this connection between us that makes me feel that way, but I know that this bonded version of me is just as real as the version that was merely a host, just as real as the me that wasn't a host. This version of me knows what I feel.

But if the bond was gone?

It was, Coen said, recalling the cold sense of dread and helplessness that had descended over him on *Halo. It was gone for six fucking weeks, and I never felt differently about you. All I wanted was you back. Us. This shared . . . whatever it is.*

She was quiet, but she understood. She didn't have to say it for him to know. They sat in silence for the next hour, their hearts beating in unison until it was time.

As promised, Sol had arranged a window for an off-planet test. Coen would watch a feed remotely from Paradox, along with Nova, Amber, Naree, and half her workers. The visuals were projected onto a wall of the crowded lab, currently showing a split-screen picture. In one, Sol was displayed aboard a mid-sized battleship that was large enough to jump Paradox's fleet of four dozen fighters directly to Xenia. The second screen depicted a view through the ship's windshield, a star field outside Casey's atmosphere.

"Nervous?" Naree asked.

"Incredibly."

"Don't be. It worked during our small-scale test. There's no reason it shouldn't work again now."

"Your daughter said the same exact thing."

Naree smiled, but her nervousness still showed in the corners of her eyes.

"Destination is plotted, along with subsequent jumps," Sol said via the feed. "Reactor powered and ready. Naree, do you read me?"

"Loud and clear."

"All right. Here goes nothing." He reached for something

313

on the dashboard. There was a muted click followed by a hum that shook the visuals. Then the feed hung, like a lag in playback before returning to normal.

Sol's smile was so large it made his narrow eyes feel less threatening. "Confirming we are currently outside Casey's southern hemisphere." The side of the screen that had previously shown stars was now filled with ice caps and oceans. "Here comes the real test. Drive will be ready in . . . thirty seconds."

"It was only a few seconds in the lab," Coen whispered to Naree.

"Bigger object to transfer, longer recharging time. But thirty seconds is still incredible."

Coen's knees bounced. The lab had fallen silent, the tension palpable. Something touched Coen's shoulder and he flinched. Naree. He reached across his body and squeezed her hand back. He sat there, eyes glued on the screen, knowing Naree was holding his hand as much as she was holding Thea's, that this was their greatest hope. Not just to stop the Radicals or keep *Psychrobacter achli* contained, but to reach Thea as well.

Deep breath, Thea told him.

Sol said, "AltCor reactor charged. Jumping home in three, two, one."

Another flicker of the feed, then updated visuals. Sol

jumping from his seat, his hands in his hair. A view of the Inansi Desert below the ship. The lab erupted in cheers. Someone was hugging Coen. But he simply sat there, staring in awe, watching as Sol made three more jumps in three minutes.

It works, Thea. It works.

Everyone was in the mess hall, celebrating. Sol had a rule about drinks only being served after dinner, but he'd gone to Bev with Naree to pick up a massive shipment of AltCor so the fleet could be fueled for the trade summit, and Paradox's crew had taken matters into their own hands. By the time Amber entered the mess in the late afternoon, half the crowd was already drunk.

Amber skirted around a dancing couple and shoved through a tight-packed group of pilots. Watching the test had been thrilling, but it had also gotten her thinking. She didn't know why she hadn't thought of it sooner—why none of them had. She spotted Nova across the way and picked up her pace. To be honest, she spotted the pilot everywhere now. Even when Amber wasn't looking for her, her eyes managed to find the other girl, latching on to her confident posture, obsessing about the way her tank top tucked into her cargo pants, lingering on her smile.

"Come to join the celebration?" Lawson said, handing

Amber a glass. The petite pilot was drinking alongside Coen and Nova, though she was the only one who looked old enough to legally be doing so.

Amber shook her head.

"Oh, come on, Amber," Nova said. "We're jumping into potential battle in barely a week. Maybe it will be the War That Never Was, like Naree and Sol are hoping for, or maybe it will be a goddamn mess. Either way, we deserve drinks."

"Sure, but I think there's an even easier way to stop Burke."

Coen set his glass on the table. "What?"

"Can I talk to you two . . . privately?"

Lawson shrugged and turned away, joining a boisterous group of Paradox pilots in a song Amber didn't recognize. Amber led the way toward a quiet corner of the mess hall, Coen and Nova following.

"Watching that feed got me thinking," she said once they were alone. "We needed the AltCor to successfully power the flux drive to its fullest capacities. That's our power source. So what powers the implants Burke's got in his hosts?"

"I assumed they were self-sufficient," Nova said.

"Have we asked Thea?"

Coen's eyes went blank for a moment. "Thea says they're not self-sufficient. Burke wanted them to be, but the Radicals are running things out of a derelict space station, and they couldn't get the tech to work perfectly in time for the summit. It's the end goal, but right now there's a computer—a logic unit, basically—that the implants transmit through."

"So they're powered by the host itself, but the logic unit establishes how they should react to any given situation? It gives them *orders*, for lack of a better term?"

Coen nodded. "Yeah. And determines if the implant should deliver a shock."

"Where's the unit stored?"

"Somewhere on Kanna7."

Amber looked at Nova and Coen pointedly. "You see where I'm going with this?"

"Turn off the logic unit and his hosts are useless," Nova muttered. "His entire plan will fall apart."

Amber winked. "And Thea can probably access it during the summit, when the Radicals are distracted. She can turn it off."

"Before you get too excited, Thea says she doesn't even know where the unit is stored, just that it exists."

"So ask Farraday," Nova said.

Coen shook his head. "He's passing Thea info, but he's not straight-up defying superior orders."

"What might make him?" Nova asked.

And just like that, Amber saw the answer. "Me. Have Thea tell my dad I'll come back if he helps her turn off the logic unit."

"Go back to him? After what he forced you to do?" Nova's brown eyes bored into Amber. It was the first time the pilot had held her gaze since that day in the infirmary.

"I'm promising to come back. I'm not promising to stay."

Coen cleared his throat. "It wouldn't change the overall plan. We'd still have to jump to Xenia to contain the Radicals."

"And containing that threat will be a lot easier if we know the hosts are free-thinking. If they can *help* us instead of answering to Burke." Amber let out an exhale. "Will you at least have Thea talk to my dad about this?"

"It means she has to admit that she can still talk to me. She's kept that hidden so far. They're confusing spikes in her brain activity with her talking to the other hosts already on Kanna7, not me."

"If this works, it will be worth it," Amber said firmly.

Coen thumbed his lip. "I know it will be. Thea's yelling the same thing at me right now. She says she'll talk to Farraday next time he draws blood. I'll keep you guys posted."

"Are you sure?" the man in shipping said to the programmer. She was back on Bev, retrieving a massive cargo container of AltCor while Sol visited Dax to handle the payment. Dax didn't want anything on the books, so a digital transfer of unnes was out of the question. The funds needed to be exchanged in person.

Naree looked up from Sol's Tab. He'd loaned it to her, the screen filled with shipping details so that she could confirm they were getting the exact number of crates they'd paid for. "Of course I'm sure," Naree said to the man. "Our men are paying yours right now."

The man grimaced behind his suit. "It's just . . . Look, I'm not supposed to show this to you, but I think you have a right to know. Especially with this shipment headed off-planet."

"What's this?" she asked, tucking Sol's Tab beneath her arm so she could accept the man's tablet. Surveillance footage from inside the base filled the screen.

"Watch."

She did, and wished she hadn't. "Has Sol seen this?"

"No, and he's not supposed to. You, either. Dax needs more

funding, so the sale is important. But you have to know. I couldn't not tell you."

A savage wind whipped through the open warehouse, nudging the programmer's back. Despite being suited, she swore she could feel its icy sting.

She watched the footage again, then motioned to the workers standing near the crate and called, "Load it up!"

"You can't," the man snapped, clapping a hand over her wrist. "Not after what I just showed you." Genuine fear flitted in his eyes. "Dax is power-hungry. All he sees is the unnes, not the risk."

"I know someone else like that, and I've survived under his roof for over a decade. We'll survive this, too." The programmer wrenched her arm free. As the man blubbered and pleaded, she bumped his Tab to Sol's, transferring the footage. She'd encrypt it on the flight home, bury it among Sol's personal files. He'd never find it, but it would be there, waiting.

Naree returned the other man's Tab and strode for her shuttle. He let her go without an argument; maybe because he knew he could lose his job for showing her the footage. His reasoning didn't matter to Naree. This changed nothing. There was only one way forward.

When Sol returned from handling payments, he found her aboard their shuttle, the cargo loaded and the crew ready to take off. "Any issues?"

"No," she said, and she meant it. For once, everything was unfolding perfectly. Perhaps even better than she'd planned.

VIII

THE ALLY

Kanna7 Station
Orbiting Sol 2 from beyond the Lethe Asteroid
Belt, Trios System

/

UBS Paramount
Trios Airspace

THEA WORKED OUT FIRST THING in the morning. It was the only time of day that Coen wasn't also awake, and the only few hours of quiet she had to herself. She could still sense him at the edges of her consciousness, but it was like a cloud divided them, a veil of fog too thick to push through. As soon as he woke it would vanish, dissipating as the connection came roaring back, all his thoughts and fears and concerns loud in her head.

She wished she could ease his nerves. The AltCor had powered the flux drive perfectly. Paradox's ships could now make numerous jumps in a short period of time. But he still longed to turn the logic unit off, because maybe, just maybe, it would make Burke fold sooner. Surrender his cause. Yield to the Union.

And because Coen wanted it, Thea did, too. It was a good plan. *If* it worked. But the next time she was brought to the lab for a blood draw, she hesitated to broach the subject with Farraday.

The doctor had passed her plenty of information over their

weekly visits, but he'd always stopped short of truly helping her. There was a freighter that came to Kanna7 every month, delivering supplies, and she'd subtly hinted that she was interested in the docking schedule. She'd mused aloud about escaping, about finding her way aboard the ship. Dr. Farraday only listened, sometimes offering an uninterested *hmm*. If he truly wanted to help her, he'd have given her the schedule, the loading bay, the window she'd have for potential escape. But his loyalties still lay with Burke.

So as Dr. Farraday inserted the needle into her arm and her blood began zipping through the tubing and into the bag, Thea wondered if she could get what she needed without mentioning Amber. She didn't want to give Farraday any ammunition to use against her, and mentioning Amber meant admitting that she was in touch with Coen. It would put him and all of Paradox at risk. She could end up back in interrogation if Farraday slipped the info to Burke.

"The logic unit you mentioned last week," she started carefully. "Where is that held?"

"In a centralized lab on the research levels. Why?"

"Just wondering. Is it guarded?"

"No. But the room is locked. You can only get to it with a key card, not that anyone would need to access it. The program has been running smoothly. Burke doesn't want anyone touching the thing."

"I need to access it," Thea said.

Dr. Farraday's gaze snapped up to meet hers.

"I need to shut it off. If the logic unit powers down, all those hosts will be able to think freely again. I don't think you truly want them—or anyone at the summit—to get hurt. And I'm positive you don't want the contagion to get out, but it can, Dr. Farraday. Burke's planning to use those hosts— to use a biological weapon—to force the Union's hand. One injury to a host, one scratch to an adult . . . It would spread like wildfire."

The doctor rubbed his chin. "Even if you somehow managed to access the unit without a key card, you wouldn't be able to power it down. It requires two sets of hands—two people to simultaneously turn a series of knobs. You should forget the whole thing."

"I know you think you want independence, but this can't be the only way."

"What I want is my daughter back."

The blood bag was nearly full. This was Thea's only chance.

"If I told you she agrees to come back if you help me, would that make a difference?"

The doctor froze. His gaze stayed on the needle for the cameras, but a vein throbbed in his forehead.

"She's with Coen," Thea continued. "I can talk to him still. The connection came back after he awoke from cryo. You've been mistaking the jump in brain activity for me communicating with the other hosts."

"Where is she?" Dr. Farraday gasped out.

"That's not part of the deal."

"Is she safe?"

"Yes."

He swallowed. Pulled the needle from Thea's arm.

"When the others leave for Xenia Station, you can get me from my cell for more blood work. We can head to the logic unit, power it down together."

"And Amber will come home if I do this?"

"Yes. But if you tell Burke, if you speak to *anyone* about our plans or the connection, the deal's off."

He nodded. Perhaps he knew Thea would be tortured if he spoke up, meaning Coen, and therefore Amber, would be at risk. Or maybe he simply feared the consequences of even considering aiding Thea. She doubted Burke would take the news well. Whatever was going in Dr. Farraday's mind, his pulse was steady, his shoulders held confidently.

"I'll come for you when it's safe," he said, standing. "We'll only have minutes before security realizes where I'm taking you. We'll have to act quickly."

"That won't be a problem."

"Then we have a deal."

❋ ❋ ❋

The week leading up to the summit was frantic. Thea kept as busy as she could, working out in her room while Coen updated her from Casey.

Sol and her mother had returned from Bev with enough AltCor to blow up a planet. The fleet was fueled with the new source of corrarium, each reactor tuned and inspected. Along with Paradox Technologies' four dozen pilots, Nova had received a crash course in charging the flux drive, inputting destinations, and initiating jumps. Outside of underground sims in the Paradox bunker, there'd be no chance for her—or any of Sol's pilots—to test if they'd truly mastered the drive. The Paradox crew would fly alongside the roughly six thousand Casey aeropilots that Sol had managed to recruit for their cause.

At least "recruiting" was the story Sol was trying to spin. If you asked General Northrop, who'd been barking orders at Sol via secured video feeds, Casey's military had recruited Paradox. Even that was a stretch. It was more like they'd allowed several Paradox workers to join their mission because they felt obligated to extend some level of gratitude for the technology their battleship was now equipped with.

According to what Coen had relayed to Thea, Northrop's crew would jump to Xenia from their own base, using their own battlecarrier. Paradox's small crew would jump via the mid-sized battlecarrier Sol had used in their initial off-planet test. There was no point traveling to Northrop's base for a singular job and risking a Radical spy picking up on the activity and reporting back to Burke.

The morning of the summit, Thea woke feeling sluggish. It wasn't a blood draw day, but she recognized the fading fog of sedation. She'd been drugged.

She lurched upright. The glass wall that had divided her cell from Coen's was gone, replaced with dark walls made of smooth, unadorned metal. There was no wash area or toilet. The cot was pushed against one wall. The lone door had a small window at its base, a water bowl resting before it.

Static filled her brain, endless, unyielding. It was like an ocean wave, but with little ebb or flow, just a steady roar of chaos.

Coen, something's wrong.

No response.

Coen!

Thea felt him jostle awake—it had to be early on Casey still—and his focus sharpened instantly, homing in on her panic.

What's wrong?

They moved me. I'm back on the Paramount.

Are you sure?

Yes. It's my old cell. I'm not capped or collared. I think they're—god, can you hear that?

Hear what?

That noise. Thea clamped her hands on her temples. *It's like when we first bonded, but worse, because this isn't even coherent thoughts, it's just static. Like a constant downpour of . . .* Thea froze, realization dawning. *It's the hosts. Coen, I'm on Paramount with all the hosts. They're bringing me to Xenia, too.*

Why? His apprehension was thick, and Thea didn't know how to abate it. This hadn't been part of the plan. She was supposed to be on Kanna7 with Dr. Farraday. They were supposed to power down the logic unit while everyone else was at the summit.

It's okay. We'll carry on like usual, Coen told her, *try to force the Radical's surrender like we always planned. The logic unit would have been a bonus, but it's not necessary.*

Thea's heart raced in her chest. She paced the small cell, trying to stay optimistic, but the static of the hosts was overwhelming, and she could barely hear Coen through them.

There's one upside to this, he said. *You'll be where I'll be in a matter of hours. We'll both be at Xenia.*

It was supposed to reassure her, set her at ease, but Thea could only focus on how she was missing something. There had to be a reason Burke suddenly wanted her with the other hosts. She just didn't know what it was.

An hour later, Thea was still in her cell, the static drilling into her head like an ice pick while Coen headed to Paradox's hangar with Nova to prep for their jump. It was still roughly six hours away, but they wanted to be ready.

Thea had no idea how to fill that time. She was helpless, isolated. The noise of the hosts was unbearable. She'd tried reaching out to them, offering reassuring words and attempting to talk them out of their frenzy. It was no use. The static blocked her from them as much as it blocked their thoughts from her.

Footsteps clanked down the hall, startling her. They paused outside her door. She could make out a shadowy pair of legs through the fogged glass window.

"It's me," came Dr. Farraday's voice.

Thea ran to the window, crouching beside it.

He reached inside, removing her water bowl and replacing it with a fresh one.

"Everything can still unfold as planned. The logic unit is onboard with us, running off auxiliary power in engineering. It won't work properly if it's not near the hosts."

"Why did they move me, too?" Thea asked. "They don't need me."

"I think Burke just wants all his investments under lock and key, where he can see them. I'll come for you when it's time. Update Amber for me?"

"Sure."

He straightened on the other side of the door, and Thea listened as his boots clanked down the corridor.

Maybe this is even better than we'd planned, Coen said excitedly. *When you finish with the logic unit, you can make your way to Docking. I can have Nova pick you up.*

I'm pretty sure Xenia is going to have incredibly sophisticated security. Nova's not going to be able to fly in.

One thing at a time. Just focus on how we'll all be together in a matter of hours.

The minutes ticked by. Having Coen with her was all that kept Thea sane.

She kept thinking about his reassurances that this was good. She wanted to believe it was as simple as Burke keeping his assets in one place, but couldn't understand why she hadn't been put in cryo if this was the case. Thea had caused too many problems for Burke, and unlike Kanna7, this small cell on *Paramount* didn't have the ability to vent sedatives.

A set of boots clicked their way down the hall. No, not a single set, but several. They marched to her cell, then tore open the door.

A half dozen guards, all in full gear. Stun guns at the ready. One carried the hot cap and collar. Another a tranquilizer.

"I'm going to inject you with a sedative now," he said, moving slowly into the room. "We've been told to use deadly force if necessary."

Thea's gaze flicked back to the guards. She'd been wrong

about their weapons. They shot bullets, not electric shocks. Coen nudged at her mind, anxious. *Where's Farraday? I thought he was coming back to get you.*

Thea didn't know, and she just wanted Coen quiet. With the static of the hosts blaring in her mind, she could barely think as it was.

Thea hooked her hands behind her head and let the guard enter the room. The needle sank into the flesh below her ear. She felt the collar latch around her neck, but things went blurry after that, darkness overtaking her.

When the drug's hold on her began to slip, she pried her eyes open. She was strapped to a table in *Paramount*'s medbay. The military crest plastered on the wall glistened beneath the harsh lighting.

"Ah, she's coming around. That didn't take long."

Thea flinched toward the voice. Lieutenant Burke was standing beside the table, Dr. Farraday behind him. They were both blurry, hazy around the edges.

"I told you it wouldn't," the doctor said. "Her body metabolizes at nearly twice the average human rate."

Panic shot through Thea's limbs. Farraday had betrayed her, told Burke everything. Coen's thoughts echoed the same concerns.

There were two other medics in the room and . . . Thea craned her neck. Aldric Vasteneur sat in a chair in the corner, legs crossed and fingers thumbing lazily through a Tab. Barely a meter away, there was a second version of him. Both were hazy. Thea shook her head, blinked. The images slid together, converging as one.

"She's still sluggish, though, correct?" Burke asked.

"Yes," the doctor replied.

"Then do it."

"It's a risk I don't want to take, sir. We agreed it's best to perfect the implants, design them so they don't need a remote computer system for logic functions. If there were a problem with upgrades, if anything went wrong . . ." The doctor frowned. "Well, then you'd be ruining our only unaltered host."

Thea's eyelids were heavy. She struggled to keep them open, sockets burning from the effort.

"We have plenty of her blood stockpiled on Kanna7," Burke argued. "I can create a new host at any time."

"You can't play god with this, Christoph. I won't do it."

Burke edged closer to the doctor, towering over him.

"I've been watching you, Farraday," the lieutenant crooned. "I know you don't think I have. It's why you've grown so sloppy this past week. It was bad enough to give her info, but to visit her just earlier, on *my* ship, to make promises to *my* property." He shook his head. "I didn't want to give you a chance to explain yourself, but Vasteneur said it was only fair. So show us. Show us right now that your loyalties lie with the Radicals over your daughter."

Burke held something out to Dr. Farraday. A scalpel. Thea caught the surgical tray out of the corner of her eye, the implant gleaming. It was a curved bit of tech, no bigger than her forefinger. A bone saw sat beside it.

Sensing her apprehension, Coen's fear crackled in the back of her mind, sharp and wired.

Thea stretched, grappling for the restraints. They were buckled over her wrists and ankles, too far out of reach. She didn't have the strength to break them with sheer force. Not yet.

"You have no proof," the doctor said, staring at the scalpel. "And as the leading expert on hosts of *Psychrobacter achli*, I urge you to take my advice. It would not be wise to implant Althea Sadik. I won't do it and you can't make—"

Lieutenant Burke thrust his hand forward, shoving the blade into Farraday's stomach. The doctor's eyes bulged with shock. His grabbed for the scalpel, but his hands came up against Burke's, still wrapped around the handle.

"I can't make you?" Burke sneered. "Is that what you were going to say?" He twisted the knife. The doctor groaned. "No, I don't suppose I can. Which makes you worthless to me."

Run! Coen shouted to her. *Get out of there!*

But she couldn't even sit.

Burke pulled his handgun from his holster and fired a bullet into Farraday's chest. The doctor dropped to the floor, gasping. Another bullet, and the noises stopped.

Farraday's pulse slowed in Thea's ears, then blipped out entirely.

Thea, now!

She tugged uselessly against the restraints.

"Your connection is still working with Coen Rivli, isn't it?" Burke said, smiling down on Thea. "There's no use denying it. I've seen you confirm it via video feeds. You explained it all to Dr. Farraday during a blood draw."

"I will die before I tell you where to find them," she grunted out.

"Unlike Dr. Farraday, you're no good to me dead. But you're not much use like this, either." He raised his gaze to the other two medics in the room. "Finish up here. I want her implanted and ready for interrogation by the time I'm back from the summit. Come now, Aldric," he said, waving a hand at Hevetz's CEO. "We'll be docking shortly."

The horror didn't truly hit Thea until Burke and Vasteneur had left the room and the medics were pulling on surgical gloves.

Coen was a fury in her head. *Get up, Thea! You have to fight back.*

I can't. I can barely keep my eyes open. They drugged me. My legs feel like lead.

Too bad. You have to figure out a way. Farraday said you'll metabolize it faster. Maybe you're stronger than you feel, but you won't know unless you try.

The ship thudded lightly, items jingling on the surgical tray.

"That'll be them docking," one of the medics said. "We better get started." He tapped at a syringe. Thea would be paralyzed in a matter of seconds, her head anchored in place, her eyes stuck staring at the overhead lights as they cut open her skull.

Come on, Thea. Get up!

The medic stepped nearer, and as his gloved hand brought the syringe closer, Thea thrust upward with her arms with as much force as possible, attempting to sit at the same time. The restraints cracked open, heat flaring at her wrists, and the man jumped back in surprise. The second medic grabbed Thea's shoulders from behind, using his weight to force her back to the table.

She fought like a feral animal. Desperate. Wild. But the original sedative still had a hold on her and she didn't feel like herself. She was sloppy, weak. The men were too strong.

She lashed out in desperation, whipping her legs free of their restraints and knocking the surgical tray to the floor.

Tools went clattering. The man with the syringe dove at Thea again, and she kicked at his chest, prying the other man's hands from her shoulders. When his grip loosened, she slipped from the table. Her legs buckled like jelly. Hands flying over the tools on the floor, her fingers closed over a spare scalpel. She turned on the men, holding it out in defense as she stood.

"She clawed me," the medic said, panting. "Like a damn cat."

The man with the syringe simply stared at his bloodied partner.

Thea glanced at her front. There was blood on her ankles and wrists from when she'd broken free of the restraints. Her cuts were only just beginning to close. Her body might have metabolized the sedative quickly, but there'd been a trade-off. Her healing had been slowed. The blood was still moist, sliding between her fingers when she rubbed them together.

Her blood, wet on her fingers.

The medic, who she'd clawed in the escape.

Thea, you need to contain them, Coen said urgently.

She was still holding the scalpel out, the blade trembling in her grasp.

Thea, now!

She raced for Dr. Farraday's dead body, fishing his key

card from his lab coat pocket. Then she flew to the door.

"Don't leave me with him!" the uninfected medic screamed behind her. "Don't lock the door."

Thea sprinted from the medical bay and toggled the control on the other side, hitting a lock button on the unit. The medic slammed into the glass doors behind her, banging, pleading. He was young, but not young enough.

"I'm sorry," she said, and ran down the hall with his screams burning in her ears.

The programmer knew something had gone wrong before Coen even spoke. The boy's face was ashen, all color having drained from his cheeks.

The contagion was loose on the Paramount, he explained. The ship was already docked on Xenia, with Burke on his way to the meeting chambers, and the contagion was bound to spread to the rest of the station.

It had been Thea's doing.

She'd contained it, temporarily, but Coen feared it wouldn't last. Someone would hear the man yelling and come to his aid. They'd open the door and it would get out. And if they were smart enough to keep the medics in isolation, it wouldn't matter. In time, the men would figure out how to open the doors—with logic or with force.

"I have to jump right to her," Coen said. "Straight into Xenia. It's more important than ever that we power down the logic unit, but it requires two people. I can help her do it, and the hosts will be able to help us protect the summit attendees. They will be the only way to keep everyone on that station safe as the contagion spreads. Just like how I kept Thea safe on Achlys."

"Coen . . ." Sol was giving a speech behind Naree, speaking to the Paradox flight crew. They were set to jump in half an hour.

"It's the only way to bypass Xenia's security," Coen insisted. "Nova can jump me straight into Docking. Thea and I can turn off the logic unit. The rest of the plan can unfold as discussed."

She looked at this boy, so young to her eyes, so hopelessly in love. Every time he spoke of Thea, the programmer knew his feelings were sincere. It was strange to know someone else loved her daughter. For so long it had been just Naree. Even stranger was the envy that roiled in her stomach. That this boy had seen Thea most recently. That this boy had held her in his arms when Naree had not touched her own daughter in well over a decade.

"Please, you have to create a distraction for me. I need a window where Nova and I can fly out ahead of the fleet to make the jump."

"We never tested jumping into closed spaces," Naree said. "Not with the AltCor-powered reactor and certainly not with something as large as a Python. The amount of radiation displaced when you appear in Docking would be massive. There's no telling what sort of damage it could cause to the station, and that's if you manage to plot your jump perfectly and actually end up in Docking rather than embedded in a wall." Naree almost couldn't believe her words. All she wanted was to save Thea. How could she be advising against it?

"I don't care how dangerous it is. I've watched an entire drilling operation fall to this contagion in a matter of hours. No one on that station stands a chance if I don't do this."

Naree swallowed. Coen seemed to know where her brain was headed because when he spoke again, it was to use her biggest fear against her.

"Galactic Disease Control will condemn the whole station when they find out what's happened. They'll blow it into stardust. You are damning your daughter."

And that's what did it. She folded immediately. Maybe it made Naree Sadik a coward. She was willing to sacrifice hundreds of lives, but she could not sacrifice her daughter. Everything she'd done for Sol, every day she'd spent dutiful and submissive, had been to get back to Thea. She wouldn't stand by and let the girl die.

"His key card is in the pocket of his suit jacket," she said, nodding to a service cart where Sol had slung his jacket before climbing onto the stage to deliver his talk.

Coen followed her gaze. "Thank you. You have no idea how much this means."

"Oh, I do. You better pray I'm wrong about the displacement effects. The results won't be pretty otherwise."

He said nothing else. The programmer watched him leave, lifting the card seamlessly from the jacket as he brushed by.

The trouble was, Naree knew she wasn't wrong. The radiation released by the jump would be disastrous, but Coen might be able to save Thea before it caused any structural damage to the station. She wished him luck, sincerely and wholeheartedly. How could she wish him anything else, when he was doing what she hadn't been able to all these years?

Saving Thea had always been—and would always be—her priority.

IX

THE SUMMIT

Xenia Station

Orbiting Eutheria, Trios System

NOVA WAS CHEERING WITH THE other pilots when Coen brushed into her shoulder and whispered, "I need a word."

Amber raised a brow, her freakishly good hearing not missing a beat. "What was that about?" She'd been standing beside Nova for the entirety of Sol's speech, much to Nova's dismay. They'd spoken rarely in the past week; Nova had been busy getting a crash course in the flux drive and was still trying to forget the things she'd said in the infirmary. Having Amber so close just made her worried she'd say something else stupid.

"No idea. Let's find out."

With Amber on her heels, Nova peeled away from the crowd and followed Coen deeper into the hangar. He rounded the battlecarrier that would jump Paradox's pilots to Xenia, climbed the gangplank, and waited in the shadows.

"What's up?" Nova asked, scrambling to meet him.

"You're really good, right? You got kicked out of the Academy for something that shouldn't have even mattered."

"My peripheral vision isn't perfect, but I can still fly a fighter with the best of them, if that's what you're asking."

"Right. So you'd be able to jump me directly into Xenia Station."

"That would be like threading a needle with my eyes closed. We'll jump *to* Xenia and go from there."

Coen shook his head. "I need to get *inside*. This is the only way."

"I'm clearly missing something," Amber interjected. "The plan was for the fleet to appear *outside* of Xenia. Put pressure on the Radicals, make sure the contagion didn't get loose."

"Yeah, well, it's too late for that."

Coen told them everything—how Thea had attacked a medic to avoid getting implanted. How she was currently hiding on *Paramount*, but worried the contagion might spread, first through the ship, then to the station. How she needed the hosts' help to protect the civilians aboard the station but couldn't turn off the logic unit without Dr. Farraday, who was now dead.

Nova glanced at Amber. The girl stood stoically until Coen delved into details about a scalpel and multiple fired shots. Tears began to glisten in her eyes.

"Coen, enough!" Nova spat. "This is her dad you're talking about."

He shot Amber a sympathetic look before turning back to Nova. "You can do it, though, right?"

"It's dangerous."

"So is letting the contagion spread."

"The drive's never been tested like this."

"It would be a leap of faith."

"I don't know, Coen. We should just talk to Weet so he can move the jump up and alert Xenia's staff."

"If we hail the station, they'll go investigate *Paramount*, get themselves infected, and just spread things quicker. And that's assuming there isn't already a Radical on Xenia's staff who will hear the transmission and intervene. I ran through our options a hundred times already. This is our best shot. And just think"—Coen cocked up an eyebrow—"if this works, you'll be considered the most skilled flux drive pilot in the galaxy. Can you think of a better way to stick it to the Academy?"

He was appealing to her ego, and even still Nova thought it sounded good. Most of the jump's plotting had already been done. She'd only need to alter a few things. Of course, they were the most dangerous of the bunch.

Xenia Station was a giant cube, with docking stations encircling it and accessible from four sides. Bays were nearly two hundred meters tall. It would still be threading a needle, but at least a fairly spacious needle. If she pulled it off, there wouldn't be a corps in the Union foolish enough to bar her from flying for them.

"Maybe you should think about sticking it to the Radicals instead," Amber said sullenly. "For what they did to you. To Coen and Thea. To my father."

"To all of Black Quarry. To your *Odyssey* crew," Coen added, eyeing Nova.

Her cousin flashed before her. Sullivan had died at her hands on Achlys, but he hadn't needed to die at all. If not for Hevetz's collusion with the Radicals, he wouldn't have even been on that damn rock. Same for Dylan Lowe or Lisbeth Tarlow, or even Toby, who Nova had hated. No one deserved the fate he'd gotten. And if she didn't try this, if the contagion got loose and everyone on Xenia Station died, she'd have to live with the knowledge that those deaths were partially her fault.

"Nova, we're kinda running out of time," Coen urged.

"All right," she said. "I'll do it. How do we get out of here without anyone noticing?"

Coen smiled crookedly and waved a key card. The name *Solomon Weet* was on its front.

Thea was barely hanging on. Coen could sense her guilt like a lead blanket, weighing on her shoulders, dragging her down. She'd fled deep into the *Paramount* and was now hiding in engineering. *We're on our way*, he assured her. Her only response was a frantic nod.

As Sol's speech continued at the other end of the hangar, Nova backed a PythonII from the battlecarrier and turned it to face the exit. A 360-degree window enveloped the cockpit, and she popped it open.

"I'm coming with you guys," Amber announced.

"It's gonna be dangerous," Coen warned.

"If you're right about everything, you're gonna need me. I can track down Burke and the hosts while you and Thea see to the logic unit. That way, as soon as it's down, there's someone nearby to communicate with them, give orders."

It was a fair point. Every second would count. Coen nodded in agreement.

"I'm gonna have to bail after the jump," Nova said. "Security will freak when I blip into the station. How do you guys plan to get out?"

"One thing at a time. Let's just get there first."

"All right, but everyone's wearing full enviro-suits."

Coen didn't argue. After what Naree had told him about the radiation dispelled after a jump, it was a precaution he was more than willing to take. Together, they scrambled onto the battlecarrier and located the appropriate gear, changing quickly as Coen told Thea to locate a suit of her own. Then they were back on the PythonII, internalized comm gear linking their helmets.

The cockpit was slightly bigger than a standard Python,

allowing room for a copilot. Coen sat beside Nova, but Amber had to curl up like a ball behind their chairs, the newly updated flux drive and its AltCor reactor likely digging into her back.

Coen gave Nova a thumbs-up, and she guided the fighter toward the exit. "Something's wonky with the diagnostics on this one," she told the hangar's security guard. "I'm supposed to take it for a quick spin before liftoff, double-check some things."

"You better be quick. Schedule says the carrier takes off in twenty. Key card?"

Nova held it up for the scanners. Coen heard the successful beep, then the hangar doors opening.

"Hang on a sec, credentials on this card are for Solomon—"

The engine roared as Nova shot them ahead. Coen swiveled in his seat. "He's running after us!"

"Let him try to catch me," Nova gritted out.

Flat desert earth blurred in the 360-degree window that enveloped the cockpit, but straight ahead, Coen could make out the fencing that corralled Paradox Technologies' base. It grew larger at frightening speed.

"Pull up, Nova," he urged. "Pull up."

"It doesn't work like that! These things usually drop out of a battleship into space, not launch from on-planet."

"Nova . . . ?" Amber said behind them.

The fence was twenty meters away, fifteen, ten . . .

Nova pulled back on the control stick, urging the ship up. The nose finally lifted.

Five meters.

The back wheels were airborne.

One meter.

They soared over the fencing, and Nova had them climbing. Coen suddenly felt like a truck was sitting on his chest. The pressure was everywhere, closing in on all sides, and then it was gone. The world was dark. Stars danced beyond the cockpit.

Nova tapped coordinates into the dash. Coen tried not to think of all the ways the jump could go wrong. To land *inside* the station, Nova would have to take into account the station's orbit around Eutheria, how each passing minute moved the station's destination, how the destination *within* that station was a docking bay with walls on five sides and a deadly force field on the sixth.

"GSA is going to catch us hovering around up here," Amber worried over the linked helmet comms.

"Sol arranged another launch for the battlecarrier," Coen reminded her. "This section of airspace has an open travel window for an entire hour."

"All set," Nova said. She leaned back in her seat, gaze still on the computer. The data entered there didn't make any sense to Coen. It might as well be another language. Still, there was a spark of challenge in Nova's eyes, a reminder of the confident, daring pilot he remembered from before her coma. "Here goes nothing."

She turned a lever on the dash, punched in a command, and the world collapsed around Coen like a dying star. For the briefest moment, he ceased to exist. He was weightless, bodiless, a million cells zipping through a vacuum. There was no light, no color, no sound.

The connection with Thea even fell away. Being cut off from her—even for a window of time smaller than a fraction of a millisecond—was horrifying. He was alone again. The silence was like a knife, cutting away half of him, leaving him empty.

Then his senses were overloaded.

Gravity returned. Sound and light and heat.

A wall appeared directly ahead and Nova yanked the control stick, spinning them away with only centimeters to spare. As the PythonII turned, Coen got his first view of the massive docking bay they'd jumped into. It sprawled out before him, filled with shuttles, ships, and refueling stations. Workers were buckled over, shocked by the sudden appearance of the fighter. At the far end of the bay was an open door framing the blue-green planet of Eutheria—no bigger than his fist at this distance—amid a sea of stars.

It was terrifying to take in—a seemingly open window to space. But of course there was no threat. Coen could make out a holographic label reading *Bay 03* on the entryway, the only obvious sign that a force field kept the station's docking bay pressurized.

"I tried to get us in the middle of this damn thing," Nova said, steering them away from the wall they'd nearly crashed into, "but I guess my plotting wasn't perfect."

"It was good enough," Coen said as she set the fighter down. They were alive. The ship hadn't exploded when jumping into a pressurized area. Xenia Station wasn't flashing warnings of radiation leaks. Maybe Naree had been wrong about the side effects.

"You guys better bail," Nova said. The security workers who had hunched over at the Python's sudden appearance were now staggering upright and closing in on the fighter.

Coen, Thea said in his mind. *You're here.*

It wasn't a question—she knew it from his own thoughts—but there was still a note of awe to her voice. His heart beat wildly knowing she was nearby.

The Paramount *is in Docking Bay Four*, she told him. There was more, too, the horror of what she'd started. It was out. It had spread. She couldn't stop it.

Dread coated Coen's limbs. *I'll be right there. Stay calm. We'll figure it out.* He scanned the force field ahead. Additional holograms were visible on the far edges, labeling the way to bays two and four.

"To the right," he told Amber. "She's in bay four."

"I gotta split and find my way to the summit chambers, remember? So that I'm ready to communicate with the hosts the second you two power down the logic unit."

"Well, you're gonna have to stick together for a minute," Nova said. "These guys don't seem too happy to see us."

The security details closing in on the Python were now yelling for credentials. Nova popped the cockpit open and Coen leapt out, Amber on his heels. Before his feet even hit the ground, Nova initiated her jump out. A wave of energy sent him reeling forward, barely able to keep his feet.

When he looked back over his shoulder, the Python was gone.

The instant one of the guards drew a stun gun and sent a sloppy shot her way, Amber knew things would be easy.

She dodged the blast and dove straight at him, tackling him around the middle. By the time they hit the ground, the weapon was in her hand. She sent a blast of electricity into her attacker and pulled a shock rod from his belt, thrusting the active end into his side for good measure. She had every intention of keeping it engaged until the safety kicked on, but the guard fell unconscious almost immediately.

Amber spun. Coen had just delivered a blow to another guard's side. The man crumpled like a sack of grain. A blur of motion caught Amber's eye—two guards closing in on her from the left. She leapt to action, working methodically with Coen, stun gun in one hand, shock rod in the other. By the time the guards were disarmed and slumped on the ground, unconscious, no one else in the massive bay was close enough to see what had transpired.

I'm headed to bay four, Coen told Amber. *I'll be in touch through our comms.*

She grabbed a key card from the unconscious guard at her feet and tore across the docking bay. Coen's retreating feet faded quickly—the enviro-suit had muted her senses—but she reminded herself that he was only a comm call away.

She used the guard's card to access the first air lock door, then stepped through. Peering through the second, she could see Xenia Station's pristine halls labeled with holographic signage. A pair of diplomats—one in a formal gown and the other in a sharp suit—were walking beneath a label pointing the way to *Main Meeting Chambers*.

Amber's heart sank. She wouldn't get anywhere in her suit. It would attract too many eyes. Her outfit beneath—a T-shirt and leggings—wasn't much better, but if someone stopped to question her, maybe she could pretend to be a diplomat's aide. Someone who was supposed to wait on the ship but needed to bring something to her boss.

"I'm gonna have to ditch this suit," she said to Coen over the comms.

Still on their shared channel, Nova hissed, "Don't you dare. There's no telling what sort of effects our jump had on that docking bay. The whole thing could be flooded with radiation."

"I'm leaving the docking bay," she explained. "Through an air lock. Which I'm sure protects the internal rooms in case the force fields ever fail. I'll be fine."

"It's not worth the risk," Nova insisted.

But Nova was already off the station, waiting at a distance for the rest of the Paradox crew to make their jump. There was nothing she could do to stop Amber, and the simple truth was that a suit would give her away too quickly. No one was wearing a suit—not the guards they'd encountered in Docking or the diplomats moving through the halls.

"Look, the suit made sense when we planned things, but now that I'm standing here, I'm telling you I'll be stopped in a matter of minutes. I have to ditch it."

"But Amber . . ."

"Take whatever risks you need to," Coen said. "This whole mission was a risk. Best we keep it going as long as possible."

Amber unlatched her helmet. She could still hear Nova arguing after the helmet hit the floor of the air lock, and even a bit longer still after stepping through the second air lock door and into Xenia's gleaming halls, suit discarded behind her.

Coen found Thea in *Paramount*'s engine room, sitting with her back to the reactor, a hand pressed to either side of her helmet.

He'd known it was bad—he couldn't block out her thoughts even if he'd wanted to—but he'd still prayed that she'd been overreacting. But on the way to her, he saw the signs. There'd been blood on the ship's floors, evidence of physical struggles in the halls and common rooms. When he passed the medical bay, his worst fears were realized.

The man Thea had claimed she'd secured there was missing. The doors were open.

Thea, he said, rushing to her.

She stared numbly at the floor, even when he grabbed her shoulders.

Thea, look at me.

She glanced up, eyes bloodshot behind her visor. She'd been crying. It was such a strange sight. He realized he'd never seen her cry. Even on Achlys, when everything fell apart around them, she'd appeared worried and angry and concerned, but never downright scared like this. Never broken.

I hid, she said, the shame thick in her voice. *I didn't even try to stop it.*

He grabbed her helmet and forced her to look at him. He wished he could touch her face, her skin. They were always separated by glass. *I hid once, too*, he reminded her.

You did that to survive. You didn't know it was already in you, that you'd be safe. She shook her head, tears still streaming. *Coen, I just let it happen. I was scared of my own hands—scared of infecting more people, but also scared of failing. I was still metabolizing that sedative. What if I couldn't fight back? What if there were too many of them and they put me back in that hot cap, or the cell, or . . . I just hid. And I heard him get out of the medbay. The other guards rushed to help him. They opened the door, but he'd already turned. It's out and it's my fault.*

Coen hadn't seen evidence of a struggle beyond the ship, but *Paramount*'s gangplank had been lowered, and the infected were smartest immediately following infection. If Docking Bay 4 had already been full of ships, Xenia's security personnel would have moved on to other bays. The infected could have walked clear out of Docking and directly into the rest of the station, searching for fresh hosts.

Thea, we have to turn off the logic unit.

She could barely look at him. She was racked with guilt. She wanted to do it all over. She'd have fought back differently in the medbay, made sure she didn't infect someone.

And if it had gotten out, she'd have killed to keep it from spreading. She'd been weak.

Her thoughts were heavy, nearly pulling Coen into misery alongside her. *Not being able to kill someone isn't a weakness,* he said.

You were able to do it on Achlys. You killed Cleaver before he could turn.

Coen remembered the feel of the man's head in his hands all too clearly. Cleaver had been asking for help, and death was the only kind Coen had been able to provide. He'd taken no joy in doing it, but it had been necessary.

And I wasn't able to do what was necessary here. Thea's voice was feeble, so unlike her.

Thea. He said her name sharply, like it was a whip that could inflict pain, like it was a name he didn't like. He'd never spoken to her like that, and it was enough to make her raise her head and look him in the eye. He'd forgotten how big her eyes were, how brown and deep. *What's necessary now is the logic unit. With the rest of the hosts thinking freely, they could help us contain this. We still have a shot at saving lives. Do you understand?*

She nodded, lip trembling. She'd stopped crying, but she still didn't look like herself. It was a lot of guilt to harbor. Coen understood all too well. It hadn't been his fault that *Psychrobacter achli* spread on Achlys, but he'd nearly drowned in survivor's guilt later. Why him? Why out of every life on that rock had *he* been the only one worthy of being spared?

It had nothing to do with worth, he'd realized later. His age had spared him, his body able to coexist with the contagion. It was nothing but dumb luck.

Even still, the guilt lingered, and he felt Thea's now as heavily as he had his own. It made Coen want to drop to his knees and quit, to hide in this engine room with her and pretend nothing had happened, to go down with the station when Galactic Disease Control inevitably blew it to stardust.

We can still right it, he said, desperate to believe his own words.

Maybe, she answered. *Most likely not.*

But we have to try. Thea, I want to try.

I want what you want, she said firmly. There was an edge to her voice, pain and doubt.

And I want what you want, he reminded her. *Even if it's something as wrong as giving up.*

Thea's features steeled with understanding. She stood and offered him her hand. *The logic unit is this way.*

Amber followed the set of diplomats to an elevator. After they disappeared, she took a solo trip of her own. Inside the car, displays advertised that all summit meetings would take place on Level 26, but even when the doors slid open at that level, Amber found the hallways shockingly quiet.

The annual UPC trade summit welcomed leaders from numerous countries on every planet in both the Trios and Cradle. But here Amber stood, barely an hour before the meetings were slated to begin, and the hall was completely empty. Even the smaller meeting rooms, used for local trade discussions between just two or three officials, were barren.

A sharp gasp sounded down the hall. Amber froze, her senses locking on to it. She could hear a flurry of heartbeats from that direction, too. Not several, but hundreds. Growing faster, if she wasn't mistaken.

Amber padded down the hall and to a set of double doors, left slightly ajar. She peered through the crack and into a high-tech lecture hall. Rows of seats descended toward a stage in the front of the room where twenty of the Union's most influential leaders sat facing the packed hall. The lights were dimmed and a giant screen was illuminated above the stage.

One look at the visuals playing there and Amber understood why every heartbeat in the room was currently elevated. Footage of a drilling technician attacking medics—*Psychrobacter achli* at work in its most dangerous form—filled the screen. Metadata in the corner declared that the footage was taken during an operation known as Black Quarry. The project Nova and Thea had been sent to investigate. The operation from which Coen had been the only survivor.

Even her own heart beat faster. Breathless, Amber squeezed through the doors and into the hall, where she took a vacant seat in the last row. No one heard her enter. Everyone was too focused on the screen, which was cycling through more visuals now—bloody noses and hemorrhaged eyes and humans that had no control over themselves. The rats her own father had tested on Kanna7. And a shot of Coen that stilled Amber's blood. He wore an orange backpack like the one she'd seen in her father's lab and was fighting a small army of infected people in a narrow hallway. His movements were fluid and precise, his accuracy deadly. Blood sprayed as he twisted and thrust. He fought with a simple blade, one boy against nearly twenty. When his attackers lay dead around him, he leapt upward with inhuman speed and disappeared from the frame.

The screen faded and the lights queued up within the hall.

"Now that you've seen the consequences—and the benefits—of this contagion, I'm sure you'll all see fit to cooperate," Lieutenant Burke said from center stage. He was seated behind a placard that read *Sylvi Meadows, Union Commander and Chief*. The real commander, Amber assumed, was either dead or being held against her will within Xenia.

Burke's small army of hosts stood to his rear, lined up

before the digital screen like dutiful soldiers. Each teen was dressed in plain white clothes, and though their eyes moved over the crowd, they all looked distant, almost detached from the situation. It sent a shiver down Amber's limbs. When she tried to reach out to the hosts, a soft static was the only response.

Which meant Coen and Thea still hadn't turned off the logic unit. Then again, they weren't exactly running late. This meeting had started early. Perhaps it had even been moved up to a new time, one Paradox's and Casey's forces had never been privy to.

Amber wished for her suit and the intercom she'd left behind. She needed to update Nova so the pilot could tell the others that they were already late. The jump needed to happen immediately.

"This group behind me is equipped with the same fighting skills you saw in that video," Burke went on. "They are all hosts, just like that boy with the orange backpack." He paused dramatically. "This can go smoothly, in that the Union recognizes the Trios as an independent system and we renegotiate all trade agreements to the Radicals' approval right here and now. *Or* you will be dealing with this new breed of Radical soldier. The choice is yours." Burke glanced over the room, speaking to the Cradle as much as he was to any Union loyalist.

"Is there a cure?" a woman said, standing in the middle of the stands.

"There is a cure in the works, but only my people know of it," Burke said.

Amber had heard nothing of a cure during her time on Kanna7. She'd even stressed how dangerous it was to play with the contagion without being able to rein it in, but the scientists from Hevetz Industries had seemed more interested in re-creating hosts than curing infection.

"So you would risk all our lives, including your own, and that of every civilian in the Union for your own agenda?"

Burke turned to the host directly behind him—a pale-skinned boy of roughly fifteen—and snapped his fingers. The boy reacted robotically, pulling a weapon from behind his back and firing. His aim was impeccable, and it took only one shot. The woman fell to the ground, and tension in the room came to a blistering edge. The pulses heightened, beating angrily in Amber's ear.

Come on, Coen, Thea. Hurry up.

But of course they couldn't hear her. She wished for a bullet-shooting weapon of her own, but she had only the stun gun and shock rod from Docking, which would do no serious damage. Worse still, she felt suddenly heavy and clumsy. Exhausted, even. The fight in Docking had caught up to her, the severity of the situation in the hall chilling her to the bone. There was nothing she could do for these ambassadors. Amber searched the crowd, praying a member of the hall might find the nerve to fire back at Burke, but they sat trembling, their fear so rancid Amber could taste it in the back of her mouth. They'd probably been forced to check all their weapons before entering the meeting hall. It was Burke who had muscled his way in.

When everyone else abided by the rules, it didn't take much to get the upper hand.

"Does anyone else want to challenge me?" Burke roared, gaze sweeping over the stands. It settled on Amber for the briefest instant, recognition gleaming in his eyes. He opened his mouth to give an order to the hosts—and the meeting hall's main doors burst open.

Finally, Amber thought.

But when she turned, it wasn't Thea or Coen bursting into the hall. It was an infected medic wearing a uniform that matched the ones Amber was used to seeing on *Paramount*. The man dove at the nearest official, dragging him from his seat as dozens of infected poured in behind him.

Thea descended the ladder to the engine room's first level, Coen following her lead. She hated that she'd hid. That she'd been useless. That this was all her fault.

It's Burke's fault, Coen said. *That's what you told me once in the thick of our testing. Remember? That we couldn't get mad at each other or even ourselves. This is on him. On the Radicals.*

Thea understood the concept perfectly, but it didn't remove the guilt she felt for what had just unfolded.

She pushed off the ladder, skipping the last few steps in favor of jumping. Her feet hit the floor, and after hearing Coen land behind her, she jogged toward an alcove labeled *Auxiliary Power*. The logic unit was the size of a compact rover, rectangular in shape, with a series of cables running from the rear and plugging into *Paramount*'s supplementary drives. The face of the unit blipped with lights.

Thea had never expected to stand before the unit without Dr. Farraday. It had always been a cautious alliance she'd formed with the doctor, but it was Amber who'd made Thea's trust in Farraday solidify. He'd been willing to risk everything for her. Thea's own mother working for Sol all those years suddenly made a little more sense.

She pulled up before the logic unit. On both ends, set behind a panel of glass, were two dials and a single lever.

We have to do it at exactly the same time, she said, sliding one of the glass panels open. *One dial, then the next, and finally the lever.*

He nodded at her from across the unit. *First dial in three, two . . .*

As he said *one*, Thea turned the first dial, clicking it to *off*. *Second dial in three, two, one.*

Another dial turned together.

Thea grabbed the lever and glanced across the logic unit at Coen. Not that long ago they'd been standing on *Celestial Envoy*, a similar lever beneath Thea's palm. He'd put his hand over hers, helping her to initiate the self-destruct sequence. She needed his help again now. Not because this was a difficult choice. This was perhaps one of the rare instances she'd faced over the last few months that was *easy*. But she was not surprised that she still needed him to make it, that they could only do it together. They were two halves of a whole. She could barely remember her life before he was in her head, before he knew her heart better than she knew it herself.

Ready? she asked.

Ready, he said.

They didn't need to count. They simply looked at each other and knew. When Thea was ready to push the lever up, Coen pushed as well.

They clicked in perfect unison, and the lights on the unit's front fell off in a cascading wave.

"Logic unit is off!" Thea said, joining the channel Coen was using to communicate with Nova.

"Good to hear you, Thea," came the pilot's reply. "I need to jump back to Xenia in about thirty seconds. Any word from Amber?"

"Not yet," Coen answered. "But we'll need your crew to secure the station regardless."

Confusion laced the pilot's voice when she replied. "You guys just freed the hosts' minds. Xenia security can probably de-escalate everything from here, right?"

"Yeah, about that . . . ," Thea began. She couldn't bring herself to state the truth.

"We couldn't contain things to the *Paramount*," Coen explained. "The infected have most likely spread into the station."

"What?!"

"You have to tell Sol," he went on. "Maybe he can radio Xenia's commanding officers. They could lower security clearance on the force fields, and you guys can help us evacuate the civilians and crew."

"There's no other way to contain it?"

Thea said, "Beyond separating the already infected from the uninfected, and getting those healthy people off Xenia, no." Admitting it made her stomach twist with guilt. "We'll find Amber in the meantime. Do what we can to keep the uninfected safe."

"And I'll do what I can with Sol," Nova said. There was a subtle beeping in the background. "That's my countdown. Time to jump."

The intercom fell silent, and Thea again took Coen's hand.

● ● ●

The hall descended into chaos. Amber watched in horror as the meeting chambers became a blur of flesh, a wave of screams. There had to be at least three dozen infected *Paramount* members present and more kept forcing their way through the doors. They attacked like rabid animals, and without weapons, the summit officials didn't stand a chance.

Amber knew she should do something—anything—but she felt glued to the spot, her limbs like rubber, her body weighted down. She coughed into her elbow, praying she wouldn't be sick from the carnage.

Desperate, she looked to the only other exit in the hall: the one at the stage's rear, where Burke and the other top officials were now fleeing for their lives. The hosts still stood in a line on the stage, but their postures had suddenly relaxed. They blinked, coming out of a daze, and glanced to one another frantically. The buzz of static they'd previously given off was gone, replaced with panicked thoughts. *Where the hell are we?—What are those things?—Why can I hear everyone's thoughts?*

Amber reached out to them, trying to ignore the way her limbs seemed to tremble. *Hello? Back here, near the rear of the hall.* She raised a hand. Dozens of eyes slid to her. *The Radicals injected you with a contagion you can host, which means the infected won't be interested in you. They're looking for* new hosts. *You have to help me move the uninfected to a secure area.*

The responses came at her in a defensive wave. *How did you get here?—Where the hell were you when we were infected?— Why didn't you help then?*

But then one that was promising: *Move them where? The exit is blocked by the infected, and I swear I can hear more of them coming from farther down the hall.*

There's an exit to your rear, Amber said. *Burke left that way with some of the other officials. If you get up here and help me fight, we can probably save about half these people.*

Don't listen to her.—Yeah, she didn't help us earlier. We can't trust her—I'm leaving now.

If you don't help me, Galactic Disease Control will destroy this entire station. But if we separate the healthy from the sick, we can evacuate. Being subjected to quarantine procedures once the GDC arrives sounds a lot better than being blown to stardust, doesn't it?

Murmurs of consideration rippled through the hosts while others argued to run.

Burke barricaded the door! came a shout from the stage exit.

Amber wasn't sure if this host was intent on helping move summit attendees through it or simply saving their own hide, but in the moment she didn't care. *Get it open!* she ordered. *The rest of you, come help me. I'm begging you.*

No need to beg, a familiar voice said. Amber spun toward

the main doors, her heart practically leaping. Coen was forcing his way into the hall. He drove something into the side of an infected *Paramount* crew member, then pulled it free. A standard butcher's knife, likely swiped from *Paramount*'s kitchen. Amber looked away, feeling sick. She coughed again, practically gagging. When she glanced back up, Thea was at Coen's side, lashing out with a shock rod. It did little to slow the infected, but it did give Coen an opening to attack with the blade.

About time you guys got here! Amber called.

We would have been faster, Thea said, *if you'd been able to tell us how bad things were.*

But someone decided they absolutely had *to ditch their suit. We had to follow blood trails.* Coen shot her a smile, then struck down another infected crew member.

How were they joking at a time like this?

Amber lurched to action, scrambling clumsily over seats and making her way down the rows. "This way!" she shouted to the diplomats. "There's an exit in the front."

Most of the panicked crowd was already headed in that direction, but they were fighting even among themselves, shoving each other, climbing over the weaker, slower officials. Anything to stay as far away from the infected as possible.

"Do it in an orderly fashion!" Amber shouted.

"Go on!" said a dark-skinned boy to the crowd. One of the hosts. He had four other teens with him. "Listen to her. We'll help hold the infected back."

Thank you, Amber said breathlessly.

He gave a curt nod and raced up the stairs, the other teen hosts trailing after him. Back on the stage, the second set of exit doors now hung open. The hosts who had not come to the crowd's aid had forced their way through Burke's barricade and fled.

That meant Amber, Coen, Thea, and five hosts against several dozen infected.

She didn't know if it was enough, especially not with how winded she felt. But it would have to be. She prayed no one else was tiring as quickly as she was.

Nova blinked back to existence with Xenia in the distance, just as Paradox's and Casey's ships glided into position against the stars.

She didn't think she'd ever get used to the sensation of jumping. How for a moment you were everything and nothing. She also didn't think her heart could beat any faster, because if what Thea and Coen had said was true, things had just escalated from dangerous and risky to goddamn disaster.

Accelerating hard, she flew toward Paradox's battle-carrier. Pythons were dropping out of the ship and cruising to various positions around the station.

"This is Nova Singh requesting a private channel with Solomon Weet," she said over the open comms.

A new channel number flashed on her dash a moment later and she switched to it, syncing up with Sol.

"You have to hail Xenia and get security measures lowered. We need to enter Docking and evacuate people."

"Whoa, whoa," Sol said. "We need to stay calm and hold firm until Eutherian forces arrive—forces we can confirm are loyal to the Union and will help rein Burke in."

"The contagion is loose. Thea and Coen just confirmed it."

There was a brief pause. Nova could almost see the anger rimming Weet's eyes. "How would they know something like that?"

She spilled it all. How Thea had devised the plan to shut down the logic unit but needed Coen's help. How Nova had jumped him directly into Xenia's docking bay.

"Do you have any idea how dangerous that was?"

"I plotted everything perfectly," she said, leaving out the bit about how she'd nearly crashed into a wall.

"I don't care. The issue is you still jumped *inside* a contained location. We have no clue what the consequences will be. After today I never want to see you on my premises, let alone near them. This is the last Paradox-owned fighter you will ever fly!"

It was like being back at the Academy, hearing she was barred for life. No matter what she did, no matter the impossible feats she pulled off, it was never good enough.

"I made the jump nearly an hour ago," she snarled, "and the only consequence is that the contagion is loose, and not at my doing. If you still want to save lives today, hail the damn station."

Coen fought methodically, the bright walls of the meeting hall morphing into deep purple skies. Seats became craggy rocks. Each row in the hall a crevice or ravine.

He was back on Achlys, a feral instinct taking over him, only this time, he wasn't alone.

Thea was in his head, letting him know where to turn and strike. For each blow of her shock rod, he'd follow it with a slash of his knife. The blade was nothing compared to the weapons he'd fashioned on Achlys. It had no reach, and while he pined for a longer handle, it still did the job. If anything, the fighting was easier because he had Thea on his side. Together, they were invincible.

It was the diplomats he needed to worry about. Despite how efficient he and Thea had become, they still weren't fast enough. There were too many infected, and too many summit attendees were being marred and attacked as they tried to escape. Bloody noses and hemorrhaged eyes filled the hall. Everywhere Coen turned, he saw the people he was supposed to be saving buckling over with spasms.

We can't keep this up much longer, Thea said. *We need to get the healthy people out of here—now!*

Coen slashed out with the blade, leaping over the nearest infected. Using the handrails of seats like stairs, he darted down to the stage, Thea on his heels.

Of course, as soon as they weren't actively engaged in a fight, the infected horde sharpened its focus on the people escaping through the stage exit.

How many did you get through? Coen asked Amber.

Fifty, maybe?

It wasn't enough. The hall could hold close to a thousand, and it had been nearly full with diplomats.

Coen leapt onto the stage and raced through the exit, finding himself in a corridor that ran parallel to the stage and presumably joined back up with the main hallway. He could make out the footsteps of fleeing summit attendees far ahead.

"Attention Xenia staff and station guests," a surly voice said over the station's intercom system. "This is the acting station commander. It has come to our attention that we've suffered a massive security breach. For your own health and safety, please make your way to Docking Bay Three in a calm and orderly fashion. Ships will be waiting to evacuate you.

Again, that is Docking Bay Three. Make your way to Docking Bay Three in a calm and orderly fashion for immediate evacuation."

Nova must have made contact with Sol, Coen said.

It was about the only thing that had gone right. Even turning off the logic unit hadn't panned out the way they'd hoped. Nearly all the hosts had bolted once free, not helped to fight off the infected.

But if they were still loyal to Burke, Thea said, *things might be even worse.* She slipped through the door, giving Coen's arm a quick squeeze. Her gaze trailed to a toppled pile of supply crates in the corridor. *Is that what Burke used to barricade the door?*

I think so, Amber said. *Which means the infected will force their way through in seconds if we use them to barricade it again.*

Don't bother with it then, said a foreign voice. *We'll hold them off as long as possible.* It was the dark-skinned host who'd been fighting alongside him earlier. From where Coen stood in the stage exit's doorway, he could see the other boy halfway up the aisle, waving them off enthusiastically. Beyond him, his host friends were fighting back the growing crowd of infected. *Get the healthy people to Docking!*

Coen didn't need to be told twice.

He tore down the corridor with Amber and Thea. It fed back to the level's main hallway. Running hard, they caught up to the diplomats they'd just helped escape the meeting chambers. The spooked bunch was packed in front of the elevator, frantically hitting the call button.

"Stairwells!" Coen shouted to them, pointing to the doorway opposite the elevator. He shouldered through it, staggering onto a landing. The emergency stairwell looked nothing like the rest of Xenia Station. Plain cement replaced gleaming tile floors. Industrial piping ran along the walls and bare metal handrails snaked downward. A strip of reflective tape marked each step.

Coen led the way with Thea while Amber brought up the rear, the survivors packed between them like a herd of sheep. They'd gone only four flights when the stairwell flashed with red warning lights. This time, it wasn't the station commander's voice that projected over the intercoms but an automated message.

Warning: Radiation detected inside shields. Air locks and seals malfunctioning. Station failure imminent.

The crowd skidded to a halt, bodies bumping into each other.

But how—? Amber searched out Coen. Her face was flushed, her forehead sweaty. *There were no issues when we jumped into Docking. Everything was fine.*

The security details were hunched over when we landed, Coen said, dread blooming in his stomach.

And they were so easy to overpower . . .

The radiation made them sick, that's why. And then it started to degrade the station itself. Air locks, reinforced walls, computers . . . Who knows how much of it is no longer structurally sound.

This was his fault. Naree Sadik had warned him, and he hadn't listened. In jumping to Xenia to save Thea and the station's occupants, he'd damned them all.

Thea froze, certain she'd heard Coen and Amber's conversation wrong. But then the announcement repeated.

Warning: Radiation detected inside shields. Air locks and seals malfunctioning. Station failure imminent.

"We need to evacuate!" someone screamed.

"We *are* evacuating," Thea reminded them. "Please keep moving."

"If the air locks fail, we're all dead!"

"If there's already radiation inside the shields, we're already being poisoned!"

"How could it be *inside*?" yet another panicked voice shouted. "The only radiation even projecting on this station is the sun's!"

"I don't know," Thea said, even though she did. Coen's guilt continued to hit her like a wave. Jumping into a confined area had proved deadly. Not at first, but the dispelled radiation must have weakened the structural integrity of the station. What was overheating and breaking down—wires, computers, the hull itself? It didn't matter. If the air locks and seals were failing as the announcement declared, it was only a matter of time before the people she was trying to save began exhibiting signs of radiation poisoning. And that was if the air locks didn't completely fail first, sucking them all into space.

"We need to stay calm," Thea insisted. "It's fifteen more flights to Docking, and when we get there, ships will be waiting."

"*If* we get there!"

"There are emergency drop pods!" a young diplomat shouted. "A dozen on every floor, and they drop straight to Eutheria!"

"If we get to one of those, we won't have to worry about reaching Docking!" another man agreed.

"No, we should stick together!" Thea said. "Quarantine procedures can take place on the larger ship waiting in Docking. But to take the drop pods straight to Eutheria means—"

"There's no time. I'm leaving now." The young diplomat shoved her way to the next landing and backed up to the door. "Who's coming with me?"

"Ker, your nose," her friend said.

Thea turned slowly, spotting the bead of red at the end of the diplomat's nostril. It dripped, spattering on the floor.

"It's in her, too!" someone shouted.

"It could be in any of us!"

"He has a bloody nose also!" A finger was thrust out in the crowd, pointing to a man Thea couldn't even see from where she stood.

Warning: Radiation detected inside shields. Air locks and seals malfunctioning. Station failure imminent.

"Wait, please!" Thea shouted. "We have to stay calm!"

But the crowd—stretched out between several flights—was already splitting, shoving their way through doors on three different landings and disappearing into the halls of Xenia Station.

The doors banged shut, and Thea found herself standing with Coen and Amber. The only other person present was the young diplomat with the bloody nose. She hunched over, clawing at her face.

When the diplomat finally straightened, one of her eyes was hemorrhaging, dark red filling the white. The young woman stared at Thea blankly. She blinked and looked to Coen, then Amber, her expression almost bored. It was as though the three of them weren't standing there, and really, to the *Psychrobacter achli* swimming through her veins, they weren't. None of them were viable hosts for the contagion that now itched to leave the woman.

But they chased me on Achlys after the outbreak, Coen said.

They chased us through the air vents and the dumbwaiter.

No, they chased me, Thea said. *I wasn't truly a host until* Paramount. *The same happened for you. They chased you in the early hours, and when you hid, they retreated to the drilling site. But we're all hosts now, fully. She doesn't see an opportunity here.*

The young diplomat cocked her head, picking up on the commotion outside the stairwell.

"It is my fault this happened to you," Thea said to her. "I'm so sorry." She took Coen's knife and ended the woman's suffering.

"Why the hell haven't they lowered their damn securities yet?" Lawson said, her voice clear in Nova's helmet. "We can't evacuate anyone if we can't access Docking."

Nova glanced out her cockpit and to the fighter beside her. Lawson was waving a hand at the docking bay's force field in disgust.

"No idea, but maybe I can find out. Gimme a sec." She switched off the public channel she'd joined with Lawson and back to the one she'd agreed to use with Coen. "Guys. Update me. We're still waiting to get access to Docking, even though Xenia told us they'd be lowering security measures on the force field."

"Slight problem there," came Coen's reply. "Our jump did damage after all. The whole station is suffering a radiation leak. Air locks and seals are failing. It's not a stretch to assume their computers are malfunctioning, too, and now Xenia can't update security features."

Lawson threw her hands out across the way, as if to say, *Well?*

Working on it, Nova mouthed, then said to Coen, "So, no evacuation?"

"We've got an even bigger problem," Thea interrupted. "People are taking escape pods now."

Nova frowned. "How's that a problem? We don't want them stranded there."

"It would be good if *Psychrobacter achli* was contained. But it's not. And people showing symptoms are now racing for escape pods. Nova, you're gonna have to shoot them down."

"What? Thea, I can't do that. They're civilians. Some of them probably aren't even infected."

"It's them or an entire planet. Dozens or billions. If this gets out on Eutheria . . . Nova, we can't let that happen."

Something flashed in her peripherals, and always aware of her less-than-perfect vision, Nova did a double take. Sure enough, a pod was detaching from Xenia. It fell away from the station, racing for the planet below like a shooting star.

Nova looked at her control stick, the trigger near her thumb, the pod in the distance. Lessons from the Academy bombarded her—lessons about sacrifice and necessary deaths and victories that would feel like nothing but loss for those who lived through them.

"I can't do it, Thea. I won't."

"You *have* to!"

"You're not my ranking officer!" Nova shouted. "You're just a damned intern and I'm a temp. That's how this started, remember? We have no business making this call! We shouldn't even be here!"

Another pod detached. Then a third.

"Dr. Tarlow once told me that the responsible path is often hard. That it has consequences and is never easy," said Thea. "This isn't easy, Nova. How could it be? But it's necessary."

Lawson's Python lurched to life, pivoting into view before Nova. Lawson slapped the side of her helmet, signaling Nova to switch her comms. She did.

"—received a call from Xenia Station," Solomon Weet was saying. "A threat to the galaxy is airborne in all drop pods. Trios military has been dispatched from Eutheria, and they'll be here in approximately eighteen minutes, but by then, it may be too late for the planet. Orders are to shoot down all drop pods. I repeat: shoot down all drop pods."

Nova's stomach churned. Casey's general came on the line next, repeating the same order to his troops. Lawson took off, missiles firing, and Nova watched in horror as the first pod exploded in a soundless burst of light.

Nova eyed the launch trigger on the control stick. She'd wanted for so long to fight for the Union, to serve and protect. Still, she'd never ended an innocent life with the push of a button before. At the Academy, it was always sims and exercises. She glanced up. Nothing about this was simulated. Drop pods were releasing in droves, and though she hated everything about it, Nova couldn't see a single reason *not* to follow orders. Thea was right.

It was one to save many.

Dozens to spare billions.

Drop pods for the security of a planet.

Nova surged forward, the fighter vibrating around her. When she found the nerve to fire, she did not miss.

Despite being without her helmet, Amber's exceptional hearing made listening to Nova's conversation with Thea and Coen easy. "What about you guys?" the pilot asked, her voice choppy as she presumably raced after drop pods. "I can't jump to you again. Not until the drop pod threat is over."

"We'll figure something out," Thea answered, but she didn't sound very convinced.

"Is Amber with you? Is she showing signs of radiation poisoning?"

Thea's eyes slid to Amber. "She's with us, and . . ." She trailed off.

Amber grimaced, feeling queasy. What had started as slight breathlessness in the meeting halls had amplified to full body aches and nausea. She'd thought it odd that she'd been so winded, especially with *Psychrobacter achli* swimming in her veins, but she'd chalked it up to the adrenaline rush of fighting the infected. But she hadn't sustained any injuries, and now they were simply standing on a stairwell landing, talking. She shouldn't be winded. Her body shouldn't tremble with chills. Still, she couldn't bring herself to share the news with Nova.

"Tell her to quit worrying about us and go save the world," Amber gritted out.

Thea relayed the message with a forced smile, and Nova disconnected to focus on the drop pods. It was only then that Amber admitted, "I think I should backtrack for my suit. Just to be safe."

Coen looked grave. "Even with excellent healing capabilities, I don't know if you can heal radiation damage. Also, this station is going to fail and a suit isn't going to save any of us. If the air locks go first, we'll end up floating around in space until our O_2 runs out. And if we take a drop pod—"

"We'll be shot down before we even enter Eutheria's atmosphere," Thea finished.

"I honestly don't see how we get out of this. Not without a pilot, and the only one who can jump to us is a bit preoccupied at the moment."

"That's not exactly true," Amber said, the idea striking her like a blow to the heart. "There's a pilot on *Paramount*. Or at least there might be." He'd been cargo, just like Thea and Coen, first held on *Paramount*, then moved to Kanna7. But Thea had been moved back to *Paramount* before the summit, and it was possible this pilot had been moved back, too. "Decklan Powell."

"Powell from Black Quarry?" Coen said.

Amber nodded, trying to ignore the way the stairwell had started to spin. "Burke intercepted him as he flew to the Trios for help. Vasteneur released a statement that Powell died during Black Quarry and Burke's been holding him ever since."

"There was no one else held on *Paramount*," Thea said. "No one human at least. It was just me and hosts. Their hearts beat in perfect unison, like robots. I'd have heard someone else in the cells."

"He was never in the cells on *Paramount*," Amber said. "They kept him in isolation in the medbay, but he went in stasis like the rest of us once we were headed to Kanna7. Pretty sure they've been keeping him that way since."

"If he's in stasis . . ." Coen's eyes lit up. "Between

Paramount's shields and the cryo chamber, there's a good chance he's still healthy. And *Paramount* already has credentials for the force field's security measures, too. He can fly us out of here on that ship or any of its shuttles!"

Amber could register the elation in Coen's and Thea's eyes, but she couldn't mirror it. When she tried to smile, she simply buckled over, coughing. Blood spattered the back of her hand.

"Amber, you okay?" Coen grabbed her arm.

"Yeah, fine," she managed. "You guys head straight for *Paramount* and find Decklan. I'll meet you there, but I need to backtrack for my suit first. Radiation levels are probably crazy down at Docking, and I don't think I can make it much longer without some added protection."

"You're sure you can manage alone?"

"Positive," she said, even though she wasn't. But she knew they'd stay to help her if she said otherwise, and they didn't have time to waste.

Amber trailed Thea and Coen down the stairs, but quickly fell behind. They were sprinting and she was barely able to walk evenly.

When she reached the docking floor, the results of their jump with the flux drive were obvious. Xenia staff were buckled over in the halls, coughed-up blood on their fronts, blisters on their faces. Some were already dead, others moaning so pitifully, death couldn't be far off.

Amber staggered by them, unable to look too closely. Her legs ached beneath her, and every few steps she had to stop to hack and cough. The sleeve of her shirt was soon red with blood from wiping her mouth.

The air lock to Docking Bay 3 came into view, and Amber crawled nearer. When had she started crawling?

She reached the air lock. The suit lay on the floor. She coughed, blood spattering the glass door.

She straightened on her knees, barely able to reach the toggle. The door slid open and Amber collapsed on top of her suit. She couldn't put it on. She had no strength left. Without *Psychrobacter achli*, she'd probably already be dead.

Maybe it was best to have it all end here. Her father had lost his life on this station. She could be buried with him in a way. She'd hated him when she'd fled from Kanna7, but knowing he'd been willing to risk everything to see her again meant more than she could say. Her vision tunneled, darkness threatening to overtake her. She blinked, fighting it off, knowing she had to find the strength. If she didn't survive this, her father's death would be for nothing.

Get up, she told herself, forcing herself to sit.

Put your suit on. She was gasping by the time it was on, her skin feeling aflame. She coughed again, wiped blood from her mouth.

Start walking. She pulled the helmet on, creating a seal with the suit, and took her first step. Suddenly, getting to *Paramount* felt possible. She breathed fresh air and put one foot in front of the other, trudging wearily toward Docking Bay 4.

The extra heartbeats were obvious to Coen long before he stepped into *Paramount*'s cryostasis room with Thea. Decklan Powell's was easily discernible: mellow, slow. It should have been alone, but two others were with him. *Infected*, his brain worried.

There's no static, Thea said. *Maybe hosts?*

Coen tried to reach out to them, but there was no response, no sign that they'd even registered his words. He shook his head to Thea.

Survivors, then, she said. *Xenia staff or summit attendees. We can take them with us.*

Coen edged into the room and froze.

Aldric Vasteneur stood before Powell's stasis chamber, ready to initiate a wake cycle. Beside Vasteneur, with a gun leveled at Coen's head, was Lieutenant Burke.

The knife in Coen's hand suddenly felt like a toy. He'd once told Thea that he could take a gun from her before she managed to fire it. He'd meant it, too. But she'd been standing so close to him that day, and her weapon only shot electricity, not bullets. If he'd been slower than he anticipated, he'd have been able to withstand the shock long enough to force her to surrender the weapon.

But this . . . Burke's gun was already aimed, and the lieutenant was smiling. They were easily two meters apart. Far enough that Coen couldn't get to the weapon. Close enough that Burke wouldn't miss.

Maybe Coen could leap aside, dodging the bullet. As soon as Burke's trigger finger flexed, he could dive out of the way.

And then I'll dive at Burke, Thea said, understanding. *Disarm him.*

"This is our pilot," Burke announced coolly. "Turn around and leave."

"He's my pilot," Coen said. "He's Black Quarry, like me."

"I will shoot if I have to."

"And you'll miss."

"Yes, I will." Burke's smile widened, and Coen realized his mistake. Coen wasn't the target. Burke's bullet wasn't meant for him.

Thea! he yelled, but she'd turned toward the hall, distracted by something. The lieutenant's aim twitched to the right. Coen watched him squeeze the trigger.

By the time Thea realized what was happening—all of Coen's fear crashing down on her like a wave—it was too late. The bullet had already left the gun.

Coen dove—not away from the bullet, but *toward* it. In front of Thea. Blocking its path.

Pain exploded near his hip, drilling deep, radiating outward.

He hit the floor gasping, and the first thing he saw was Thea's face overhead, her thoughts attacking him. *Why would you do that? You stupid—Are you okay? Oh my god you're bleeding. You're bleeding everywhere.*

There was her hand, applying pressure on his side. And the pain. The pain, everywhere. Even when his body started healing, it didn't lessen.

Thea held him in her lap.

He was wondering if the bullet was lodged somewhere. If he was bleeding internally, if his organs were intact. He wondered if this was how Lisbeth Tarlow had died, and Thea couldn't keep the truth from him. Even if she wanted to, even as she desperately tried to hide her thoughts, he knew everything.

Coen turned away from her, managing to glance at Lieutenant Burke. The man was sharpening his aim on Thea again, and Thea didn't care. Coen screamed at her to fight, to run, to do anything. But he hadn't heard what she had just earlier, what had pulled her attention away from Burke and his gun to begin with. When they'd first entered the cryostasis room, she'd picked up on it. Faint then, now louder. A cacophony of static in her mind. Feet clambering through the halls. Pulses pounding like a thousand drums.

Oh, Coen said, noticing it now as well. *You always did have the better hearing.*

Thea looked at Burke, staring past the gun and into his eyes. "There's a saying," she said, "about getting what you deserve."

Something caught the lieutenant's attention—a noise in the hall. His gaze jerked toward the door just as the first infected body stormed through. Burke turned, adjusting his aim. He wasn't quick enough. An infected crew member tackled him to the ground before he could loose a shot. A dozen other infected followed, jumping on Burke, on Vasteneur. The sounds they made were inhuman.

Thea leaned over Coen, unable to watch.

When the struggle ended, she risked a glance. The infected crowd stood over the men they'd just attacked, glancing around the room. Their eyes skirted over the cryostasis pod holding Decklan Powell, but he hadn't been revived yet. His pulse was still too low, making him look like an incapable host to the infected. Their gazes shifted to Thea and Coen and drifted away, uninterested. They turned and staggered out of the room.

Burke and Vasteneur groaned where they'd fallen. The

lieutenant's leg was bent at an unnatural angle. Vasteneur clutched his head. Rivers of blood marred both their faces and necks. They had five minutes, no more.

Thea lowered Coen from her lap, then ran for the stasis pod. She threw the switches Vasteneur had yet to initiate and heaved open Powell's door. He flopped forward into her arms and she lowered him onto the floor.

"Come on," she said, slapping the pilot's cheek. "Wake up."

He blinked his eyes, groggy, and searched Thea's face. When he looked behind her, finding Coen, his eyes widened. "I remember you," he managed.

"Black Quarry," Coen grunted out.

"Where are we?"

"I'll explain when you land us on Eutheria," Thea said. "Right now we need to get to a shuttle. Can you walk?"

He nodded and pushed himself wearily to his feet. Good. She'd have to carry Coen. His face was pale behind his visor, and if Thea was being honest with herself, it didn't look like he'd last long. Dr. Tarlow had been shot in the stomach. Maybe a bullet to the pelvis was better. And he'd had all those layers of the enviro-suit as added protection. Was she lying to herself?

She grabbed Burke's gun from the floor, then scooped Coen up in her arms. He seemed to weigh nothing. His head lolled against her chest.

I wasn't worth it.

You were. You are, he managed. *I'd do it again.*

She turned back toward Burke and Vasteneur. Blood was beginning to drip from the lieutenant's nose. She raised his gun, her aim perfect.

"I will shoot if I have to," she said, throwing the lieutenant's words back at him. "But I won't miss."

A primal fear spread across his face.

A blink. Blood-filled eyes.

"I guess I have to," she said, and squeezed the trigger twice.

As Amber staggered toward cryostasis, exhausted but no longer coughing up blood, two figures appeared farther up the hall. One had a hand on the wall for support. The other was bulky and awkward, too wide at the middle. As they drew nearer, Amber realized the oddly shaped figure was actually Thea, carrying Coen.

Bullet to the hip, the girl explained.

Amber tried to hide her worries. Blood loss in that area would be high. There were all the organs that could be compromised, too.

Help Powell? Thea went on, nodding to the man leaning into the wall for support. *He's queasy and slow from stasis.*

Amber slung the man's arm behind her shoulder. He was

significantly taller, perhaps forty kilograms heavier as well. They leaned into each other, keeping one another upright as they followed Thea through the ship.

A muted thrum of heartbeats reached Amber's ears.

They're coming back, Thea said.

Infected?

A nod. *They left after attacking Burke and Vasteneur. They didn't sense any other potential hosts. But now that Powell's out of stasis . . .*

Amber could put the rest together. They went as fast as they could manage, making their way toward the hold and boarding one of *Paramount*'s short-range military shuttles. Not a second after they safely boarded the the shuttle did the infected horde begin climbing *Paramount*'s gangplank.

"Get us out of here," Amber barked.

Powell jumped to action, tearing for the cockpit.

Amber turned back to Thea. She'd set Coen on the floor and had stripped off his suit. His pants were soaked with blood at the hip. "You have to do something. Please, Amber."

She knelt beside him, touching his forehead. His skin was clammy and cold. Pulling at the waistband of his pants, she couldn't see the bullet. The wound had seemingly vanished. "He's healing himself, but the bullet must be lodged somewhere. And if it hit something vital . . ." She glanced around the military shuttle. "That medical kit on the wall. Bring it to me."

The shuttle rumbled to life and barreled forward. Amber could hear the bodies in *Paramount*'s hold getting pushed and struck aside as the shuttle rolled down the gangplank and into Xenia's docking bay. Then there was a surge of acceleration, the undeniable sensation of flight as Decklan guided them for the stars.

Thea reappeared with the kit and dropped it before Amber. Inside was everything needed for tending to field wounds. She willed herself to focus, tried to ignore the exhaustion that troubled her limbs. If she closed her eyes now, she would sleep for hours.

She'd start with the bullet, Amber decided, assuming she could get to it. *Please don't let your healing abilities be what kills you*, she thought, and grabbed a pair of medical pliers and scissors.

Behind her, Thea spoke on the shared intercom channel. "Nova, we're off Xenia. We're in *Paramount*'s short-range shuttle. It probably has Trios military markings. Make sure they don't shoot us!"

Nova passed the information up the chain of command, although she couldn't do much more than hope it was heard.

She banked her fighter hard and began to chase a new drop pod. They'd been detaching in droves. If Xenia Station was a boat, the drop pods were the life rafts, and there were thousands—enough for every visitor.

Nova had already taken care of nine. The first had been the hardest, but each one grew a bit easier. It helped that she couldn't see the faces inside. She could tell herself they were all infected or already showing symptoms. It was easiest that way. Later, she'd have to live with what she was doing, but right now she focused on her crosshairs.

The pod she was chasing was finally within range and she fired off another missile. Brilliance exploded outside the cockpit window and she banked aside again.

"What's that make, ten?" Lawson said in her ear. "You're putting me to shame, Singh."

"You know, you probably shouldn't treat this like a game. It's a shit situation."

"Go suck the fun out of everything, why don't you."

"I'm not kidding, Lawson."

"Maybe you should. Lighten up a little and—"

Her voice cut off with a crackle.

"Lawson? Lawson!"

Nova brought the fighter around, scanning in all directions. They'd been working together, watching out for one another. With so many drop pods falling, and so many being shot from the sky, it was impossible to keep your eyes everywhere. Too many blind spots.

Remnants of a blast lingered in Nova's peripherals.

"Lawson?" she tried again, already knowing what had happened. Cross fire. Or maybe a collision with another fighter or pod.

This was Nova's fault. She was shooting potentially innocent lives from the sky and she'd managed to let another one die on her watch, too. She shouldn't be in this situation. Maybe the Academy was right. Maybe her eye condition *was* too much of a risk.

"Nova, did you give them the order?!" Thea screamed through the intercoms.

"Yes. Why?"

"We've been hit and—SHIT!"

"Where are you?"

"I have no idea. Powell's saying it was cross fire."

"Who the hell is Powell?"

"Decklan Powell, from Black Quarry. Our pilot."

Nova fired on another drop pod, blasting it to pieces before turning the fighter back toward the action. Streaks of light filled the darkness beyond her windshield, fighters and pods cutting across the black canvas like shooting stars. Explosions peppered the expanse. And there, gunning toward Eutheria with smoke billowing from the tail, was a short-range shuttle with Trios military markings plastered on the hull.

"I see you. I'll trail you guys, be your outside eyes. Tell Powell to join my channel."

She gave Thea the channel number and engaged the thrusters for the hundredth time. Zipping after the shuttle, she dodged cross fire and rolled away from other fighters as she gave chase.

"Powell here," a deep voice crackled in her ear.

"Good to meet you, Powell. Your tail's smoking pretty bad, but with both wings and a decent amount of power, you should make it down fine."

"I'm feeling like shit, just warning you. The girls mentioned something about radiation. I keep thinking I'm gonna puke."

"Just do what I say. I'm watching your back and—BANK LEFT!"

Nova watched as the shuttle tilted to the side, narrowly avoiding a blow with cross fire.

"Orders are to shoot drop pods, not the military shuttle!" Nova screamed on the open channels.

There was no response except another series of missiles coming in at the ship. Nova wondered briefly if Sol and Casey's general had even given an order to avoid the *Paramount* shuttle. Maybe they'd agreed to shoot down everything—containment to the fullest degree.

She watched the missiles coming in, stomach filling with dread.

"You've got a series coming after you," she said to Powell. "Three, it looks like."

"I've got alerts they're locked on."

Nova checked her peripherals, pushing her eyes as far as she could. "Here they come. Do what I say exactly as I say it." Nova pulled to the side, getting a better view. "SPIN LEFT. Keep spinning." One missile soared past. "Okay, stop. Hold true. BANK RIGHT!" Another missile passed. "BANK LEFT." A third.

The sky was suddenly dark, the streaking missiles gone. The shuttle was still smoking, but they'd be entering Eutheria's atmo in a matter of seconds. Nova let out an exhale. "You're good. I'm gonna pull off now."

"There's a fourth," Powell replied.

"What?"

"Four missiles! There's a fourth locked on."

"I didn't see a fourth. There were only three. Three miss—" Something bright flashed overhead, streaking past Nova's fighter, coming into view too late, and Nova knew with sickening dread that it was her less-than-perfect peripheral vision that had just damned them.

"SPIN RIGHT!" she shouted. "SPIN."

Powell spun, but not fast enough, not soon enough.

The missile clipped the shuttle's left wing, and Nova watched in horror as Powell lost control, the shuttle corkscrewing as it entered atmo and plummeted toward Eutheria.

Standing on the observation deck of Paradox's battlecarrier, the programmer could barely breathe.

She hadn't been able to sit behind on Casey, not when Thea was in jeopardy, and certainly not when Sol was jumping his crew right to her. She'd known she wouldn't be able to see Thea until it was over, but she'd wanted to be there. She'd pleaded her case and Sol had listened. He was beginning to do that more lately. A part of her wondered if maybe he could change, or if this was just another way to appease her temporarily.

Then word had come in from Xenia.

There was no hope of containing things. Infected people were escaping. Drop pods were to be shot. The station would likely be destroyed. And Thea was on it.

The programmer had felt her daughter's death again, just as real as when she'd been reported dead at Northwood Point. How many times would she need to live through a moment like this—fearing it was over, that there was no hope?

And then word had come in that Thea was on a shuttle. They were going to land on Eutheria. Everything was fine.

She'd run to the observation deck, desperate for a view. The updates in the war room didn't matter anymore. The only update she needed was something she could see.

Now she wished she could unsee it.

Someone hadn't listened to the orders Sol had given. Or maybe they'd simply missed them in the heat of the fight.

She'd come all this way to see her daughter again. They'd been separated for thirteen years, and after jumping back to her in the blink of an eye, all her effort had done was get her there in time to see Althea's funeral. Because with the way the ship was spiraling, with the smoke billowing off it like a bonfire, Naree Sadik didn't see how anyone aboard would survive.

X

THE CURE

Hearth City

Eutheria, Trios System

POWELL HAD TOLD THEM OVER the shuttle's intercoms that the crash was coming, and even though Thea had strapped into one of the shuttle's rear harnesses, nothing could have prepared her for the full force of impact.

She was holding Coen because he was too limp to wrestle into a harness of his own. Amber was buckled in across the way, but on impact, Thea lost sight of her. Her head whipped forward, forehead cracking against the top of Coen's skull. White pain roared behind her eyes. Something lanced her arm and she felt burning agony, followed by the immediate relief of her body healing.

All the while, she whispered to Coen. *Hang in there. Hold on just a minute longer. We're nearly there. I'll get you to a hospital. Just hold on.*

Amber had managed to get some of the bullet out before the first missile struck the shuttle's tail. She'd had to literally cut Coen open to get to it. His body had kept trying to heal, but the bullet had struck his pelvis, shattering bone before deflecting into part of his intestines. Amber had removed what she could of the bullet, and his skin had healed back up, but inside, he needed attention. If they didn't get to a doctor, he would die. Within an hour, if the internal bleeding was bad enough. There was also the surgery he'd need for his intestines. Dr. Tarlow's death on Achlys had proved that while a host could heal many injuries, reversing major organ damage was impossible.

When the shuttle sagged still, Thea opened her eyes. A piece of jagged metal protruded into the ship to her right. It must have been what lanced her shoulder through her suit. Amber unclipped from her harness and staggered for the cockpit, medkit in hand.

Thea unclipped as well and stood. Everything hurt, but she was whole. She'd only lived because of the contagion in her veins, this she was sure of. Even Coen, weak and fading in her arms, had lived only because of it.

"Powell's dead," Amber said, reappearing. "We have to go. The shuttle's corrarium reactor was probably damaged. I'm surprised it didn't blow when we crashed."

Thea dragged Coen toward the exit, every limb in her body aching. The ship was ungodly hot—she could feel it even through her suit—and Coen's skin was beaded with sweat.

Hang in there. Please don't leave me. Please don't go.

He remained silent. His pulse was shallow and weak, but she could feel his drive to live, a stubborn refusal to quit.

She fought her way through the rippling air and into the hold. The gangplank was ruined, crushed in the weight of the crash and buckled partially into the hold. There'd be no lowering it. Where the seams had warped, a gap of sunlight bled through.

Thea passed Coen to Amber and went to work with her hands. The metal was scorching. Beneath the lining of her suit, her hands began to blister, then heal, then blister again. But the insane heat meant the hull had softened slightly, and if she could just widen the gap . . . Thea ignored the pain and pulled back with all her might, bending the metal toward her.

Light plunged into the hold, blinding, foreign. She winced. It had been forever since she'd seen anything so naturally brilliant. Thea tugged again, and the metal snapped, a section of the gangplank clattering to the floor. The gap was now just wide enough to climb through.

She gasped, breathless, then turned back to Amber. "I'll climb through. You lower him to me."

After some awkward maneuvering, Coen was back in Thea's arms and she was staggering away from the wrecked ship, Amber on her heels. Thea ran, squinting in the brilliant light.

They'd landed in a grassy field, the ship creating a crater in the otherwise manicured earth. There was a children's park in the distance, a familiar skyline beyond.

Hearth City.

Of all the places they could have crashed, she was just kilometers from home.

Behind her, the shuttle exploded without warning. Thea was propelled forward, falling to her knees and buckling over Coen as scrap metal rained down. Pain flared across her back, then quickly faded. Thank goodness for her suit.

She risked a glance at Amber—whole, and staggering to her feet beside Thea—then back to Coen. His eyes were fluttering, his heart beating too fast. Much faster than her own. They'd been in sync since bonding. Even with entire systems between them, they'd beat as one.

Thea tore off her helmet and ripped her arms from the suit. She pressed her bare palm to Coen's forehead, finding it cold and clammy despite how profusely he was sweating.

"Thea . . . ," he managed. "I can't . . . I feel . . ."

"He's lost too much blood, is probably bleeding internally. I'm a universal donor. I can give him a blood transfusion."

"We *need* to get him to a hospital," Amber said.

"He's not going to make it to the hospital! I need to do this. To keep him with us until they get here."

Sirens sounded in the distance. Help was coming and they had a giant plume of smoke to follow, but Thea knew what she'd have to say when they arrived. Coen would need to be quarantined for all of Eutheria's protection. Any doctors working on him would need to be fully suited. As soon as she mentioned these things, they'd lose precious time. She needed to buy more.

"Now, Amber!"

The medic pulled a blood transfusion field kit from the medkit and went to work. Soon there was a needle in Thea's arm, her blood zipping through the tubing and into Coen. She held his hand through it all. *Please stay with me*, she begged. *It's like you said. I need you to stay. I don't know how to do any of this alone anymore. Please stay. PLEASE.*

His head lolled. His eyes struggled to focus on her, and it killed her to see him like this. "Thea," he whispered. That was it. Just her name. She bent down, putting her forehead to his, cupping his face in her hands.

"Hang on, Coen."

He was fading. She could feel him leaving her. His thoughts, his wants, everything—dissipating like fog, vanishing before her eyes.

"Don't go," she pleaded.

Then, like a rib snapping in her chest, their connection broke. The emptiness scorched her core and she gasped at the shock of it.

"No." She was sobbing now, uncontrollable. "*No.*"

"I'm right here," he said. His voice was strained, but

stronger now somehow. "Thea, I'm right here."

She pulled back. His heart had slowed to a healthier beat. The transfusion was working, but the silence in her head was endless.

Coen? she asked mentally, searching his eyes.

He remained silent.

"Coen?" she said again.

When he looked at her, she knew. It was written in his eyes, in the utter shock on his face. "I can't reach you," he said wearily. "I can't hear your pulse."

She threw herself at him, kissing him once, twice, again. She could pass it back to him. It was how he'd infected her, after all. She could do the same.

When he cringed in pain beneath her, she pulled away, searching his face. His brows were drawn, his eyes weary. He shook his head and the quiet was everywhere.

Coen's world became a blur. There was an ambulance and stretchers and medical lights. Doctors. A fog that descended after someone mentioned the word *surgery*. The only constant through all of it was that Thea was gone. He couldn't reach her, hear her. Couldn't hear anything, really.

The doctors surrounding him were pulseless machines. Every light and color in the operating room seemed muted. And the very weight of his own body was unbearable. He felt like a shell of himself, a pathetic excuse for a human. The pain was so intense, seemingly endless.

When he came to after the surgery, she was still gone. The absence stung in his core. It was like leaving her behind on Kanna7 all over again, only this time, he didn't even know where she was.

A pair of faces bent over his bed, blurry before coming into focus. It took him a moment to recognize them as his parents. "Coen," his mom murmured, gathering him in her arms. Her shirt was soft and smelled of the fabric softener she always used. He smiled at the fact that he could recall something so inconsequential.

"Where's Gina?" he managed.

"At Northside, across town."

"How is she?"

His father laid his personal Tab on Coen's bedspread. A picture of Gina filled the screen.

She didn't look how Coen remembered her. The little meat she'd had left on her frame when he flew out for Black Quarry was gone. Now skin and bones, her complexion was sickly. Her collarbone was visible through her shirt, and the scarf he'd given her for her last birthday, deep blue with an octopus print, was wrapped around her head.

He gasped out a sob.

"She's barely hanging on, but we spoke with a Trios official just this morning. There should be a settlement from your ordeal on Kanna7. We'd like to use some of the money for the treatment Gina needs."

"Yes. Use all of it. Anything she needs," Coen said. "Can I see her? I want to see her."

His mother shook her head sadly. "You have another surgery scheduled for tomorrow. Maybe even a third, depending on how tomorrow's goes. When you're discharged, when they say it's safe, it will be the first thing we do."

Coen exhaled heavily, tears building in his eyes.

A salary from Black Quarry hadn't provided the help Gina needed, but the contagion, in a way, had. All he'd suffered—all he'd endured—would be worthwhile if the settlement was enough to buy Gina the care she needed.

Coen's mother brushed hair from his eyes and he drifted into a dreamless sleep.

Everything had gone to hell.

After watching the shuttle plummet to Eutheria, Nova had been called back to the Paradox battlecarrier. She'd considered avoiding the order and chasing after her friends, but the Trios's military ships were finally flying into the vicinity and she hadn't wanted to get blown from the sky.

Back on the carrier, news was awful.

Most of the drop pods had been destroyed. The few to make

it on-planet were being rounded up by Eutheria's local GDC branch and quarantined. Occupants proven to be healthy would be released. The others, terminated.

The entire flux drive crew—both Paradox's and Casey's fleets—was berated by Trios officials.

You should have alerted the Union, not staged a rogue mission.

This flux drive tech isn't tested to UPC standards. You had no business jumping to our airspace.

A deadly outbreak that could have killed an entire system is completely on your hands!

It was on the Radicals' hands, Nova maintained, but this was exactly why Paradox had acted as it did. There was no way of knowing if any of the officials berating them now were Radicals themselves. If they were, the only reason they'd helped was because of the contagion. Everyone had their own motives, and no one could accomplish those if they died.

Xenia Station eventually failed. The force fields blinked out and equipment flew from the docking bays, sucked into space. Paradox's and Casey's fleets were permitted to land on Eutheria. In part to avoid the various debris now in orbit around Eutheria, and also to make room for the GDC cleanup crew that would sweep the station.

Once on-planet, Nova sought out Naree Sadik. "You're going to see Thea, right?" It was a question, even when

Nova knew the answer. The woman had waited so long to see her daughter. If they'd survived that crash—and whispers around the battlecarrier suggested they did—Naree would be making demands to see her. "I want to come with you."

"Don't you have your own family to reunite with?"

Nova thought of her mother, who'd kicked her out of the house over a year earlier. "Thea and Coen and Amber are more family to me than my own blood. I guess that happens when you've been through what we have together."

Naree gave an understanding smile and arranged for a car.

"I keep thinking about all those people on Xenia that we failed," Nova said as they sped for a GDC building in downtown Hearth City. "We jumped to the station to contain things and look what happened."

"It didn't go as planned, but imagine what might have happened if we didn't jump at all. The contagion would have gotten loose. People would have raced for the drop pods. And no one would have been there to stop them from traveling to Eutheria. The outbreak would have been disastrous."

"But I jumped Coen and Amber into Xenia. *That's* what caused the station to fail. The radiation. All those deaths are on my hands."

"Once people started falling sick and attacking each other, people would have raced for the drop pods anyway."

"But the station wouldn't have failed. Maybe we'd have been able to save some of them."

"And maybe if I never helped Sol make the flux drive, none of this would have happened. Thea would have grown up with a mother. Maybe she wouldn't have taken the Hevetz internship, or become a host, or released the contagion while fighting for her life on *Paramount*." Naree Sadik gave Nova a hard look. It was the kind of look she was used to getting from her own mother, and she wondered if all parents had this expression wired into their DNA. "You see why you can't go down this route, trying to find the source of blame? I have blamed myself for Thea's predicament for years, but Sol is just as guilty. The world is a complicated place, Nova. People are complicated, too. Throw us all together and you get one horrible mess."

The car rolled to a stop.

"Coen's been taken to a Hearth City hospital. Apparently he suffered some pretty substantial injuries, but he's been cured of *Psychrobacter achli*."

"Cured?" Nova gaped. "How?"

"I don't know those details yet, only that GDC took multiple blood samples from him and tried infecting those samples with various strains of *Psychrobacter achli* taken from the infected who made it to Eutheria via drop pod." Nova must have looked startled because Naree added, "Don't worry. Those subjects have been terminated, and it's common practice for the GDC to maintain secure samples of any contagion of this magnitude. Regardless, Coen's results are good news. It means a treatment—a cure—is possible."

Nova was still gaping at the programmer, trying to make sense of this turn in events. Dr. Tarlow hadn't managed to save Sullivan on Achlys. Nova's cousin was dead, but now a treatment seemed possible? It broke her heart and also made it swell. It had been so long since she felt any semblance of hope, of safety.

Naree unbuckled and opened the car door. "I'm going to see my daughter. You'll understand when I ask for a moment alone?"

Nova nodded. "I'll see Amber first."

Thea sat in a debriefing room, trying to make sense of everything. Coen had been cured.

It was something in her blood. It had to be.

Maybe each iteration of *Psychrobacter achli* was different. Once it found a home in a host, multiplying and spreading, maybe it mutated slightly, becoming unique to *that* person. Thea's blood had successfully infected the teens Burke brought to Kanna7 because no version of the contagion existed in their system. But with Coen, another host . . . Maybe their unique versions of *Psychrobacter achli* had, for a lack of a better word, canceled each other out—destroyed each other.

Thea had cured him.

When she looked at it scientifically it wasn't all that surprising. Antibiotics were created by finding an organism with a natural resistance to a certain bacteria, then isolating the right antibiotic compound and producing it on a large scale to be used as a drug. Thea *was* that organism. Her universal blood, already a host to *Psychrobacter achli*, had been the cure for another host.

It should have made her happy. An antibiotic could be made with this knowledge. Any host could be cured. Anyone infected by the disease might stand a chance as well, depending on how quickly antibiotics were administered and how fast they worked. There would be months of research and testing ahead of Galactic Disease Control, but it could mean protection for Eutheria and the entire UPC.

Because of this promising possibility, Thea told the GDC and Trios authorities everything. She left nothing out.

Black Quarry. Hevetz Industries. The Radicals. Kanna7 and Casey and the showdown on Xenia.

Still, she felt numb. She'd weathered the silence in her head for six weeks already. She'd never expected to have to do it again. And this time it wouldn't come back. Even when she was eventually released and allowed to visit Coen, he'd still be distant. She could stand right before him and not know what he was thinking. She'd never hear him in her head again.

She hadn't realized how intimate it had been, how truly close they were, until it was gone for good.

"There's someone here to see you," the official questioning her said. Thea couldn't remember his department. After the first three interviews, they'd all started to blend together.

She nodded numbly.

The man left.

A woman took his place.

"Are you the last one, because I really—" Thea fell silent when she looked up.

"Althea?" The sound of her voice triggered a million memories. Thea had already experienced this once with Coen as her proxy, but being on *this* end of the experience was beyond words. She leapt from the seat, threw her arms around her mother, and cried into her chest.

In that moment she cried for everything. Their lost time. All she'd weathered on Achlys and Kanna7. The broken bond. She didn't care if her mother's first impression of her was that she was weak and a child. Thea wanted to be exactly those things. She wanted to relish the feeling of this embrace. Above all, she wished she was still naive enough to believe that her mother could fix everything.

● ● ●

Nova was permitted to step inside the windowless questioning room only if she put on a suit.

"I've been in close contact with her for weeks and I'm not sick," she snapped at the GDC officer. "Neither is anyone on Casey. I'm not putting on a damn suit. I want to *see* her."

"You have to keep your distance, then."

"Fine."

The officer opened the door. Nova stepped through.

Amber straightened quickly, chair skidding back. Her strawberry hair hung at her chin, limp and flat from the theatrics of the past day. Her cheeks were flushed with heat, but her shoulders sagged slightly, like the effort to hold herself tall was draining. There was a bandage at the crook of her left arm, an empty IV rack in the corner of the room. She'd suffered radiation poisoning, according to the GDC officer.

Nova wanted to say how sorry she was for the missile that took down Amber's shuttle, but Naree's warning about trying to find the source of blame echoed in her head. It hadn't been Nova's fault, not truly. Powell was flying. Someone else had fired the shots. Nova had done her best—done all she could—and it hadn't been enough. Sometimes, that was just the way of it.

She wanted also to say that she was sorry for being an ass

on Casey. It seemed so petty now, to hold Amber at a distance because of jealousy or envy or *whatever* it had been.

"I've never been good at needing other people," Nova said, knowing she had to start somewhere, "and I needed you a lot. During the coma, the healing and PT, getting off Kanna7. I needed you so much and it went against everything I pride myself on."

"I know." Amber's voice sounded smaller than Nova remembered. "I needed you, too, though. You were right about my suit and Xenia. I suffered some pretty bad radiation poisoning. I think I only survived because of the . . ." She gazed at her front, as though she could see the contagion pumping through her veins.

"Right. Well, it's good to need someone," Nova said.

"Is that what you've figured out?"

"Yeah. Of course. I mean, it's good to not *need* need someone, but it's nice to have backup. To know someone else will be there for you when the time comes. I always thought I was attracted to the wrong people. Turns out I was just picking people who didn't want to need someone else, too."

"Oh, I don't need anybody," Amber said, smiling. "I love lonely, depressing solitude."

She winked, and that's what did it.

Nova strode forward, closing the space between them. She'd clamped a palm over Amber's mouth and kissed the back of her own hand before the GDC official had caught up and pulled Nova back.

Amber just stood there, smiling as she touched her lips.

"Do you realize how stupid that was?" the official roared.

"I've never been the best with quick thinking," Nova said. "That's Amber's area of expertise."

"Thea's pretty good, too," Amber admitted.

Nova shook her head, laughing. "Forgive me for favoring you."

Thea was allowed to visit the hospital after three days of interrogation. In reality, they'd wanted to keep her there for another two, but her mother had put her foot down. Sometimes it was nice to be a minor, Thea reasoned as the escort car combed the busy Hearth City streets. There were perks to having a guardian who could fight battles on your behalf.

When she stepped out of the car to face the hospital, her stomach was unsteady. The sun was brilliant and foreign. Too bright. She hated that she'd adjusted to artificial lighting in the past months, that a brilliant blue sky and thick humid air felt strange.

Thea walked through the automatic doors and into the lobby, where a receptionist told her how to find Coen.

"Do you want me to come with you?" her mom asked.

Thea shook her head. She had to do this alone. Or, as alone

as she could, given the two GDC officials who now followed her everywhere.

"I'll wait in the lobby." One of the officers put a finger to his ear, then leaned in and whispered something to Naree. Her smile vanished. "Turns out they have a few more questions for me back at GDC headquarters."

"Go on," Thea said. "I'll meet you there."

She watched her mother hustle off, one of the officers ushering her to the exit. The other trailed Thea to the elevator, then down Coen's floor. She kneaded her hands as she walked, feeling skittish. Heartbeats were audible from each room she passed, some weaker than others, and Thea was stung again by the realization that Coen could no longer hear this symphony of life. She couldn't give the gift back to him even if she wanted to. Her mother had explained how additional tests had been run on samples of Coen's blood.

Coen wasn't just cured. He was *immune*.

She planned to be the same one day, when the right treatment was developed. It was too dangerous to live like this, posing a constant threat to others. Even now, Thea was forced to wear a mask in the hospital despite the fact that the contagion wasn't passed by air.

When she reached Coen's door, she paused. What would she say? What if everything was different? Maybe the only reason they'd even been close was because of the bacteria— their bond.

She knocked before she could lose her nerve. No one answered. Pushing the door open, Thea edged her way inside. The bed was empty, but he couldn't have checked out. He'd had his final surgery just yesterday, the receptionist had told her. Maybe something had gone wrong—maybe there were complications the woman hadn't known about.

"Hey."

She spun.

Coen stood on crutches in the doorway. "I'll give you a few minutes," the nurse accompanying him said, and closed the door. When it clicked shut, Thea wasn't sure if she was glad the GDC agent was waiting in the hall or not. They were very alone.

"I had a session in a regen bed this morning. Surgery is rough when you don't have superhuman healing skills." He smiled and it lit up his whole face. His hair was pulled back in its typical fashion, half of it in a bun at the crown of his head, the rest falling to his shoulders.

"You can take that mask off," he added. "It's just the two of us in here."

She pulled it off and held it by her knee, letting it dangle by the elastic.

"Thea, say something, please."

"Is this the hospital your sister is at?" she asked. It was the first thought that came to mind.

"She's across town. I haven't seen her yet."

"But she's well?"

His gaze fell to the floor. "She's holding on. If she can last just a little longer, we might get the money for the treatment she actually needs. My parents mentioned a settlement."

Thea would have known all this if they were still bonded. Her chest ached—for what they'd lost, for what his family still had to endure. She'd been so focused on the good to come from the last few days—the realization that an antibiotic for *Psychrobacter achli* would likely be developed in the coming months—that she'd forgotten how broken things still were. The Radicals had been thwarted and the Trios was still a part of the UPC, but the Union had its problems. For someone to suffer from something treatable, to toe death's doorstep when a richer person would recover quickly . . .

Civilization had come so far. In tech. In resources. And yet some things were still so backward. A settlement shouldn't have to be Gina's only hope.

"They're going to start work on an antibiotic," Thea said.

"I heard."

"Do you want to sit?" She glanced at the visitor's chair, the bed. Coen was hunched over the crutches in a way that looked completely uncomfortable, and anything would be better than this awkward meter between them. Close enough to see the pain in his brow and the longing in his eyes, but far enough that she didn't feel like she could close the distance.

"How are you feeling?" she asked when he didn't answer.

"Stop it. That's not what you came here to say."

"I didn't come here to check on you?"

He sighed, shook his head. "You're acting like you don't even know me."

"I don't," she admitted. "Not really. We were what we had to be to survive. Maybe now we're supposed to go back to how things were."

"When? When we didn't know each other? I don't want to go back to that."

She couldn't look at him. Everything was awkward. If she could just *hear* his thoughts, if she could just *know* what he was thinking, she'd be able to say the right thing.

He hobbled nearer, stopping before her. Crutches still hooked beneath his arms, he used a finger to nudge her chin up so she was forced to look him.

"Tell me you don't want to try, and you can walk out of here and I'll never see you again. Tell me that's really what you want and I won't argue. But it's supposed to be hard, Thea. And sloppy and awkward and new. That's how it was when we first bonded, remember? Now we just have to do it again. Without being in each other's heads."

His eyes were urgent, their brown depths practically glowing. It dawned on her how little time she'd really spent with him like this—up close and personal. There were those few days when they'd been bunked together, but otherwise, so much of their relationship had been between walls and space suits.

He reached out and took her hand, threading his fingers between them. Pulling her nearer.

"You know what I'm thinking," she said, realizing it was true. Not about *everything*—what they'd had before was a special kind of magic—but partially. He still knew.

"What's that?" he said with a smile.

"I *do* want to try. I do. But I'm scared. To screw it up. For it to not be as amazing."

"You said it was only happening on Kanna7 because we had no other choice. Remember that?" He was staring straight at her—into her. "Well, we have all the choices in the galaxy now, Thea. Six-point-five billion people on Eutheria alone and we can choose any of them. I still choose you."

"I didn't have a choice then, and I don't have one now," she said. "It's just you. The bond broke, but it didn't. You know?"

"God, do I know." He took her face in his hands and kissed her.

In that moment, with their lips pressed together, he knew everything. It wouldn't be easy, and he was sure to read her wrong at times. They'd misunderstand or judge unfairly. They'd communicate poorly. It would be messy and real and perfectly human. But as they kissed, he knew that she'd meant it. She hadn't said it just to appease him. She wanted to be here. She wanted *him*.

They broke apart and smiled. He'd forgotten how beautiful her smile was.

"Amber told me she's going to catch a movie with Nova tonight," Thea said. "She said we should come."

"That sounds so . . . normal."

"Doesn't it?" Her eyes flashed with excitement, but he couldn't mirror it. All those people dead on Xenia. His sister's fate still uncertain. "Coen, we have to let ourselves live a little. We're all grieving, and the Union isn't perfect, and fighting to make everything right will be exhausting. We can't always be on full alert. We did that the past few months, and I gotta be honest, I don't think my body can handle that level of stress constantly. We can do something for ourselves. It's allowed."

He let out a sigh. This girl. He didn't understand how the worst thing that had ever happened to him had led him to her.

"Show is at seven. Private screening because . . ." Thea made a gesture at her front. "Well, me *and* Amber, I guess. We get followed everywhere by GDC staff right now. There's an agent outside your room. Anyway, you can pick me up and it will almost be like a date. A date with a pair of creepy chaperones shadowing us. And I'll have to wear my mask. Sexy, I know."

He laughed. It made his stitches ache, a reminder of how different they now were.

"So I'll see you later?" she asked.

"No."

She frowned at the response, confused.

He'd been discharged after the regen bed session. His parents were getting the car so they could head across town to Gina's hospital. "There's someone I want you to meet first." He hadn't told her where they were going, but somehow, he could sense that she knew.

Coen took her hand, and they faced the door the way they'd faced everything the past few months: together.

"Explain."

The programmer fidgeted in her chair. Four GDC officers stood rigid along the room's perimeter, watching as the head agent scowled down at her.

She'd known it would come to this. Everything she'd done—every decision she'd made in the last thirteen years, and especially in the last few weeks—had always been about getting to this moment.

"I don't know what you're talking about," she said glibly.

The head agent set his Tab in front of her. A familiar freeze-frame filled the screen. "This was sent to us from Bev. Apparently someone saw the news about Xenia and couldn't remain quiet. He said his company's fuel powers your flux drives."

"It does. It's wonderfully stable, remarkably powerful."

"And incredibly dangerous," the agent snarled. "You were shown this footage, according to him. Did you forget?"

Naree hadn't forgotten. She knew everything she would see, even as the agent reached out and pressed the play prompt.

Devon in his medical bed, pale and sweaty and stripped to his underwear. His veins black from the blood poisoning, a cobweb of darkness pulsing beneath his skin. His eyes bloodshot. A bead of blood dripping from his nose.

The footage sped on as he thrashed, clawed at his face, batted away a sedation needle. He blinked, eyes filling with blood, and burst free of his restraints.

That was when Dax entered the medbay and shot his brother in the head.

"Devon fell on the job several months earlier, didn't he?" the agent asked.

"So I've heard." There was no use lying. "His suit was breached and he suffered terrible burns from the cold. They thought the blood poisoning was somehow related to the burns."

"But it wasn't. This video proves it. He came in contact with something. Some sort of contagion in the AltCor, much like what your daughter encountered on Achlys, only this strand of the parasite takes months to fully infect its host. All of which you knew after seeing this footage, and you still accepted the shipment of AltCor. Brought it to Casey and put it in your drives. Flew it to the Union! The fact that the losses on Xenia were from Psychrobacter achli doesn't invalidate your guilt in this. You ignored the risks. You endangered an entire system!"

Naree raised her chin, looked him in the eye, and spoke the words she'd been planning since she bumped Sol's Tab against the man's from shipping, transferring the damning footage. "Solomon Weet ordered me to accept the AltCor. He abducted me years ago, held me hostage all this time. He only sees unnes, just like Dax, who killed his own twin in that video. You'll notice there's no record of Sol buying the fuel. He and Dax don't like records. But you'll find the footage of Devon's reaction on Sol's personal Tab, buried in an encrypted folder. He saw the risks. He knew about them and he didn't care. I followed his orders because I feared for my life. I have since he abducted me."

The agent's brows furrowed. He licked his lips, then brought a hand to his ear. "Get Solomon Weet in here and confiscate his Tab. Also, I want that containment briefing from Bev already! Get me updates!" His gaze homed in on Naree. "Take her outside and get a written statement," he said to one of his men, "but don't let her leave. We could have an outbreak on our hands—on hers and Weet's. He may take most of the fall, but she's not getting off free."

Naree smiled as they hauled her from the chair. It was her word against Sol's, but she was the victim and he had the criminal record. A fugitive from Eutheria. A company with a history of illegal black market purchases. A drive built outside of UPC laws. A damning video saved on his personal Tab.

She'd take her chances. If she went down with him, it would be worth it.

The officer guided Naree from interrogation. In the hall, Sol was being escorted by a pair of agents. His feline eyes were narrowed, his lips curled in a snarl. He'd already been briefed, she imagined. He knew what fate awaited him in that room.

"How could you?" he growled as they passed.

"I would do anything to get back to my daughter. You of all people should know that."

Panic flicked over his features. "Naree, please. I'm sorry about what I did to you, but you have to help me. You have Thea now. Why won't you help me?"

They dragged him on.

"Help me, you ungrateful, backstabbing traitor!"

She squared her shoulders and spoke to him one final time, a smile on her lips. "I promised I would ruin you one day. I promised."

His face paled. The guards shoved at his back.

When she blinked, he was gone.

ACKNOWLEDGMENTS

There was a time when I thought I'd never finish this book, and yet here I am, writing the acknowledgments. I did it. (Somehow.)

Many thanks to my agent, Sara Crowe, and the team at Pippin Properties, who do so much behind-the-scenes work to ensure my books succeed.

Additional thanks to my editor, Erica Sussman, and everyone at HarperTeen who worked on this project. Many of you touched *Contagion* and *Immunity* without me even knowing it. Thank you for your time and efforts.

Many friends supported me in various ways as I worked on this book, checking in with me via text, brainstorming plot points aloud, cheering me on when I was in a rut, or simply listening when I had to vent my frustrations. To Alex Bracken, Susan Dennard, Jodi Meadows, Mackenzi Lee,

Sara Raasch, and Tara Sonin: thank you.

I couldn't do any of this without the support of my family—a family that grew between the day I drafted these acknowledgments and the last time I drafted them for *Contagion*. Rob, who is patient and never loses faith in me. Casey, who keeps me humble (and is starting to grasp what I do for a living and show excitement when finished copies arrive, which brings me the greatest joy). And Jeff, who keeps me humble to the max (and has no idea what I do in my office three days a week)—this one's for you, buddy. If I'm really lucky, maybe I'll be able to write long enough that you get another book dedicated to you. Your sister also!

To everyone who has supported me in one way or another—booksellers who push my books, librarians who stock me on their shelves, teachers who recommend my titles to readers—thank you.

And because I like to end acknowledgments the same way all the time, thanks to *You*, person holding this book. You are the most important piece of this puzzle. I wouldn't be an author without readers, so thank you for seeing this duology through to the end. I am so very grateful.